Clouds of Destiny

Books by Lou Ellen Davis

Clouds of Destiny
There Was an Old Woman (by Elizabeth Davis)

Clouds of Destiny

by

Lou Ellen Davis

G. P. Putnam's Sons
New York

 Published simultaneously in Canada by Longman Canada Limited, Toronto.

SBN: 399-12055-6

Library of Congress Cataloging in Publication Data

Davis, Lou Ellen, 1936–
Clouds of destiny.

I. Title.
PZ4.D26198Cl 1978 [PS3554.A9355] 813'.5'4
77-15567

PRINTED IN THE UNITED STATES OF AMERICA

ACKNOWLEDGMENTS

I am deeply indebted to John Clemm, chairman, History Department, Bentley School, New York City, for so generously sharing with me, page by page throughout the writing of this manuscript, his extensive knowledge of England and its American colonies in 1775. I am also indebted to Mrs. Alfred W. Dater, Jr., curator of the Stamford Historical Society, for her time and her love of the history of Stamford which helped so much to bring "New Hereford" to life. I also thank Julia Weinstein Tossell for the use of her beautifully researched and written master's degree thesis, "The Loyalists of Stamford, Connecticut, 1754–1785."

My thanks also to my uncle-in-law Pat Broach, for sharing his expertise on antique locks, chains and Newgate Prison, and to my friend Julie Ellis, for her eagerly solicited, fully incorporated suggestions on plot structure.

L. E. D.

Dedication

FOR MICHAEL, DAVID AND LESLIE

Clouds of Destiny

CHAPTER ONE

A cloud shifted. Moonlight spilled onto the open road.

Sarah Carrington tightened her arms around her five-year-old son. The road was already too visible, the hour far too late. Her husband, Charles Carrington, and brother-in-law, Edward, quickened the pace of their horses, Sarah's horse promptly falling in with the new rhythm. Did they, her husband and his brother, also feel the fear, a strange new coldness unrelated to anything this bitter February 1775 night wind might bring? A coldness of the soul, thought Sarah, momentarily grateful for the physical numbness and exhaustion the night and long trip back to the colonies from England had produced. A welcome sense of unreality washed over her. She was twenty-five, yet in that instant felt oddly timeless, a disembodied spirit immune to pain, immune to fear, but even as the instant was born, it passed. The beating of her heart ever reminded her that she was not disembodied. She was mortal, vulnerable and, above all else in the sight of God responsible for the safety of the child she held in her arms, nestled so gently, sleepily in the folds of her scarlet riding cape.

"How much farther?" she asked her husband.

"How much farther?" her husband echoed, his voice directed to his brother, Edward, as colonial in dress as Charles and Sarah were British.

"Quite a distance," Edward answered. "We'd best stay the night at the Twin Stallion, then move on in the morning."

Carefully concealed among the tall trees and winter-brown underbrush, James Devant knelt close to the leaf-packed soil. To his left, beyond and below the clearing, the moonlit Connecticut shoreline met the waters of Long Island Sound.

"I don't like it," whispered Garth Chandler, a massive black man of indeterminate age, although he figured he was about twenty-five.

James was twenty-eight; his black hair pulled back into the tie-wig style of the day, his features finely chiseled yet strong, starkly handsome. Both men wore tricorn hats, buckskin jackets, black wool trousers and wooden-soled leather boots that reached to their knees.

"It don't feel right," Garth continued.

James sank down onto his haunches. With his back firmly braced against an oak tree behind him, he drew his gun, held it loosely, his finger resting on the first trigger. The gun was unusual, a double-barreled two-trigger flintlock; the underside of the lower eight-inch steel barrel was equipped with a folding spring bayonet. Although the gun was American made, the handle was intricately ornamented silver, in midcentury Scottish tradition. There was no other gun quite like it in all the thirteen colonies. Garth carried a more common steel bell-mouthed pistol, but the weapon with which he felt most comfortable was the brass-handled machete that hung like a sword from his side.

"If it is a trap," said James, "they're probably down that way." He pointed south, toward a particular stretch of coastline where the woods ran close to the shore. Farther down, he knew of several caves which offered an even better hiding place for anyone who might wish to attack an incoming smuggling ship. The crew and the entire shore group waiting to help unload and move the contraband could be captured or slaughtered with relative ease, depending on which group awaited them. The revenue agents were bad enough, the British soldiers worse because there were more of them, better armed and better trained, but James' main concern was Nathaniel Shyrie. Certainly Shyrie knew the coastline as well as James. For many years both men had worked together under Thomas Kyle, before Thomas was finally taken by the British last year and hanged. His death left what had been one of the most efficient smuggling organizations in all the thirteen colonies divided into two major factions, one headed by James Devant, the other by Nathaniel Shyrie. Both men knew only one of them could survive.

"I don't know," said James. "We could bring it in at Stamford."

"Stamford? With a British fort less than five miles across the Sound?"

"Even Nat would never expect us to do it." The use of Nathaniel's nickname indicated clearly James' contempt for the man. Nicknames were never used where respect was present.

"Greenwich be safer," Garth answered.

"No. It's farther from the fort than Stamford, but they could still spot us. If they sent over even two ships, they could box us in. At Stamford at least we could run. No, it's got to be Norwalk, New Hereford or Stamford, and I'm afraid Nat's expecting us here at Norwalk."

"New Hereford then?"

James hesitated, then shook his head. "Even if we missed the British, Nat's men could still make it down from here and be on us before we were a mile inland."

"New Hereford still better than Stamford," insisted Garth. "Better chance we miss British. I'd rather fight Shyrie than British soldiers."

James remained silent. Then, keeping the oak tree at his back, he rose slowly to his feet. "You're right," he said. "New Hereford it is."

Garth nodded.

Carefully, close within the shadows, they made their way up over the wooded incline back to where Jeremy Porter waited with their horses. Jeremy, tall, gangly, fifteen years old, born on a farm outside Norwalk, was eager to earn the kind of money James Devant offered, regardless of the risks. Unlike James, however, whose primary incentive was money, Jeremy considered himself a patriot, his smuggling activities a contribution to his country. If, on occasions more numerous than Jeremy cared to consider, James' cargoes contained goods which competed with American-manufactured goods or included tea and other English items officially boycotted by American patriots, there was always the consolation of shiploads like the one due in tonight. It included English-made guns and gunpowder to be used someday against the British by other patriots like Jeremy, although on this particular peaceful February 1775 night, the prospect of an actual war between England and its American colonies seemed slightly incredible.

He greeted James with: "All quiet here, sir."

James nodded, started to untether his horse, then abruptly held up his hand for silence. Almost in unison James, Garth and Jeremy lowered themselves to the ground. Horses! At least two, possibly more. But probably not Nat's men, James decided. The pace was wrong.

More likely Nat Shyrie's men would be either slow, careful and watchful or fast, so that no adversary would have a chance to catch up with or outdistance them. The pace of these horses was moderate. Still keeping to the shadows, James rose to one knee. The road was maybe ten feet ahead of him; his view was restricted by the same trees that shielded him. He waited as the sounds grew louder.

Three riders appeared, two men and a woman, traveling south. No—four riders. The woman had a young child with her, almost hidden by her scarlet riding cape. She rode sidesaddle, the child astride in front of her. The distance was too great for him to make out anyone's features. He waited until they were well down the road, then signaled Garth and Jeremy to rise.

"Unimportant," said James as he untethered his horse and mounted.

About two miles inland a loosely organized group of some thirty men awaited his instructions. They knew only that a smuggling ship was due somewhere in the general area of Norwalk, sometime between sunset and dawn. Only the ship's captain and one other carefully selected backup man on board the ship knew where to expect the signals from shore and how to interpret them. Now, the first signal would read, continue past Norwalk. The second signal would come from the Twin Stallion Inn, located in an otherwise isolated area about ten miles north of New Hereford. The inn was three stories high with a tower almost the height of a full fourth story, from which a signal light would be visible for miles over the Sound.

Assuming, of course, that the ship even made it as far as Norwalk. When James had announced his intention to bring a full-rigged eighteen-gun brigantine as far down the Sound as Norwalk, there were those who whispered he had gone mad. Yet, with the overland routes infested with British soldiers, loyalist spies, Shyrie's men and American rebels all too willing to excuse their theft of smuggled goods in the name of patriotism, perhaps James' decision to stick with the sea was not as rash as immediate appearances might indicate. The *Silver Hawk*, posing as a legal merchant vessel, could not simply put in at any Connecticut port, since such vessels were subject to search. The *Hawk* was nonetheless the most valuable of all of James' larger ships. Built for speed, she contained no false bottom, none of the usual structural hiding places which added weight. Her illegal cargoes, in plain sight belowdecks, were in no way limited to an amount which could be hidden. Of the eighteen guns, only eight were real. The others were wood, painted black, their sole purpose to discourage attack and mislead even the most sophisticated revenue cutter captain as to just how fast the *Hawk* could fly, free of the weight of the additional ten guns. Only the small, fast revenue sloops worried James, and none too seriously. Of the larger, more heavily armed ships, James was sure there was not one which could catch the *Hawk*. The *Hawk* also carried two sets of sails, one a respectable buff color, the other, to facilitate clandestine nighttime landings, black. If all went well, the black sails would carry her down the Sound this night.

With Garth and Jeremy slightly behind him, James drew rein on the other side of the hill, about a mile and three-quarters beyond the road. He took a good look at the Stanton farm, apparently quiet and peaceful in the moonlight except for the unusually persistent barking of dogs, an eerie windborne disruption in an otherwise seemingly ordinary February night. To an outsider, however, even the dogs' barking might seem natural. Perhaps a skunk was on the loose; perhaps a deer had ventured beyond the meadow.

James waited, his senses tuned to mood as much as to actual sound. Still in the protection of the trees, he looked at Garth, who nodded. To proceed seemed safe. James affirmed and passed the reaction to Jeremy. After dismounting and walking out of the woods into the cleared area, Jeremy followed the route which led to the main house, a large, yet unpretentious building of weathered clapboard with bright-red shutters. Approximately ten minutes later a lantern light appeared at the door, was waved to and fro twice, then disappeared.

With Jeremy's horse in tow, James and Garth rode past the oversize barn, now packed with horses, and drew rein at the house. The barking of the dogs grew frantic.

The door was unlocked. A trail of mud and dead leaves across the wide-beam oak floor left little doubt where those who had preceded James had gone. A whale oil lamp with polished tin reflector glowed steadily in a wrought-iron holder attached to the whitewashed stucco wall opposite the doorway, a courtesy to James. Whale oil was expensive.

James walked into the kitchen with Garth beside him. Jeremy reluctantly left the warmth of the fireplace to take the three horses still at the hitching rail outside the house into the barn. Voices from the group waiting in the secret cellar extension below were clearly audible. The cellar extension and oversize barn had been planned and financed by the legendary Thomas Kyle, James' and Nat Shyrie's now-dead former employer and mentor, as a meeting and hiding place for smugglers. Shyrie now used a similar farm farther north. The Stanton family, a widow with six daughters and two young sons, stayed out of the way except to stand watch at an upper window, prepared to warn those below should anything irregular occur.

The kitchen fireplace with its orderly assortment of

well-scrubbed iron and tin utensils still retained some of the heat from the fire that had cooked the evening meal. Two flickering candles stood in tin holders on the table. Followed by Garth, James took one of the candles and made his way through the open trapdoor to the cellar and down the stairs to the cold, hard-packed earth below. The "official" cellar was small, used mainly to keep certain foods handy and cool in summer. The ceiling was about five feet high; the walls were lined with stone. Two barrels of dried apples had been moved to the right, out of the way of the stone-lined iron door, which stood open, a masterpiece of deception and engineering. When closed, the stones set into the iron blended so well with the wall that the door was virtually undetectable. To open it, one particular stone had to be removed to accommodate the key, but the stone was near the base, not at all the normal location for a keyhole. Since the door was always unlocked when the smugglers met, few even knew it required a key. Two years before, a loyalist spy had joined the smugglers and dutifully reported the farmhouse. When the soldiers came into the official cellar, however, they were unable to locate the secret room and, with shrewd encouragement from Mrs. Stanton and her family, subsequently decided that their spy was either mad or hopelessly incompetent and had confused the houses. Since then the Stanton place had become one of the safest meeting places on the coast. The cellar door could be and often was left open during meetings.

The open door made a significant difference. For all of Thomas Kyle's engineering prowess in designing the room's somewhat intricate ventilating system, he had neglected to take into consideration the quantity of oxygen consumed by even five or six candles. At the moment well over a dozen illuminated the meeting room, which began where the official cellar left off, underground, but outside the house. Three steps led down from the official cellar to the meeting room's equally cold dirt floor. The rough-hewn stone walls were uneven and eternally damp from the surrounding earth. The furniture consisted of half a dozen rude wooden benches and two tables.

As James, followed closely by Garth, entered the room, the general conversational hum died. Most of the men in the group were, during the day, respectable tradesmen, artisans, farmers or laborers. Shyrie's group was dominated by a considerably rougher element, many of its members imported from the gutters of London.

Stopping a few steps inside the doorway, James stood with his back against the wall and was comforted by its feel. Even in social situations, even in bed with a woman, having his back exposed made James Devant uncomfortable. Quietly, his voice carrying well in the now silent room, he announced, "New Hereford."

Maybe half a dozen voices echoed, "New Hereford!" Their tone conveyed a mixture of surprise and objections to the distance.

"That's right," James answered, "New Hereford." He paused, for only an instant, an open challenge to anyone who might seriously question his judgment. No one did, and why should they? Over the years the mistakes James had made had resulted in only a minimal loss of life and cargo. James was an "honest" smuggler, well respected. He paid his men promptly and fairly and had never placed the safety of his cargo over the safety of any man who worked for him.

He smiled. "I agree with you. The night is cold." Then, more seriously, he continued. "By midnight be on the shore about a mile down from the Twin Stallion Inn. That gives us a little less than two hours. We'll leave quietly in groups of twos and threes. I doubt if anyone would expect us to go as far as New Hereford, but still, there may be trouble. Stay alert. Bruce, I want you, George and Michael to leave first. Contact Matthew Hewett. We'll store the goods at his farm. John, I want you to remain here with Jeremy to signal the *Hawk* that she's to move on to New Hereford." Directing his voice to the entire group, he added, "Any questions?"

"I have one," answered a farmer from Darien. "You got muskets and pistols and gunpowder on board, right?"

In the silence that followed, James could hear his own breathing. It was not customary to question the cargo.

"And why might the cargo be of any concern to you?" asked James.

"Well, I don't mind guns to fight the British," the farmer answered, "but what else you got?"

For the first time James realized the man had been drinking. Although a mug of ale or flip was acceptable, especially in winter, this man had gone too far.

"When the group you go with reaches Darien, you are to leave," James said. "Any other questions?"

A carpenter from Norwalk rose to his feet, faced James. His manner was respectful, even frightened, but firm. "You see, sir, a bunch of us was wondering what else might be aboard. None of us wants to help the British."

The reaction was mixed, but support for what the man had just said was too strong to be ignored.

Quietly, carefully, James answered, "Goods from England are aboard that ship, and when she returns to England, she'll be carrying New England codfish, beaver hats and rum, which will bring us profits, as we shall sell for profit what we unload tonight. Gentlemen, the only politics with which this group concerns itself are the politics of pounds and pence."

The answering signs of approval left much to be desired, primarily because only about half of those present participated, and of that half, James realized, only a few had any really thought-out convictions. The rest were basically followers, who might just as easily follow some other path if appropriate leadership emerged. Against his better judgment, James took one last look at the carpenter—the wave of the future perhaps. Already most of the American leadership was actively polarized between pro- and anti-British forces. Not that most ordinary people really cared much one way or the other, but unfortunately the tension between the two groups created platforms and power bases for too many radicals. Like too many other rebel-dominated towns throughout the colonies, New Hereford, where James had spent the early years of his youth, had a Committee of Correspondence, supposedly a communications vehicle among patriot groups throughout the colonies, but actually a disturbingly powerful political organization, whose extralegal harassment of loyalists provided the rabble with much amusement. Basically, James' own sentiments leaned toward the rebel cause, but not to any extreme which might affect his business. However, that same sentiment in others was apparently now beginning to undermine his organization. It was a situation he realized he could no longer afford to ignore.

"Bruce, George, Michael," he continued, "be on your way to the Hewett farm. The next group, follow in about five minutes. Matthew, I think you know the New Hereford coastline as well as anyone else here. See to it that everyone goes to the right area. It's a cove, about a mile down from the inn. There are three large boulders, and the trees come right to the water's edge."

Matthew nodded.

James went on. "I'll be at the inn with Garth. As soon as we see her, I'll give the signal; then we'll join you. John, William, Jeremy—see me now. I'll tell you the signal to send her to New Hereford."

As John, William and Jeremy approached James, the group assigned to the Hewett farm left and the rest of the group began to select companions for the long ride ahead. The room was cold, candles now flickering as moving bodies disrupted the air currents.

James rode with Garth. By the time they spotted the familiar shape of the Twin Stallion Inn, James' hands and face had passed from painfully cold into an almost welcome numbness.

The inn, from this distance a silhouette against the moonlit February sky, except for the single lantern which glowed from the tower, stood on a slight rise in the land, about ten miles from the town of New Hereford, and roughly defined the northern outer boundary of the New Hereford area. The owner, John McCaylan, in his early fifties, was the father of fourteen sons and three daughters. All three of the girls and eleven of his sons were still living, most of them married with children of their own, all but one settled in the New Hereford area.

Respected not only by his own children but also by the families united with his by marriage, John McCaylan was a powerful man. He was also, by his own standards, an honest man. The Twin Stallion was well known as one of the safest inns in New England. It was also well known in appropriate circles as a favorite rendezvous for smugglers and as a neutral meeting ground for opposing groups of smugglers. However, unlike many similar inns along the coast, no smuggled goods were ever stored at the Twin Stallion, although certainly Mr. McCaylan was not opposed to accepting reasonable quantities of such goods as a tip for services rendered—services such as access to the inn's tower to project signals. If questioned by the British, officially John McCaylan would not even have known anyone was in the tower.

His relationship with both British soldiers and civilian

loyalists was satisfactory, as was his relationship with the opposing New Hereford Committee of Correspondence, which dominated the area politically. He also got along with both James Devant and Nathaniel Shyrie, a delicate balance on all fronts maintained primarily by the judicious use of his influence through family connections, which prompted most men who knew him either to fear or to court him. Like most inns in politically polarized sections of the colonies, the Twin Stallion tended to draw patrons whose political beliefs at least ran in the same direction. At the Twin Stallion, that direction was antiloyalist.

As James and Garth approached the inn, they slowed the pace of their horses. The first-floor windows and an occasional second- and third-floor window showed light, indicating that business was good tonight, unfortunately, but not unexpectedly in the cold weather. The wooden sign, jarred by the wind, jutted out at a right angle beside the door. The sign pictured two simplified, stylized horses to identify the inn for those who could not read. For those who could, THE TWIN STALLION was lettered over the horses' bodies in now weather-beaten, once-bright yellow paint. A lantern hung from the same wrought-iron support which held the sign. As James and Garth rode past the main building to tether their horses in the carriage house, the pungent smell of flip mingled with the kitchen odors of roast beef and hot apple pie. Indistinct male voices and laughter became audible.

Both men dismounted. Garth opened the carriage house door, as James stood to the side, his hand resting loosely on his pistol butt. There were fourteen horses. They tethered their own, then routinely checked the others. Two had expensive saddles, apparently made in England, an unusual sight in the carriage house of a rebel-dominated inn. None had military saddles. Both men specifically kept an eye out for the horse Jack Logan generally used. Logan, Shyrie's second-in-command, came to the Twin Stallion fairly regularly because it was one of the few places along the coast where he could get drunk in reasonable safety. However, Logan's horse was not there tonight, nor were any of the other horses immediately recognizable as belonging to any of Shyrie's men.

On foot, James and Garth started back to the inn, James' shoulders hunched, head down against the cold. Garth, as usual, walked tall and straight, even though, having been born and reared in the South, he probably felt the cold even more severely than James.

"I haven't seen, haven't heard of Logan long time," said Garth.

"Last I heard," James answered, "he was in England."

"Long time ago. Before Christmas."

"You think something happened to him?"

"Maybe. I hear Logan wants to take over Shyrie's men."

"I've heard the same rumors about you and me."

Garth laughed. "Nobody would follow me. But Shyrie's men would follow Logan."

"I hope you're right," said James. "Maybe they'll kill each other, all of them, down to the last man."

Garth laughed.

Upon reaching the inn, James pulled open the heavy oak door and stepped inside with Garth. The floor was also oak, with wide beams five or six inches thick, noticeably worn by the entranceway and touched by a special glow from the fire in the enormous brick fireplace dominating the twenty-five-by-forty-foot room, to the left, which was called the fireroom. There visitors who planned to spend the night might warm themselves while their own rooms were made ready. To the right was a smaller area, dominated by the steps which led to the upper floors and tower. Straight ahead was the taproom, brightly lit and, at the moment, noisy. The kitchen and John McCaylan's living quarters were beyond the taproom, the ceilings throughout supported by roughhewn oak beams, stained unevenly black by years of candle smoke.

With the door closed behind them, the pleasantly sour odor of flip from the taproom mingled with the pungent scent of burning birch logs in the fireroom, an aromatic welcome beyond description. For the first time that night, full consciousness of the fact that he was tired, cold and hungry flooded James' senses. He cast an almost wistful look into the fireroom. Abruptly he froze. The woman who stared back at him appeared just as startled as James. A strikingly beautiful woman, she still wore her scarlet riding cape, the hood thrown back now, revealing long medium-brown hair intricately styled high on her head with soft curls touching her shoulders, an expensive observation of current British fashion. Although he had not seen her in many years, he knew her at once. Sarah Howgate. No, not Howgate. She was married now. Had been for many years.

As he looked at her, his memory played tricks. He was a boy of twelve again. His mother no longer scrubbed and cooked for the Rev. Howgate and his hawk-faced driving wife. His mother was dead. His French father, who had permanently left both his English wife and his half-English son to join the French army and fight the British in Canada, was also dead. James, an arrogant, cunning whelp, according to Mr. Howgate, was promptly apprenticed to a local shipbuilder, but he remained in touch with the Howgate household, specifically with the reverend's grand-niece, Sarah, who had arrived from England to live with her great-aunt and great-uncle a week or so before James' mother died. Sarah was only nine then, but already anyone could see that the beautiful child would someday become an even more beautiful woman.

Sarah and James had immediately liked each other, but when James' mother died, the shared grief of both children over the loss of their parents created a bond between them which stepped beyond the domain of mere liking somewhere into the general area of love. Mr. Howgate heartily disapproved. Although there was little money in the Howgate family, the Howgates were accepted as a very fine, very old family. Virtually from the moment Sarah stepped off the ship, Mr. Howgate had determined that she would marry money, although as a clergyman he was never in a position to admit it openly. Over the next four years, although no longer part of the Howgate household, James still saw Sarah regularly at church and on any other occasion he could manage. He was still not sure at what point his love for the child began to grow into a man's love for a woman, but when Mr. Howgate forcefully attempted to arrange a marriage for James, at age sixteen, to the local blacksmith's daughter, James flatly refused. The old man retaliated by using all his influence to have James transferred to a shipyard in Boston. It was in Boston that James met Thomas Kyle and was introduced to his current profession.

With James removed from the scene, at age sixteen Sarah Howgate—a dutiful and obedient niece, although her Whig political inclinations at times disturbed her Tory uncle—married the man her uncle had chosen for her, Charles Carrington, the second son of the wealthiest, most powerful Tory landowner in New Hereford. With the first son, Edward, a leader in the then fledgling patriot movement and unwelcome in his loyalist father's house, Charles stood as crown prince to his father's fortune.

A hesitant, almost questioning smile touched Sarah's

lips. Did she, too, for one instant, remember the sweetness of those cool summer evenings, the playful snowball fights, the long, quiet walks together, suitably chaperoned, of course, by the local shipbuilding family James worked for then?

James' eyes turned suddenly cold, the warm memories of those early years replaced by later, bitter memories. Eventually she had refused to speak to him, because her great-uncle forbade her to do so. She had married Charles Carrington because her great-uncle had arranged it, even though James had refused to marry the blacksmith's daughter, refused in some vague adolescent hope that his love for Sarah might someday work the miracle of marriage to her.

His bow to her in the doorway of the fireroom was almost a mockery. Drawing himself back up to his full height, he greeted her, now remembering well her married name. "Good evening, Mrs. Carrington."

Olanthia Jones, a black servant girl, born into slavery and now free on Connecticut soil, started down the hall from the taproom, carrying a large tray of food and ale. She walked quickly and gracefully, apparently headed for the staircase which led to the upper floor rooms. James barely noticed her.

Abruptly Sarah Carrington's eyes reflected the success of his sarcasm. Good. Unfortunately, too quickly she seemed to recover completely. In a voice neither pleasant nor unpleasant she answered, "Good evening, Mr. Devant."

For the first time James noticed the child. A boy, maybe five or six, sleeping on a bench near the fire. Yes, the group he had seen earlier near Norwalk had probably been Sarah's group. Two men with her. Strange. Sarah and Charles Carrington were well known as staunch loyalists. The Twin Stallion catered to patriots, and a few of the more radical patriots, especially with a few drinks, could be dangerous to loyalists.

Her manner subtly protective, Sarah stepped between her sleeping child and James. The action surprised James. Was she actually afraid of him? The idea was so ludicrous he wanted to laugh. Did she think him a drunken rebel, a source of physical danger to her and the child? With an almost curt nod indicating that their conversation was ended—Lord, she was beautiful, standing there with the firelight dancing in her hair—he turned to face Garth, who stood near the base of the staircase opposite the fire-room in conversation with the black servant girl, their voices hushed.

Two men started down the hall from the taproom, one dressed much the same as James and Garth were dressed, the other decked out like an English dandy, complete with white tieback wig. The dandy appeared to be in his late twenties, the other somewhat older, both tall, slim, similar in their physical features. Both carried trays similar to the one carried by Olanthia.

"Is he dead?" James heard Garth ask.

"I don't know," she answered.

"Who?" asked James, joining them.

Keeping his voice low, Garth answered, "Logan. They caught him in England, put him in Newgate. She don't know if he been hung yet. Some say it was a trap. Some say you planned it."

James frowned. Smugglers did not bring in the law. It was not done. He doubted whether anyone with any intelligence would take such an accusation seriously.

"I go," said Olanthia as the sound of approaching footsteps grew louder. With one last adoring look at Garth she walked quickly up the staircase which led to the upper-floor private rooms.

James nodded toward the taproom. It was time for Garth to find John McCaylan and tell him the tower room would be in use that night. As Garth started down the hall, James found himself being carefully observed by one of the approaching two men. Both men walked into the fireroom, but the one whose clothing was American rather than British merely deposited his tray on a long table near the center of the room, his eyes scarcely leaving James, who still stood by the stairs across the hall. Feigning casual disinterest, James turned his back, but the intensity of his concentration on everything he heard was not casual. He opened his jacket, permitted his hand to rest near his pistol. Although the voices in the fireroom were not really distinct, Sarah definitely spoke the name "Charles." Charles Carrington, probably, her husband, the English dandy. The sound which most concerned James, however, was the sound of footsteps. They drew nearer to him. Still maintaining his casual stance, he turned and found himself face to face with the second man, the one who had accompanied Charles Carrington into the fireroom. The man's eyes were sharp, guarded; his face was intelligent, not handsome, but his features were regular, well formed, somewhat aristocratic. Like James, the other man's hand rested close to his pistol.

Two men approached from the taproom. One was perhaps forty years of age, heavy, stocky, while the other was younger than James; his gait was awkward, his hair blond. If one judged by their clothing, the two men who had just arrived were not well-to-do. From their open interest in James, it seemed likely the man who stood in front of James had summoned them.

Not unpleasantly the man who had been in the fire-room with Sarah addressed James. "Good evening, sir."

"Good evening."

"I don't believe I've had the pleasure of seeing you before."

"And why might you assume it would be a pleasure?"

"It's a pleasure to know any man who supports the cause of freedom against the tyranny of King George," the man answered promptly, "and since I find you here at this hour, I know you have a pass, signed by a member of one of the local Committees of Correspondence. I am Edward Carrington, chairman of the New Hereford Committee, but I know most of the officers of the other committees in this area. In friendship I greet a stranger obviously known to one of my colleagues. Which colleague? May I see your pass, sir?"

James froze, tried to keep his eyes from the two men backing Edward Carrington. He had a pass. No stranger dared enter a patriot-dominated area without one. However, since no member of any Committee of Correspondence would dare openly support a man who smuggled British goods, the pass was forged. The name it bore, so convincingly copied from the man's genuine signature, was Edward Carrington.

CHAPTER TWO

Midway up the curved marble staircase Isobel Browne stopped, overwhelmed by her surroundings. The molded ceiling was a three-dimensional tapestry of gilded leaves and flowers, culminating in a magnificent crystal chandelier, unlit at the moment, supplemented by crystal candleholders which lined the wall along the staircase, alternately lit, providing a soft, glowing path to the darker regions above. The stuccoed wall was niched to accommodate a display of statuary worldwide in origin. Below, the semidark entrance hall boasted larger-scale art treasures, rising up in stark patterns of light and shadow against the silver-tone marble floor. The portraits, all in intricately patterned heavy gold frames, were mainly of stern-faced gentlemen of varying ages all in opulent costumes reaching back in time at least a century, possibly even longer.

Designed in the William Kent tradition back in the 1730s, Lord Henry Marlowe's house was considered by many one of the finest in London, although others now, in 1775, considered it dated. At the establishment where

Isobel Browne lived and worked, only one other girl had seen it. Henry Marlowe, sixth Earl of Lanchester, did not usually bring ladies of pleasure into his home, but to-night, with his wife, son, daughter-in-law and four grand-sons away in the country for at least another week, to-night, giddy from the wine and entranced by Isobel's beauty, his lordship had made an exception.

She stood on the stairs like an additional art treasure, wisps of copper-gold hair escaping from under her fur-trimmed green velvet bonnet. Her coat, also green velvet trimmed in fur, was open. Her beige and gold satin bro-cade gown was cut low, revealing an ample bosom which somehow emphasized and complemented the smallness of her waist. In conjunction with the painted rouge, the natural flush brought on by the February cold outside gave an almost-scarlet tone to her cheeks, but in the soft candle glow, her deep blue eyes, her youth—she was nineteen—and natural loveliness predominated.

Several feet ahead of her, near the top of the stairs, Lord Marlowe turned and looked at her, his gaunt, aged face shadowed, hawklike, in the candle glow. His cape was black with liberal traces of white powder which had fall-en from his Cadogan-puffed horseshoe toupet wig. His waistcoat and breeches were blue-gray satin; his shirt was French silk with an abundant quantity of English lace.

He held out his hand to Isobel, a quiet command that she disengage her attention from the house and return her thoughts to their proper focal point—himself.

With well-practiced grace, she caught her skirt in her right hand and lifted it high enough to enable her to con-tinue up the stairs without tripping. At the top of the stairs Lord Marlowe drew her into his arms and kissed her, his breath heavy with the stench of stale alcohol and rotting teeth, mingled with the too-sweet scent of per-fume, primarily musk, applied to his person far too liberally many hours earlier. She laughed, drew back from him playfully, but permitted him to encircle her waist with his arm and lead her down the hall to a large paneled door set off from the others by lit candles in ornate gilded holders which protruded from the walls on both sides.

He opened the door which led into a bedroom. Again, Isobel found her attention trapped by the house. The room was large, with blue damask-covered walls matching the draperies in the glow of perhaps two dozen burning candles. The bed was enormous, West Indian mahogany, richly canopied and draped with a carved lion motif carried through the fabric and wood, even to lion's paw casters. The fireplace was of a blue-tone marble, its mantel shelf supported by two columns on which a fantasy of moving lights and shadows kept pace with the crackling fire. A fire! Isobel ran to it, removed her coat and bonnet, then tossed them onto a nearby scarlet brocade chair. The room, she decided now that its initial impression had worn off, was a bit old-fashioned, but still stunning. Any of the light, modern French influences which predominated the house where she worked would be grossly out of place here. Here everything was large and heavy, ornate, gilded, marbled, carved, exquisitely coordinated and exquisitely expensive.

The warmth from the fire flooded her body. She threw her head back, drank it in, her movements deliberately, yet subtly sensual, provocative. She knew he was watching her. Sir Henry's arms encircled her waist. For one brief instant she tried to imagine that he was young, strong, handsome and in love with her, but the image disappeared quickly. Gently she turned, within his arms, and kissed his lips, almost shyly. Her feigned embarrassment, she knew, was part of his pleasure. A product of London's slums, father unknown, mother dead, beneath her carefully learned upper-class accent, which still occasionally slipped into cockney, Isobel Browne was rapidly becoming a master of her craft. She had been with her current madam, one of the finest in London, only six months. Six months to "improve" herself, to rise to a level where some fine rich gentleman might take her out of the house and set her up as his mistress, possibly even his wife. Allowing Lord Henry to lead her to the bed, she feigned a tremor of excitement as he unpinned her handkerchief and gown, then unlaced her stays. Parchment-like spidery fingers groped hungrily over her now-naked breasts; thin and wet lips delighted in the taste of her flesh.

"Isobel," he whispered, "Is-o-bel, the whore, the strumpet, *my* strumpet!"

Abruptly tending to his own clothes, he nodded toward an enameled Bristol-glass decanter set on a blue-green marble-topped table near the window. "Wine," he ordered, his voice suddenly sharp and commanding, "much wine. For both of us."

Quickly she brought two glasses. His waistcoat now removed, he continued to work on the buttons of his shirt with his right hand, his left hand holding the wineglass, its contents drained in a matter of seconds. "That is exquisite wine," he announced, his words beginning to slur. "French. Old. Rare. But you wouldn't know that, would you, girl?"

"I—I like it, milord."

"You like it! You don't know. Ah, but I'll bet you know a real diamond from a Cheap Street bauble." He held out his glass for a refill. Quickly, dutifully, Isobel obliged. With luck, he would get so drunk he would fall asleep.

For the third time, while he removed his shirt, Isobel filled his wineglass. How funny he looked, now spilling some of the wine, his elegant powdered wig still in place, the upper part of his body thin, his chest somewhat concave supporting a leather pouch which hung from his spindly neck by a golden chain. Not a money pouch, Isobel realized. More likely it contained papers. Important papers, she concluded, if he carried them so closely and constantly about his person. His eyes followed her gaze, his lips curving into a supercilious smile.

"Can you read?" he asked.

"No, milord," she answered truthfully, "except for a few words, of course. And I can read and write my own name."

"Can write it! Good girl!"

The leather packet around his neck became even more interesting to her. Were its contents something she should not read, if she could read? The fact that he had even mentioned the subject convinced her even further that the papers it probably contained must be valuable indeed, but no external reaction betrayed her thoughts. Of course, she concluded, there was no reason for him to be suspicious, no reason whatsoever for an illiterate harlot to be interested in whatever papers he might carry.

Depositing the wineglass none too safely on a table edge, he drew her body against his and undressed her completely, then stepped—or staggered—backward, his eyes taking in all of her naked body.

Slowly, nodding his approval, he removed the remainder of his own clothing, including his wig. Except for a few stray wisps of white hair, which somehow made him appear even more comical, he was totally bald.

Quickly, to avoid any external indication of the laughter which threatened to break from her lips of its own accord, against every measure of her own will, she ran to him, embraced him. "Milord," she whispered, "take me now!"

With a violence that amazed her, he shoved her away from him. If not for the bedpost, which she grabbed and clung to with both hands, she would have landed on the floor!

Initially she simply stared at him, more confused than frightened. Then, slowly, she felt the color rise in her face. How awful! His naked body plainly showed the source of his anger, a complete lack of the masculine response which would be required of him if they were to complete the purpose of her visit. The wine had indeed been good. *She* had drunk too much of it!

"Laugh at *me*, will you?" he exploded.

"No, milord, never! I—" Her voice broke, twisted into a sudden scream as he grabbed a heavy carved-mahogany walking stick and crashed it against the canopy support, inches away from where her head had been only seconds ago.

Drunk, beyond reason now, again he might have killed her with a blow, but this time, before he had the chance to raise the walking stick again, she caught its end with both hands, struggling and twisting, yanking, pulling, and what a grotesque dance he did at the other end of it, like a puppet, but a puppet made of steel, the steel forged to the wood of the walking stick.

"Let *go* of it!" screamed Isobel, still holding it, but now, instead of continuing to pull and twist, she lunged at him, shoved it toward him.

The carved lion's head handle rammed into his chest, threw him completely off-balance. His hands flew from the stick, leaving it completely in Isobel's grasp, and flayed the air. The rest of his body turned toward the bed, as though the bed might provide support, break his fall.

The fall was not broken, and what an awful fall it was! His head crashed against the bed leg to the right of the one where Isobel stood, the whole of his body now on the floor, still like a puppet but now a puppet twisted and discarded as though the strings had suddenly snapped.

Horror-stricken, wet with sweat, breathing as though no amount of air could ever be sufficient, Isobel looked down at him. He was unconscious now. Oh, how furious he would be when he awoke! As she continued to look at him, slowly, gradually, she realized that the carved lion's head which ornamented the base of the bed had something red all over it. Red? How still he lay, his mouth and eyes wide open.

Unconscious? No, he was not unconscious, he was—no! She shook her head as though sheer denial could erase the scene.

Abruptly, she swung around, faced the door. Someone might come in. No, that was unlikely. He had probably left instructions not to be disturbed until morning.

Morning! The horror, the reality of it began to penetrate. They would take her to prison. Hang her! The madam she worked for would not protect her. No one would help her.

Turning away from the corpse, she dropped to her knees, tried to collect her thoughts.

A sound—or had she only imagined it? A sound from the corpse. She swung around, looked at it. No, there had been no sound unless some final muscle twitch had caused one of the limbs to touch something. Henry Marlowe, sixth Earl of Lanchester, was unquestionably dead.

Slowly, unsteadily, Isobel rose to ther feet. Her mind was clear now. She must run. Leave London. Leave England, if possible.

Barely able to control her trembling hands, she walked wide around Lord Henry, gathered her clothes and dressed.

She would need money.

His purse lay on the table which supported his wig stand. She lifted it, dumped the contents into her hand. Four gold pieces! Might have been better, but not bad.

Instinct more than a direct thought gnawed at the back of her mind. Something he had said. Something about—diamonds. Yes! She looked at his waistcoat, draped over a chair. The buttons were diamonds! When he had said she could probably tell a real diamond from a Cheap Street bauble, he was answering the unspoken question she had asked with her eyes every time she had looked at the coat all evening.

She grabbed it. With fingers and teeth, she tore and gnawed at the thread which held the buttons. One by one, they came loose into her hands. She dropped them into her purse, fixed her cloak and bonnet, then walked to the door.

Compulsively she hesitated, drawn to one last look at the corpse. His left hand caught her attention. His fingers were adorned with rings, gold rings rich with precious stones.

Repugnance almost stopped her, but she forced herself to walk to the bed, kneel down beside him. It was not like stealing, she told herself determinedly. He had done this to her, gone after her with the stick; it was his fault he lay there, his fault she had to run, had to have money. At first she tried not to look at him. Then, angrily, she lifted his hand. The touch of his dead flesh brought bile to her mouth, washed away any lingering sweetness of the wine. She dropped the hand. How cold and clammy it was, so quickly. His eyes seemed to be staring at her.

Bracing herself, she tried again. This time she closed her eyes and, strictly by feel, stripped the rings from his fingers. One ring refused to budge. Angrily she shoved the hand away, then drew back as it seemed to move toward her of its own accord, a mere gravitational response to the angle and force with which she had pushed it.

Quickly she stuffed the six rings strewn about her on the floor into her purse.

For the first time it occurred to her that someone might indeed come to the room before morning. Lord Henry was an important man, a Member of Parliament. If a message arrived, the servants might very well interrupt him to deliver it.

She must not run. She must walk, quickly, quietly. Perhaps a servant was waiting to call a cab for her. If so, smile at him.

She hesitated. The leather packet was still around his neck. To remove it, she would have to touch him again, move his head.

It might be worth it. If whatever it contained was that valuable to him, perhaps it might also be valuable to Isobel. Perhaps it had something to do with someone else important, as Lord Henry had been important. And perhaps, if Isobel were arrested, that someone else might be willing to help her in exchange for the papers. She would, of course, have to find someone to read them to her—someone she could trust. Trust! Offhand, she could think of no one, even among those with whom she had a friendly relationship, who would not cut her throat in an instant if to do so might profit him.

Still, if Lord Henry valued these papers so highly, they were probably worth taking. With trembling hands and necessary force she removed the chain from his neck and slipped the packet, including the chain, down under her corset.

She walked to the door and opened it. Her heart seemed to stop. Had the door made that much noise when he had opened it? It seemed somehow all London must have heard it this time.

Carefully, her heart pounding, her skirt gently lifted, the silver buckles on her shoes reflecting the dim candlelight with each nervous step, she made her way down the hallway to the top of the stairs. Directly below, in front of her, a thousand miles and a thousand years away, she saw the front door. More carefully now, more frightened now, for the entranceway was more brightly lit than the upper hallway, she started down the stairs, her purse drawstring wrapped around her left wrist, her right hand leaving a trail of sweat smears on the West Indian mahogany carved railing. Step by step—only a few more steps to go. She was fully two-thirds of the way down, and so far at least, no servant had appeared.

With dreamlike semireality the front door seemed to open. She imagined she heard voices. Her mother's voice, back from the dead, to laugh at her.

No, not her mother's voice. And the moving door was not a dream.

"Wake Millicent," the woman said. "I'm famished."

"Yes, Mother," a man answered.

And another woman's voice, a younger voice: "I have never been so cold. I—"

All of a sudden the voices stopped. A group of people were inside the house now. They stared at Isobel. The old woman, the younger woman and the man, probably her husband, and four boys, all foppishly dressed, ranging in age from perhaps five to eleven.

It was the man who finally broke the silence. He seemed more stunned than angry.

"Who are you?" he demanded.

She knew who they were. Lord Marlowe's family, according to Lord Henry supposed to be in the country for at least another week. In that instant the adult son's physical resemblance to his father seemed grotesque.

This time with anger, he repeated, "Who are you?"

Clinging to the banister for more support than she dared let any of them know, she straightened her back, tossed her head and answered in her best upper-class accent, "I am a guest of your father, sir."

Both women at the base of the stairs looked stunned. The older one was first to turn her back. The younger promptly followed suit, as the children continued to stare.

"And I was just leaving," she concluded, releasing her grip on the banister. By some miracle for which she was fully grateful, her legs carried her to the base of the stairs, where she managed a curtsy to Lord Marlowe's son, proper in every respect except for the way in which her eyes met his, teasing, challenging. "Good night, sir. I'd not disturb him. He's quite tired."

The younger Lord Marlowe gave her a slight nod which indicated his familiarity with the courtesies of fashionable whorehouses. His eyes, however, did not respond to her teasing. They seemed instead to have picked up something else about her, something not quite right.

She started for the door.

His voice, behind her now, was authoritative. "One moment, please."

Momentarily panic-stricken, she felt the color drain from her face. Did he know? No, of course not. There was no way he could possbily know. She turned and again curtsied, but this time was unable to muster anything flirtatious. "Yes, milord?"

"My apologies, but I must insist you show me the contents of your purse."

The senior Lady Marlowe swung around, faced her son. "Apologies! You apologize to this creature in my home? I've heard all I can bear!" Head high, she started up the stairs.

Apparently upset and momentarily distracted by his mother's reaction, he half turned in the direction of the staircase. "Mother—"

Isobel ran for the door, lifted the latch.

"Henry!" cried his wife.

Startled, the younger Lord Marlowe seemed immediately to grasp at least part of the situation. He ran to the door, grabbed Isobel around the waist with one arm and, with his other hand, wrenched the purse from her wrist. In almost the same gesture he worked the purse open with his fingers and spilled its contents onto the dimly lit marble floor.

The clink of the coins, diamond buttons and gold rings seemed to Isobel incredibly loud. Not fully comprehending at first, the entire family looked at the scattered objects. Then, slowly, young Lord Marlowe's wife stooped and lifted one of the rings. His mother, watching from the stairs, stepped down again, drawn by her daughter-in-law's shocked expression.

After closer examination, the senior Lady Marlowe seemed equally shocked, then frightened by a dawning suspicion she seemed unwilling fully to consider. Clutching the ring in her hand, she turned and started quickly back up the stairs.

"He give it to me," screamed Isobel, lapsing into full cockney. "Don't go in his room. He's asleep. He give it to me!"

Physically unable to stop his mother because it would have meant releasing Isobel, who now employed every ounce of her strength to break from his grip, Lord Marlowe called, "Mother, no! Wait!" More quietly, he instructed his wife, "Ring for Thomas. Tell him to fetch the constable."

"Let me go!" cried Isobel, her voice now choked with sobs. "I didn't do it! He fell! It was an accident."

A piercing scream echoed from somewhere beyond the top of the stairs, followed by words growing rapidly louder as the senior Lady Marlowe, ghostly white and barely able to stand, came into view at the top of the stairs.

"She's murdered him," she cried. "God help us all, she's murdered him!"

Taken to Newgate Prison by carriage, her hands handcuffed behind her back, with a stern-faced elderly magistrate and one guard seated opposite her, Isobel found herself almost grateful for the shock which numbed her senses. She knew the February night air was cold, she felt each jolt of the carriage, heard the sound of the horses' racing hooves, the shrill London street noises as the fashionable section in which his lordship's house stood became part of the past in distance and time, yet somehow none of it seemed real. They would kill her, of course. Although she had never actually witnessed an execution, on more than one occasion she had seen the horse-drawn carts carrying condemned prisoners along the road to the Tyburn gallows. Would the crowds that generally turned out to enjoy the executions pelt her with rocks, or would they cheer for her, or would they merely laugh at her in her agony? Oh, God, oh, why had God not taken her the same minute she had been born?

She looked at the guard, who was young and seemed to enjoy watching her. His eyes were cruel. More than once he ran his tongue over his lips. The magistrate was old and self-righteous in fulfilling his promise to Lord Henry's widow to deliver Isobel to the prison personally. A rider on horseback had been sent ahead to notify the prison authorities of her pending arrival, for Isobel was no ordinary prisoner. The man they believed she had killed was too important.

The magistrate lifted part of the curtain and glanced out the window. "Almost there," he announced. As though in response to his words, the sound of the horses' hooves, clattering against the cobblestone street, slowed, then stopped.

As the guard reached over to open the door, Isobel turned her head, but the rest of her body seemed suddenly made of rags, icy cold and immobile. The carriage stood directly in front of the gate to Newgate Prison. Two guards, each holding a lighted torch, stood like sentries on either side of the latticework iron gate which sealed the arched entrance to the prison area. How ominously dark and thick the stone walls seemed, stretching up from the torchlit entrance area to accommodate three life-size statues in symmetrical niches, flanked by two grand Tuscan pilasters eventually lost in black silhouette against the cold, moonlit sky.

While the guard climbed out of the carriage, two officials from the prison stepped forward and held out their hands to Isobel, whose hands were still cuffed behind her back.

"Step out, girl," ordered the magistrate angrily.

Since she made no move, he prodded her with his cane. The hands that finally removed her belonged to one of the officials, rough at first, but less rough as the torchlight revealed her face to those who awaited her arrival.

"Sorry, sir," she heard someone tell the magistrate, "we was unable to reach the warden. But don't you worry none. We'll take proper care of her."

One of the officials guided her to a short flight of stone stairs leading to a door at the base of one of the pillars. Instinctively the muscles of her right arm tightened, the beginning of a gesture to pick up her gown so she could ascend the stairs without tripping, but her hands were still handcuffed behind her back. The magistrate apparently misread her hesitation. Again he prodded her with his cane. She cried out, tried to move forward more as an attempt to escape pain than in any spirit of cooperation, but on the second step, her balance was lost in a tangle of brocade and she fell forward, striking her head against the massive open door in front of her. Her breath caught in her throat and pain brought a flood of nausea as blurred faces surrounded her, hands lifted her, moved her forward, half dragged, half carried her up the remaining stairs and through the doorway. Indistinct words were spoken. Supported by two men, she was on her feet again, her senses still reeling, the nausea growing worse. She heard the magistrate's voice, somewhere behind her, concluding the formalities of her transfer.

She stood in a small room with stone walls and a stone floor, cold, eerie and foreboding in the flickering glow of the thick, cheap candles which lined the walls. For the first time she got a good look at the two men who were with her. One was tall and thin, slightly stoop-shouldered, young—maybe in his early twenties—and his clothes seemed not quite clean. He wore leg irons! The other man was older, perhaps in his early fifties. Three of his front teeth were missing. He needed a shave, and his white hair was unkempt. The odor she had vaguely noticed when she first entered the prison was now stronger—stale, sour, fetid.

The older man addressed her, his voice all business. "Well, girl, and what money have you to pay your fee?"

Blankly she looked at him. "Fee?"

"The fee for your jailer," he snapped. "Surely you don't expect the man to take proper care of you if you don't pay him."

Still not understanding, she answered, "I—I had some gold pieces, but when they arrested me, they took my purse."

Under his breath the man swore, then continued. "But surely a lady so fine as yourself has friends—"

Someone who would give her money? Someone who

would admit to friendship with her in the position she was in? She wanted to laugh. "No, sir," she answered, fear growing inside her like a disease. "I have no one."

The two men exchanged irritable glances. "Then get a move on with you," snarled the older one.

Roughly they escorted her from the small room into a far larger one. The larger room contained an incredible variety of manacles which hung from the walls, supported by large iron hooks. Instinctively Isobel drew back, looked at both men, tried to read their eyes. Did they intend to torture her, try to make her confess? If so, then she must confess quickly, for the rope which awaited her neck would have her, she knew, no matter what she said.

"I did it," she said. "I killed him."

The older man shook his head. "That's too bad. They'll hang you." He took a key from the large ring which hung by his side, then stepped behind her to remove the handcuffs. Quickly she rubbed her wrists and looked at him. His attention, however, seemed focused on the walls. After only a brief hesitation, he stepped forward to select a set of leg irons, then motioned for Isobel to be seated on a long wooden bench next to the wall.

Kneeling on the floor in front of her, the man in the leg irons, a fellow prisoner, she realized, lifted her gown and found her ankles, his hand wandering up her leg considerably farther than necessary.

"You won't like the place where we have to put you," the man with white hair said. "Women's ward. All them pretty clothes—they'll tear 'em right off you."

The leg irons the man had selected for her were different, she noticed, than those worn by the other prisoner. Hers merely snapped closed. The cuffs on the man appeared to be welded. Even while she was seated, the weight of the irons was uncomfortable. The chain between them was maybe twenty-four inches long. As with her initial shock when she had first discovered Lord Henry was dead, this shock also began to recede, leaving in its wake an exceptionally sharp awareness of her immediate situation, every thought and instinct abruptly mobilized to deal with it.

As best she could, she watched his eyes as the male prisoner fastened handcuffs to her wrists. His eyes terrified her—because they were so blank, so dead. It was the other man she must listen to, learn from.

"A fine lady like you," the older man went on, "layin' around in all that filth. A lot of them's gone mad up there. They'll cut up your face just 'cause you're young and pretty."

Her eyes, bright and alert now, remained on the older man. His words were a threat. Threats implied alternatives. They wanted something from her. Sex? *A fine lady like you.* Perhaps they assumed she had merely been his lordship's mistress. But was there really an alternative, or was it merely a game to see what they could get from her? Dear Lord, did they still not believe her that there was no one who would give them money on her behalf? Perhaps it was, indeed, sex they wanted. A cooperative woman could be considerably more pleasurable than one who resisted. The thought sickened her—what would she have to do, and for how many of them? And yet—no, sex was not his game. At least not his primary concern.

Again the older man stepped to the wall and returned with an additional chain, this one attached to a hinged iron collar. Eyes wide, Isobel stared at him, then rose to her feet and drew back. "No!" she cried. "*Why?*"

"Oh, now you mustn't give us no trouble, milady," he said quickly. "Anyone going to be hanged, we got to put lots of irons on 'em so they can't run away."

Run away? The man was mad. No, not mad. More of the game. Helplessly she remained standing as the younger man snapped the collar into place around her neck, then attached the end of the dangling chain in front to the middle link in the chain between her handcuffs. Again engulfed by shock which threatened to numb her thought processes, she realized she could no longer stretch her arms full length, no longer even rest them at her sides. The cold iron weight on both her neck and her arms was already uncomfortable, with the full promise of later pain. But why were they torturing her? She had already confessed.

Methodically the older man selected yet another set of chains, then—part of the game, she was sure—he appeared to hesitate. "Of course, if you're truly repentant of all your sins—"

"I'm truly repentant," she answered quickly, fighting hysteria.

He smiled, his grizzled face with the missing teeth twisted and demonlike in the flickering candle glow. *This is like hell,* she thought. Only hell was supposed to smell of brimstone, not feces, urine, vomit and sweat. The stench seemed even stronger now. A subtle shift in the direction of some hidden air current perhaps. "Well, if you're truly repentant, then maybe you don't need to be so heavily ironed. But you see, that's a problem. We don't get no pay for taking chains off. Not until they hang you, and that might not be for weeks, even months. You got to have your trial and everything."

At first she merely stared at him. Then, abruptly, she understood. "I have no money," she cried. "They took it. All of it."

"A lady like you can get some," he snarled. "Do you think us fools? A relative. A friend. A gentleman friend, perhaps."

Abruptly she remembered the papers she had taken in

the leather pouch from Lord Henry's corpse. "I . . . might."

His body seemed to relax. Obviously pleased with himself, he answered, "Good. Give us his name. We'll get a message to him."

No, she dared not show them the papers, and she could not read them herself because she could not read. Desperately she answered, "I don't know!"

"You don't know his name?"

The assistant made a circular motion with his finger and tapped his head, indicating that he believed her to be at least slightly mad. Speaking for the first time since she had seen him, he said, "Maybe somebody in stateside might want her. Maybe Logan."

"Why Logan?" asked the older man.

"Because they're hanging him next week. Give us the best price for her, I'll wager. What else he got to spend his money for?"

"Stateside?" asked Isobel.

"Oh, that's where we keeps the quality folk like yourself," answered the older man. "If they got money to pay for it, that is. We got some fine gentlemen over there. Not like the wards. Each man got his own room, with a door and a bed, decent food, clean water. Now Logan, they'll be hanging him soon, but there's other gentlemen over there." His mind seemed to have taken off with enthusiasm in this new direction. "Only start with Logan," he went on. "He'll pay to get them chains off you, I'll wager, and maybe even give you some money for yourself. He's ugly, but he's going to die, he's got money and not much time left to spend it."

She swallowed hard. "What did he do?"

"Logan? Jack Logan's a smuggler. Come over from America. Should have hanged him right where they caught him. Killed two guards who was bringing him here, with just his hands, I heard. Got clean away, but they caught him again. Won't get away this time."

Carefully Isobel asked, "If he has that much money—"

The prisoner shook his head. "Anybody helped Jack Logan escape, they'd get hanged themselves. No, he'll hang."

The older man patted her cheek, then, his eyes never leaving hers, his hand cupped her breast over the fabric of her dress. The gesture was neither lustful nor rough—it merely asked the question. "A young girl like you needs friends in here. Friends like me."

She froze, yet somehow managed to smile at him. "It's not me you want," she said, hoping desperately that none of her repugnance showed. "At least not as much as you want the money," she continued. "Let me be clean and fresh and eager for Mr. Logan. You say he'll be dead in a few days. See what money you can get from him. I'll see what I can get." Her smile was soft, inviting. "Then we'll meet again."

Laughing, he withdrew his hand. "You're a sly one, aren't you? Come on." He and the prisoner walked with her back into the hall, the prisoner carrying two candles, their trailing flames slicing an eerie path through the tomblike darkness. It was the first time Isobel had actually attempted much movement under the weight of chains. At first even the sound frightened her; then the desire merely to stretch out her arms without constriction, without pain, overwhelmed her. The odor was now definitely stronger. Mingled with voices, there was laughter, but the laughter one might expect in a madhouse, not a prison.

Someone screamed, high and piercing. More laughter followed.

At the top of the stairs, occasional torches lit the hallway. She felt dizzy, partially from the stench, partially from the muscular pain caused by the chains, but something new seemed the predominant factor. How easy it would be, she thought suddenly, to break from her captors and throw herself down the stairs. Kill herself, with luck! The iron collar could easily break her neck. They would never hang her then. The devil-faced jailor would never know her living body against his, and neither would the American murderer, the condemned ugly man with so much money to spend.

The impulse lasted only a second. With luck she would die, but without luck she would merely cripple herself. Crippled, she would be thrown into one of the women's wards, of no further interest to anyone, at least of no interest that might be at all advantageous to herself.

And yet—to die! The mere thought gave her a sense of light-headed comfort. If she had to die, she decided, it would not be by the hangman's noose. It would be by her own hand.

She felt radiant, sustained, the weight of her chains somehow distant, part of another body, another life.

The wards she passed, candlelit and noisy behind their heavy iron doors with small gratings one could look through, seemed distantly interesting. She was an observer, no longer a participant. Her body was merely a weight, the chains a part of that weight which, unfortunately, she was still connected to, but the connection was now merely a thin thread, a thread soon to be snapped, at her convenience, by means of her choosing, quickly, effectively. Oh, what fools they were to think they could use her so cruelly, control her so completely!

Abruptly, a man's voice cut through the torchlit pitch-scented corridor ahead. "Hey, who's there?" They were on the second floor now, three floors up, with the street-level floor counted. The voice was heavy cockney, not frightened, merely guarded, alert—uneasy perhaps.

"Just me, William and a prisoner," the younger man answered promptly.

William. To Isobel, the man with white hair now had a name.

Two men appeared from around the corner, the sound of their footsteps lost in the clatter of Isobel's leg irons against a floor which consisted of thick oaken planks. One of the men carried a candle. Both were armed. The man without the candle had a large ring of keys dangling from his wide leather belt. Voices in this section of the prison were more subdued than in the other sections Isobel had just passed through. The intensity was still there, but the atmosphere was less high-pitched, less frantic. Also, she realized, the air was cleaner. The predominant odor was pitch, but even the pitch did not overwhelm.

The man with the keys at his side stared at her, obviously both startled and pleased. To William, he said, "What's she in for?"

"Killed her lover," came William's prompt reply. "Used his walking stick on him. Important man he was, too. Lord Henry Marlowe. Member of Parliament."

All within hearing distance seemed impressed. The man without the keys stepped forward. "Well, we'll find a nice room for you, milady."

William laughed. "She's not got a shilling to her name."

The man who had started forward froze. His expression changed from confusion to expectation. An explanation was in order. He knew William. William would give him an explanation.

William grinned. "We figured Logan might be willing

to pay her fees, seeing as how he has so little time left. If not—well, we'll let some of the gentlemen take a look at her."

Yes, she thought, let someone pay her fees. Then she would die. Then let them fight over whether the money should be returned.

Accompanied now by the four men, she walked to the end of the corridor, then turned left.

The corridor was wider here, and more brightly lit. Other guards were visible, most of them slightly shabby, not quite clean. Three of the cell doors were open. The far end of the hallway between the two rows of cells was dominated by a fireplace in which a roaring, crackling fire at least removed some of the chill in the air all the way back to where Isobel stood.

Awkwardly, again painfully aware not only of the weight of the chains but also of her flesh which she feared might actually be scraped bloody by them, Isobel permitted herself to be led down the hallway, past one of the cells with an open door. A card game was in progress inside, between one of the guards and a warmly dressed older man whose feet and hands were shackled. The room's furnishings would have suited a comfortable inn, even down to the bottle of wine on a bedside table.

Some of the horror she had felt in passing the wards began to subside.

Most of the guards at least looked at her , and several asked questions, but no one slackened his pace to answer.

"Here we are," announced the man with the keys who had greeted them in the outer corridor. They stood outside the fourth cell on the left. The door was closed, with an iron grating near the top.

"He's got only one more day here, you know," the man

with the keys told William, almost as an aside. "Day after tomorrow they're taking him down to the condemned hold. He swings on Friday."

"One day?" William frowned. "I thought it was longer. All her fees for just one day. Think he'll do it?"

The man with the keys gave William a careful sidelong glance. "Get whatever you can. Make a bargain with him." To Isobel, he added, "There's one part of the prison is better than here—the Castle—that's where they got the real fine gentlemen, but you might do better here. The Castle, that's where most ladies pretty as you who comes from outside to spend the night with some of the gentlemen wants to go. Not so many want to come here, so you might get even more money. You get whatever you can from Logan. We'll take good care of you."

His smile, if it could be called a smile, made her flesh crawl.

He rapped with his keys on the door. "Hey, Jack—"

A few seconds later a covering over the inside of the iron grating at the top of the door was pulled back, and a face became visible: a shadowy pockmarked face framed by long, stringy black hair. "What do you want?" he asked. His voice had a slight accent—American, she supposed.

"We're going to open the door," the man with the keys answered, promptly inserting the proper key into the lock.

The door opened, heavy and creaking on its large iron hinges.

Jack Logan stood about a foot back from the doorway, fully visible in a heavy black woolen shirt tucked into dark-gray breeches. His ankles were joined by a long chain. He was a big man, and William had not lied when he had said Jack Logan was ugly. His face was deeply marked from the pox, sections of his left cheek merely masses of scar tissue. His jaw was hard and square, his lips thick, fishlike, his eyes narrow, his body stocky, but well built, solid through the middle. Something other than his ugliness, however—his eyes, Isobel realized—caught and held her attention. Perhaps he was merely mad and refused to believe he would soon be hanged, but perhaps he was not mad. Mad or sane, however, these were not the eyes of a man resigned to death. She lowered her head in apparent shyness as she had learned to present herself to many of her clients, yet the direct eye contact between them which had begun almost the instant he saw her remained.

"This poor lady," began the man with the keys, "has no money. A new prisoner. Says she'd be ever so grateful if you was to help her—pay her fees so she could get some of them chains took off. Says she don't want to go to the felons' ward."

He was interested. She was sure of it.

He shook his head, turned his eyes to the man with the keys. "No. Tomorrow's visiting day. For the last time I'll be seeing the woman I was going to marry, and I'll not see her with the taste of another woman on my lips."

His answer startled her. He was lying. But why? There had to be a reason, a good reason. But what was it? Tomorrow would be his last full day here, in this loosely guarded section. Wherever they took those condemned to die—the "condemned hold," someone had said—it was probably far more tightly guarded.

Far less chance of escape?

Escape! In that instant, for the first time since she had entered the prison, Isobel felt fully alive. A smuggler, they had told her. From America. A big, important smuggler. That meant he owned or worked for or with someone who owned ships. A ship to take him back to America? Obviously they had not broken the whole smuggling operation because Jack Logan had money, an ample supply which continued to pour into the prison. Money, power, an organization and ships. Could he do it? Was it really possible to get an important condemned prisoner out of Newgate and onto a ship bound for some other faraway part of the world?

Of course it was possible. Not easy, that was all. Dangerous probably. Very dangerous.

The man with the keys looked surprised, then disappointed.

Whatever he intended to try, Isobel realized, was probably planned for tonight or tomorrow. That was why he had said he did not want her. He did not want her in the way!

She looked at William. "May I speak to him, sir? Alone?"

Quickly exchanged glances among the three officials who had accompanied her to the cell promptly settled the matter. With the cell door closed behind her, she checked to make sure the covering over the iron grating at the top of the door was also closed. Now she turned her full attention to Jack Logan.

"I'll not take you, girl." Almost awkwardly, he corrected himself: "Milady."

"I'm no lady," she answered quietly, allowing her voice to slip into its natural heavy cockney accent, "as you are no gentleman. Take me with you."

He looked at her as though her meaning were unclear.

"I want to go with you," she continued, her voice intense yet now barely more than a whisper, "to America."

Surprise turned quickly to biting cynicism, as he touched his short thick fingers to a mass of scar tissue on his pockmarked left cheek. "I see. You find me so beautiful you cannot wait to fulfill your part of the bargain."

"No," she answered, her head as high as the weight of the iron collar permitted. "They told me you were ugly, and you are ugly. But you're strong, and you're big, and you have courage. And you're new—a whole new world. America. I want you. I want you very much."

He was vulnerable, she realized. His reaction lasted only an instant before the guarded look returned, but in that instant she saw that he wanted to believe her. Yes, she decided, she could manage him. At least she could try and know the odds were in her favor. As well as Jack Logan might know ships and selected sections of the English and American coastlines, Isobel Browne knew men.

He hesitated, then walked to the door, the chain between his ankles dragging on the oaken floor. The door was unlocked. He merely pushed it open and faced the three men awaiting his decision.

"All right," he said. "How much do you want for her?"

CHAPTER THREE

As Charles Carrington placed the tray which held food and drink on a table to the left of the blazing fire in the fireroom of the Twin Stallion Inn, Sarah Carrington, still standing, barely acknowledged his entrance. Rather, she continued to look at James Devant. James, near the base of the staircase across the hall, was now in conversation with Sarah's rebel brother-in-law and two other men, obviously known to Edward. Was James Devant one of them, she wondered—James Devant! By what alchemy had the boy she had once known and loved and desired so desperately not to love turned into this incredibly handsome man? Had he, like she, married? But what difference did it make? James Devant was no part of her life. A stranger now. And yet, shamelessly, her eyes refused to leave him; her heart refused to slow to the same pace it had held before he appeared.

Was James one of them, she wondered—one of the rebels? The young James Devant had seemed so much more sensitive than Edward, so much more . . . vulnerable. Indeed, politics produced unlikely sets of companions. The politics of treason. Treason. Somehow the word still sounded strange, foreign, when applied to Edward, yet it was the word her husband, Charles, had lately begun to apply more and more frequently when speaking of his older brother. Of course, Charles was and always had been a strict Tory. The king could do no wrong. Sarah, however, as in the days when she had been much younger, was still basically a Whig. Yes, the king could do wrong. As far as Sarah was concerned, he was indeed wrong in many of the laws and restrictions he had tried to force on the colonies, but he was not an evil man. He was merely misguided, poorly advised.

This was where Edward had gone wrong. One does not seriously consider disowning a loving parent merely because the parent makes mistakes; one does not talk of open rebellion, even war; one does not physically attack those who remain loyal to the parent, the protector, the king. At least, that is, if one is sane and honorable. Sarah was sure that given time, King George would recognize and correct his too-authoritarian attitude toward the colonies. But they must give him the necessary time; they must not force him into a corner where British subjects would have no other choice than to take up arms against other British subjects, brother against brother, as even now political differences threatened the love between her own husband and his brother Edward.

How incredible that she and Charles should need Edward's protection to travel to their own home in New Hereford, in fear that some unruly rebel mob might actually attack them. Including the time spent at sea, Sarah, Charles and their son had been away from New Hereford only five months, their ship docking in Boston yesterday morning. Boston, because Charles had had some business to attend to there. Could the whole world—their world—really have changed so radically in only five months?

Of course, even in London they had heard stories—

exaggerated rumors, they had initially believed—of rebels gone mad with power throughout New England, but it was not until Edward's last letter arrived that the gravity of the situation began to penetrate. The letter urged them to sell the house in New Hereford and, for their own safety, to remain in England. Their father, Joseph Carrington, the letter further stated, was in failing health but safely out of New Hereford, lodged in a strongly loyalist-dominated section of New York.

Furious that anyone might dare even suggest a threat to his person or property and with no comprehension of the very real danger, Charles made arrangements at once to return to America. Charles had been born in New Hereford. He knew or was at least known by most of the people who lived there. It was important, he told Sarah, to show the local residents that those within the Carrington family still loyal to the king were not to be intimidated.

Yet, gradually, even prior to their trip to England, Charles had seen the stature and power of New Hereford loyalists in local government diminish. He knew of some of the harassments and injustices other New Hereford loyalists had suffered, but none of the others were nearly as wealthy or influential as the Carringtons.

They should never have left for England, Charles told his wife. Clearly, their duty had been to remain in New Hereford, an example to other loyalists, whose courage might otherwise falter. Sarah, however, far more concerned with the safety of her only surviving child, had begged Charles to let the boy remain in England. Still not seriously believing New Hereford could actually be dangerous to him, Charles had merely admonished her for what he called her lack of patriotism.

Now, however, Sarah knew Charles, too, was frightened and grateful for the protection he had so condescendingly accepted from his brother, at Edward's insistence. Last night, in the privacy of their shared bed at another rebel-dominated inn, Charles suggested that it might well be best if they remained in New Hereford only long enough to take what steps they could to preserve as many of their possessions as possible, then, like his father, waited in New York for the storm to subside. Wait for King George to send in the necessary troops to restore proper order. To Charles, it was beginning to look as though the king would soon have no other reasonable alternative. Yet, although in his anger the prospect of seeing these rebels cut down to proper size was basically appealing, it also frightened him. Edward was one of the rebels, an outspoken, eloquent, powerful leader in league with other equally scurrilous leaders, throughout the entire thirteen colonies. When all of them were finally rounded up, tried for treason and hanged, would Edward Carrington be among them?

"Who is he?" Charles asked his wife.

Startled, Sarah answered, "Oh, I'm sorry. I did not mean to ignore you. His name is James Devant. I knew him when we were children. His mother worked for Uncle Ezra. I met her when I came to America after my parents died. Then she died, only a week or so later. James and I were—" She broke off. How strange the words sounded as memory clashed with the reality of this adult man, who, only a moment or so ago, had greeted her so coldly, yet, at the same time, unleashed such emotional turmoil within her. "We were fond of each other," she concluded.

"How old were you?" asked Charles.

She looked at her husband, then laughed. "Charles, we were children. I was—I don't even remember, maybe twelve or thirteen when he left New Hereford. He went to work in a shipyard, in Boston, I think. I'll admit, I'd hoped he might write to me, but he never did. It doesn't matter. So long ago." She stopped talking. It did matter. She had not merely hoped he might write; she had prayed for it and in those same prayers had begged God to forgive her for praying for something so obviously contrary to her uncle's wishes. Even after she had married Charles, there were still moments when James Devant came into her mind and refused to leave in spite of her occasionally painful determination to be a faithful and dutiful wife to Charles in thought as well as in action.

"I suppose he's one of them," she added almost abstractedly, trying to turn her attention to the food her ever considerate husband had brought for her.

Perhaps it would have been better, she thought, had she never seen James Devant again. Although time had been kind to him—no one could deny that the slender, somewhat awkward youth had grown into an extremely handsome man—still, a man's soul was far more important than his appearance, and apparently James Devant's soul had become so twisted with disloyalty to his king, even the friendship he had once had with Sarah counted for nothing. How cold he had been. A reaction, no doubt, to the well-known loyalist politics of all her family, except Edward. She must dismiss James Devant from her thoughts. Remember, rather, the young boy. But why remember, why think of him at all? Like some unrelenting demon, however, he stayed in her mind. Had she wanted to, she could have walked across the hall and touched him. What an odd thought. Touch him in what way? As a mother might touch her child, gently, tenderly, so Sarah might this night lovingly touch the child James had once been, should the man suddenly step back in time and re-present himself to her as a boy.

Oh, no! What a lie! It was not as a child that she longed to touch him, even hold him in her arms.

"Edward seems to know him," she added. Guilt brought a flush of color to her cheeks. She had made her voice sound casual, a deliberate attempt to hide the intensity of her true feelings. She must pray for forgiveness, pray that God release her from any interest in James Devant. She sat facing her husband and began to eat.

"No," said Charles quietly, a deliberate understatement, "I do not think he is one of them."

Attracted by the same sounds which had caught her husband's attention, Sarah looked back across the hall. The two men who had stood slightly behind Edward a few moments ago now forceably held James Devant. Stunned, she started to rise, then caught herself quickly. She must remain seated. Edward was searching him! Apparently unnoticed by Edward, the tall black man, who had been with James when he first came in, started down the hall from the taproom, saw James being held by the others and quickly ducked back out of sight beyond Sarah's line of vision. No longer able to control herself, Sarah rose to her feet.

Charles caught her arm, stopped her. "Have you gone mad? Stay out of it!" As he spoke, his eyes searched hers.

Awkwardly, helplessly, her face deeply flushed, she answered, "But . . . he was a child."

"He is not a child now."

"What will they do to him?"

"I don't know," Charles answered, his voice sharp, tinged with anger—jealousy, perhaps? No, that was ridiculous. Charles had no reason to be jealous. She had never given him cause. "Depends on what he's done, I suppose," Charles continued. "Sit. Eat. He is no concern of yours."

Returning to her seat, Sarah leaned forward, her voice

low. "They took a paper from him. Whatever it was, Edward is furious. Charles, I think he's one of us. God help him, I think he's a loyalist. Perhaps that's why he greeted me so coldly. Any show of friendship might have given him away. Surely there must be something we could—"

"What?" snapped Charles. "What would you suggest we do? If they murder him, would you suggest we invite them to murder us also? There is a point beyond which even Edward cannot protect us. Be still, wife, and tend to your own proper concerns."

She felt as though he had slapped her. Anger mingled with guilt. He was right, of course, yet compulsively, though carefully, she took one last look at James. Disarmed now, he faced Edward Carrington's pistol as the older man who had held him stepped to the fireroom entrance. His question was directed to both Sarah and Charles. With a nod of his head, he indicated James. "Do you know this man?"

Charles was initially startled, then frightened, Sarah realized, although someone who did not know him might not see it. Their son still slept on the bench by the fire. She had waited in the fireroom for the fire to be lit to warm the room where they would spend the night, but now she wished she had gone to the room directly, never to have known that James Devant had even visited the inn that night.

As though speaking to an unruly servant, Charles answered, "Why do you ask?"

Edward also looked startled. Apparently he had neither authorized nor anticipated the older man's actions.

"Because you look so interested. Because I think he's a damned Tory, just like you two."

"Mark!" The voice was Edward's, firm, authoritative. "They've no connection with this."

"No? I think they know him. I think they planned to

meet him here. What for? To pass information? What information?"

With his pistol, a bell-mouthed flintlock, Edward motioned James into the fireroom. Apparently intending to put Mark in his proper place once and for all, he asked, "Sarah, Charles, do either of you know this man?

"No," answered Charles, promptly.

Sarah's awkward hesitation hit Edward like a slap. "I—I knew him when we were children," she answered finally. Perhaps too quickly she added, "Tonight's the first time I've seen him in years." Her eyes met James' and held. She saw that he was afraid, yet somehow sensed that his fear worked for him, sharpened his instincts like those of an animal, quick and sure with intensified strength in the face of danger. She searched his eyes and read—what? Irony? Why? Abruptly she wondered, was it her connection with Edward, who now held him at gunpoint and seemed ready to—what? What would they do to him?

"Hasn't seen him in years!" scoffed Mark.

"Leave us," commanded Edward.

A new element—confusion—appeared in Mark's anger. "*Leave*?"

The younger man stepped fully into the room. Apparently uneasy, he watched both Edward and Mark.

With obvious yet quiet rage boiling directly below the surface, Edward addressed Mark, "Do you dare question my loyalty to the cause of American freedom?"

The older man seemed somewhat taken aback. "I never said—"

"I tell you, leave us. I am in command here. Leave us and say nothing of this." To the younger man, he added, "Stay with him. See to it that he holds his tongue better than he holds his liquor."

The older man hesitated; then, apparently disconcerted, with an unconvincing show of face-saving indignation, he left the room. The younger man followed, awkwardly but closely.

When they were gone, his gun still trained on James, Edward spoke to his brother, his voice barely more than a whisper. "Do you know this man?"

Apparently surprised by Edward's anger, Charles answered, "I already told you, I do not."

To James, Edward repeated the question, this time indicating Charles as the subject, "Do you know this man?"

James remained silent.

Edward leveled his pistol, aimed at James' heart. His voice was quiet. "Answer me."

"Edward, no!" The voice was Sarah's. "We knew each other when we were children. His mother worked for Uncle Ezra. What I said before is true. We haven't seen each other in years."

"Then you have no idea why he might carry a forged pass with a signature so like mine I doubt whether any man other than myself would know it was false."

"No," answered Sarah, looking now at James. Her eyes searched his for some explanation, some effort to save himself.

To Charles, Edward continued, "If you're lying to me, using me—"

"Edward," Charles answered, his voice sharp with fear as much as with anger, "for God's sake, have you gone mad? I told you, I never saw him before."

Edward hesitated, then seemed to relax, momentarily at least, in the familiar trust of his brother's love, if not his politics. He shook his head. "I never should have agreed to bring you here. I should have forceably kept you away."

"We'll be safe enough in the morning," offered Charles. "You handled that man—Mark—you handled him well," Charles continued. "Tomorrow they'll all be sober." The statement contained more hope than real belief.

Dryly, Edward answered, "It was not your safety I was thinking of. It was mine. I cannot help you anymore, Charles. I'll see you through the night, ride with you to the house in the morning and give you a pass to leave the area. I recommend you use that pass quickly, before nightfall. Go to Stamford. I'll see to it that a boat is made available to take you across the Sound to Fort Franklin. I'm sure the soldiers will give you the protection you need to reach the house where Father is staying. If you are truly wise, you will take Father with you and return to England."

"I've asked you for nothing," said Charles with tattered dignity.

Sarah turned her back, stepped over to her child. How like Charles, unable to admit his indebtedness to Edward—or anyone else. Of course, Charles had always resented Edward. Prior to the political gulf which now separated Edward from both his brother and father, Edward—the more charming, more attractive, more intelligent firstborn son—had been openly his father's favorite.

With the unemotional logic typical of Edward he ignored his brother's gibe and answered quietly, "I know." His attention now directed to James, Edward continued, "All right—outside." He nodded toward the hallway. "I'll learn your true business if it takes all night."

Sarah closed her eyes against the sound of their footsteps receding across the oaken floor toward the hallway. Charles was right. Stay out of it. Edward was also right. Those who served the king were in mortal danger in New

Hereford. But dear God, surely there must be something she could do.

No, there was nothing. She must think of other things. Think of her child, lying safely, sweetly asleep in front of the fire, her only surviving child, the other three all dead, two of the pox and one of lung fever.

"Forgive me," she whispered, meaning it. What a sinful creature she was.

Charles answered gently, "Of course I forgive you. The times are . . . difficult. For all of us."

Gratefully she closed her hands over his, yet her thoughts continued to flow in forbidden channels. Edward Carrington! Kind? Generous? No! In that instant—the sensation it produced was eerie—her brother-in-law seemed a stranger to her. Perhaps, when King George finally did send troops in to restore order, to protect innocent men like her husband and James Devant—when, finally, Edward Carrington was hanged for treason—perhaps memories of this night would enable her still to love her king without bitterness on Edward's behalf.

Sounds from the hallway. Startled, Sarah and Charles broke away from each other. A sudden scuffle, a stifled cry. James and Edward returned to the fireroom, Edward held by the enormous black man, one arm around his throat, the other arm pinning both of Edward's arms behind his back.

Quietly James addressed Sarah and Charles. "One sound, and we'll kill him." He nodded in the direction of the taproom. "They will hold you responsible for his death and tear you apart." His pistol aimed at Edward, James continued, "My friend will release you now. Hold steady. Make no sudden move."

Slowly, carefully, Garth Chandler released Edward Carrington.

With quiet, seething anger Edward asked James, "Who are you?"

"I must ask you to accompany me outside," James answered. Apparently the black man intended to remain behind, with Sarah and Charles.

Before any of them could move, the outside door at the end of the hall opened. The abruptly audible sound of the wind mingled with male voices. One of the men stopped at the doorway to the fireroom. He was in his late forties, portly, with friendly, guileless eyes. The red woolen scarf wrapped about his neck covered most of his face.

"Mr. Carrington," he said. "Good to see you." To James, he added, "Good evening, Mr. Devant." Apparently misinterpreting the cool reception he received from both men, he continued awkwardly, "Well, I imagine you two have business to discuss. I'll not disturb you."

As he took even two steps down the hall, James noticed his slight limp, a constant reminder to him, no doubt, that he had once worked for James. Two dead and four wounded. It was a night James would not soon forget.

Incredulously Edward looked at James, then turned again to the newcomer. "Wait," he ordered.

The instant hung suspended. In calling them back, Edward had also called James' hand. If James were to kill him, it must be now, for as soon as the other two men—Carrington's men—entered the fireroom, Edward Carrington would no longer be unprotected.

No, James did not choose to kill Edward and unleash the consequent general slaughter. Instead, he quickly whispered something to Garth, who immediately left the room.

The man with the scarf turned, limped back and waited, accompanied by a second man, who had come into the inn with him. The second man was considerably younger than the first, in his early twenties perhaps. The physical resemblance between the two suggested father and son.

"Stop him," commanded Edward, indicating Garth.

Startled, confused at first, the older man quickly oriented himself to the order and drew his pistol, aimed at Garth, while Edward retrieved his own firearm from James' belt. In almost the same gesture, Edward also reached for James' pistol. James drew back, lowered his arm, but retained his weapon.

"What you now possess is your own property, " James told Edward. "I'll thank you to leave me with what is mine." To the older man, whose pistol was now aimed at Garth, James said, "Let him go, Michael. You know as well as I, John McCaylan permits no violence at the Twin Stallion, no drawn weapons. Shall I call him?"

"You drew on me," said Edward.

"In self-defense and hopes that I might speak with you rationally, I drew on you and I threatened you."

"You ordered me outside."

"In hopes that we might talk"—with a sidelong glance at Sarah and Charles, he concluded—"privately."

The color of Edward's face deepened. Obviously he had assumed James was a Tory spy. But if James was not a spy, then certainly there were many possibilities which might warrant privacy. "You carried a forged pass with my name on it."

"Which you took from me by force. And now, if you gentlemen will kindly excuse us—"

The older man, Michael, still held the gun, but his wrist seemed to go limp as he looked from Edward to James, then back again.

"You'll not get far from this inn," said Edward quietly. "Unless you'd care to state your full business to me.

When you forge my name to a pass, your business becomes my business."

James hesitated, then addressed Garth. "Go to our room," he said.

Garth started across the hallway toward the stairs. At first the man with the red scarf seemed tense, but no one made any real move to stop him.

With Garth now ascending the staircase, James, obviously more at ease, addressed Edward. "You have me at a disadvantage, sir. Except for my friend, I am quite alone in these parts. Therefore, I will tell you my business. As Mrs. Carrington told you, as a child I lived with the Reverend Howgate and his wife. I came here tonight hoping to go on to New Hereford in the morning to pay my respects to Mr. Howgate. Word reached me several days ago that he was in poor health. Many years ago I received similar news about his wife. By the time I acted on that news it was too late."

"Uncle Ezra is ill?" cut in Sarah, her voice filled with concern.

"I don't know how seriously," answered James. "Let us all pray he is well by now, but he is nonetheless an old man, and I wish to see him. However, since Ezra Howgate is also well known as an active loyalist, I dared not apply for a pass in fear that I might mistakenly be identified with his politics."

His disbelief obvious, Edward Carrington answered dryly, "I see. In your soul, you are truly a patriot."

"My soul," answered James, "is my own private concern. But my business is the building of ships and boats, which I sell to both loyalist and patriot alike, antagonizing neither with any politics of my own."

His disbelief wavering, Edward answered, "And all this because you heard the Reverend Howgate was ill."

"The man was like a father to me."

Uncomfortably Sarah listened to his words and knew he was lying. That he owned a small shipyard in the colony of Massachusetts she knew was true, but she also knew no love had ever existed between James Devant and Ezra Howgate. The irony of his statement suddenly struck her. No, he was not lying. He had implied that he loved Ezra Howgate as much as he had loved his own father—the father who had left James and his mother penniless social outcasts the day he donned his French uniform and, with a new and younger woman on his arm, left America to fight the British in Canada. James had told her the whole story long ago. Had he forgotten that he had told her? Apparently.

She said nothing. The feeling her silence evoked in her was eerie. By silence she chose James Devant, whatever his politics might really be, over her brother-in-law.

Abruptly Edward faced Sarah. "From what you know of this man," he demanded, "does what he say ring true?"

Her heart seemed to stop. "Yes," she answered.

God forgive me, she thought. The choice was final now, a commitment as irretrievable as words chiseled into stone.

Edward nodded, turned his attention back to James. "Very well. See me in the morning. I'll give you a pass. A twenty-four hour pass to see the Reverend Howgate and be on your way back to wherever you came from in Massachusetts."

Sick with guilt and shame, Sarah found herself unable to look at either of them.

"Thank you," answered James with a slight bow. "And now, if all of you will be kind enough to excuse me, I bid you good night." His eyes lingered on Sarah perhaps a second longer than necessary. This time they were not cold. Had her lie actually saved his life? Her lie which Edward had believed because he loved and trusted her.

As James crossed the hall to the stairs, Sarah turned to her husband and clutched his shoulders. Could she ever again face Edward?

"Sarah—" Her husband's voice, tense with concern.

"I—I'm sorry," she said, able to stand free of him now. No, she had not lied to Edward. Ezra Howgate had, indeed, been like a father to James—a father to be despised, had he actually been James' father, but, nonetheless, a father. And as far as she knew, James did own a small shipyard. No, it was not Edward she had betrayed; it was Charles. Charles, because of how much she had admired the quick intelligence with which James Devant had seized and capitalized on every opportunity by which he might survive the forged pass.

But Charles was her husband, her life, the father of her child. With an intensity which both shamed and excited her, she tightened her hand in his and hoped that he would make love to her that night.

CHAPTER FOUR

When out of sight and hearing of the others, James quickened his pace. Approximately two years had passed since Michael had worked for James, quitting at his wife's insistence following a night when he had barely made it home, a pistol ball in his leg, courtesy of Nat Shyrie, although Shyrie still denied any knowledge of the attack. Two years. Certainly far enough in his past that Edward Carrington would forgive him when Michael told Carrington, as James was sure Michael would, before this night was through, that James Devant was a smuggler. Carrington would not be pleased. The rebels' answer to those who smuggled English goods into America to enrich England and compete with American-made goods for American dollars was swift and ugly, often deadly. British-made guns eventually to be used against British soldiers would, of course, be acceptable to men like Carrington, but the other 75 percent of James' cargo this night would not be. There would be no pass from Edward Carrington, not the following morning or at any other time.

Damn the irony of it. So far James had managed to avoid becoming as well known as Shyrie, mainly through the judicious use of middlemen in most dealings outside his immediate organization. The middleman who would tonight make the arrangements with Carrington for that part of James' cargo which would be of interest to Carrington was a local farmer named Luke Thompson.

Walking carefully now, alert to the possible sound of following footsteps, James continued up the stairs. Of course, John McCaylan permitted no violence at his inn, and yet a few moments ago, violence had almost occurred. Times were changing. Political fanatics like Carrington made their own rules, and Edward Carrington was a powerful man. Perhaps even powerful enough to break John McCaylan's rules and suffer no major consequences.

Barely breathing, James paused when he reached the third-floor hallway. Sounds from the taproom below were audible, now mingled with a sharp wind outside, but the relative silence of the area immediately surrounding him reinforced the conclusion born of his instincts. He was alone. How much longer he might remain so, he knew, could very well depend on which moment Michael chose to tell Carrington of his past association with James. On the other hand, perhaps Carrington did respect John McCaylan enough not to go after James inside the inn. Perhaps, rather, Carrington would merely post some men where they could observe both the front and back entrances, with some prearranged signal to follow James when he left, then take him prisoner. He doubted that they would try to kill him—at least not right away. First, there would be questions. What was he really doing in this area? Was a ship due in? When? Where? What was the cargo? Which local men were part of his organization? Ironic how the "higher good" excused outright theft of smuggled cargo if the cargo might be of value to the cause.

Theft, that is, from those who did not support the cause. Those who did were fairly paid. They were also protected by men like Edward Carrington, whose power now was a force to be reckoned with throughout New England.

Perhaps, James decided, the time was right for James Devant to become a patriot. Perhaps.

He stepped from the staircase into the third-floor hallway, then from the lighted area to a small dark alcove midway down the hall. Although officially the tower light was strictly to guide travelers by night to the inn, the small room to which the alcove led contained, along with the stairs to the tower, an exit hidden within the fireplace wall. The exit led to a flight of stairs down to the storage cellar of the inn which connected, by a second passageway, with the carriage house. The passageways, however, as James had discovered about a year ago, were dangerous. The stair boards and beams that supported the underground route were badly rotted with an abundance of rats and spiders. With luck there would be no need to leave by any route other than the one by which he had entered.

The door to the room which led to the tower staircase was like the other doors throughout the inn's upper floors except that it was set back in the alcove, an alcove in which a man might hide if his pursuers were careless. Carefully James pushed the latch release and eased the door open. He waited, barely breathing.

A single candle stood on the table near the window, its flame unsteady in the sudden draft created by the open door. James stepped inside, closed the door and slipped the bolt into place.

The candle flame grew taller, brighter. The room contained a bed, a rough-hewn table, three chairs and a large fireplace. At the far end the stairs to the tower began.

James, his pistol drawn, crossed the room as far as the fireplace escape exit, then made the sound of an owl, a sound promptly repeated from the tower. Garth was in the tower, alone and safe. James mounted the stairs and climbed, above ceiling level, to the loft. The wind was loud, icy cold. Garth's face so merged into the darkness James found it difficult to distinguish the black man's features until carefully, deliberately, Garth permitted the glow of the tower lantern to touch more fully his entire body. Strange, James thought, how Garth, born into slavery on a Louisiana sugar plantation, bore up so well under the New England cold. James' body was hunched, braced against the wind. Garth seemed, as usual, alert but physically at ease.

"I see no ship," said Garth.

James sat on the floor of the loft, his back against the wall, his pistol still in his hand. "When we try to leave here, we may have trouble," he said.

Garth sank to his haunches, still keeping an eye on the distant waters of the Sound. "McCaylan says he don't want us back. Not for no ship with British goods."

Surprised, James answered, "Since when does John McCaylan care, as long as he gets a share of whatever we carry?"

"He don't want to fight Carrington."

More surprised, James wondered why. John McCaylan would probably win. The same people who were loyal to Edward Carrington were also loyal to John McCaylan. More loyal, in most cases. John McCaylan was a self-made man, and well respected as such. Edward Carrington, on the other hand, had grown up with his own sort—always had money he had never had to work for, and his family was Tory, wealthy before they even came to America. What an odd place America was. In Europe aristocratic bloodlines and wealth paved the road to power.

In America a man's lineage stood far behind the fruits of his own hard labor.

"McCaylan don't want to fight with Carrington because he believe Carrington is right," Garth continued, answering James' unspoken question. "We can still use the inn, he say, to meet, but not to signal no ship that carries British goods. He say he want to see you."

James leaned his head back, closed his eyes. His body ached from the cold, and abruptly he felt very tired. It would take years to establish new contacts in new countries to continue a smuggling operation anywhere near the size of his current operation, if he excluded his British suppliers. To cut off the British suppliers would also, in many cases, cut off his outlets in Britain for American and West Indian goods since the same men often controlled both channels. In addition, the process of establishing new contacts in new countries was dangerous. One incident of misplaced trust could put a knife in his back by anyone whose territory James' expansion might threaten, or a rope around his neck by the authorities. "We'll have to do business directly with Carrington," he said. "Bring in only what Carrington approves."

"Carrington? Why?"

"Because most of our men don't care about politics, but most of the ones who do support what Carrington supports. And now, from what you've just told me, Carrington's got John McCaylan behind him. We'd have to be mad to try and fight the two of them."

"What about Shyrie? He do business with Carrington, but he don't bring in only what Carrington want."

"Very different. Most of Shyrie's men are not local." In anger, James added, "Nat Shyrie! He'll probably pick up whatever markets we leave. Markets we built. He's already bigger than we are." More thoughtfully, he went on. "Of course, if there is a war, soldiers can't fight and work at their trades at the same time. There'll be shortages. Certain English goods not welcome now because they compete with American-made goods will become welcome. Welcomed by men like Carrington."

Surprised, Garth asked, "War? Between the colonies and England?"

James shook his head. "I don't know. Some say it's possible. Most of the men I know, I don't think they'd want to fight, but with men like Edward Carrington, John McCaylan, Patrick Henry, Samuel Adams, Thomas Paine—with men like these behind them, pushing them—I just don't know."

"Fight for *what?*"

James smiled. "Freedom. The right to govern themselves, still a part of England, with the king's blessing, some say. Others would have us break with England completely, but all want at least the same rights enjoyed by British subjects living in England. They want the right to protect their lives and property. They want free trade. Now, by English law, whatever the colonies export has to be sent to England. Then England resells it to countries willing to pay higher prices. Same with goods the colonies want to import. Have to go through England, we pay English prices and then, having already enriched itself so mightily at our expense, it levies taxes on us which indeed we are hard pressed to pay."

"So you want to deal with Carrington. You trust Carrington?"

James hesitated, then nodded. "Within limits. In his way, I think he's honorable." Bracing himself against the wind through the open tower, he rose to his feet and followed Garth's line of vision to the moonlit waters of Long Island Sound. "We can't stay here all night."

"Listen!" said Garth.

Barely breathing, James listened. The distant clatter of

horses' hooves echoed through the night, drew nearer. Quickly, quietly, both men stepped back into the shadows. Let there be no silhouettes, no sign of movement against the tower light.

"Soldiers," announced Garth, in a better position to see than James. "Redcoats. Ten, twelve, no, more. Maybe fifteen."

"What in—" James broke off, waited and watched.

The group split. Four rode to the back entrance and drew rein while the others continued to the front, where four more remained posted outside. A man's voice carried to the tower, the words indistinguishable in the whistling wind, but the tone was clear, sharp. These men were on duty, well disciplined. Of the group in front, two rode to the carriage house, cutting off access should anyone in the inn attempt to reach his horse.

"Maybe it got nothing do with us," said Garth.

"Maybe. But if we signal the ship, it will. They'll see it. No way those two by the carriage house could miss it."

"What happen if ship don't get signal?"

"She'll keep going, eventually dump the cargo and run. We'll loose at least two-thirds of all she carries to water damage. I'll see what I can find out."

"And if it is us they want?"

Quietly James answered, "Then protect your life as best you can. Forget the ship, forget me."

Garth made no answer. Garth's chances to survive, James knew, were better than his own, if a chase ensued. Garth was black, like the night. Garth was also an escaped slave, with instincts honed by years of running before he was finally caught. He had been working for James then, in the shipyard, although James had not really had much contact with him. Then the men came with their hard faces and that peculiar intonation of speech so common to the Southern colonies. They came with legal papers and told James that Garth was not a free man. James bought him, took his word that he would stay and work off the debt, a debt James canceled the first time they fought side by side.

Hunched low, James made his way beyond the light of the tower lantern, down the stairs to the tower room. The candle on the rough-hewn table still burned.

He opened and closed behind him the door to the outside hallway, acts covered by the darkness of the alcove, sounds lost in the sound of fast footsteps mounting the stairs.

The voice James heard was female. Olanthia, the black girl who had told Garth that Jack Logan was either in Newgate waiting to be hanged or already dead.

"Ow," she said. "Nobody here. What do you want?"

"Open each door," commanded a male voice.

James flattened himself as best he could into the corner where the alcove wall met the door. He had been a fool to leave the room under the tower. He had been greedy to hope he might still be able to bring in his ship, greedy and stupid to gamble his life on the mere chance it might not be himself the soldiers sought. More intolerant of his own mistakes than of the mistakes of others, possibly because he made so few, rage—at himself—brought a slight tremor to his hands which anyone who did not know him might well assume was motivated by fear.

Then—no, he decided, it was not greed that had brought him into the hallway. His decision to investigate rather than run was, at the time he made it, a reasonably responsible course of action. By all ordinary procedures, no soldiers should have reached the third floor so quickly. Rather, for the number concentrated on blocking exits, most of the remainder should still be on the lower floors since unless one knew of the secret escape stairway, an escape from the third floor or lantern tower, with all known exits blocked and the lower inside floors well covered, would seem virtually impossible.

Still protected by the dark, he squatted low, quietly drew his pistol and ventured a look out into the hall.

Olanthia, accompanied by two soldiers stood at the first door. In her left hand, she held a lantern. In her right, she held a large ring of keys, one of the keys inserted into the lock. As she turned it, both soldiers stepped to the side, removing themselves as possible targets for anyone in the room.

"No one is here," she repeated.

"Open the door and walk inside," commanded one of the soldiers.

She opened the door and stepped inside, out of James' view. The soldiers waited a second or two, then carefully followed her.

Quickly James turned his attention to the other end of the hall. One redcoat was posted by the stairway which led down to the second floor. James dared not move. Even to start to open the door back into the tower room would draw their attention. In a matter of seconds all three of them would be upon him.

More footsteps, soldiers' boots, this time slowing as they reached the second floor.

Barely breathing, James drew himself up to his full height. The beat of his heart was too fast, every muscle in his body alert, catlike. He would have to kill the three soldiers on the third floor. Even if it were someone else they sought, which he now doubted, if they found James there in the doorway, there would be questions, an investigation into his background. The end result would be a British rope around his neck, assuming, of course, that he did not die first under the "stress" of their questions. Everyone he knew or had ever been seen with would be in jeopardy.

From the sounds of the soldiers' boots on the heavy oaken floor and the rattle of Olanthia's keys he realized they had left the first room. Covered by the sound of her key inserted into the lock of the next door, James released the spring bayonet on his pistol. Kill the first one with the knife. Go for his throat. Avoid entangling the blade in the winter-thick cloth of the uniform in search of mortal targets deep within the man's body. Move quickly, for once he moved, his only advantage—surprise—would be gone. When the surprise was gone, use the first trigger, a pistol ball from the top barrel. By then the third soldier, the one now posted at the far end of the hall, would probably be upon him. Use the second trigger; fire from the lower barrel. Go into the tower room. Close and bolt the door behind him. With Garth, use the secret staircase while the soldiers from the floor below, summoned by the noise, worked to break down the tower room door.

Following Olanthia, the soldiers emerged from the second room. From the sounds of their boots, easy, heavy, James was sure they would be unprepared when he struck. The light of the lantern was visible now, a stark line on the floor outside the alcove.

"No one here," said Olanthia irritably, her voice too loud to James, an obvious attempt to warn Garth and himself.

"Move along," commanded a male voice.

James braced himself. In a matter of seconds all would stand within the alcove. Slash rather than stab the throat. The man would probably not die right away, but at least he would be incapacitated while James shot the other two.

Olanthia led the way, holding the lantern. Her eyes met James'! A stifled cry caught in her throat as he motioned her out of the way, the spring bayonet on his pistol open and ready. In the same instant a male voice called from another floor, "Sergeant Harris. . . ."

The first soldier's face turned toward the sound, away from the position in which he would have seen James within the second had he not turned.

"We got him," the voice continued.

James held his breath. Sweat broke out on his forehead, threatened to drip into his eyes and impair his vision. His legs felt suddenly weak. If they found him now, would he even be able to defend himself?

The footsteps of the soldiers began again, receded down the hall, mingling with the jangle of the keys still carried by Olanthia. Slowly, James let out the deep breath he had held so long. The sensation was eerie! A few seconds ago he had been prepared to kill, steeled to die, if necessary. Now life flowed through him, and with it, fear of death, shock at how close to death he had actually been.

Still in the alcove, he tuned his senses to the other end of the hall. The lone soldier who had been posted there was apparently also gone. James waited, then ventured a look, his eyes now well accustomed to the near-black darkness of only one candle on the wall at each end of the now-empty hallway.

Carefully he made his way along the wall, drawn by the sound of loud voices coming from at least one, probably two floors below. He recognized John McCaylan's voice, the faint Scottish clip, but full sentences were not audible. Remaining close to the wall, he descended the stairs to the second floor.

Sarah Carrington stood by the landing above the staircase which led to the front entranceway. She stood with her back against the wall, a position in which she could not be seen from below. Her face was turned in the direction of the voices which now clearly carried up the staircase. The effect the sight of her standing there alone and unprotected had on him was staggering. Beyond all sense and reason, he longed to take her into his arms, gently, tenderly, because he cared for her, had always cared for her, yet at the same time, roughly, cruelly, because she had hurt him. Charles Carrington's wife! James would have her, if she would have him. The thought was absurd, a dream. How shocked dutiful, virtuous Sarah Carrington would be, could she read his thoughts.

"To protect ourselves," said a male voice, thick with fear, yet defiant.

"Good, loyal subjects of his majesty are protected by British troops," came an answer—one of the soldiers probably. "They need no guns."

Gently James touched the soft, now-warm scarlet velvet of the riding cloak where it covered Sarah's arm. She swung around, startled, eyes wide. As she recognized him, her initial tension seemed to relax, but only for an instant, promptly replaced by something else. Discomfort? No, more than discomfort. Not *fear* exactly, yet something closely akin to it. Fear of *James?* In the name of heaven, what must he do to show her he meant her no harm?

Irritably he placed his finger to his lips, then spoke softly. "What happened?"

"He—he's a local farmer," she answered. "They found a stockpile of guns on his property. Someone told them he was here."

"What's his name?"

"Thompson, I think. Luke Thompson."

Under his breath James swore. Luke Thompson was the contact to whom James' middleman had planned to sell the guns and gunpowder due in any moment on the *Hawk*.

"Do you know him?" asked Sarah.

"The name is familiar to me," James answered.

Tentatively, at first, then fully, her eyes met and searched his. As though speaking from some other time and place, she asked abruptly, quietly, "Who are you?"

"You know who I am," he answered, surprised by his own words. "You've always known me."

"Are you in the king's service?"

"I am in the service of James Devant."

Low, angry murmurs drifted up the staircase, followed by heavy footsteps and a flood of cold air as the outside door opened, then closed. One distinct voice carried above the others: "We can't let them take him. They'll kill him!"

"Keep your voice down!"

The sounds became more subdued, words no longer distinguishable, but the air remained filled with tension.

"What will they do?" Sarah asked. "Go after him? Draw weapons on the soldiers?"

"The times are unsettled, madame. Dangerous. You should leave New Hereford as quickly as possible."

"Are you one of them? One of the rebels? No, you couldn't be. Edward would have known you."

As though tracing the finest silk, abruptly, gently, James touched the tips of his fingers to her face, brushing back into place a stray lock of hair.

Quickly she drew back against the wall. "You've no right to touch me!"

"I've every right. Once, we made a commitment that we would always be the best of loving friends."

"A child's game. No more."

"Why did you lie to Edward—tell him you believed I was here to pay my respects to Mr. Howgate? If you hadn't, most likely I should be dead by now or much desiring the release of death."

"You punish me for helping you stay alive?"

Dropping both his arms to his sides, he answered, "No. Forgive me. I am in your debt."

"Then pay it by leaving me, at once, sir."

Certainly the words were plain, yet her eyes—such pain, such sadness. "A debt so large cannot be canceled so lightly, yet if this is your desire as a beginning, most certainly I shall—"

Movement on the steps below quickly drew his attention. Charles Carrington seemed to recognize James in the same instant James recognized Charles. Charles' face indicated first surprise, then anger as his eyes moved from James to Sarah, then back again. With a courteous nod, all of it a lie, James addressed him. "Good evening."

Reluctantly Charles returned, by gesture, the courtesy.

At a speed grown slack by the intense, lingering distraction of his encounter with Sarah, James turned and started up the stairs to the third floor. God willing, if there were a God, he would never see her again.

Had the ship passed, with Garth unable to signal? As he approached the third-floor hallway, his pace quickened. He reached the alcove and rapped on the door, two short knocks followed by three more.

No answer. Carefully, as quietly as possible, he opened the door. The sound seemed to reverberate throughout the inn, although he knew logically that probably no one else had heard it.

Inside the room he closed and locked the door behind him, then mimicked an owl.

Again, no answer.

The candle on the table burned low. Within a matter of minutes, the room would be dark, except for the faint glow which filtered down the staircase from the tower lantern above.

Less careful now, he climbed the stairs and dared speak for the first time. "Garth?"

Still no answer.

Angrily, helplessly, James crouched back against the tower framework, taking care not to be visible from below. The soldiers were gone, the sound of their horses fading into the distance. Garth was also gone. Probably he had heard Olanthia's deliberately loud words to the soldiers, to Garth obviously a warning. And the soldier's words, "We've got him!" "Him" might well have been James.

But had the ship passed? Should he wait or try to find Garth?

He decided to wait, at least an hour or so. If the ship had already passed, at least he would be able to catch her coming back up. At least he would know she had arrived safely; he would know the goods had been dumped. Perhaps his men could begin retrieval that same night, thereby minimizing the water damage.

Sounds outside the inn drew his attention. Voices, unnaturally subdued, mingled with the wind. Still careful to avoid becoming a silhouette against the tower lantern, James made his way to the side railing and looked over the edge. The carriage house door was open. Horses were led out, mounted. A confrontation with the soldiers? No—at least not immediately. Only about half a dozen men were visible. Probably messengers to spread the news of Luke Thompson's capture or to gather reinforcements.

Again James looked at the waters of the Sound, then turned away. The wind was biting, icy, painfully cold. If those poor fools actually attempted to rescue Luke Thompson, the soldiers, properly reinforced, might well return to the inn. No corner would remain unsearched, no occupant unquestioned. On the other hand, perhaps

Carrington's organization had little choice. Luke Thompson knew too much.

To hell with it. Even if the soldiers did not return, once Edward Carrington discovered the true nature of James' business in the area, even John McCaylan's protection would be unreliable. At least James knew Garth had not signaled the ship. There had been no opportunity. The soldiers had arrived before James left Garth's side and had remained until only a moment ago, when James returned to the room. Better to disband the men, return tomorrow and fish out the dumped goods. Unless whatever attempt was made to rescue Luke Thompson produced some dead soldiers. If any redcoats actually died, with Fort Franklin directly across the Sound from Stamford, the whole New Hereford area could well be occupied by dawn. Could so small an incident actually trigger open armed conflict?

He hesitated. Damn it! If the ship did come in, right now, perhaps they could unload her before any trouble began. With soldiers occupying the area, fishing for dumped goods could be twice as dangerous, if not impossible.

His eyes scanned the horizon. Perhaps something had gone wrong back at the first signal station. Perhaps the goods had already been dumped, farther up the Sound. Or perhaps Nat Shyrie really was in the area, really had intercepted James' ship. The *Silver Hawk!* The most valuable of James' larger ships.

No, he must not remain at the inn even an hour longer. From the position of the ship when sighted that morning, she should already have arrived. Perhaps she had, but since there had been no signal, the goods may have already been dumped. More important, however, Luke Thompson had been arrested. There were British troops in the area. James' identity, if not already known to Carrington, soon would be, and once Carrington knew who

James was, he would also know why James was at the inn. He would know that somewhere on the shore a group of men awaited a ship carrying goods unacceptable to Edward Carrington. Not only James' life, but also the lives of his men were in jeopardy. Even the *Hawk* was not worth the risk. James must ride now to the shore. Set up communication lines to deal with whatever additional information he might have by tomorrow night, then disperse the men. Send them back to their homes. The night was wasted.

He walked down the stairs, into the room below the tower. The candle had burned away. Carefully, in the dark, he made his way to the door, out into the hallway. He must walk tall and straight, show no sign of uneasiness. Walk out the front door. If he were caught in an attempt to exit by any but the most normal means, even John McCaylan might not be able to protect him.

It never seriously occurred to him to worry about Garth. There was something not quite human in Garth's past-demonstrated abilities to remain alive and free.

Slowly James walked from the alcove to the top of the stairs. The atmosphere of John McCaylan's inn was starkly different. No more laughter drifted up from the taproom. The voices were low, careful.

He descended to the second floor, abruptly conscious of Charles and Sarah Carrington, husband and wife, behind one of those closed doors. It angered him that he cared. Until tonight she had been only a memory to him, a fantasy figure occasionally permeating quiet moments with a bittersweet sense of something missing, something lost.

He continued down the stairs to the first floor. Before he reached the bottom step, he heard voices, realized several other men were also about to leave. For a split second he stopped, his back against the wall. No, he must keep going. Use his wits. There was now no way he could avoid being seen. He walked into the hallway, directly opposite the fireroom, several steps ahead of the other men who were leaving. The instant he became visible, their conversation stopped. One lone man—more boy than man—sat in the fireroom. When he saw James, his body stiffened. Had he been posted there in case James attempted to leave? The answer seemed obvious. When his eyes moved from James to whoever was behind James, his body relaxed.

"Allow us to walk with you, Mr. Devant," came a male voice, followed by: "Samuel, inform Mr. Carrington that Mr. Devant is leaving."

The boy in the fireroom reacted quickly.

James turned, faced the men behind him. There were three of them. Two, he recognized immediately. One was the older man—Mark—who had challenged him when he first came in. The man had even challenged Edward Carrington. The second was the boy who had been with Mark. The third man was about James' age, and voices suited to faces, apparently the third man was the one who had spoken. The assumption was confirmed when the third man continued, "But, Mr. Devant, you have no pass. Was not Mr. Carrington prepared to give you one in the morning?"

Trapped, playing the game because there was no other immediate alternative, James answered, "I must thank you for your concern. The need for a pass completely slipped my mind. But then, as we all know, I am perfectly capable of writing Mr. Carrington's signature myself."

"He's a bloody spy for the British!" spat Mark. "Sent here to find out whatever he could about Luke Thompson, about all of us! Where's your black man?"

"I don't know," James answered.

What might have been a violent reaction was stayed by the arrival of Edward Carrington.

"You're leaving us, Mr. Devant? I take it that means your ship arrived successfully? I'm interested in your cargo. Perhaps we can do business."

The whole thing was too easy, too direct. Something was wrong. James remained silent.

Calmly, but with subtle, visible anger, Carrington continued, "Mr. Devant, I shall speak plainly. When we parted company, I posted a man by the carriage house to watch the inn. He left his post only when the soldiers arrived. Therefore, had you signaled your ship at any time except while the soldiers were here, my man would have seen the signal. Does it not seem odd to you that British soldiers seeking a man they consider a dangerous rebel would ignore such a signal? Unless, of course, they supported the man who gave it."

"Supported me?" James' incredulity gave voice to what was a purely instinctive reaction.

"The seas are dangerous," Carrington went on. "The ships of those who support us seem regularly to fall into British hands. Yet yours do not."

"Perhaps those who support you are inexperienced," James answered dryly. "Perhaps, to smuggle successfully, one needs more than dedication to a cause and courage."

"Or perhaps the men who support our work do not make deals with the British. Perhaps they do not supply information on patriot activities in exchange for the safe conduct of smuggled goods."

Carefully, masking his fear as best he could, James answered, "You appear to possess many conclusions and few facts."

"It is a fact that you forged my name to a pass. It is a fact that when caught, you lied as to your business in this area. It is a fact that you signaled your ship in the presence of British soldiers, who took no action against you. It is a fact that indirectly you did business with Luke Thompson and knew of the weapons hidden on his property—information which obviously someone passed on to the British. It is a fact that as a child you were part of Mr. Howgate's household—Ezra Howgate, probably the most powerful Tory leader in New Hereford."

Stunned, James stared at his accuser. "Is this your 'patriot' justice?" he asked quietly. "No responsible court would convict on such thin evidence."

Just as quietly, Carrington answered, "You are a smuggler. You bring into these colonies English goods we are sworn not to consume. You carry our goods back to England. You corrupt our organization. You and those like you weaken our economic leverage with England. If this leverage fails, we have no alternative but force. If force becomes necessary, many on both sides will die. Your profits are blood money."

His voice rising slightly above Carrington's, James' words were sharp and clear. "I did not create the times. I corrupt no one. If, in contempt for the king's laws men choose to work for me, to buy my goods, to sell their goods through me, they do so by free choice. You say you would have these colonies free of the trade restrictions imposed on us by England. You talk of force. But what if your force fails? Then what course of defiance—what course of escape—is left to you, except men like me who have the ships and remain willing to break the law? Do you really believe these few lonely disorganized colonies can challenge the entire British Empire to either economic or actual war, and prevail? No, Mr. Carrington, before you tell me there is blood on my hands, take a look at your own."

Taken aback, Carrington recovered quickly. "I see.

You believe our cause is lost. Therefore, you cast your lot with the British."

John McCaylan joined the group. He was not a tall man, but he was heavy, with big bones and a straight back, which somehow gave the impression of height and physical strength, the latter an accurate impression in spite of his age.

Contemptuously, angrily, James directed his answer to both McCaylan and Carrington: "I am no British spy!"

McCaylan shook his head and spoke in the Scotch brogue so familiar to all who knew him, a brogue still thick even after all these years in America. "Don't lie no more, Jamie. Save your soul. You gave them Luke Thompson. For what? Safe conduct for a ship. Thirty pieces of silver! And I make no judgment as to what truth there might be in it, but they say it was you helped the British get Jack Logan."

"Rumors!" spat James. "Lies! If the British had help to get Logan, we both know where it came from. Shyrie was afraid of Logan. Logan was too popular with Shyrie's organization."

"I'd like to believe you," said McCaylan.

Desperately James changed direction. Although he had never really thought of John McCaylan as a friend, at least he knew the man's mind and conscience far better than he knew Edward Carrington's. "Whether or not you believe me," he began quietly, "I still remember a time when John McCaylan's word meant something. A time when any man could enter this inn and know he was safe."

Sharply McCaylan faced Carrington. "You'll not harm him here. You'll not dishonor my word and hold my support."

Others drifting into the hall from the taproom included two of McCaylan's sons. One, about eighteen, resembled

McCaylan's second wife, tall and sandy-haired, small-boned. The third, no more than perhaps ten, looked more like his father than his mother, McCaylan's third and present wife.

Carrington hesitated, then nodded consent. It seemed to James a political rather than a moral decision.

Directing his words to James, Carrington answered, "I'll give you a twenty-four-hour pass. You're free to leave. At the end of those twenty-four hours, your name and description will be sent to all the American Committees of Correspondence, and Mr. Devant, if you are still in these colonies, you are a dead man." To McCaylan, he added, "John, give me pen and paper."

McCaylan nodded in the direction of the taproom, the same direction as his living quarters, where Carrington would find the necessary supplies.

Together, McCaylan and Carrington started down the hall, followed by McCaylan's younger son. James took a step toward the fireroom. Mark seemed unsure whether he should interfere, then apparently decided not to.

In the fireroom, alone, James sat by the fire, his back to the group in the hall. The stance was deliberate, a challenge to any of them to defy both Edward Carrington and John McCaylan by shooting him in the back. Somehow it seemed safer than facing them. Face to face, any of them might claim James had attempted to draw his pistol. What sheep they were, what headless sheep. Edward Carrington was their head, and what a head! Carrington had now even managed to recruit John McCaylan.

Twenty-four hours! He felt reasonably sure Carrington would stick to his word, but what about those other than the McCaylan clan who supported Carrington?

Twenty-four hours! Did they really expect him to leave everything he had worked and fought for through the years, his ships, his home, his organization, and run? Run for his life. Run where? Not England. Shyrie's cutthroats would make short work of him, stripped of his money and organization, in England. France? At least he had money in France, but not enough. His dream to settle in France one day, take a French girl as his wife and live out his life as a country gentleman in reasonable comfort and security was years away. The true irony was that he knew it was not really the smuggling for which Carrington condemned him. Carrington needed smugglers—probably he did at least some business with Nat Shyrie, as some of the men who supported Carrington's politics had also done business with James. Rather, their condemnation of James was based on their impossibly ludicrous assumption that James was in the pay of the British, the pay of men like Ezra Howgate, who had worked James' mother to death and cast James away like a rabid dog because he had dared show a most honorable affection for Sarah. For the first time, James realized why he had so disliked Edward Carrington, even before they met. In spite of the man's American style of dress and antiloyalist politics, he still, by virtue of birth, former position and inherited money, carried about him the stench of the English aristocracy.

James a spy! Surely the guns and gunpowder on board the *Hawk* at this moment would convince that arrogant, self-appointed judge it was not true. Tea, rum, fish, beaver pelts—these were goods the British might allow to pass, but not guns, not pistols and muskets to be used against British soldiers. But where was the *Hawk*? Tonight the guns could prove not only James' innocence, but also his potential value to Carrington. Tomorrow, however, guns either on board one of James' ships or in the water with the rest of his cargo could very well be merely part of a British plan to protect James, to ingratiate him with Carrington.

He needed his men, he needed his ships—tonight. Give the guns to Carrington. It might not convince him, but at least it could create a doubt in James' favor; at least it could stay the death sentence, give James time to prove his genuine willingness at this point to work in all good faith for Carrington. It would also sit well with James' men. Most of them were at least sympathetic to Carrington. Those whose feelings were stronger than mere sympathy would be even more strongly tied to James, more personally supportive. With spy rumors in the wind, personal support might well be crucial, at least until Edward Carrington admitted even the possibility of a mistake and realized James could be useful—very useful—to Carrington's fanatical cause. Not that James really intended to see it through to the end. If men like Carrington could not be stopped, obviously the colonies were doomed—as doomed as Carrington. When the time was right, James would simply sell his ships and get out. When the time was right.

In the meantime, survive! Get to the shore; talk to his men. Introduce and meet the spy accusations head-on. If humanly possible, regardless of the danger, take those men still willing to follow him, and get the guns, deliver them to Carrington—tonight.

The door to the inn burst open. Startled, James turned and faced the fireroom entranceway.

A young boy, no more than twelve, maybe thirteen, stood in the hallway. His coat was improperly buttoned, as though thrown on too quickly, and his words were at first difficult to understand because he had not yet fully caught his breath. His lips, cracked from the cold, may very well have been partially frozen.

"Dead. . . . "

"Who? Take it easy, son. Who's dead?" The voice was Mark's.

"Luke Thompson. Tried to get away. They killed him."

A shocked silence prevailed. Finally, Mark spoke. "Thomas, go tell Mr. Carrington." The sentence completed, Mark looked at James, a look which James met and held. Defiantly James rose to his feet. He was innocent of any part of it, damn it. He crossed the fireroom, stepped into the hallway and started for the door.

Mark stepped in front of him, eyes blazing. "And where do you think you're going?"

"As a free man and a guest in John McCaylan's inn, I am leaving. In peace and safety." Deliberately, he kept his hands far to his sides, far from his weapons.

"You'll wait for Mr. Carrington," announced Mark.

Indeed, times were changing. Luke Thompson's death could well mean the end of John McCaylan's no-violence-at-the-inn policy, the complete conversion of John McCaylan to Edward Carrington's cause. Doubtless within a matter of seconds both McCaylan and Carrington would reappear in the hallway. Although there was still the chance that Carrington would stick to his promise of a twenty-four-hour pass, at this point James was unwilling to bet his life on it. Ah, but the sheep would not know. Without either Carrington or McCaylan present to express whatever changes may have taken place in their thinking, what they had said before they left would still stand in the minds of the sheep. Use it! Use these few seconds.

"I'll wait for no man," James answered. "If you would stop me, then kill me. Here, in the hallway of the Twin Stallion. But if you would honor John McCaylan, then step aside."

Disoriented, Mark remained where he was.

James used the disorientation. Calmly, sacrificing no dignity, he walked around Mark, opened the door and stepped out into the icy New England night. He must not show his fear; he must not run—not yet. One lone horse was tethered in front of the inn—the boy's horse probably, cold and for the moment apparently forgotten. Take it? No. He heard footsteps behind him, the crack of frozen leaves and twigs. At least two men, maybe more, had regained their bearings and followed him from the inn. They were too close. To run for the horse would probably be his last free movement. Would they let him get as far as the carriage house? They did not rush or attack; their footsteps merely kept pace with his own. No one spoke.

He reached the carriage house. Would they shoot him in the back? If there were only two of them, in face-to-face combat he might have a chance, unless guns were drawn. One shot would probably bring out everyone in the inn.

He lifted and dropped to the ground the wooden bar which held the carriage house doors closed. As though in response to the noise, a human voice cried out from somewhere on the other side of the door. A man's voice, angry, frightened, a voice that was no more than loud, wordless sounds. With the board removed, both doors burst open. A man, his arms and legs bound, his mouth gagged, fell forward onto the ground by James' feet. Startled, James stepped back, instinctively reached out to help him, then consciously stopped the movement. In that instant he got his first look at the men who had followed him. They also seemed momentarily fully concerned with the man on the ground. There were two of them—Mark and a younger man. The younger man, James remembered, had been present when Carrington made his spy accusation to James. There was something else about him, though. Something familiar. A name James should know, yet somehow could not recall.

Quickly, but still not obviously running, James

stepped past Mark and his companion, into the carriage house, as the other two men worked to sever the third man's ropes and gag. With the gag removed, James heard the man answer, "Black man. Came out of nowhere. . . . "

To James, the rest fell into place. Garth had used the tower-room fireplace exit all the way to the carriage house. The carriage house contained two windows. Garth had opened and gone through one of the windows, found and overpowered Carrington's man, then dragged him inside. Yes, Garth's horse was gone. He had probably walked it outside, rebolted the door, then continued to walk until both master and horse were well beyond earshot of the inn.

As inconspicuously as possible, but not slowly, James untethered his own horse.

Abruptly Mark looked up from the entranceway and yelled, "Hey!"

With well-practiced speed, James mounted his horse, landed low in the saddle, the reins in his left hand. In his right hand, he held his pistol, aimed at Mark. "I would prefer not to kill you," he announced quietly. "Be kind enough to remain as you are."

His pistol steady, James turned his horse to face the open doorway; then master and animal became as one with the night. As the Twin Stallion Inn grew rapidly part of the past, the wind stung James' face, impaired his vision and hearing, yet he knew the others were behind him, perhaps only two of them, perhaps all three.

He rode inland, slightly north, away from the shore. If his men saw him with shadowy figures in pursuit, they would defend him. The odds were too great that his pursuers would be killed, and James could not afford to kill any of Carrington's men, at least not while one shred of hope remained that Carrington might eventually reverse his present position and support James, accept the smuggling organization and expertise James was prepared to offer.

A heavily wooded section lay ahead near the top of a hill to James' right. Interspersed with the winter-barren oak and maple were numerous pine, hemlock and spruce, trees ever thick and green regardless of season. From about halfway up the particular spruce James had in mind, he could await his pursuers and with luck disarm them and scatter their horses. He hoped there were only two. If three arrived, he would need his wits indeed. Perhaps he could convince them Garth was with him, that they had met by prearrangement at the top of the hill. In truth, he had met Garth and others there on more than one previous occasion.

The hill was well known—Cotter's Hill. Legend had it that sometime back in the 1600s a man named Cotter had survived an Indian massacre by running all the way to the crest of the hill, where he climbed to and hid in the uppermost branches of the same spruce James now sought. The trees gave good cover. It was a logical meeting place for anyone with illegal business to discuss, a high rise in the land which gave a good view of the surrounding area. As far back as a hundred years before the Twin Stallion Inn had been built, Cotter's Hill had been a popular base for signals to smuggling ships.

James reached the base of the hill. With Carrington's men disarmed, he could ride from their sight, switch direction, go back down past the inn, south toward Stamford, then cut across and up the coast to where his men waited. If more men were sent to find him, odds were they would look above, not below, the inn.

He dug his heels into his horse, urged it on to speed faster up the hill. Those behind him, still on level ground, seemed to be gaining on him.

He reached the first clump of evergreen trees.

A sharp sound split through the wind, a sound James knew well. A pistol ball. He leaned farther forward, head low, but the fully lowered position he sought was never reached. A second shot rang out. Pain ripped through his right arm, high, near the shoulder. His body jerked spasmodically. His hands tightened on the reins as his back arched, the upper part of his body now high and vulnerable. The horse reared in response to the sharply yanked reins. A third shot brought pain to James head and a flood of warmth over his left ear. He fell from the horse, landed on the frozen earth amid dead leaves, twigs and pine needles. The force of the fall seemed to have worsened matters. He tried to pull himself up, but his head now seemed an intolerable, immovable, throbbing weight. Even his right arm was useless. No amount of will seemed able to overcome the immobility dictated by the pain which had begun near his shoulder but which now, doubtless partially because of the fall, seemed to have taken over the entire upper right side of his body. He lay on his back and heard their horses. With pain-fogged detachment, he watched as three horses drew in and surrounded him.

Three shots had been fired. Three men. Their guns were empty. Mark dismounted. The man Garth had bound and gagged remained in the saddle, reloaded his gun. The man who had come out of the inn with Mark also dismounted. His voice was low, hoarse. "Is he dead?"

"Don't know," Mark answered. He drew his knife and approached James. "No," he called back.

"What'll we do with him?" asked the second man.

The man still in the saddle answered, "Hang him. Let everyone see how we handle British spies!"

"Got no rope," Mark answered. "You got rope?"

"Just kill him and be done with it," said the second man.

Mark looked at the knife in his hand. Obviously he was not accustomed to killing people.

"Well, go on. What are you waiting for?" asked the man on horseback.

"You kill him," said Mark.

"What the hell's the matter with you?"

"I got no belly for it," snapped Mark.

"After what he did to Luke Thompson?"

James' gun was within reach. In his mind, he held it in his hand. In one last desperate surge of strength he reached for it, but the pain was excruciating, immobilizing. As though of its own accord, his body jerked, twisted, wrenched him from his back onto his belly, his head oddly twisted, eyes still observing his surroundings. The sudden movement seemed to disconcert, even frighten the others.

"Look out!" cried the man on horseback. Mark jumped out of the way as the man who had spoken quickly aimed his now-loaded pistol.

A shot rang out. The face of the man on horseback was suddenly a mask of pain mingled with amazement. His pistol flew from his hand. He cried out, a shrill, agonized scream. His body, rigid with pain, fell from the horse. Desperately he clutched at saddle and stirrups to break the fall, the right side of his gray wool coat now dominated by the still-spreading stain of his blood.

Garth Chandler stepped from the shadowy protection of a gigantic hemlock tree, a smoking pistol in his left hand, a drawn machete in his right.

The man who stood beside Mark reacted, reached for the loaded pistol the first man had dropped when Garth shot him. Apparently the movement caught Garth by surprise. The machete sliced through the night with such speed it seemed as though magic had cleft the man's skull in two, drenching him in his own blood.

Mark's jaw fell open. Stunned by the sudden reversal, but still physically unharmed, he staggered backwards.

Summoning all his strength, James called to Garth, "No. . . . "

Garth froze, the machete still in his hand. The instant in which he might have killed Mark merely as an extension of the will to destroy all who threatened his life was gone.

Breathing heavily, his senses blurred, consciousness fading, James said, "Disarm him. Send him back with the one who is still alive, both on the same horse. Scatter the other horses." To Mark, James added, "Tell Mr. Carrington. . . . " His brain refused to function. Tell Carrington what? Something nagged at his memory. The man Garth had killed with the machete—James knew him, had seen him before. Where?

Yes. Now he remembered. The man who had accompanied Mark from the inn, the vaguely familiar face to which James had been unable to connect a name.

The man Garth had just killed was one of John McCaylan's sons.

CHAPTER FIVE

"I say, kill her. Throw her overboard."

Isobel Browne backed even more closely against the wall of the tiny cabin, as though by sheer will she could make herself disappear. The cabin was belowdecks, used by the first mate when more important passengers, like Nathaniel Shyrie or Jack Logan, were not aboard. It was up to Logan now. He looked at Isobel, then turned his attention back to the captain, a bearded sea-weathered man in his mid-fifties. With less authoritativeness than Isobel would have wished for, Logan answered, "We can get her through. She's little. We'll hide her."

"They're searching every ship in London," the captain roared. "No—not just London, all England! I never told Mr. Shyrie I'd take a woman. You think Mr. Shyrie would let you take her? That man she killed—a personal friend of his majesty, he was. A friend of Lord North, the prime minister of all England!"

The first mate, also crowded into the small cabin, remained expressionless. To Isobel, he was even more frightening than the captain. His face was lean, with parchment-like skin pulled tight over high cheekbones. His eyes were gray, cautious, cold.

"He weren't no friend to them," ventured Isobel in thick cockney. "Something about some land Lord Marlowe said should of come to him when his wife's brother died, but the crown claimed it. He knew the king and he knew Lord North, but they weren't no friends to him."

"Oh, I see," said the captain dryly. "He told you all about it."

"No," Isobel answered, holding in both her fear and temper in the face of the man's obvious contempt for her. "He didn't tell nobody *all* about it. He told a little bit to me and a little bit to some of the other girls where I worked. One day we was talking about him, and the pieces come together. He seemed to think the king would change his mind and give him the land. I don't know why. It had something to do with Lord North. Something Lord Marlowe had that Lord North wanted. He usually drank a lot when he was with us, and he thought we was all stupid. I don't think he even knew how much he told us. I only know he weren't no friend to King George."

"Then why are they looking so hard for you?" demanded Logan.

"You sure it is me they want? Maybe it's you."

"No," snapped the captain, "it's you, girl, and they want you alive! I think they'll get you, too. They know you're with Jack, they know he'll head for America, and when they do get you, I'll not have you tell them my name and the name of my ship!"

Isobel clutched her hand to her bosom, a thoughtless gesture. Her dress was gray wool, simple, warm and unlikely to attract attention. With her face scrubbed clean of powder and rouge, her copper-gold hair long and loose about her shoulders, she looked even younger than her nineteen years. Stripped of cosmetics and elegant clothing, she felt grossly unattractive, and that frightened her. From the moment they walked out of Newgate, the center link of their ankle chains sawed through, the remainder of each chain wrapped tightly against their legs to prevent the giveaway sound of rattling links, Isobel's life had been in Jack Logan's hands. Together, they had simply walked out of the prison with a flood of departing visitors, Jack dressed in woman's clothes, Isobel wearing the scarlet hooded cape worn in by the pale, thin woman who had brought the female clothes in which Jack disguised himself. Once out, however, their three-day route to London Harbor included a complicated maze of squalid little rooms, attics, basements, secret passageways and carefully spoken code words. Occasionally money changed hands, but more often those who assisted Jack Logan seemed motivated by either fear or friendship. However, no one had welcomed Isobel. The search for her was too intense. At first she had assumed it was really Logan they sought, focusing on Isobel only because everyone knew she was with Jack and was more striking to describe than Jack. Now, however, she wondered. England was full of smugglers, some of them far bigger than Jack Logan. A search of this scope and intensity for Jack Logan—it made no sense. And yet, since Lord Marlowe had not been on good terms with either the king or Lord North, a search of this scope and intensity for Isobel made even less sense.

The floor of the ship swayed slightly beneath her feet, a sensation none of the others seemed even to notice. A hundred-and-fifteen-ton red cedar Bermuda sloop exceptionally well designed for both speed and stability in rough weather, the *Sally Anne* lay at anchor in London Harbor in full view between two far larger ships, one British built and one West Indian. Perhaps Jack was right. She hoped so. Perhaps any of the many coves along the coast where the mere presence of a ship might arouse suspicion would be far more dangerous. Perhaps ships searched in London Harbor would indeed be searched less carefully.

Still, it would certainly be to Jack Logan's advantage and the advantage of all directly concerned with his escape if she simply disappeared, a nameless body washed up on the English coast.

A knock sounded on the cabin door.

"Wait a minute," growled the captain. He stepped to the door and opened it slightly while Jack pushed Isobel against the wall behind the door, out of sight of anyone who might now be able to look into the room. Although most of the crew knew that about half an hour ago as the first traces of dawn transformed the night-black sky to still starlit blue Jack Logan had been smuggled aboard, few knew anyone was with him, and even fewer knew the second person was a woman. Only the captain, the first mate and one crew member knew the woman was Isobel Browne.

The voice Isobel heard from the area of the open door was young, respectful, almost servile.

"Beggin' yer pardon, sir," he began awkwardly, "but there's a party of soldiers boardin' the ship next to this one. Mr. Barrett said to tell you, looks like we'll be next."

Wordlessly the captain shut the door.

Jack's hand slid down Isobel's arm, not gently, yet somehow protectively.

With no more communication between them than a look, the first mate and Jack upended the trunk which contained most of the first mate's belongings. Jack climbed from the narrow bed to the top of the trunk and carefully pushed up, then slid back a wide beam in the ceiling, revealing a narrow area between the cabin ceiling and the floor of the captain's cabin on deck above. It was a space in which a man—or several men—could lie hidden. Only someone sharply looking for it would be likely to notice that the cabin ceiling was slightly lower than the belowdecks ceiling outside the cabin. The displaced cabin ceiling beam had a thin foot-long extension nailed to its top on both sides. It rested on these extensions, aligned with the other ceiling boards, undetectable when properly in place.

With the board pushed aside, Jack hoisted himself the short distance from the top of the trunk into the hollow area. Lying on his belly between the ceiling and the floor above, he held out his hand to Isobel. Quickly she followed his route from the bed to the top of the trunk and grabbed his hand. If they survived the search, there would be no reason to kill her. Unless, of course, one of the people who had helped Jack along the way and knew the name of the ship talked, and word got back to the authorities. But no, it was insane to think that the king might actually give chase to the *Sally Anne*, might even continue the search into America. On the other hand, was it really any stranger than the intensity of the search so far?

As she lay beside Jack now, the board back in place, the darkness seemed suddenly to overwhelm Isobel, as though she had abruptly gone blind. The groaning of the timbers, even though the ship still lay at anchor, seemed starkly magnified, like moaning spirits, like souls in torment, the souls of those who had filled their lives with sin, as Isobel had sinned. The air was stale, tinged with the odor of rot, dead fish and the sweat of her own and Jack Logan's body, in spite of the cold which threatened to numb her extremities. Or was it fear? Tears flooded her eyes. No, she must not cry; she must not make a sound. Logan's arm was around her, her body now so familiar to him. Logan might kill her, but at that moment it was good to be close to him. Logan was strong, so much stronger than Isobel. They might have hanged him, but never could they have broken him.

Jack's hand moved from her breast to her throat, his fingers toying with the chain around her neck, the chain attached to the leather packet she had taken from Lord Marlowe.

His voice barely audible, Jack whispered, "This last letter from your dear mother which you guard so carefully . . . you must read it to me sometime."

The beat of her heart quickened. "I can't read."

"No? Well, the captain can read. And another man on board, Thomas Norris. So can Ira."

"Ira?"

"The first mate. Be careful of him."

"Why? What do you mean?"

"He's Shyrie's man."

"I thought all of you worked for Mr. Shyrie."

"Aye. Shyrie arranged the escape. He sent this ship for me—with Ira as first mate. We've at least thirty days ahead of us—maybe more. Stay close to me, and watch Ira. I may have to kill him."

He was trusting her. Fool! Perhaps, if Jack became an imminent threat to her, she could cast her lot with Ira against him. Taking advantage of his mood, she sought, with an appropriately naïve tone in her voice, further information.

"You mean Mr. Shyrie may have sent Ira to kill you? But why? Why not just leave you in Newgate? Let them hang you?"

He laughed. "Because then they'd all know Shyrie done it, left me there to die." Tight-lipped, he added, "Maybe even put me there. It was a trap we walked into, it weren't no accident."

"You think Mr. Shyrie—"

"I don't know. He has his reasons. *Thinks* he has his reasons. Thinks there's those who'd leave him to follow me. Thinks I might decide to take some of what's his—or all of it."

Quietly, almost teasingly, continuing to take advantage of his mood, his anger, because the better she knew Jack Logan, the better able she would be to manipulate him, she asked, "Is he right?"

He clamped his hand over her mouth. A sharp cry stuck in her throat as both her hands grabbed his.

"Quiet!" he whispered.

Suddenly she understood, let her hands go limp as Jack removed his hand from her mouth. His action had not been motivated by her question. Someone—no, several people—had entered the captain's cabin above.

They'll find us, she thought. They would throw her back into Newgate, into the wards this time, and if she were still alive when it came time to hang her, they would hang her. The pounding in her skull grew loud and painful. She heard only part of the conversation above, tried to hear none of it. They would all die—herself, Logan, the captain, the crew.

She heard a man's voice. "The *Sally Anne,* British registration, bound for the West Indies."

Sounds overlapped. She realized someone had entered the first mate's tiny cabin below her. A loud slam. Had they slammed closed the first mate's trunk? She envisioned herself hiding in it, dragged out, now, screaming. Or was it the door they had slammed? If it was the door, so soon, they were moving quickly, probably not overly suspicious of the *Sally Anne.*

If she made a sound, Logan would probably kill her. Some devil inside of her told her to make a sound, cry out, scream. If Logan killed her, it would be quick. It would be over. She would never again have to feel such terror. *Scream*, yelled the devil.

"No," she whispered.

Logan's hand covered her mouth. His fingers dug into the flesh of her cheeks and chin as though, in blind and silent rage, he were seeking to crush her skull.

She whimpered. The devil was wrong. She, Isobel, did not want Jack to kill her.

His hand relaxed, but his anger remained, engulfing her, crushing her even more than the previous weight of his hand. She started to cry, silently at first except for the heavy and uneven breathing, but then her voice became part of it, her voice as uncontrollable as the first silent tears.

Something pounded against the ceiling with a quick, rhythmic beat. After only a brief hesitation she heard Jack move, heard the scrape of wood against wood before the light struck her eyes, as the board was displaced. With apparently practiced agility, Jack lowered himself through the opening onto the upturned trunk. Still balanced on the trunk, he grabbed Isobel's wrist, yanked with such force that she screamed and tried to fight him. He pulled her through the opening, pulled by her clothes, her flesh, wherever he could grab and feel movement in response to his will.

She came through, down against the bed, then onto the floor, the weight of her body toppling the trunk and, with the trunk, Jack Logan. Almost as a part of the same movement, he regained his balance, grabbed her arm and smashed his hand across her face.

Tasting blood, she found herself on the floor by the bed, looking up at Jack, now on his feet. The captain and Ira were also in the cabin. For the first time she realized the four of them were alone. No soldiers were present.

"They're gone," announced the captain. "We've hoisted anchor, the tide's with us, and it's a fair wind."

"Tend to your duties," Jack snapped at Ira.

If Ira was startled, it showed only for an instant in his eyes. He left the room. Jack held up his hand for silence, apparently checking to make sure the younger man's footsteps actually receded.

Quickly Jack stepped to where Isobel half sat, half knelt by the bed. He grabbed the chain around her neck. In near panic that it would cut her neck, she used both hands, twisted her head to assist him. At last she was free of it, her neck sore but not bleeding, her face bearing a sharp scrape from it. The chain partially dangling, the leather packet firmly in his grip, Logan thrust the packet at the captain.

"There's papers in here. Read 'em," he commanded.

Had they been anywhere but on a moving ship, Isobel would have taken the moment to run. Instead, she carefully ran her fingers through her hair. Her lip was cut, her eyes no doubt red in flesh swollen from the tears. Not an attractive picture. Her hands were wet with sweat. She wiped them on her dress and was further intimidated by the coarseness of the unattractive gray wool fabric. Oh, for some powder, rouge, a comb, some decent clothing!

The captain withdrew the papers, then scowled, almost contemptuously. "Whatever it is," he said, "it's fake."

"How do you know?" asked Logan.

"Right here." With two fingers, he tapped the broken wax seal. "I've seen that seal before—seen the real one, I mean. Was first mate on a ship once that took an emissary to Spain. The pouch he was carrying got wet, and we had to take the letters out. He's having fits, saying the ones with this seal was most important—letters from the king of England, they were." Barely looking at Isobel, he indicated her with a nod and continued. "Now where do you suppose the likes of her could get a letter from—" He broke off, his eyes still sharply trained on Jack. As though the same thought had grown simultaneously in both men's minds, both abruptly looked at Isobel. Not that either the intensity of the search for her or the access to nobility granted her by her former profession confirmed the validity of the letter; it was merely that together they raised the possibility.

Jack's voice was tough, directed at Isobel and permitted no answer but absolute truth. "Where did you get it?"

Trembling, she answered, "I got it from Lord Marlowe. He carried it on his person as I've carried it on mine since I took it from him. I told you I can't read, and it's true, but it seemed if he carried it with him like that, it might be valuable."

Lowering his voice, betraying his interest only with his eyes, Jack turned again to the captain. "Read it," he ordered.

"It's not to no Lord Marlowe," said the captain. "It's to Lord North."

Stumbling over some of the words, grossly mispronouncing others, he began to read:

Lord North,

I charge you to hold this letter in strictest confidence, neither to show nor to mention it to anyone, for reasons which shall become clear as the writing proceeds. I have given much thought to our conversation of Thursday last and have reached some conclusions which I shall pass on to you here, so that you may give them careful consideration before we meet again to determine in detail those areas in which I shall rely most heavily on your support.

As you know, there are those in Parliament,

whose names you know, who by public speeches and in private use of their influence continue to encourage the ungrateful, rebellious American rabble in their outrageous pretensions to a self-government independent of this nation. It is, therefore, my royal will and pleasure to take the following actions: first, I shall revoke all outstanding original patents. . . .

"What's them?" cut in Jack.

"I'm not sure," answered the captain. "I think it's charters. Way back in the 1600s the king gave some land to some of the people who come over to start the colonies. The charters gave them certain rights to govern theirselves. I know Connecticut's got one. And Massachusetts. Some others, too. The ones that don't the king just appoints a governor, and the governor's got to do what the king tells him. Revoke, I'm not sure, but I think that means take away. Why, I was born in Massachusetts. Take away our charter—we'd be nothing more than slaves!"

Momentarily impressed and distracted by the older man's knowledge, Jack asked, "Where did you learn all that?"

"My people was farm folk," the captain answered. "Sent me to school, they did, right up until I was ten and run away to sea. Good thing, too," he added, his voice softening. "Fever killed 'em all the next spring."

No longer interested, Jack turned his attention back to the letter. "Go on," he said.

The captain continued:

. . . revoke all outstanding original patents. Unlike my predecessors, I shall tolerate in this matter no interference from Parliament. That Parliament may pass certain laws affecting my dominions beyond the seas is indeed their right, but the king alone granted the patents, and the king alone has the power to revoke them. However, with a backward glance at my predecessors' errors in even permitting Parliament to discuss the matter, I count on you and selected others whose loyalty to me is beyond question to see to it that those who might consider taking action to oppose such a move on my part fully understand in advance that to do so would be beyond their jurisdiction, an infringement on the rights granted me by the constitution and Divine Providence. More plainly stated, to defy me in this matter would be treason and would be dealt with accordingly.

Second, I have this day ordered Lord Dartmouth to communicate to General Gage my determination that order be restored in the colonies. What further troops General Gage may request will be dispatched at once. In addition, should the Provincial Congress dare assemble again to promote further the treasonable aims already so arrogantly espoused throughout America, I have empowered General Gage to arrest its leaders, at his discretion, but with full precaution and secrecy of the intent and moment of execution, to avoid any further spur to mob action.

Gladly would I see all of them hanged, but my servants inform me there is little hope that a penalty so severe would at this time be inflicted on them by an American court, even if the courts were open. Their indefinite imprisonment until the courts reopen, however, will at least keep them from further mischief and perhaps also somewhat dampen their rebellious spirits with even a small taste of the punishment they deserve.

In my prayers, I daily ask guidance of Divine Providence, and lately I seem to hear in answer my mother's words spoken so often to me as a child, "George, be king." My duty as regards my colonies in America is now clear. Even my own Parliament, it would seem, stands to be reminded that I am, indeed, king.

GEORGE R.

His face red with anger, the captain tossed the letter onto the bed. "He is indeed king!" he spat. "That bloody little German bastard, king of England! Food for fish, that's what he ought to be."

Carefully Jack picked up the letter, returned it to its leather container, then placed the chain around his own neck, tucking the packet beneath his shirt. Addressing the captain, he added, "Keep quiet about this."

Incredulously the captain answered. "Quiet? The minute we land, it should go to Edward Carrington. He'll see the right people gets it. He'll see everybody in the colonies finds out about it, so they can arm theirselves, stop trying to make peace with him. Take back our charters, will he! Arrest anybody who says anything he don't like. Send troops to murder us!"

"I said, keep your mouth shut!" ordered Jack. "We do business with Edward Carrington, that's all. You think Nathaniel Shyrie really gives a damn whether there's a war—except that if there is, we get even higher prices for the arms and gunpowder we bring into America. We're all in this for the same reason—money. The only question to do with this letter is, where can we get the best price for it? Edward Carrington—or Lord North?"

"Lord North!" The captain laughed, a raucous sound born of amazement. More calmly he continued. "Lord North. And you think you'd live long enough to spend it? My God, man, you're talking about the prime minister, a man who takes his tea with the king of England as regular as you and me and Mr. Shyrie might share a keg of rum. He'd track you down to the ends of the earth, put a price on your head so high your own mother would turn you in."

It seemed to Jack a point worth considering. He went on. "North must be pretty sure she's got it. Tells why he's looking so hard for her, why he wants her brought in alive. Must have knowed Marlowe had it."

"The land—" ventured Isobel.

Both men looked at her. "What land?" demanded Jack, irritated by the interruption.

"Remember? Some land the crown claimed when Lady Marlowe's brother died without children. Lord Marlowe said it should have gone to him, through his wife, for their children. He said someone close to the king was going to use his influence with the king to get it for him."

Jack raised an eyebrow, turned his attention back to the captain. Jack smiled. "King probably don't even know the letter's missing. King finds out, Lord North might just as well go hang his self. It's North is behind this search. 'On the king's business.' It's all he'd need to say. They'd do whatever he told them. He'd pay *anything*. Must have sent some men to Marlowe's house, soon as he heard he was dead, to search for it." To Isobel, he added, "You tell anybody you had it?"

Awkwardly she answered, "I didn't even know what it was. I did ask one of the jailors at Newgate if he could read, but I wasn't thinking clear; then I didn't say no more."

Jack nodded. "Marlowe's wife would of knowed he carried a packet around his neck. Packet's gone, and you ask a jailor if he can read. Wonder how Marlowe got it."

"Stole it probably," ventured Isobel. "Or hired somebody to steal it. He really wanted that land."

"You know you're crazy," said Jack, the old anger flaring again. "Could have got us all hanged, screaming like you did."

"No!"insisted Isobel. "I'd never do it again, I know I wouldn't."

"You don't need her," the captain added, his voice slightly quickened by the taste of potential victory. "If you do decide to sell it to North, North knows you was with her. When he hears your name, he'll know it's probably the real letter, that you got it from her."

Barely able to support herself, Isobel rose to her feet. The same devil that had made her scream was now a protecting angel, giving her words to say when her own mind contained no words, refused to function. "You do need me," she announced sharply, directing her voice slightly more to the captain than to Jack. "You both work for Mr. Shyrie. What if Mr. Shyrie don't want to sell the letter to Lord North? What if he wants to sell it to—to the other man? The one in the colonies?"

"Carrington," said the captain, his voice flat, but at least he was listening.

"How is Mr. Carrington to know the letter's real?" She went on, this time concentrating on Jack. "It could be a lie, a fake, something you made up to get money from him. If you was to give it to him, like the captain wanted, then you'd have no reason to lie, but if Mr. Shyrie wants to sell it, how do you prove it's real, how do you prove where it come from?"

"Why should he believe her?" snapped the captain.

"Because Edward Carrington's a smart man," countered Jack irritably. "He'll question her. He's smarter than she is. He'll get the truth."

"Then he'll know Shyrie has it," said the captain. "And once he knows that, why should he buy it? What's to keep him from taking it?"

Jack laughed. "Because he don't want his throat cut. He don't want war with Shyrie. Who else is he got to bring him the supplies he needs?"

The captain shrugged. "Devant?"

"Devant's as good as dead," answered Jack contemptuously. "Most of his men is American farmers and tradesmen. They don't know how to fight, and they don't want to fight Carrington, not the way things is now. And Carrington will fight them if they stick with Devant because Carrington don't want nobody to bring in the kind of English goods Devant brings in, except for the guns and gunpowder, and Shyrie don't like that, because it cuts into our market. Maybe you're right, though. Maybe we should make sure Carrington don't get the choice. Finish Devant before we offer the letter."

"It's up to Mr. Shyrie," said the captain, his voice a reprimand.

"I know it," snapped Jack. "Nobody never said it wasn't."

"And until it's decided—Lord North or Edward Carrington—the girl stays alive," added the captain, with obvious displeasure.

He frightened Isobel. If anything happened to Jack, would the captain dare simply give the letter to Mr. Carrington? Without a price tag on the letter, Isobel would be unnecessary—an unnecessary, possibly mortal danger to the captain.

Jack looked at her. He also did not seemed pleased. "Alive," he repeated.

She sat on the bed and covered her face with her hands. Watch Ira, Jack had told her. If Ira—or anyone else—killed Jack, Isobel would be lucky to survive him by even so much as an hour. Unless, of course, the captain were also dead. She heard the cabin door open and close, then she looked up and saw the captain was gone. Her eyes met Logan's and she realized she hated him. How strange. Lord Marlowe had tried to kill her, yet it had never occurred to her to hate him.

A slow smile touched Logan's lips. "Ah, you don't care for me anymore."

Quietly she answered, "I hate you."

His hand smashed across her face. She jerked away from him, as far back against the wall as she could get, tears flooding her eyes. "Go on," she cried, "beat me! I've been beaten before. Yes, I cared for you. I even respected you. But you let the captain bully you like a stupid schoolboy. And you're afraid of Mr. Shyrie, aren't you? You're afraid of the captain, Mr. Shyrie, Ira—you're so afraid, all you can do is hit a woman!"

Jack stared at her.

"Well?" she persisted. "Look at you! That's *your* letter. What's it got to do with Mr. Shyrie? But the captain says give it to Mr. Shyrie, so you hold it for Mr. Shyrie. The only reason the captain even knows anything about it is because he can read." More quietly she added, "And he's the only one, outside of us, knows anything about it."

Abruptly Jack grinned, leaned forward on the bed and drew his finger across her throat. "Ah, then, would you have me slit the captain's throat?"

Instinctively she shoved his hand away. "Would you have him slit yours?" she countered. "You saw how much he wants to give the letter to Mr. Carrington. What if Mr. Shyrie says, sell it to Lord North? You think the captain would take that chance? You think he'll really give Mr. Shyrie the choice?"

Jack drew back from her. Confusion mingled with anger. "You're a witch," he answered. "You put thoughts in my head with your witchcraft."

Carefully, with forced lightness, she went on. "You don't really believe in witchcraft. I put no thoughts in your head. These are your own thoughts. I only speak them. What if the captain does let Mr. Shyrie decide, and Mr. Shyrie decides to sell it to Lord North? The captain's right, Mr. Shyrie would need only you, not me. He'd need you to prove it was real—you, to be caught and hanged, and who'd ever believe it was Mr. Shyrie made sure you got caught? You as good as said Mr. Shyrie wants you dead, that he's afraid of you, that he put Ira on this ship to kill you!"

Jack rose to his feet, leaned against the wall, apparently deep in thought. Concerned that the mixture of newfound hope and old fear she felt might show, she kept her eyes turned from him.

His voice through the heavy silence struck her like the crack of a whip. "For one who hates me, you say much to keep me safe."

"Of course, I want you safe," she snapped. "Anything happens to you, the captain will feed me to the fish a minute later. I know about the letter. I know him, I know his ship. The British want me. I know every person and place you used to get out of England. That's too much for Mr. Shyrie, too. You're all I have." Abruptly she jumped from the bed, grabbed his arms, her voice startlingly calm, eyes never leaving his. "Get rid of the captain," she said. "Use me to sell that letter to Mr. Carrington. Mr. Carrington's safer than Lord North. I'll help you kill the captain; I'll help you kill Ira; I'll help you kill Shyrie. You'll be safe; you can take over everything. I can use a gun or a knife. I'm little; I look helpless. They'll never expect it. Use me!"

The moment hung suspended in time. Jack looked at her. She tried to pick up his thoughts but saw only confusion, a whirlpool of emotion.

Abruptly, angrily, he shoved her away. "Witchcraft!"

he exploded. "You cloud my mind. I can't see, I can't think!" In almost the same gesture he yanked open the cabin door.

The captain stood in the entranceway, his face in the belowdecks lantern light an eerie mask of exaggerated lines and shadows. Isobel drew back, her hands flat against the cabin wall.

Jack found his voice. "Do you now listen at doors like a scullery maid or Ira?"

"I heard nothing," the captain answered in an almost-believable tone of surprise and indignation. "I was about to knock when you opened the door. What's the matter with you?"

Jack persisted, "You didn't hear the witch offer to help me kill you?"

Yes, Isobel realized, the captain had heard. Jack knew it and was covering himself—or trying to.

"Kill me?"

"Come on," said Jack. He stepped toward the open doorway, his arm extended as to touch a friend. "We'll keep her locked in here. She's mad, you know. I need some rum and sunlight and fresh sea air."

CHAPTER SIX

Still backed against the cabin wall, Isobel watched both Jack and the captain. The captain accepted Jack's gesture of apparent friendship, but the acceptance was an act. She could tell from his face, his eyes, the wariness in the way he held his body. Not only had he heard her offer to help Jack kill him, but—more important—he had also heard Jack's indecisive reaction. And if she could see it so clearly, then Jack also saw it.

The two men walked out, closed the door and bolted it from the outside. Odd that the door should have an outside lock. In addition to men like Jack who welcomed the voyage, had they also transported prisoners in that cabin?

With one trembling hand she covered her mouth and smiled. Tears flooded her eyes, but the sound which broke from her lips resembled laughter, high-pitched and frightened. She tightened her hand over her mouth and sank to her knees, leaned her head back against the wall, her hands now clasped in front of her as though in prayer. Now neither Jack nor the captain could really afford to let the other live, for to do so, each believed, would be a constant source of peril to his own life.

Jack had to win. Jack had to kill the captain. If the captain killed Jack, Isobel would be next, probably immediately. Or perhaps not immediately. Now the captain was angry at her. Perhaps, first, he would throw her to the crew. Nightmare visions of the Newgate wards filled her mind. She saw her body stripped, then torn apart; only now the faces were male, the bodies clothed in sailor's garb.

She needed a weapon—a knife, a gun. If the captain killed Jack, then at least she could—her mind seemed to go blank. As though from a great distance, the thought continued, faint and unwelcome—she could kill herself.

Her eyes scanned the room. Where might a weapon be stored or hidden? The room was so small. Her eyes rested on the trunk at the foot of the bed. This was the first mate's cabin—Ira's cabin. The trunk was probably Ira's. It was wooden, sealed closed with a slat of wood jammed through two loops of heavy rope, one extending from the lid down over the one which protruded from the area directly below the lid. It had no lock.

She hesitated, then bolted the cabin door from the inside, returned to the trunk, knelt beside it and opened it.

Nothing but clothing. At least on top. She pulled out a pair of trousers and held them up. Yes, they looked as though they would fit Ira. Ira's trunk.

She dug deeper, piling the clothing on the floor beside her. Her hand touched something hard—a book. She had forgotten; Jack had told her Ira could read. She pulled out the book and recognized it—a Bible. With instinctive respect she carefully laid it aside, then continued to dig.

A razor! A long, straight-blade razor folded back into a leather case. She flipped the blade out, examined it. The blade was very sharp. Heart pounding, she stood up and searched for someplace in the cabin to hide it, a place where she would be able to get to it quickly, if necessary.

Of course, Ira would probably miss it, but why should he say anything? Not knowing the relationship between Jack and Isobel, it would probably appear to Ira that Jack had stolen it, and a stolen razor was hardly sufficient reason openly to antagonize Jack Logan.

She closed the razor and dropped it down into the bodice of her dress. Hide it later. She did not know how much time she might have alone and the contents of the trunk still had to be returned to their proper order.

Quickly she ran her hands through the rest of it but felt only another book, way down in the corner, tightly wrapped in what seemed to be a rough wool shirt.

Or was it a book? It might be a box with something of value inside. The Bible had been obvious. This was wrapped up, not at all obvious.

She dug it out, unwrapped the shirt.

Her heart sank. Another book. She started to rewrap it, then hesitated. Maybe there was something special about this book. If only she could read! She started to leaf through the pages, then stopped, startled by the illustrations. Most of them might have been drawn from scenes in the London establishment where she had worked, except that no man's sex organ could ever really be that large, nor could any female frame support such enormous breasts.

She snapped the book closed. She wanted to laugh, to sing! With trembling hands she wrapped it back up and replaced the entire contents of the trunk, with the exception of the razor.

Ira, Ira, Ira! How long had he dreamed of a girl like Isobel? Had he ever had one? she wondered. Probably not. The house where Isobel had worked catered to nobility. A common sailor, even with an enormous bankroll—well, even if they did admit him, they would not give him a girl like Isobel. If the captain killed Jack, tell Ira about the letter. Ira was Mr. Shyrie's man. Jack said so. Especially with Jack dead, Mr. Shyrie would need Isobel to sell that letter. Ira would protect her from the captain, keep her alive—to help Mr. Shyrie sell the letter and to take Jack's place in bed with her for the duration of the voyage.

The outside latch on the cabin door was lifted.

Her heart quickened. She reached down the neck of her dress and grabbed the razor.

Someone pushed against the door, discovered it was locked and started to pound.

"Who is it?" she called. Because no other place immediately occurred to her, she shoved the razor between the mattress and the board on which it rested—the first place anyone would look, she supposed, but so far no one had any reason to look.

"It's Jack," snarled the voice from the other side of the door.

Quickly she crossed the cabin, opened the latch, then stepped back.

Jack entered, closed and locked the door behind him.

She leaned against the wall, arms folded. "Well?"

"Well, now you've done it," he snarled. "He made like he believed me, but he don't. He's afraid. What did you lock the door for?"

"Why did *you* lock it?" she snapped back.

"Because I'm not willing to have a madwoman run free on this ship."

"I don't like to be caged," she answered quietly, almost petulantly. "And I'm not a madwoman." More quietly she went on. "Why do we have to fight—you and I?"

Surprise melted quickly into suspicion. "What are you up to now?"

"Do you want me to pretend I'm not glad he heard us? Now you have to do something about it. Maybe I was wrong. Maybe it never entered his head to kill us—us. Me, as well as you. You're strong. If he tried to kill you, you might have a chance, but what chance would I have?"

Quietly Jack answered, "He'll not kill us."

Her eyes met his. "Can you do it alone?" Deliberately she looked away from him and continued awkwardly. "I know I said I'd help, but I'm not really sure I could. I never said this before because it didn't matter, but now I have to tell you. I didn't really kill Lord Marlowe. It was an accident. He was very drunk, and he fell. I knew I'd be blamed, so I ran, and everybody thought I did it, but"—she broke off, then looked at him again, this time with real tears in her eyes, but the tears were a product of raw nerves, not the seeming contriteness which accompanied them—"but, Jack, I don't think I *can* kill. Please help me. I need you. I'm so afraid." She threw her arms around him, held her body close to his, a vulnerable child-woman now, not a whore. The whore, she knew, no longer appealed to him. Briefly his body retained the tension of distrust; then, slowly, his arms encircled her.

"There, there," he whispered, "it's all right."

He kissed her, gently at first, then with growing sexual interest. She ran her fingers through his hair, down over the pox scars, over the unshaved stubble on his chin, down over his throat, now starkly conscious of how the veins in his throat protruded and throbbed, the veins which carried blood from his heart to his head. Use the razor. Cut these veins. Not that she really had any reason to kill him—at least not at that moment—but nonetheless, the knowledge that she could kill him, quickly and quietly, some night while he slept somehow comforted her, made her less frightened of him.

As his passion grew, momentarily Isobel's lips left his and lingered on his throat. With the tip of her tongue she touched the particular vein which so intrigued her. "Lock the door," she whispered.

The following morning the captain could not be found. The ship was thoroughly searched. His bed seemed to have been slept in, but otherwise, his cabin was in perfect order with apparently nothing missing.

Jack and Ira spent most of the morning questioning the crew. By afternoon rumors among the crew ranged from witchcraft to suicide to foul play. Perhaps it had happened because there was a woman on board. Or perhaps he had left of his own accord, perhaps in a boat hidden in any one of the many smugglers' crannies within the ship, to return to England via some other ship, or perhaps some other ship had sent a boat to carry him off to betray, in some way, Nathaniel Shyrie's organization for the captain's own profit, although no one who really knew him considered this a likely explanation. Had the weather been rough, it might have been assumed he had been washed overboard and accidentally drowned, but the weather was beautiful, the wind continuing fair.

"Unless he was drunk," Jack suggested. It was Jack who discovered that a startling quantity of rum was missing. The crew was reassembled and, this time, examined for sobriety. All appeared perfectly sober.

The logbook entry made by Ira, now by default serving as captain, gave this last explanation as the one he and Jack considered most likely, although both he and Jack, according to the log entry, were not completely satisfied since the captain was well known to be basically a sober man.

Isobel said nothing. All she really knew was that late the previous night Jack had left her side, then returned perhaps half an hour later, breathing hard, covered with sweat and sexually aroused. After roughly using her, he had fallen into what to Isobel seemed an unnaturally deep sleep.

The excitement and confusion of the captain's disappearance delayed until late afternoon what would probably otherwise have been first order of the day. To Isobel's surprise, the snow-white sails of the *Sally Anne* were replaced by cream-colored sails, and a canvas flap was dropped and fastened over the words "Sally Anne" on the side of the ship. The letters on the canvas flap read "Wayfarer." The masthead figurine of a nymphlike woman was also removed, replaced by a large carved wooden figure of a man in Pilgrim's garb holding his hand over his eyes as though to shield them from the sun. In the captain's cabin the *Sally Anne*'s papers were appropriately replaced with the carefully forged *Wayfarer* papers. By nightfall anyone searching for the *Sally Anne*—on sea, or later in America—might well assume the sea had swallowed her.

That night sleep came slowly to Isobel. Jack Logan had killed the captain as surely and smoothly as doubtless someday, directly or indirectly, he would kill Isobel. At this point, Jack's safest course would be to destroy both the letter and Isobel before the ship even landed, thereby eliminating any opportunity for Nathaniel Shyrie to make sure Jack was captured in the process of selling the letter to Lord North. Of course, Jack Logan did not always choose the safest route. Perhaps she would actually live long enough to verify the letter to Edward Carrington—but no longer. She had revealed herself too clearly to Jack Logan. He knew, and was right, that she could not be trusted. Especially now. Now she knew not only his escape route, but also that he had killed the captain and, further, that he was equally well prepared, already half-intending, to kill Ira. As long as she remained alive, if ever it became to her advantage to do so, she could talk—to the British, to Mr. Shyrie, to Ira.

In truth, she was no freer, no safer now than when she had been in Newgate. Except that now she at least had the run of the ship. Once they landed, however, she would not be overly surprised should Jack produce a set of handcuffs.

In the pitch black of their cabin she reached out and allowed her fingers to rest on the chain around his neck. Abruptly his breathing changed as a subtle muscular tension came into his shoulders. Quickly, angrily, she withdrew her hand. The man was a cat! How could she ever possibly kill him in his sleep, how could she ever trust her own judgment as to whether he was asleep, or how deeply? And even if she did kill him—what then? Obviously Jack had thrown the captain's body overboard. The prospect of Isobel dragging Jack's body even from the bed to the door of the cabin was ludicrous. Surely by now Jack realized Isobel knew he intended to kill her eventually, yet he continued to sleep in the same bed with her. And why not? Why not, indeed?

Tears flooded her eyes. That letter was *hers*. If she had it, perhaps she could make her own arrangements with Edward Carrington. The price would be cheap: some money, clothes and safe, secret passage to some other country—France perhaps. At least to Edward Carrington, as witness to the letter's validity, Isobel Browne would be more valuable alive than dead.

There was, of course, only one solution, one shred of hope. Ira. Before the ship docked, Ira must kill Jack.

Two days later Isobel used an opportunity to brush against Ira on the steps leading belowdecks. The physical contact might have been a pure chance, but the look in her eyes and his reaction—startled confusion followed by obviously heightened interest—could not at all be construed as accidental.

From that moment on, whenever Jack was around, both Ira and Isobel went out of their ways to avoid eye contact, but the mutual deliberateness of their avoidance began to build an almost-tangible bond between them.

By the end of the first week Isobel was a familiar sight on deck, a blanket wrapped about the shoulders of her gray wool dress like a shawl. She had only one change of clothing—a man's shirt and pants, commandeered by Jack from the smallest crew member. These she wore when she washed the dress and found it not yet dry by morning. Once, alone in the cabin, she tucked her hair up into one of Jack's stocking caps. She realized that wearing the man's loose jacket and trousers, she might well be able to pass as a boy, once she reached shore. Not that her plans were at all definite; it was merely an observation she filed away, like a tool which someday might or might not be useful.

She knew, from talking carefully, casually, indirectly with Jack, where she must go when the ship landed—an inn near a town called New Hereford, somewhere in the colony of Connecticut. The Twin Stallion. There no one would turn her over to the British, and she would be able to make contact with Edward Carrington. She would have to be careful, though. Apparently Mr. Shyrie also frequented the Twin Stallion.

The problem was, she needed the letter. It occurred to her to attempt to take it from the packet some night while Jack slept and hope he would not notice the contents were missing as long as the packet remained around his neck, but what if he did notice? Far better to remove it after he was dead. But how? She would have to be alone with his body.

Ira. So much depended on Ira!

By the end of the second week, the wind fair again after a brief storm, Isobel wrapped the blanket around her shoulders and prepared to go on deck. She wore her gray dress and white lace-trimmed cap. It was early morning. She knew it had to be her imagination, but yesterday she could have sworn a taste of spring blew over the water, even though the month of February was barely behind them. If the wind held, surely not even another three weeks would be required to reach the colonies. Jack rarely touched her these days, even though they still shared the same bed. Their game of getting along with each other had worn thin, although apparently Jack also preferred to avoid any overt antagonism. She knew he had told all the crew not to speak to her, and she suspected he had even assigned a select few to watch her, to report back to him should Isobel attempt to initiate contact. Any meaningful communication with Ira had so far been impossible. Initially she had been afraid Jack might kill Ira, as swiftly and neatly as Jack had killed the captain, but now, with two weeks passed since the captain's death, it seemed apparent that Jack did not intend to kill Ira until or unless he had to. Ira was now captain, and a good captain. According to Jack, no one else on board knew as well as Ira which sail configurations best suited which winds and what weather a day not yet begun would bring. As for Ira killing Jack—if this was his intention, he gave no sign of it. Perhaps Jack had misjudged him. A chill swept over her. If Jack Logan stepped off this ship onto American soil, without question, shortly thereafter Isobel Browne would be dead.

She ran her hand over the coarse material of the blanket shawl around her shoulders, then started for the door. Unexpectedly, she caught a glimpse of herself in Jack's shaving mirror. No! She did not want to see her reflection. Usually he packed the mirror away with his other belongings when he finished with it, but that morning he had been interrupted by one of the crew members, a message—something on deck had required his immediate attention. With morbid fascination, she turned back to face her reflection. Her hands against the blanket were red and chafed by the wind, no longer soft and pretty. Her eyes seemed hollow, her cheekbones grossly sharp, her lips hard, her whole face aged and ghostly pale between the sun and windburned splotches of red. The mirror seemed to whisper to her, taunt her. Even Jack no longer wanted her. Why should Ira? The mirror told the truth. It was not fear of Jack that had curtailed Ira's desiring glances—it was Isobel. The young, desirable girl who had started the flirtation no longer existed.

She thought of Ira's razor, still under the mattress. Ironically there had been no need to steal it. Jack left his own razor lying about freely.

First Jack, she thought, then herself. Funny if the crew simply threw both of them overboard. Poor fat Lord North. How long would he continue to search frantically for a hopelessly blurred, washed-out letter long buried around the neck of a corpse at the bottom of the sea?

She closed the cabin door behind her, climbed the short flight of steps to the deck and immediately realized something was wrong. Instead of attending to their regular duties, the men stood in small groups, whispering among themselves. Most of the activity seemed to center on the captain's cabin. The door opened, and Jack stepped out into the crisp March sunlight. He stood with his hands on his hips. There was something about him, dressed in red stocking cap, sailor's jacket, gray woolen pants and knee-high boots, strongly reminiscent of a masthead figurine.

"Well?" he bellowed at the crew. "What are you all gaping at? Get to your duties!"

A few hesitated, but only for an instant. Jack walked to the man nearest him and slapped him on the back. "Come on," he said. "Am I to take over your work, or shall we set the girl to it?"

Initially startled, the man laughed, then left the area of the cabin along with the others. Yes, Isobel concluded, Jack handled the men well. They seemed to like him, a feeling Jack encouraged, but never at the expense of any relinquished authority. In addition to the force of his own personality, Jack Logan was Nat Shyrie's second-in-command, and apparently to these men the name Shyrie had a magic ring to it. For the first time Isobel tried to picture Nathaniel Shyrie, wondered what he was like.

Drawing the blanket tighter around her shoulders, she walked to where Jack stood in front of the cabin.

"What's wrong?" she asked.

Tight-lipped, his voice barely more than a whisper, he answered, "Ira's dying."

She felt the color drain from her face. For an instant she feared her legs would no longer support her.

Jack caught the reaction. Voice low, he watched her very carefully. "I did not know Ira was so dear a friend to you."

"You said he knows the sea better than any man aboard," she snapped. "Would you kill them all, one by one, till there's nobody left can handle the ship?"

Apparently without thought, he raised his hand as though to strike her but stopped himself. Too many of the crew would have seen it. Obviously he preferred to keep the antagonism he felt toward Isobel a secret. Otherwise, Isobel concluded, he might be hard pressed to explain why he kept her alive and protected. Quietly he answered, "I've nothing to do with it. He has a cut on his arm, a little cut, an accident he did hisself three days ago. Now the whole arm is red and swollen, and you can see the fever in his eyes. That's what Thomas come to tell me this morning while I was shaving."

"But—does he have to die?"

Dryly Jack answered, "You know a way to save him?"

Head high, her heart beating far too rapidly, she lied. "I might. If the cook can supply even a few of the right herbs. Let me see him—Ira, I mean."

With a curious mixture of hope and suspicion, Jack asked, "You've knowledge of these things?"

"One of the girls I worked with in London was from the country. She taught me much. Let me see him."

Jack hesitated. Then, decisively, he opened the cabin door and led the way for Isobel, closing the door behind her, perhaps to shut off the sight from any lingering curious crew members. Immediately Isobel turned her head and covered her nose with the blanket. The room stank of sweat, excrement, disease, death. Yes, the man was really dying. Somehow she had walked into that room with one last desperate hope that he might recover, that she might finally have found an opportunity to talk to him.

She let the blanket slip back into place around her shoulders and accepted the stench of the cabin, even though she feared she might vomit. His breathing was heavy, loud and labored, his eyes and mouth wide open. Carrying through on the game, led by instinct rather than any conscious plan, she walked to the side of his bed. The cut had been bandaged, the bandage now stained more with fluid than blood. His eyes met hers and for an instant appeared lucid; then as though a shade had been drawn, the blank, unseeing quality returned.

"Well?" said Jack.

"I—I must unwrap the wound."

Suspiciously Jack answered, "What are you up to?"

"All right," she snapped, stepping back, "then you unwrap it."

He walked to Ira's bed and complied with Isobel's request. In that instant, with Jack's full attention turned to Ira, Isobel realized why she had continued to play the game even after she realized Ira was really dying. She had remained in the cabin to secure a weapon. A *real* weapon, not a mere razor. A razor could be wrenched from her hand long before the job was finished. Where would Ira keep a weapon? Somewhere close to him—very close. No matter what explanation of the captain's death he genuinely considered most logical, surely he was not stupid enough to have eliminated the possibility of murder completely. In addition, he knew Jack was hardly his friend.

The weapon would be close enough for him to reach if he were attacked while sleeping. The bed! Under the covers or the pillow.

The wound now unwrapped, Jack stepped aside. A fresh wave of nausea overcame Isobel. The man's breathing was louder, his sight now apparently completely gone.

"I've seen men die of this before," said Jack contemptuously. "He'll be dead before I could even get to the cook."

"First," said Isobel, "raise his head. Find something to place under the pillow. Hurry!"

Without any real show of enthusiasm Jack turned his attention to other parts of the room.

Isobel, in a stance of adjusting the pillow, slipped her hand underneath it, her back covering the details of her movements from Jack's view.

Tears flooded her eyes. Her heart pounded with a mixture of joy and fear. God had forgiven her and wanted her to live. Quickly her fingers traced the barrel of the pistol under his pillow down to the handle. She grasped the handle.

Ira's breathing stopped, the sudden silence so stark, so startling that all movement by both Jack and Isobel stopped in the same instant. Then, again, sound, but not really breathing except to the extent that somehow it seemed related to his general breathing mechanism. A last gagging, rattling, wheezing sound. His head lolled to the side, facing Isobel, his eyes and mouth open.

No! Not *now*. A few more minutes, even seconds, and Jack would have been close enough for her to use the gun with no fear of merely wounding him.

With a gesture of contempt Jack dropped the clothing he had been carrying to place under Ira's pillow in line with Isobel's instructions. He let out a deep breath, then started for the cabin door. "I'll have to tell the crew," he said.

"Jack—"

"What?"

Her tears flowed freely now; her voice was small and tremulous. With her left hand she held the shawl-blanket tight around her shoulders. In her right hand, hidden by the blanket, she held the gun, her finger tightly positioned on the trigger. "Jack," she went on, "I'm sick. Please help me. Take my arm."

His irritation turned to near exasperation, but perhaps through the habit of generally avoiding overt trouble with her, he walked to where she stood and held out his hand.

With her left hand she released the blanket, let it fall to the floor. With her right hand she quickly brought the gun up, level with his forehead, and pulled the trigger.

He looked so surprised. Not even angry. No time for anger. Whatever secondary reaction might have followed, she would never know, because not enough of his face was left to express any emotion. The impact of the shot sent his body reeling backward, arms flailing. He fell to the floor, crumpled, lifeless, yet still, Isobel could not believe he was dead.

She screamed—a sharp, mechanical sound—only a split second after the last reverberation of the pistol shot. Almost stumbling over Jack, she ran to the cabin door and locked it. No, that was all wrong. The gun was still in her hand. So little time! She ran back to the bed and placed the pistol near Ira's hand. Again she screamed, kept screaming. She must remember to scream.

Now the letter! She knelt on the floor beside Jack's body and grabbed the chain around his neck. To release it, she had to lift what was left of his head, that heavy blood-wet mass of ripped tissue, raw shattered bone and whatever else, now in pieces, God had placed whole in the man's head. By now her hands and clothing were soaked with blood. Someone pounded on the door. So little time. More pounding on the door now. Voices, shouting. Soon they would break it down. How long? Not too soon probably. The door was heavy; the lock was good.

The chain yielded to the pressure of her hands. The letter was again hers. She stuffed the badly blood-wet leather packet down into the bodice of her dress.

A pane of glass shattered. The scream it evoked from Isobel was real. One of the crew had climbed to the cabin window and smashed the glass. His face appeared from behind the drawn draperies, rapidly followed by the rest of his body. He was young—no older than Isobel, if even that old. With an expression sharply akin to awe he took in the scene before him, then ran to the door and opened it.

The rest of the crew poured into the room, but stopped, as though suddenly frozen.

It was the cook who spoke, his voice filled with incredulity. "What happened?"

As though in shock, Isobel answered, "Ira shot him.

Called him over to the bed, then sat up and shot him. Used all the strength he had, shot Jack, then died himself. Oh, God!" she whispered. Then, as though overcome by grief, she explained the blood on herself by leaning over Jack as though again to caress what was left of him. "Jack, Jack!"

"Ira shot him?"

"*Why*?"

Repelled in a way she dared not show, she rose to her feet, where at least Jack was not directly in her line of vision. "He told me Ira threatened to kill him," she said softly, "but Jack didn't believe it. He thought Ira was just mad at him."

"About what?" She heard only the words, did not even notice which man had spoken them.

Directing herself to the former first mate, Thomas Norris, now—she supposed—captain, she answered quietly, "I was Mr. Shyrie's woman. Jack was bringing me to America for Nathaniel Shyrie. When Jack and I shared the same cabin, Ira said Jack was betraying Nathaniel."

After a brief pause Thomas Norris answered, "I don't think you ever even met Mr. Shyrie."

"I met him in England," she answered firmly, fighting panic. She did not even know what he looked like. "Last November," she added. Jack had told her Shyrie was in England last November. Her eyes almost pleading, she went on. "But Ira was wrong. Nathaniel wouldn't have cared, as long as Jack let me alone once we got to America. At least that's what Jack told me. I don't know. Maybe he lied." Voice firm again, she continued. "I only know I boarded this ship with Jack's promise that him and Mr. Shyrie would protect me. I expect that protection to continue."

"Must have been the fever," said the cook. "Ira

wouldn't kill Jack over some skinny little whore. Must have been out of his head with the fever."

Skinny little whore! She bristled. Some of the most powerful men in all England had laid out fortunes—well, small fortunes—to be with her.

But that, of course, was a long time ago. It might have been a hundred years.

"Mr. Shyrie wants me!" she cried. Starkly conscious of her stringy hair and bloodstained dress, she added awkwardly, "I—I didn't used to look like this."

"Yeah?" answered Thomas Norris angrily, obviously holding her at least partially responsible for Jack's death. Yet at the same time he seemed unsure. Perhaps she did know Shyrie. Best to be careful. "Well, we'll see if he still wants you." To the assembled crew, his voice far more authoritative now, he said, "All right. Let's get to work. We've this cabin to clean out and a ship to bring home to America." Fully in charge now, he continued. "No one's to touch the girl. You hear me? You touch her, it's mutiny. Same orders Jack gave us about her still go."

Slowly Isobel lifted her now-bloodstained blanket from the floor beside the bed, tightened it about her shoulders and left the cabin.

CHAPTER SEVEN

Sarah Carrington, one arm around her son's waist, held her horse to a fast trot as the New Hereford Anglican Church came into view. The church somehow resembled a neglected child, oddly forlorn in the late-afternoon light rain, a rain so light it seemed more mist than rain. It was late March now. The bitter snows of February had been replaced by mud. Even during those brief intervals when the rain stopped, the mud remained, oozing over the cobblestone walkways of the town, seeping through the matted grass and weeds of the countryside.

New Hereford was starkly changed, yet perhaps not as starkly as Sarah had at first imagined. Perhaps the basic current already flowing when she had left for England was now merely stronger, now too striking to be overlooked. Thoughts whispered when she had left were spoken out loud. Treasonous words met equally strong arguments in support of the king and mingled with more words by those who, often out of fear and sometimes out of genuine Christian charity toward all men, tried with increasing difficulty to remain neutral. A local merchant, a man Sarah had known since childhood, had actually been hanged for selling tea, in accord with a law passed by the Town Committee last December. To Sarah, the event still seemed unreal. How could any law so directly opposed to the king's best interests be legal? Yet the rebels now completely controlled the Town Committee. God alone knew what other "laws" might suddenly be passed. Charles was wrong to have remained in New Hereford, wrong to have let himself be drawn into the underground loyalist movement, which supplied information to the British on rebel armament stockpiles and activities. In spite of the fact that even the most powerful members of the Town Committee dared not—yet—openly attack the person, family or property of Charles Carrington, how could Charles not see how thin the protective shield of his name and money had become?

But no, not Charles. How like Charles to see only what he wanted to see. He saw the British garrison at Lloyd's Point directly across the Sound from Stamford, which was only a few miles south of New Hereford. He saw other New Hereford loyalists going about their business with no overt interference. He saw the underground loyalist group grow stronger, more numerous, more daring. He invited to his home and listened too well to British officers who laughed at the idea of any real danger from the rebel movement. Did he also, she wondered, see this time in New Hereford as an opportunity to win favor in the king's eyes—favor which might be used as leverage in his brother's behalf when Edward and others like him, their cause in ruins, stood trembling in the shadow of the king's justice? Or was it, rather, to prove beyond question his own loyalty in order to avoid any stigma from Edward's politics?

But whatever his motives, noble or ignoble, she found

herself unable to forgive him for continuing to subject little Charles, not quite six, the only surviving child of the four she had given birth to, to the dangers of New Hereford. How easy for any of the rebels who knew of Charles' loyalist activities to take the child as hostage for—what? Money? Information? But it was not merely the adults she feared. Last Thursday, when young Charles wandered too far from her side in the town, larger children infused with the poison of treasonous parents had actually attacked him. His father saw no more to the incident than children's play, children's fights, but Charles had not been present. Sarah had seen the attack, seen their faces, felt their hatred.

Charles seemed unwilling or unable to see the critical point—the speed with which New Hereford was changing. With the rebels now in complete control of the Town Committee, no stranger dared use the previously free and open roadways through and around New Hereford without a signed pass from one of the local Committees of Correspondence, ostensibly a communications network among rebel leaders throughout the colonies, but actually an increasingly dangerous power group not above physical violence if violence suited their aims at any given moment.

Even more than politics, however, personalities frightened Sarah. In England everyone knew his proper place. In America one's "proper place" seemed to be as high as one could rise, and many of those who had not risen seemed to resent those who had. For all the respect the Carrington name commanded in New Hereford, the name also evoked resentment. At what point in the current New Hereford atmosphere of fear and hovering violence might old resentments, in the false name of politics, explode into very real violence against the Carrington family? Even now Sarah found herself unable fully to trust all her servants, some of whom had been with her many years. Even now, in the rain, she dared not leave her son alone in the care of her own servants in her own home.

At the entrance to the church she dismounted into the mud and carefully lifted her son into her arms. How frail he seemed, how quiet, withdrawn so much of the time into a world of his own making. A world free of the tension between his parents, free of the fear which sometimes hung in the air almost as tangibly as the rain-mist which now engulfed both mother and child.

The church was in the Georgian style, rectangular with two tiers of arched windows. The walls, today darkened by the rain, were laid in English bond brickwork, the roof topped by a brick and wood octagonal spire reaching to a height of a hundred and seventy-two feet. The belfry contained four bells. The church, with its adjoining graveyard where Sarah's three other children lay at rest, was about a mile from town on a rocky slope inhospitable to trees and greenery, although like the church itself, two nearby hemlocks, one white pine and—in spring—a profusion of mountain laurel somehow seemed to survive and flourish. The far larger Congregationalist Meetinghouse was part of the town, a considerably older squareline weathered clapboard building in a choice location. Although before she had left for England, no clear distinction among rebels, loyalists and ambivalents was discernible between the two congregations, a polarization was now emerging. Unquestionably the rebels now dominated the Congregationalist Meetinghouse, the loyalists the Anglican Church.

Still holding young Charles, she tried to open the church door and realized it was locked. A sudden, unnatural coldness gripped her. Must even a house of worship now lock its doors in fear? Having stopped at her uncle's house on the way and been told he was at the church, she had no reason to believe he was not there. She had assumed his horse was in the carriage house to the left of the main entrance. With her own horse now loosely tethered at the hitching rail and young Charles growing heavy in her arms, she pounded on the door and called out repeatedly, "Uncle Ezra!"

The door was opened by a young boy, fourteen or fifteen. In his right hand he held a pistol, which he promptly lowered.

Startled, Sarah stepped inside and lowered Charles to his feet. She looked from the teenage boy's face to the gun, then back again. Although she recognized the boy, she could not recall his name. She knew only that he was part of the active loyalist movement. Obviously he recognized her.

"Sorry, Mrs. Carrington," he promptly apologized. "Something's happened."

She lowered her riding cloak hood and, with a handkerchief, wiped some of the rain from her face. They stood in the narrow foyer area of the church, the sanctuary directly ahead of them. To her right was a small vestry with an entranceway to the winding staircase which led to the bell tower. To her left was the entrance to the minister's office.

"What's happened?" she asked.

"They went and used our bell tower," the boy answered. "The rebels. Under the staircase. Loosened some boards and loaded it with firearms. Smuggled firearms, probably. One of the steps was rotted and gave way, and when we saw what was underneath, we couldn't believe it."

Incredulous, Sarah said, "They must be mad!"

"Perhaps not. Who'd ever look here? It's the one place in New Hereford no soldier would think to search. They're stockpiling arms, you know. Arms and gunpowder."

The door to the minister's office abruptly swung open. The Reverend Ezra Howgate, bundled up against the cold like some white-wigged snow gnome, stood framed in the doorway, a thin, bent man well into his seventies.

"Sarah!" he said. "You bring the boy out in this inclement weather. He'll catch his death of cold. And the church is not safe. We're packing everything of value—the silver, papers—taking it to my home, where we'll hide it. We still don't know how they got in. Perhaps over the roof, down the bell-tower stairs and unlocked the front door. But, you see, they'll come back, and when they find their weapons no longer here, we don't know what they'll do. We gave the guns to the soldiers. We asked for their protection, but they won't do it. Won't be bothered, that's what it comes down to. Too busy drinking, gambling, chasing women. At least they'll not find many women to suit their tastes in New Hereford!"

"The guns—where did they come from?"

"Smuggling group. Man named Shyrie. Slippery as an eel. Works for the rebels now, but the soldiers can't prove it. Or it might be another one. You remember little Jamie Devant? About three weeks ago they captured a ship little ways down from Norwalk. The *Silver Hawk*. Designed for smuggling like no ship they'd ever seen before. Got it out of the captain who he worked for—Jamie Devant; only they can't find Devant. Like the earth just swallowed him up. Ungrateful whelp!"

Momentarily distracted from the purpose of her visit, she asked haltingly, "Mr. Devant—if they catch him, what will they do to him?"

"Hang him! They've enough proof now. Serve him

right, too. I gave that boy every chance to learn the ways of the Lord, the good and holy life. Took him in from nowhere, him and his mother, gave her honest work, gave them both a good home. Of course, you'd remember him. I forgot. You were little then. My mind wanders sometimes. Step in by the stove."

He stepped aside, permitting access to his office. "Won't warm you," he went on, "but at least it'll take a little of the chill out of your bones. Come, Charles." To the teenage boy, he said, "Bring the wagon around, John. Start loading some of the boxes." As Sarah and young Charles entered his office, he continued. "Maybe we should have kept the guns. The soldiers won't protect us. We need to protect ourselves, God willing. Perhaps the Lord intended us to find those guns so we could keep them."

The office was carpeted, the walls paneled and stained maple, giving the room a deceptive appearance of warmth in this season. The furnishings were primarily a mixture of Chippendale and Queen Anne. A small stove, partially hidden from view by an ornamented screen depicting Jesus as an infant in the stable, stood near the corner of the room. The stove was most often used to boil water for tea throughout the year, but even the limited heat it gave off into the surrounding area was more than welcome in winter.

"So hard to know," he went on, shaking his head. "Surely He doesn't want us to lie down like lambs to be slaughtered, not we who faithfully serve the king He has ordained to rule us."

Sympathetic to her uncle's nervousness, but at the same time irritated by it and driven by her own, she closed the door and interrupted, "Uncle Ezra, I must speak with you."

"Of course, child. Of course."

To Charles, she said, "Go warm yourself by the stove, darling."

Slowly, sadly, the boy crossed the room to the stove. Lowering her voice, Sarah continued. "Uncle Ezra, I'm frightened. Monday night Charles went out. Some kind of meeting. You know he rarely tells me anything about what he's doing. He tells me the less I know about organized loyalist activities, the safer I'll be."

"Organized loyalist activities. No, child, we mustn't talk of these things. God will bless us, I promise you. To doubt is to doubt the Lord, and to doubt the Lord is a sin. If God meant for us to keep those guns and we, in our human imperfections, misunderstood, then other guns will be supplied to us. Don't be frightened. To fear is to doubt the Lord."

Then why are you so afraid? she thought. Straining to keep any trace of impatience from her voice, she continued. "Uncle Ezra, I'm worried about Charles. He went out Monday night. I waited all through Tuesday and most of today for his return. Then, about an hour ago, his horse came back . . . alone. I thought you might be able to help me, that there might be someone in the congregation who might be able at least to get some information about him. Is he hurt? Has he been taken prisoner? Is anyone else missing?"

"Anyone else missing? Yes. John's older brother. Also went out Monday night."

"Dear God!" she whispered. Then, sharply: "Uncle Ezra, I must get young Charles out of New Hereford into New York to stay with his grandfather."

Sternly her uncle answered, "A wife's duty is to remain at her husband's side."

"If"—she braced herself and continued—"if Charles is

all right and insists I remain, I'll do so, but"—her voice cracked—"I'll not see my last child join his sisters and brother in the cemetery simply because I did nothing to prevent it!"

"It's not for you to prevent anything," her uncle snapped. "It's in the hands of the Lord."

Startled, even somewhat amazed by the strength of her reaction, she answered just as sharply, "The Lord helps those who help themselves. He did not tell Joshua to remain home and be safe. He sent him into battle and blessed the battle. Right now I pray that God may bless my son's journey and guide me in making the safest possible arrangements for that journey."

Anger quickly replaced her uncle's initial reaction, shock. "I brought you up, loved you as my own child, arranged a proper marriage for you, and now you dare speak to me with such bold disrespect."

"Dear Uncle, I intend no disrespect."

"If Charles has decided that his son's place is by his side, it's not for you to interfere. A wife's first duty is to obey her husband. Have you so soon forgotten the wifely virtues I taught you through the years of your youth?"

"No," she answered quietly, "I've not forgotten. In the sight of God, at your insistence, I made the commitment to become and remain Charles' wife. I was sixteen and knew very little of marriage. Nonetheless, it is a commitment I intend to fulfill honorably, but I will not sacrifice my son to it. I came to you for help. Help in locating Charles, and help in getting my son safely out of New Hereford."

Abruptly young Charles left the stove, walked to his mother and tentatively took her hand in his. "Don't leave me, Mother. I want to stay with you."

"See how you frighten him, when you put no faith in the Lord's protection!"

She knelt down, faced her son. "You'll be safer with Grandpa, darling. I'll come to you as soon as I can, if your father says I may."

"You turn the boy against his father!" said Ezra in a voice appropriate to damnation pronouncements from the pulpit. She looked up at him. His eyes seemed almost glowing, like some distant saint or devil. Yes, she supposed he had loved her, to the best of his ability, to the best of his knowledge of what love was. She herself had never really known what love was until her children were born, until one by one, with the exception of Charles, they died. She looked away from her uncle and briefly tightened her arms around her son. All that remained of all she had ever really loved, in that instant, she held in her arms.

Her sense of being in the church seemed to overwhelm, almost to suffocate her. Was it really only her son she loved? Certainly one should also love God, but in that instant God and the white-wigged stern-faced figure of her uncle seemed so inextricably intertwined that she found her soul flooded with nothing but anger, fear and resentment.

She rose to her feet, faced her uncle. Voice unsteady, she asked, "Will you help me?"

"I'll help you find Charles," he answered firmly. "I'll see to it that those who are looking for John's brother also look for Charles."

Lips tight, she took young Charles' hand and started for the door; then, abruptly, she turned again to face Ezra. "I need a boat," she said. "A boat can take him across the Sound to the British garrison at Lloyd's Point. I know Charles' loyalist group has access to boats. I know they sometimes slip through the shoreline guards posted by the rebels. I'll tell you, I've already been to see Edward. Last week."

"You saw your husband's rebellious, treasonous brother without your husband's knowledge?"

"Edward didn't believe Charles didn't know of the visit. He was furious at me because he thought I was lying to him. He knows Charles is involved in the loyalist movement. He seemed to think Charles was using me and the boy—that all of us were trying to use Edward to help us carry information to the British. He refused me a pass even to leave New Hereford, so I can't travel overland." Voice less steady, she went on. "Edward told me to tell Charles to forget they are brothers." More quietly she continued. "I looked at Edward, and it was as though I had never seen him before. Uncle Ezra, I think Edward's afraid. He's even afraid of some of the people in his own movement, afraid because there's a point beyond which even he can't really control them."

"Disorganized rabble," spat her uncle. "No one can control them, and it'll be their downfall, I promise you. By what right does Edward Carrington tell you you cannot leave New Hereford?"

Dryly Sarah answered, "By right of his power to enforce it. There are rumors that the Town Council may soon create a committee to investigate the loyalty of all New Hereford citizens to the American cause, with legal penalties for those who show themselves loyal to the crown. Charles refuses to take it seriously. I don't know. Maybe it is important that Charles remain here, and I remain with him. Maybe it does give courage to others who defy the rebels." More firmly she added, "But I am still not willing to keep young Charles with us. We can say we sent him for reasons of health or as a comfort and companion to his grandfather, now so old and ill—"

"Bang!" It was young Charles who spoke. Both Sarah and Ezra quickly turned and looked at him. He stood by

Ezra's secretary desk, a Chippendale prototype with an enclosed hooded and scrolled top, in true New England tradition. The desk was one of the newest pieces of furniture in the room and one of the finest in design and workmanship. Below the slant top, open now and cluttered with papers, were four oxbow-shaped drawers. The second drawer was open, the drawer in which Ezra stored sweets for his own consumption, but fairly often shared with young Charles. Apparently seeking the sweets, Charles had, instead, found a bell-mouthed flintlock pistol, which he now pointed, teasingly, at his uncle.

"No!" cried Ezra, wrenching the weapon from his hand. Almost as part of the same gesture, he shoved the child, knocking him to the floor. "Would you come here and steal from me?"

"He did not steal it!" Sarah exploded as she rushed to Charles to help him to his feet. He did not cry. There was a time when he would have cried. To Sarah, his silence seemed ominous, an additional indication of even further emotional withdrawal, a reminder to her that it was not merely his physical safety which concerned her.

Obviously shaken, Ezra stood there, with the pistol in his hand.

For the first time the fact that the pistol had been in his desk drawer fully registered with Sarah. She looked at him, tried to reconcile his purported faith in the Lord's protection with his possession of the weapon.

Awkwardly, as though trapped and ashamed, yet refusing to admit to either, he said, "The others insisted I keep it. One finds one must compromise. As you know, in the church service I no longer pray for the good health of King George and Queen Charlotte. Rather, we merely pray for the well-being of all Christian kings and queens everywhere. Of course, by so doing, I am actually praying for our own king and queen—a minor compromise, a slight change in words. The meaning remains the same."

Still shocked, Sarah asked, "Is it loaded?"

"They insist I keep it loaded." He returned it to the drawer, then took out a sweet, which he handed to young Charles. After only an instant's hesitation the boy accepted it eagerly.

It was not, however, his pleasure with the sweet which so impressed Sarah. Rather, it was the quickness with which he had forgiven, possibly even forgotten Ezra's roughness of a moment ago. Sarah looked again at her uncle and, to her amazement, found herself caught in a wave of compassion. All his life Ezra Howgate had lived by rigidly defined standards of right and wrong, standards which, in more settled times, might well have carried him with reasonable emotional comfort and dignity to his grave. Standards which he had passed on to Sarah and how many others with such an aura of authority that who might dare question? And yet now many did question, and the answers he gave and had given through the years no longer fitted, no longer satisfied. Yes, he was afraid, but only part of it was physical. Far more, she realized, he was afraid of seeing himself as she saw him in that moment—a confused, inept, lonely old man.

Had young Charles sensed it even before Sarah saw it? Was this why the child bore him no ill will?

Suddenly driven by compassion, she lifted her riding hood back over her head, stepped to her uncle's side and kissed his cheek. Gently she said, "God bless and keep you, Uncle." She took young Charles' hand and started for the door.

"Sarah—"

She turned and waited.

He looked at her but apparently changed his mind about whatever he had intended to say. Instead, clutching at the remaining shreds of his tattered dignity, he offered, "As soon as I hear anything of Charles, I'll send word to you."

She nodded, walked out of the office. She felt strangely free. Her fear was still with her, yet now her image of God and Ezra Howgate were no longer so confusingly intertwined. Now she at least felt free enough to pray, in the silence of her own mind, that God would reveal to her the path she must take, no matter how difficult, and bless the journey.

Outside the church, John, the teenage boy who had opened the door for her, stood in the rain beside a partially loaded wagon. The rain was heavier now, colder. A man in his forties stood beside John, his voice soft, the words inaudible to Sarah. She recognized him. He was a shopkeeper, an ambivalent, but his inclinations were unquestionably Tory. Perhaps it was the rain and coldness of the day in conjunction with her own imagination, but John looked ill—too pale, almost waxen.

Concerned, holding tightly to young Charles' hand, Sarah approached them, her dress and riding cape dragging in the mud. With a brief nod to John's companion, she spoke softly to John. "Are you all right?"

She would have thought it impossible, but even more color drained from his face. The older man's eyes frightened her. Pity. Pity was what she read in those soft brown eyes.

He nodded towards the church and offered his arm. "Let us step inside, Mrs. Carrington. I have something to tell you."

The cold which until now had been merely uncomfortable became painful. It particularly penetrated her feet and hands. Very quietly she answered, "It's about Charles, isn't it?"

He hesitated, nodded, then guided her back into the church along with young Charles and John.

Ezra stepped into the foyer and quickly surveyed the situation. Obviously something was wrong. To young Charles he said, "Would you like another sweet? You know where they are, but touch only the sweets."

Sensing his mother's distress, the boy hesitated.

"Go, child, go now," said Ezra with a sharpness probably not intended.

Obediently, not really drawn by the sweet, Charles left the adults and walked into Ezra's office.

"I don't know fancy words," the man began quietly, "so I'll just say it plain. Mr. Carrington's dead. They beat him; then they hanged him. Might even have been dead before they hanged him. Back behind Seth Jackson's house, where the meeting was Monday night. A few feet farther they found John's brother. Shot in the head."

Abruptly Sarah found herself seated on the floor, her mud-splattered dress and riding cape billowing out around her. How she had come to be in this utterly absurd position remained unclear to her.

"Get a chair," someone said, "and some water."

She did not notice who spoke. She did not want a chair, and as damp as she was from the rain, the suggestion that additional water be brought struck her as ludicrous. All she really wanted was to remain exactly as she was. Charles was dead. Ridiculous. Charles could not possibly be dead. His face and voice, in her mind, were far too vivid.

Hands reached out, lifted her.

"Let me alone," she said.

They helped her onto the chair the shopkeeper had fetched from the office. None of their words seemed coordinated, coherent. Only sounds. One sound, above all others, tore at her heart. Young Charles was crying. She could not remember the last time she had heard him cry. He must have listened from the office. Slowly, almost tentatively, he came to her. She embraced him, drawing him to the icy cold of her own body. Was his heart really beating that fast, or was the hammering pulsation which filled her ears the frantic beating of her own frightened heart?

"Now, now," Ezra said to the boy, "we must be brave. Your father wouldn't want you to cry."

"Let him cry!" Sarah exploded, her own eyes suddenly wet and stinging. Legs still unsteady, she rose to her feet, and her arms perhaps too tightly around young Charles, she addressed the shopkeeper. "I need a boat. I need to get my son safely into New York. The rebels have forbidden me to leave New Hereford. Can you help me?"

Awkwardly, almost as though he were embarrassed, the man answered, "Well, I was never really into the group deep, like your husband, but I can tell you this, his life gave them courage. His death—I tell you, ma'am, the ones I've seen are scared now. Really scared."

"The ones like you," spat John. Yes, Sarah suddenly remembered. John's brother had also been killed. For a boy of fifteen, John's face seemed incredibly aged. "The ones like you who try to sit in the middle and pretend you're not in any more danger than the rest of us." John continued, still addressing the shopkeeper. "I knew my brother, I know what he'd do, if he was still alive. He'd ride down their homes, scatter their livestock, burn their barns, kill six of them for every one of us they dared touch!"

"Oh, yes," said Sarah, her voice suddenly shrill, "and then whoever killed Charles and your brother could do the same, until finally there'd be nothing left but half-burned buildings and half-mad women and children. Who are *they*, John? *They* killed my husband and your brother, *they* have decided to terrify us, perhaps hoping it will stop us, but *who are they*? I'll tell you—a handful of madmen! I know Charles' brother. Oh, yes, he's changed very much from the man I used to know, but not that much. Edward Carrington does not kill for sport, for pleasure. If he can, he'll avoid war. The name Carrington is not unknown at court. Do you really believe any responsible member of whatever Edward's group wants to call itself would so endanger their hope for peace as to sanction the butchery of a Carrington? No—these are madmen, lunatics, drunkards, those who merely attach themselves to the edge of a cause, that they may justify and feed their own appetite for blood in the name of that cause, any cause."

Amazed by her outburst, the three men merely stared at her. Awkwardly, yet sharply, Ezra finally answered, "These are men's affairs. Tend to your womanly duties."

With almost equal sharpness Sarah countered, "My first womanly duty at this moment is to protect my son." Addressing herself to all three of them, she added, "Will any of you help us leave New Hereford?"

"Charles was killed because of his politics," Ezra answered firmly. "You and the boy are in no danger. No, I'll not ask any man to risk his life to satisfy your headstrong foolish fancies. Go home, child, and take the boy with you. Put these fantasies of madmen out of your head. Yes, they are mad, but it's power they lust for, not blood."

Very quietly Sarah asked, "Do you believe Edward gave his consent that his brother be killed?"

Without hesitation Ezra answered, "Yes."

"I cannot agree. Imprisonment perhaps, but not death."

Lips tight, as though even to acknowledge her defiance of his authority would be beneath his dignity, Ezra turned to the shopkeeper. "Would you be kind enough to see Mrs. Carrington safely to her home?"

"I know the way," answered Sarah coldly. *The Lord will protect me,* she thought sarcastically, bitterly, an answer to her uncle which she lacked the courage to speak.

Her horse at a fast trot, her thoughts seemed to race in time with the now-beating icy rain. A boat, a boat. But how? Even if she secured a boat, she herself did not know the coastline, nor would she have the strength to row all the way from New Hereford to Long Island. She needed help, but who? Ezra was right. Anyone, rebel or loyalist, who tried to cross the Sound now would do so at the risk of his life.

She thought of the British officers who had dined at her home, friends of Charles. Surely they would help her, at no risk to their lives, but she had no way to get in touch with them, no way to let them know how badly she needed their help.

Suddenly the answer came to her. She had known it all along, yet not seen it because the solution was so obvious. She did have something to offer.

Money!

She slowed her horse. She had to think. The motion and sound were too much. All right, she would pay someone.

Tears flooded her eyes. No good. An error in judgment—hers or in the person she hired—could be fatal for all of them. It had to be a very special person. Someone who knew the coast, someone able to protect himself should trouble occur, yet honorable enough to protect Sarah and young Charles as well.

Someone in the loyalist movement. Who? Perhaps John could help her find someone. His entire family was part of the movement. How difficult it was to concentrate. No, John would be unlikely to help her, with Ezra's obvious opposition.

Perhaps she could hire someone to take a letter to the garrison, to any one of several officers. Yes! That should do it.

How long might she wait for an answer—how many days, weeks—only to discover the message had never been delivered? No, she could not assume the letter would get through.

The rain struck her face like needles, the sky almost dark now. Against her arm she felt a movement from Charles which seemed to sweep his entire body. At first she thought he had started to cry again; then she realized it was a cough, deep and racking.

She sped the pace of her horse. Get him home, get him warm.

Tight-lipped, she thought how ironic that smugglers seemed able to roam the coast, hide weapons in churches, in short, do pretty well as they pleased, while honest, God-fearing, loyal subjects of his majesty lived in terror for their lives. She thought of James Devant, working for the rebels, so well hidden from the British authorities. A smuggler! Well, at least now she knew why that night at the inn he—she broke off. No, she did not know. Edward Carrington and James Devant were *not* friends—or at least had not been that night at the inn. *Was* James a smuggler? Ezra had said he was, but Ezra, she had realized many years ago much to her uncle's consternation, was not always right.

James. Something strange about James. Where exactly did he stand politically?

I am in the service of James Devant, he had told her. Memories of those few moments she had spent alone with him in the hallway at the inn warmed and at the same time frightened her.

I am in your debt, he had told her. A pretty speech, or had he meant it?

She must find out. She must find James Devant, ask him to help her. She would send word to everyone she knew who had known him as a child, everyone from New Hereford to Boston, and back down the coast again. Send word and pray that he would care and trust her enough to come.

CHAPTER EIGHT

"Carrington want to see you," said Garth.

In the dimly lit kitchen of the Taylor farmhouse on the outskirts of New Hereford, behind the now-deserted broken-down mill once run by Samuel Taylor, James Devant sat on a rough-hewn bench abstractedly finishing the straw broom he had started earlier that evening for the Widow Taylor. To Alma Taylor, even the hands of a man recovering from gunshot wounds could and should be put to work. Well into her sixties and a staunch Congregationalist, Alma still remembered little Jamie Devant and his mother, virtual prisoners in the home of that upstart Anglican minister. Worked the mother to death, that was what those hypocrite Howgates did, then sent the boy off to godless Boston. Certainly simple Christian charity, in conjunction with the appreciable sum of money James was paying her, warranted refuge for him in her home, the home she shared with her widowed daughter-in-law and two teenage grandsons. Both grandsons had at one time or another worked for James. Alma, however, was far too practical to refuse when Nathaniel Shyrie outbid James for use of the farm as a drop for smuggled goods. With the deserted old mill such an obvious hiding place, periodically searched by the revenue agents and found empty of any contraband, the rest of the farm seemed somehow above suspicion—certainly not a place where anyone, especially Nathaniel Shyrie, would expect to find James Devant.

Keeping his voice low, even though he had no reason not to believe the entire Taylor family was asleep in their beds, James answered, "Carrington? See me? What for?"

"Make a deal maybe," said Garth. "Howgate find the guns Shyrie hide in the church. Give them to British soldiers. Maybe Carrington know you got guns and gunpowder hid somewhere."

Dryly James answered, "Maybe. And maybe it's a trap." He shook his head, remembering the *Silver Hawk,* the ship he had been waiting for the night Mark, McCaylan's son and the other man almost killed him. The British had seized the ship when it arrived at Norwalk, as initially scheduled. With all three men James had left to signal against the Norwalk landing murdered, James strongly suspected that Nat Shyrie had had a hand in it. Soldiers tended to use their guns, not knives; they tended to arrest, not to murder. The *Hawk!* To build another ship even comparable to it would require months. What disturbed him even more, however, was the manner in which his three signal men—Jeremy hardly more than a boy—had died. Certainly anyone who joined any smuggling group knew the risks, but damn Nat Shyrie, a man had the right to die with a weapon in his hand, facing his opponent.

No. To dwell on it was no good. The men were dead, the ship taken, and that was the end of it.

"Now soldiers look for you," Garth continued. "Somebody tell them about you."

"I think it was Shyrie," James answered. "Somehow he

found out when the ship was due and told them. Like he turned in Logan, in England."

"Logan alive. Got out of prison."

Startled, James answered, "You sure?"

Garth nodded. "On his way back here, some say. Others say he's already back. Lots of soldiers come here from New York and Boston, more come from England. They want Logan."

James frowned. "Sounds like a lot of effort for one smuggler."

"They say he have some girl with him. He find her in prison. They say she kill somebody good friend to the king."

Placing the broom beside him, James stood up and flinched more from stiffness than actual pain. Moving slowly, with minimal muscle strain, he stepped to where he could more fully appreciate the heat given off by the still-warm bricks of the gigantic kitchen fireplace, with its well-scoured array of cast-iron pots and cooking utensils. The faint odor of hasty pudding and apple pie still lingered.

"Sounds like he's gone mad," said James. Abruptly he laughed. "Over a woman! Jack Logan! She must be quite a woman." In spite of the discomfort, he swung around, faced Garth. "Yes, I'll see Carrington. If Logan's got himself a woman who's bringing a flood of British troops into New Hereford, Carrington will need help."

"Shyrie kill Logan and woman."

James' smile turned to a full grin. "He can't. Too many of his own men wouldn't follow him anymore. But they won't follow Logan either, not with their own lives endangered by troops chasing Logan's woman. The whole damned organization could fall apart, with all of them killing each other for control of it."

"You think Carrington see what coming? Want somebody new bring arms and gunpowder? Want you maybe?"

"Maybe. Maybe not. Arrange a meeting for the top of Cotter's Hill. Tell him to come alone."

"You go alone?"

"No. You'll be there, but he'll never know it, unless it is a trap. Make it for tomorrow night. Eleven o'clock. Any word on the *Dolphin*?"

Garth nodded. "Should be in end of next week."

"We'd better unload her in Massachusetts, then bring her down here empty. The goods she's to take back with her are stored at the Haydon farm." With the loss of the *Hawk*, caution had become the watchword for James' remaining ships. "Anything else?"

"Mrs. Carrington want to see you."

James frowned, as he tried to envision Edward's wife. Somehow he was under the impression that she had died several years ago. "Edward's wife?" he asked.

"No, the other one. The one you see at Twin Stallion."

"Sarah?" The beat of his heart quickened.

Garth nodded. "Her husband dead. About a week now."

"Yes, I heard."

And the news had, initially, evoked in James a feeling he had rarely experienced before in his adult life—guilt. Guilt because he had no reason to wish the man harm, or Sarah the grief of widowhood, yet he had been pleased to hear that Sarah Carrington no longer belonged to any man. Not that James could ever have her. Although even in England, a man of James' lowly breeding and background might buy himself a wife of Sarah's social standing, if she were poor, Sarah—James was sure—would not be for sale. At least not to James Devant, with Ezra Howgate and Edward Carrington behind her.

She wanted to see him. Why? That night they had met at the Twin Stallion, she had seemed so—what? Frightened of him? No, more than that—or, rather, something else. Something he did not understand, and not for lack of trying.

But whatever had prompted her to send the message must be important.

"Any idea what she wants?" he asked Garth.

"No. You trust her?"

Without thought, James found himself moving his thumb over the tips of his fingers, slowly, delicately, the mere sensation of touch unleashing memories, the incredibly sensual memory of these same fingertips caressing her face, replacing one stray silken lock of hair. "Yes," he answered so quietly even he barely heard his own voice. *Loving friends forever.* "I trust her."

Carrington, Edward Carrington. He must tend to the business at hand. Although now he realized he did trust her, without question, Sarah would be difficult to see. Too many others who did not trust her, whose interest was in her family's politics, might follow her. To arrange a meeting with Sarah would take time—a day or so, at best.

Edward Carrington was another matter. Again turning his attention to Garth, James continued. "Tell Edward that if my terms are satisfactory, he is to put two lights in the Twin Stallion tower, one above the other, tomorrow night as soon as it's dark. My terms are, we meet tomorrow night, eleven o'clock, at the top of Cotter's Hill. He is to come alone. Do you intend to see him yourself, or is this through someone else?"

"Not myself. McCaylan say what his son do was wrong, but I still think he want blood of the men who kill him."

James shook his head. "You don't understand John McCaylan. If he could find some other reason to kill us, he'd probably do it himself. But his own son violated the code he established. If he sought vengeance, in the eyes of the whole town, he'd be a hypocrite." Quickly, modifying his vocabulary to meet Garth's uncomprehending look, James added, "He'd be a liar. No, I don't think he could bring himself to kill us for that reason." Dryly he went on. "At least not so anybody might know he did it."

Garth shrugged. The intricacies of James' logic often lost his attention. "What difference, what reason? Dead is dead."

Unable to disagree, James smiled, nodded. Slowly, he raised his arm and flexed his fingers. His shoulder was still stiff, but the wound had completely healed. Perhaps someday the slight stiffness would also be gone. Alma Taylor was a good nurse. She had stopped the bleeding with spider webs. With a potion made largely from various winter-dead herbs drawn from the storage cellar of her house and from beneath the snow, she had reduced his fever, eased his pain. The hair she had shaved to treat his head wound was starting to grow back, the scar tissue of the wound itself not really noticeable with the rest of his hair pulled back and tied. How fortunate that the pistol ball had merely grazed his head. Once he had known a man who had survived a far more serious head wound, but had eventually gone mad.

Garth looked at him questioningly.

James nodded. "I'm still weak, though. I need to get out in the sun, move around." A chill swept through his body. The fireplace was cooling rapidly. Still dressed for the outdoors, Garth seemed unaware of it.

"You have message for Mrs. Carrington?" Garth asked.

"No," James answered. Awkwardly he added, "Not yet."

"I go now."

"Yes."

With Garth gone, James resigned himself to another night in the small secret section of the attic where he had slept ever since his arrival at the house. His blankets were up there and, at the moment, seemed especially appealing. After lifting the candle from the table, he stopped, then quickly returned it and blew it out. Horses were approaching the house. At least three or four, maybe more. Their pace was cautious, a minimum of noise. Could be revenue agents or soldiers searching for James, now that he was known to them, or perhaps some of Carrington's men had managed to follow Garth, although that was unlikely. He hoped it was Shyrie. Shyrie would have no reason to come into the house. In the near six weeks James had been at the farm, Shyrie had appeared once, to drop off some goods, his lone visit followed by two groups of his agents, who had picked them up. In any case, James had best make his way to the attic, but without light. Moving light through the old leaded glass windows at this hour would be far too likely to draw attention.

Guided by faint traces of moonlight, partially feeling his way, he walked from the kitchen into the mainroom, then started up the curved staircase.

A knock sounded at the door, and a hoarse voice, although restrained in volume, conveyed urgency. "Widow Taylor!" The caller tried the door, then apparently threw his body against it. One or two more such assaults, and the nails which held the latch brace would give out. The door would open. No revenue agent or military detachment would have reason to lower their voices, and anyone else in search of James would hardly come to the door and speak, even in a low voice. Who then? Members of Shyrie's group? Or cutthroats? But cutthroats were virtually unheard of in the colony of Connecticut. Of course, rumors that the Widow Taylor had and kept about the house more money than most of the other farmers in the area were, James knew, well grounded.

Quickly he made his way back into the kitchen and stationed himself where he would be able to see when the door opened. Shyrie's men knew she had money. Some of the men from England who sailed his ships would kill a man as soon as say good morning. His mind told him he was a fool to risk his own life because the Widow Taylor might need assistance. The only sensible course would be to take the stairs, hide himself in the attic. Perhaps, like others he had known, the head wound had affected his judgment. He drew his pistol, waited.

The older of the two Taylor boys—he was fifteen—came into James' view on the staircase, a semisilhouette in the flickering glow of a candle apparently held by someone behind him, whom James could not see. The boy's feet were bare, his only garments a nightshirt and cap. In his hands he held a musket, braced and ready, aimed at the door.

The door crashed open, the bolt slamming onto the floor.

Three men stood in the doorway. One was barely standing, and another had a fourth man over his shoulders.

The boy lowered his musket. "Mr. Shyrie!" he said.

"Get your grandmother, boy!" roared Shyrie. "I got two wounded men here, and four dead laying back by the ship."

Nathaniel Shyrie was a big man in both height and

bulk. His hair was gray and wild, his face chronically in need of a shave. His clothes at that moment, from his tricorn hat to his boots, were splattered with mud, and a faint odor of seawater seemed to carry all the way into the kitchen, or perhaps it was merely a part of Nat Shyrie so firmly ingrained in James' memories of the years they had worked together under Tom Kyle's leadership that James merely imagined it.

Alma Taylor, wearing a coarse wool robe, edged past her grandson, down the stairs into the mainroom, followed by her daughter-in-law. The daughter-in-law, close to forty, although not unattractive, seemed pale and weak in the light of Alma's vitality.

"Redcoats!" spat Shyrie. "The whole coastline's crawling with them!"

Alma hesitated, obviously not enthused by the prospect of two additional patients. "All right," she answered finally, "but you and the other man who's not hurt, be on your way."

"But, Grandma, what if some soldiers come and find them here?" asked the younger grandson, who had now joined his family group.

As though the answer were obvious, Alma countered, "I'll just tell them the truth. These men came to the door needing help. Being a good Christian family, we helped them."

The man who had been carrying the fourth man unloaded him onto the floor. Shyrie took a good look at him, then kicked him, carefully watching the man's face. "Dead, damn him!" he announced contemptuously.

"Then get him out of here," said Alma. Her daughter-in-law looked ill, and both grandsons seemed disconcerted.

"Wrap a blanket around him," said Shyrie. "We'll bury him back in the woods, tomorrow morning."

"You'll get out of here tonight and take him with you," announced Alma, her voice sharp. "And I've no blanket I can spare."

The second wounded man half sat, half lay on the floor. From the darkness of the kitchen, James saw that it was a head wound, a bad one. Even with Alma's magic healing hands, James would not have laid any wager on the man's chances to survive.

"You'll do as I tell you, woman!" Shyrie exploded. To her grandson, he added, "And you, boy, put down that gun. I'll not have some child hold a gun on Nathaniel Shyrie! I'll use my own gun and leave every one of you dead where you stand!"

Slowly, almost lazily, the man with Shyrie stepped back and drew his pistol.

The boy froze. The musket fell from his hands and clattered partially down the staircase.

Alma Taylor was an intelligent woman. Although proud, she was obviously not too proud to admit she had misjudged the seriousness of Nathaniel Shyrie's quick, violent temper at that moment.

His voice barely more than a whisper, the younger grandson said, "Grandma, if soldiers come and find them here, we'll all be taken and put in prison or killed like Luke Thompson."

With a spryness surprising for a woman her age, Alma quickly stepped between the boy and the drawn gun aimed at him. Almost as part of the same movement, the boy's mother also positioned herself in front of her son, behind Alma. The older boy still seemed frozen, frightened, stunned.

"Hush, Robert," said his mother.

"Walter," said Alma, addressing herself to the older boy, "go fetch a blanket."

His mother walked to a table beside the staircase and

placed the candle on it. Free of her trembling hands, the flame became more steady, brighter. The boy made only a slight movement, apparently still disoriented. The man on the floor slumped all the way down, onto his back, groaning, holding his head with both hands in some pain-filled twilight reality.

"Move!" yelled Shyrie, drawing his gun. The order seemed directed at the entire family. "I need him," he went on. "He dies, you'll not see the light of day, not one of you!"

Must be drunk, James decided. Or maybe not. Maybe just gone crazy with the loss of his ship and so many of his men. Crazy for blood? Crazy enough to slaughter the Taylor family?

The older boy seemed to come alive. He started back up the stairs, presumably to comply with his grandmother's request for a blanket.

"Fetch some water," Alma directed her daughter-in-law.

The daughter-in-law lit a second candle and started toward the kitchen. No good. Once light hit the area where James stood, he would be revealed. Nor could he move—surely the sound would draw their attention. With icy calm, he stepped from the kitchen, his gun drawn and aimed at Nathaniel Shyrie. "Mrs. Taylor told you to get out," he announced quietly.

Shyrie swung around, so startled that James half expected the older man's gun to fire of its own accord. The second man also swung toward James, but James' pistol remained trained on Shyrie. If either Shyrie or the other man actually fired, odds were, Shyrie would receive the answering fire of James' gun.

Frozen, Nathaniel Shyrie stared at James Devant. From the corner of his eye, James saw Alma Taylor grab the musket, her aim concentrated on the second man, avoiding James.

Slowly Shyrie lowered his gun. The tension level in the room visibly dropped.

"Jamie Devant!" spat Shyrie. "I thought you was dead. Thought McCaylan's boy got you, before Chandler got him. Thought you bled to death, and Chandler buried you somewheres secret so he could say you was still alive and take over for a while."

"Widow Taylor asked you to leave," James repeated. "And take your dead men with you."

Shyrie swung around, saw for the first time Alma with the musket in her hands, now trained on him. Surprise mingled with rising anger. "Would you kill me, Widow Taylor?"

"If you threaten me and mine, I would," she answered firmly. "That man on the floor is as good as dead."

"You'd threaten me and you'd nurse that bloody bastard back to health!"

"You've the use of the farm to store your smuggled goods. That's all you're paying for."

"Oh, I see. It's all the money, is it? And what's Jamie paying you?"

"He's paying me," she answered quietly.

Abruptly Shyrie laughed. "You'll be a rich woman, Alma Taylor. Leave it to your daughter-in-law and I might marry her."

Even in the dim glow of the candle the rush of color into Alma's daughter-in-law's face was visible even from where James stood. The idea was obviously as unappealing to Alma as to her daughter-in-law, but neither woman spoke.

Shyrie returned his pistol to his belt and signaled for the other uninjured man with him to do the same. "I hope they don't find you, Jamie," he said. "The revenue agents, the redcoats, Carrington, McCaylan. I hope they don't find you because I want to kill you myself."

More in a desire to gain information than to antagonize, James answered, "You mean you wouldn't even let Logan do it?"

Shyrie's lips became a thin white line, his eyes questioning. How much did James know?

"And the girl," James continued. "The one he pulled out of Newgate. The one the redcoats are after."

Enraged, Shyrie sprang at James. The humiliation of his own second-in-command's stupidity—James knew of it. Perhaps the whole countryside knew.

Voice sharp, loud and directed at Alma, James called, "No!" No, do not use the musket. The man with Shyrie had again drawn his pistol. The night would be drenched in blood, some of it Taylor blood. Releasing the spring bayonet on his own pistol, James waited.

Shyrie pulled up short, stopped. "I'll kill you, Jamie," he said quietly. "It won't be fast."

James nodded. He—or Carrington, if Carrington wanted James to replace Shyrie—would have to kill Shyrie. Nat Shyrie and James Devant could no longer coexist.

His attention apparently diverted, Shyrie stepped to the second man on the floor, the one still alive.

Abruptly he stopped, listened. Everyone in the room heard it—the sound of horses' hooves, distant now, but moving fast in the direction of the house. The same thought seemed to hit everyone in the room simultaneously. Soldiers.

"I'll have to leave you with the dead," Shyrie announced. Quickly he straightened up, signaled the man with him who was unhurt and backed toward the door.

James' mind flashed to the attic, the hidden section

where he had slept all these weeks. Outside the house, even if the redcoats failed to find him, Shyrie might well be more successful.

With a quick glance at the men on the floor James said to Alma, "Tell the soldiers they forced their way in, with a third man who left when he heard them coming. The door speaks for you that you did not willingly admit them."

Alma leaned back against the wall. For an instant she closed her eyes—a tired, silent prayer perhaps. She opened her eyes, nodded.

James started across the floor, too close he suddenly realized, to the man not yet dead. Like a vise, two spidery pasty white hands gripped his boot, threw him completely off-balance. He fell, his pistol skittering out of his hand across the floor, lost in some shadow unpenetrated by the candle glow. He twisted his body, yanked and dug at the fingers. The man's face was partially missing, eyes wide, teeth bared. Muddied and bloodied, it was the face of a corpse crawled from the grave. Alma's daughter-in-law and younger grandson joined the struggle as the horses' hooves grew louder. The gun! If James had his gun, he could use the bayonet to cut the man's throat.

Whatever devil had gifted those fingers with the strength to attack abruptly withdrew. The hands loosened. Free now but with no time to retrieve his pistol, James tried for the stairs as riders drew rein outside the house. With the door still open, the scene inside was clearly visible. Her eyes speaking an apology she dared not verbalize, Alma Taylor leveled the musket at James as six British soldiers entered the house.

"Thank the Lord," said Alma, slightly lowering the gun. James was well covered now by the soldiers. More soldiers continued to ride, past the house, on out into the woods beyond. Unmoving except for the too-heavy rise and fall of his chest, James remained on the second step of the staircase.

"Forced their way in here," said Alma. "Threatened to kill us all if we didn't help them."

With a quick glance at the broken latch brace, the captain seemed to accept her explanation. Addressing himself to James, he demanded, "All right. Who are you? What's your name?"

James remained silent.

Quietly the captain continued. "You'll tell us soon enough. One of Shyrie's men, aren't you? We know you've got weapons hidden all along the coast. Tell us, where's Jack Logan? Come on, it's not you we want. A man like you just might walk away with a pardon. It's only three men we really want. We want the leaders. Nathaniel Shyrie, Jack Logan and James Devant. We'll get them, too, and they'll all hang. But you don't have to. What's your name?"

"Nathaniel Shyrie," James answered. Let it be now, let it be quick. A soldier's musket. A rope frightened him.

Although he was obviously angered, the captain's control of his temper was too good. He merely nodded to the soldier on his right. "Take him," he said.

CHAPTER NINE

Although the late-afternoon sun was warm on the deck of the *Wayfarer,* formerly the *Sally Anne* out of London Harbor, a sudden chill struck Isobel Browne. It started in her back and worked its way throughout her body until every extremity seemed to ache with it. She looked up, into the sun, beyond the seemingly endless expanse of masts and rigging, then lowered her eyes. It was April 7, 1775, forty-one days since she had boarded the sloop. Two of those days had been spent at a small island, where the canvas flaps with the name "Wayfarer" had been destroyed, replaced by paint. The paint barely dry, the word "Wayfarer" now thoroughly replaced "Sally Anne," the entire ship ready for close inspection. A death ship, with the captain, Ira and Logan now beneath the sea.

Ahead, New London Harbor in the colony of Connecticut stood dotted with ships, a tiny, toy harbor in a foreign land. She shoved her hands into the pockets of her heavy sailor's jacket, largely to help resist the almost compulsive urge to readjust continually, conspicuously the red woolen stocking cap which covered her long, dull copper-gold hair.

As the ship drew nearer the harbor, a square-rigged brig passed them, on her way out to sea. Other ships, still in port, also became more clearly discernible, their size, shape and sail configurations telling much of countries of origin and the nature of their business. A considerable distance from the docks two frigates lay at anchor. The distance between them was about the same as that of each from the shore. Uncomfortably Isobel found herself counting the guns on the one nearest the *Wayfarer* and lost count at sixteen. Sixteen on one side meant a total of at least thirty-two. Guns to kill people, to sink other ships. As the *Wayfarer* drew even closer, someone on deck of the nearest frigate signaled them.

Isobel swung around, found herself face to face with Thomas Norris, the tall, dark-haired, well-built American-born man in his late twenties who had assumed the captain's post when Ira died. "What does it mean?" she asked.

"I don't know," he answered, "but she's flying a British flag. Go to the galley, and behave like the cabin boy you're supposed to be."

Frantically she answered, "Let me hide!"

"No! You'd have to get off sometime, and if they catch you sneaking off, it'll be all our necks!"

She started toward the galley. Someone on board the frigate called, "Ahoy! Haul your wind, cast anchor and identify yourself."

"The *Wayfarer,* sir," answered Norris, "by the grace of God safely home from the West Indies."

"We're coming aboard. Have your papers ready."

Angrily Norris called to the crew, "You heard him. Cast anchor."

The next question indicated that those in charge of the frigate were not seriously suspicious of the *Wayfarer.*

"Have you any knowledge," the voice continued in the same loud virtual monotone, "of a sloop called the *Sally Anne*?"

"None, sir," answered Norris, perhaps too quickly.

Isobel grabbed the mainmast for support. From the quarterdeck of the frigate, she realized, they could see her. All she had to do was tear off her stocking cap and show them her hair. Of course, she would be killed, but so would everyone else on board. The blood on the leather packet which contained the letter was long dry now. The packet itself felt warm and good against her bosom. No one on board even knew she had it.

No, she would not waste her life on the crew of the *Wayfarer.* Not when it was now within her grasp to do almost equally serious harm to the prime minister and king of all England.

From the galley she came back onto deck and stood with the crew members while the ship was rather carelessly searched.

"The lad looks ill," commented the relatively minor officer who had led the boarding party.

Isobel looked away from him, fastened her eyes on the wide-planked deck.

"First trip," answered Norris. "Sea don't agree with him." Quickly, probably to keep the officer from questioning Isobel directly, the acting captain added, "What did you say was the name of the ship you're looking for?"

"The *Sally Anne.* Don't really think they'll try to bring her into a known harbor, though. Any of the little coves along the coast seem more likely."

Thomas Norris shook his head. "Might even be the sea swallowed her. Rough weather this last week."

The officer nodded, his manner noncommittal. The weather had indeed been rough.

As the boarding party departed, another sloop, following the same instructions the *Wayfarer* had followed, pulled up on the other side of the frigate.

Even before the *Wayfarer* docked, noise from the shore along the gray, garbage-infested waters of New London Harbor permeated the ship. Small children called to one another, a herd of mixed-breed dogs ran about barking, officers of other ships called instructions to their crews, and the loading and unloading of ships continued. Kegs of rum from the inland distilleries lined the wharf, along with goods from the local ironworks. To the left of the *Wayfarer,* six cows bellowed their indignation at being forced into a habitat so unnatural as a ketch. Passengers, arriving and about to depart, milled about. Among them, a gentleman of obvious quality stood in what was apparently a farewell family gathering. Obvious quality, yet the cut of his clothes and the clothes of those with him seemed slightly irregular, not quite the proper fashion or fit. American-cut, Isobel suddenly realized. She knew Americans were frequently secretly, sometimes even openly, laughed at in London society for their pretensions to knowledge of current fashion. The most solidly English aspect of the whole scene was the sprinkling of British soldiers, their red uniforms stark against the relatively colorless warehouses and small shops.

Her feet again on solid if somewhat muddy ground, Isobel took a deep breath and found the smell of the sea still too strong. She carried, bundled under her arm, the gray wool dress she had worn when she boarded the *Sally Anne* in London. Wrapped in the dress were Ira's razor, her woman's shoes, some bread and a pearl comb which had been in her hair the night she was captured.

With the cargo unloading process barely begun, Thomas Norris walked to Isobel's side. Quietly he said, "Keep your eyes from the soldiers. You've the look of a slut, and we'll all hang for it."

"I'll spit on you," she answered. "See what they make of a cabin boy who spits on his captain."

His mouth opened, then snapped shut. "You're raving mad," he said.

"Your teeth are rotten, and you stink of the sea."

"Mr. Norris!"

Thomas Norris turned to the sound of his name. The boy who spoke was no more than nine or ten, slightly breathless, his round face raw with windburn, his breeches worn through at the knees. "Mr. Norris," he continued, "Dr. Ward wants to see Mr. Logan right away."

"Logan's dead," Norris answered.

The boy looked shocked. Groping, he continued. "The captain then."

"Dead," Norris repeated.

"Then who?"

Norris shrugged. "Me? I brought her into port."

More surprised, the boy continued. "The first mate?"

"Dead."

As though only now conscious of Isobel, the boy went on. "Is he . . . the girl?"

Norris frowned. "How much is known? No. Wait. We can't talk here."

"Come with me then," the boy answered.

Isobel hesitated, stepped back.

Norris drew his pistol. "Then you'll have no face left, no mouth to tell them all you know, and I'll take my chances with Mr. Shyrie. In my position he'd do the same."

Isobel's eyes widened. "I meant no harm. I was only angry."

Thomas bared his teeth in what from a distance might be mistaken for a smile. "Then laugh, you bloody little slut." He returned his gun to his belt and went on. "Then laugh, loud, like a boy, so the soldier coming this way will think it was a joke that I drew my pistol on you—and don't look at him."

She laughed. Her eyes filling with tears, she laughed as Thomas Norris also laughed, his loud male voice mingling with the equally forced laughter of the red-faced boy who had brought them the message. Several other children, also a few adults, looked over and smiled, the apparent gaiety contagious. With one arm around Isobel, the other around the boy, Norris started the three of them walking, the set of his lips still a smile to anyone who did not look into his eyes. "What arrangements have been made for horses?" he asked the boy.

"At the livery stable, sir. Been there six days."

"You go back to the ship. Tell them I'm bound for—no, don't tell them where. Just tell them I've gone." He reached into his purse, fished out a coin and handed it to him.

The boy left. Isobel hesitated.

"The stable is this way," Norris informed her.

"I never rode a horse before. I'll fall off."

Surprise was quickly replaced by controlled annoyance. "We'll move slowly then. It's not far."

"Can't I ride with you?" she asked sadly, her voice childlike, yet unmistakably a very female child.

"Aye," he answered, "ride with my arms around your whore body, then lie with you and explain to Mr. Shyrie why. I'll not lie with you. I've a wife in Hartford, a good and godly woman who's borne me two sons. It's her I'll lie with, God willing, before tomorrow is through."

Her lips tightened, her eyes abruptly as cold and hard

as his. Good and godly woman! Then why did she marry a cutthroat smuggler? Summoning all her courage, she asked, "When will I see Nathaniel?"

"Soon enough, girl. You want to see him? You want him to see you?"

With all the control she could summon, she continued to meet his eyes. "Yes!" she snapped. How far was she, she wondered, from the town called New Hereford, an inn called the Twin Stallion? It was Edward Carrington she wanted to see, not Nathaniel Shyrie. A meeting with Nathaniel Shyrie after all the trouble she had caused him would surely mark the end of her life.

How quickly the town of New London seemed to disappear behind them. The woods, to Isobel, who had not anticipated them, were beautiful, alive with the first signs of awakening spring, in spite of the cold. How crisp and clean the air smelled, how unlike anywhere she had ever been in London. She rode astride the horse, like a boy, her body tense with the fear of falling, but after a while she grew to accept both the fear and the tension, somehow lessening both. Still, if only she knew how to ride! Break from Thomas Norris, ride to—where?

"You go too fast," she called.

"We go any slower," he answered dryly, "the horses will fall asleep."

As abruptly as the woods had begun, they ended. The trees were scattered now, an occasional farm visible, small farms, some with dogs that barked as they passed, and a mill. A woman in a homespun checkered dress and knitted red wool shawl drew water from a well, pausing only long enough to take a good look at Thomas and Isobel. Thomas nodded courteously. Although he was obviously not known to her, the woman returned the nod.

About half a mile farther up the road he turned his

horse sharply to the right, off the main road. The path they now followed, although not as wide as the road, was obviously well traveled. It was then that Isobel remembered. Dr. Ward. They were going to a doctor's house.

Dr. Ward's house stood on a slight rise in the land. It was old, with a gabled roof and small windows set high, but freshly painted, white with black shutters, in generally good repair. Thomas and Isobel approached the door through which most of Dr. Ward's patients left, the one which led from his consultation room to the outside. Climbing the two steps, Thomas listened, then said to Isobel, "Don't seem to be anybody there." He rapped on the door, then pounded.

The door opened.

The man who opened it looked to be in his late sixties, his body bespeaking age, yet his eyes were youthful, alert, intelligent. He wore a black suit with white lace visible at his chin and on his shirt sleeves, in the manner of a city doctor.

"Come in, come in," he said, stepping back. "We heard the horses, and the dog barked. Where's Mr. Logan?"

The consultation room was small, and little warmer than the outside, except that the dark, paneled walls at least provided shelter from the wind. However, they also seemed to absorb much of the already-fading daylight. The furniture, like the rest of the house, was a mixture of old and relatively new. An iron stove stood in the corner, unlit. The wall opposite the outside entranceway consisted primarily of shelves which supported numerous books, many with Latin titles, and a staggering assortment of chemicals and herbs.

"Jack Logan is dead," Thomas answered.

Visibly shocked, Dr. Ward paused only long enough to lock the outside door. With Isobel and Thomas behind him, he led the way into a small carpeted study, larger than the office but considerably smaller and easier to heat than the mainroom. Again the old and relatively new came together in a comfortable blend. The once-beamed ceiling had been plastered over, yet the run moldings remained on a large scale with minimal carved decoration. Like the consultation room, the study walls were paneled. A birchwood fire crackled and spit in the fireplace. Isobel ran to it, tore off her stocking cap and held out her hands. Her hair, tangled and dirty, fell about her shoulders as, quickly, she opened her bulky sailor's jacket to welcome the heat against her body. Tears flooded her eyes as her nerves began to tingle with renewed feeling. She was alive, out of Newgate, away from England, safe from Jack Logan. Sleepy, sleepy, but she dared not sleep. Completely removing the jacket, she sat on the floor, closer to the fire. With more attention than anything about her might indicate, she listened to the voices behind her. Listened as Thomas Norris related to Dr. Ward all major events of the voyage.

"Yes," Thomas continued, in answer to another question from Dr. Ward, "she's the one they want. Isobel Browne. Don't know much about her except she killed somebody important to the king. Jack brought her out of Newgate. She says she's Mr. Shyrie's woman. Don't know if I believe her. I know she was Jack's woman for a while."

Still on the floor, Isobel turned and looked up at them, her movements cautious, catlike.

Contempt flashed across Dr. Ward's gray-blue eyes. His voice was soft, yet there was an edge to it. "You killed a man in England?"

She rose to her feet. "I killed nobody," she announced quietly. "I am completely innocent."

"I see." Obviously he did not believe her. Seating himself in an easy chair at a right angle to the Chippendale sofa which faced the fire, he continued. "And what are we to do with you?"

Thomas answered, "Give her to Mr. Shyrie."

"And what then? The soldiers remain on our shores, looking for her. They uncover our ships, our supplies of arms and gunpowder. Even now, Nathaniel Shyrie is a hunted man. James Devant has been taken prisoner. You tell me Mr. Logan is dead. Even Ira might have been able to help, to bring us at least some of the supplies we need."

Quietly Thomas answered, "Better she'd drowned at sea."

"No." Dr. Ward's voice was firm. "Regardless of her sins, I'll not sanction her murder."

"If they find her, she knows enough to hang us all. Here and in England."

"Then we must see to it that she is not found."

"I say what I think Mr. Shyrie will say—kill her and be done with it."

Dr. Ward's distaste for the companions forced on him by the cause for which he had already risked so much was evident. "And I say," he answered quietly, his aged voice unwavering, "one cannot build a free and just society on the murder of helpless women. For if this is done, who is to say who will live and who will die?" Yet even as he spoke, he seemed to realize the words meant nothing to Thomas Norris. He tried again, other words this time. "You are not to harm her."

Voice firm, Thomas held his ground. "That's for Mr. Shyrie to say. She's his woman; it's his neck if she's caught."

"Mr. Shyrie now works for Edward Carrington," Dr.

Ward answered, controlling his anger. "It is Mr. Carrington's decision."

Isobel's eyes widened. Carrington! "May I speak with you alone, sir?" she asked Dr. Ward.

Suspiciously Thomas asked, "What for?"

"It's a female ailment," she spat, "and I've need to speak to a doctor. Alone!"

Thomas stared at her. Was she lying? French pox maybe. Lord knew, she had been in enough beds.

"Thomas, go to the kitchen," Dr. Ward answered. "There's cake and rum."

Hesitantly at first, then angrily, Thomas walked from the room, through the door which led to the mainroom. Quickly Isobel closed the door behind him, then hurried to where Dr. Ward still sat. She threw herself on her knees in front of him, not in a position of supplication, but, rather, one of intimacy. Voice low and intense, she began. "I must see Edward Carrington."

Startled, Dr. Ward drew back from her.

"Please," she continued, "help me! I have a message for him from Jack Logan. Jack knew someone on that ship might kill him. He said Mr. Shyrie didn't want him saved, Mr. Shyrie wanted him dead. There's much more, but I can only tell Mr. Carrington—"

"What rubbish you talk!" exploded Dr. Ward. "I'll not hear another word of it."

She rose to her feet, her voice loud. "Mr. Shyrie made a deal with the British," she lied. "Jack found out."

Dr. Ward also rose to his feet. "*Silence!*" he ordered.

"No, I'll not be silent! Whatever Mr. Carrington is working for, it's what you want, too. You're not one of Mr. Shyrie's cutthroats—"

A loud, shrill squeak interrupted her. She swung around and looked. A whole section of the paneling at a right angle to the window swung open, revealing a doorway. Through the doorway, a man stepped into the room. He looked to be in his mid-fifties, heavyset, dirty and badly in need of a shave. In his hand he held a bell-mouthed pistol, aimed at Isobel. "Tell me your message," he said. "Tell me all your bloody lies before I kill you."

Her mouth open, eyes wide, she turned to Dr. Ward. In the slump of his body she read defeat. Yes, he had known the man was there; certainly he had tried to silence her.

Dryly Dr. Ward spoke. "Mistress Browne, permit me to introduce Nathaniel Shyrie."

Pausing only long enough to take one last look in the first of the two English gilt ornamental mirrors which, side by side, adorned the drawing-room wall of her exquisite home on the outskirts of New Hereford, Sarah Carrington seated herself on the American-made French-style Chippendale sofa. The three nearest chairs were Queen Anne-Chippendale transition pieces with pierced-vase splats. The tripod tea table was mahogany, made in Philadelphia with the carved ornamentation common to Philadelphia, rare on tea tables made in New England. The walls were paneled and painted white, a stark, rich setting for three family-member portraits in heavy gilt frames. Two predominantly blue-print easy chairs and a second tea table stood in front of the fireplace, where a softly crackling fire blended pleasantly with the late-afternoon sunlight. It was April 7, 1775.

Raising her eyes slightly, trying to hide her fear and physical discomfort even from those few servants she still trusted, Sarah spoke quietly. "All right, Mary, you may show him in."

With an appropriate curtsy, Mary left the room. Dear

Mary Sullivan. Over the last week, sometimes separately, sometimes together, Sarah and Mary had dug in the earth, primarily near the grape arbors, to hide some of the more valuable objects of the house, especially the gold and silver. Not that Sarah really expected the house and its contents to be confiscated. Of all the ridiculous radical rumors intended to terrorize loyalists, that one was probably the most absurd. Rather, she was frightened by the prospect of looters and vandals once the house was empty.

In full-dress British uniform, Captain George Adams, appropriately announced by Mary, entered the drawing room.

"Mrs. Carrington," he began, his tone formal, courteous, yet somehow cautious, "I came as soon as I received your message."

Heart pounding, she rose to accept his outstretched hand and subsequent kiss on her own hand. "That will be all, Mary," she said. "Please bring us some tea."

With Mary gone, Sarah returned to her seat on the couch as Captain Adams settled himself on an adjacent chair.

"I was shocked to hear of your husband's death," he offered quietly. "I and my friends remain in his debt for many enjoyable evenings spent in this house."

"The debt is ours," answered Sarah, playing the game, fighting nausea, which in this pregnancy more than in any of her others seemed to persist throughout the day. How ironic that Charles had not lived long enough to know she was with child. Before he died, she had suspected but had chosen not to say anything because she was not sure. Now, however, she was quite sure, her feelings a mixture of supreme joy and terror—terror that she might lose the baby or possibly become so incapacitated in the later months that she would be unable to protect the living child she already had. Certainly, if the child were born in New Hereford—but, no. Whatever her sins, God was kind, God was love. Not all prayers went unanswered. Addressing Captain Adams, still playing the game, she continued. "And I am afraid I must implore you to allow me to place myself even further in your debt."

"Implore?"

"Allow me to present my case plainly, sir. I must leave New Hereford. My few remaining servants have been threatened and spit upon in the town streets. As you may have heard, a child of another loyalist family in this area—a child the same age as my son—was badly beaten by a mob of rebel children. I myself have been forced to bare indignities so cruel I dare not venture from the house. When I heard you were in New Hereford, I felt that my prayers had been answered. With your help, I know my son and I may safely join my father-in-law in New York."

His caution now more apparent, Captain Adams shifted his position in the chair. "I hope you will forgive me, madame, but I find what you have just told me difficult to understand."

His words startled and confused her. She merely looked at him, waited.

"You are Edward Carrington's sister-in-law," he continued. "Yet you tell me you find it difficult to move freely in an area so dominated by—well, shall we say, other gentlemen of Mr. Edward Carrington's political persuasions?"

Sarah felt the color drain from her face, then rise again with such force; her entire head seemed momentarily throbbing in pain. "Edward and Charles were hardly of the same political persuasion. I am *Charles'* widow."

"Yet how often here in your husband's home you spoke of a need for his majesty to recognize certain demands made by the rebel elements within these colonies."

"But I—" Words failed her. Shock and embarrassment gave way to anger. "I see. You feel I am a spy. That I could really leave anytime I chose, but that if I could do so in the company of British soldiers—what? That I might gather information which might be of value to the rebel cause?"

"Or have you already information gained here, which you wish to pass on to others in New York?"

"How dare you!" The words had a hollow ring, the last retreat before tears—indignation.

"And may I ask," he continued, his tone now openly contemptuous, "when was the last time you saw Edward Carrington?"

Trembling, she rose to her feet. "Last week I saw him. To beg him for a pass. He refused."

A knock sounded at the drawing-room doors. Abstractedly Sarah answered, "Come in."

Mary entered, carrying a large ornamented silver tea set, scheduled for burial by the grape arbor within the next day or so. Quickly and quietly the girl crossed the room and placed it on the tea table by the couch.

Rising, Captain Adams addressed himself to Mary. "I understand you had a brother named Brian."

Surprised and obviously uncomfortable, Mary answered, "I have a brother named Brian."

"No. My condolences, Mistress Sullivan. Your brother is dead. He was killed while unloading a smuggling ship for James Devant."

Stunned, tears flooding her eyes, Mary answered, "No! He was taken prisoner, but that was weeks ago. He was not killed!"

"I am afraid you have been misinformed."

"No!"

James Devant! Sarah stared at her servant, this girl she so loved and trusted and thought she had known. How desperately Sarah had tried to reach James, yet Mary was one person she had never told. But surely Mary must have known Sarah was searching for him. And Mary had never told Sarah that Brian had been captured. The tears, the concern, the obvious desire not to discuss the cause—Sarah had somehow assumed Mary had become involved with a lover, as occasionally happened with young and pretty servant girls.

Disregarding the amenities of a respectful departure, Mary ran from the room.

Turning his attention back to Sarah, Captain Adams continued. "I cannot imagine why your rebel servants might be spit upon in the town streets, Mrs. Carrington."

Words failed her. The humiliation, the injustice—the murder of her servant's brother! And now not only her own life, but also the life of her son and the unborn child within her—all were in mortal danger. Where was the king's protection? Drawing herself up to her full height, yet crippled, stifled by an upbringing which still denied her the freedom to express anger in any but the most conservative terms, she spoke words which at least partially met the demands of some stronger, fiercer part of herself, a part she had never before fully realized existed. "I find your insults insufferable, sir. I do not forgive you."

His bow was a mockery. "Indeed, madame, you grieve me. To have the"— the pause was short, yet obvious—"the 'goodwill' of a lady as attractive as yourself would please me greatly."

Nausea rose and choked her. For an instant an image, a vision of his spotless uniform drenched in blood, flooded her senses. He was a soldier. Soldiers were often killed. Yet even more than the vision, the force of her hatred, the power of her own emotions terrified her. She wanted to strike him. Charles would have done so, as a gentleman, as an insult. Edward—at one time—would have attacked him with his fists.

Quietly, unable to hide her tears, Sarah answered, "May God keep His protection from you in battle. Kindly leave my home."

Yes, the words had hurt him! Dropping any pretense of courtesy, he responded, "Well spoken, for a rebel! No doubt we shall meet again, Mrs. Carrington." He strode from the room.

She stared after him. Her tears flowed freely now, blurred his image. Panic mingled with rage. A rebel! How he had twisted her words, turned her personal insult into—what? A confession of political beliefs she did *not* hold! A confession to be repeated, no doubt, with all the weight of a British captain's "honor." Of its own accord, her body began to tremble. "No!" she whispered. Then, screaming, she ran from the room. "Mary," she cried, *"Mary!"*

The hallway, with its richly patterned carpeting, white paneling and Irish cut-glass wall sconces, became a blur, distorted into an infinitely long tunnel with the kitchen at the far end, the servants' quarters beyond.

Startled, the cook looked up from her baking as Sarah, breathless and disheveled, entered the room with no word, no acknowledgment of the older woman's presence.

Sarah continued directly to the servants' quarters. Without knocking she opened the door to the room Mary had formerly shared with another servant before the other girl, a loyalist, in fear for herself and the safety of her family, had left Sarah's employ. Indeed, the other girl had been more than spat upon in the streets.

Mary lay on the old scratched and marred Queen Anne bed, long ago discarded from one of the upper-floor bedrooms. Her face was hidden in the goose-down pillow with its much-mended linen case, her body racked by muffled sobs.

Carefully, in control of herself now although the control was so fragile she dared not rely on it, Sarah closed the door. Slowly, gently, she sat on the bed and laid her hand on Mary's shoulder.

With a startled cry the girl raised her head, then quickly pulled herself onto her knees and faced her mistress.

"Mary," Sarah began, her voice barely more than a whisper, "I'm so sorry—about your brother."

"He was not a clever lad," said Mary, her lips twisted by emotional pain which made the words barely comprehensible, "but he was strong and good. I've no one here now. I want to go home—back to Ireland. I've relatives there. I could make a place for myself."

"I'll help you," said Sarah.

"I've no money!"

"I'll give you money. I haven't much here. Most of it's in a bank in Boston, but I can give you some of my jewels. You can sell them."

Startled, Mary stared at Sarah. No, Mary's brother had not been clever, but Mary was.

Gathering all her courage, Sarah continued. "Mary, I need your help. Your brother worked for James Devant."

A wariness came into the girl's eyes. No other reaction was discernible.

It was hopeless. Mary would never trust her—at least not enough. Overcome again by her own tears, Sarah cried out, "Dear God, Mary, please, I need your help. I need to reach Mr. Devant. Without his help, surely I shall be killed." *And my child,* she thought, *and the unborn child within me.*

Momentarily driven by emotion, forgetting her position as servant, Mary answered, "*Mr. Devant?* You, who have so many loyalist friends, how could you possibly not know?"

Bewildered, Sarah answered, "Not know what?"

"That James Devant—" she broke off.

"*What?*"

"James Devant was captured by the British. If they killed my poor brother, surely by now they've killed James Devant!"

CHAPTER TEN

Guarding the northern end of Long Island, almost directly across the Sound from Stamford, Connecticut, the nearly completed Fort Franklin stood high on a bluff overlooking Oyster Bay and Cold Spring Harbor. Behind it, facing the waters to the east stood a second fort, but Fort Franklin was the larger of the two, serving as a barracks for approximately four hundred British soldiers. Perhaps twenty-five or thirty loyalist refugees, forced from their homes by zealous rebel groups, also lived within the boundaries of the fort, in far more comfortable quarters than the prisoners awaiting shipment to England for trial in English courts, where conviction for death-penalty crimes against the crown was virtually assured. The prison, within the walls of the fort but away from the barracks and other important buildings, was constructed of brick, with small, high barred windows. The cell floors consisted of wide oak beams liberally sprinkled with straw. The cells were of varying sizes, the smaller ones intended for individual important prisoners, the larger for groups of less important prisoners, although all prisoners worth the cost of a trip to England were considered both reasonably important and potentially dangerous. Embedded into the walls of all cells were iron loops to which each prisoner's leg irons could be attached.

Heavily ironed, his wrists and ankles chafed raw and bloody, James Devant sat among seven other prisoners on the floor of one of the larger cells. His belly growled for want of food, yet the stench of excrement, urine and vomit so overwhelmed his senses he had been unable to eat that morning. Toilet facilities consisted of a throne-like box in a corner opposite the door, but in addition to the number of men too sick to reach it, some still present, some already departed, the box itself had become an offense to the senses. What exquisite torture the chains were! His body was infested with lice, which grew more active at any trace of warm spring air through the two small windows, yet any attempt to scratch brought fresh blood to his wrists with attendant pain shooting up the entire length of his arms. Of the other seven men in the cell with him, six were Shyrie's. The seventh was an outsider, like James unknown to the others, although had James been clean-shaved when the fifth and sixth arrived, they might have recognized him. Certainly he had recognized them.

It was twilight, April 7, 1775. James hoped the moon would be bright that night. Without moonlight, at night the whole experience seemed dreamlike, a black world of odors, groans, whispers and pain, a world in which a man had only his pain to remind him his body really existed.

Abruptly all movement and conversation within the cell stopped. Footsteps, voices and the rattle of chains were audible from the corridor outside. A new load of prisoners had arrived. A cell door either beside or opposite the cell James occupied was opened. Continuing sounds carried a picture of the action as each new arrival's leg chain was attached to the wall.

Someone spoke quietly to the man next to James. "They'll hang us all, every last man in all the colonies who ever smuggled so much as a codfish."

"No," answered the man he had spoken to, "we'll die here or on the ship. Or in an English jail. I been here two weeks. Man used to be where you are bled to death. Dead two days before they took him away. No, we'll die, but we'll not all hang."

"Die killing us some redcoats!"

From across the room a voice answered dryly, "How?"

"Next one comes near any of us, get your chains around his neck, break his neck. Swear it!" He looked at James, the man's eyes oddly bright in their islands of puffy, bluish flesh surrounded by a matted beard and unkempt hair. "Swear it!" he demanded.

Thoughtlessly, irritably, James answered, "I've no quarrel with the British."

Stunned silence followed, finally broken by a voice at the other end of the room. "You'll not get off the ship alive, I promise you."

Recovering quickly, James answered, "Kill a redcoat, they'll at least beat you senseless, if not kill you. What chance have you then to escape?"

"Escape?"

"It's a long way from here to England to the gallows. Keep your wits about you."

The tension in the room seemed to shift. James was no longer a target. Escape? Did anyone dare hope? What sheep they were, James thought. No, not sheep. Edward Carrington's men were sheep. These men were wolves. Wolves wanting a wolf like Shyrie to lead them. James could lead them. Lead them where? Their only real hope might be if a pirate ship attacked the ship which returned them to England, but a ship as obviously well armed and guarded as the kind of vessel likely to transport this cargo would be an unlikely target for pirates. Pirates sought treasure, not convicts. Of course, Carrington might feel a rescue attempt would be worth the danger. Carrington could use every experienced smuggler he could get, but the ships Carrington had access to were mainly smuggling vessels, relatively small and fast, not men-of-war. Besides, who could be sure the British would not simply kill their cargo, rather than set them free?

The door to the cell swung open. Two soldiers, their muskets aimed in at the prisoners, flanked a captain, all clean and fresh in their stark red and white uniforms. The captain paused, looked carefully at each prisoner, then pointed to James and one other, a man who, with his black hair, blue eyes and lean, muscular build, bore a notable resemblance to James.

A clean-shaven prisoner in relatively clean clothing, encumbered only by leg chains, entered the cell. In his hands he carried a hammer and chisel. No one spoke, yet no words could have been more powerful, more threatening than the hatred with which most of the other men in the cell watched him. One of them to begin with, the man had sold his soul for a bath, a razor, sufficient food and an indefinite delay in the voyage which would someday doubtless send him, like the others, to England, to the gallows. With hammer and chisel he bent open one of the chain links by which James' leg irons were attached to the loop embedded into the wall. The second man selected by the soldiers was also freed of the wall.

"On your feet," the captain ordered.

Painfully James rose to his feet. In addition to the sudden surge of blood into chained wrists and ankles already raw and bleeding, long-cramped muscles now forced into action produced even further, starker pain so widespread no individual source seemed separable from any other. The straw under his feet felt cold and damp. They had taken his boots. *His* boots, damn it!

Outside the prison, four other men in chains, closely guarded, waited. All four also bore a marked resemblance in height, age, build and coloring to James and the other prisoner taken from the same cell with James. One of them James recognized. He was Alma Taylor's nephew, Robert Hulton, a farmer. Although he had never worked for James—or Nathaniel Shyrie, either, as far as James knew—as children, James and Robert had occasionally played together. As adults, more than once they had shared rum in Alma Taylor's kitchen. The recognition was mutual. Quickly James turned his eyes from Robert Hulton. Whatever the man had done, should James Devant be identified, to be known as even an acquaintance of James Devant would be of no assistance to Robert Hulton.

"Line up," the captain commanded, indicating the side wall of the prison. Although the evening air was uncomfortably cold, its taste was so clean and fresh that physical discomfort seemed a small price. James joined the others in line. Perhaps a dozen armed soldiers faced them. An execution? Anger mingled with fear, an icy fear, a peculiar sense of detachment from his body. The thought that he might actually be killed by British soldiers here, in chains, in America had never before seriously occurred to him. Additional soldiers and a few civilians were also visible. Some watched; some apparently chose to avoid any involvement.

"All right," the captain began briskly, addressing all the prisoners, "we know that one of you is James Devant. Which one?"

James felt his knees go weak, not in fear that he would probably soon be known to them, but rather because the physical tension with which he had braced himself to meet imminent death subsided so quickly it took with it even the normal muscle tension necessary for support. As he fell to his knees, the chains on his wrists cut even more deeply into his flesh. Oddly the pain helped, sharpened his nerves, renewed the tension. His mind also seemed sharper. Would they take him for a coward? Perhaps not. To appear a coward could cost him the respect of his men. Perhaps, with luck, they would conclude that through hunger and pain he had merely grown physically weak.

"On your feet!" the captain commanded.

Although James was included in the order, he realized it was directed primarily at another man—one of Shyrie's men—who had also fallen. This time deliberately stretching his arms, intensifying the pain, using it, James returned to his feet. Now, however, nausea accompanied the pain, the combination so severe it threatened to obliterate whatever capacity to think clearly might still be left to him.

"I said," the captain continued, his lips tight, "which of you is James Devant?"

As before, no one answered.

Addressing himself to each man, the captain began with the first, one of Shyrie's men. "What's your name?"

"Robert Smith," the man answered contemptuously.

Taking his cue from the first man, the second answered, "Robert Smith."

The third, the unknown man who had been in the cell with James, was obviously frightened by the soldiers but more frightened of Nathaniel Shyrie's men. His voice barely more than a whisper, he answered, "Smith."

The captain broke in irritably, yet with careful emphasis on each word. "We know that the man taken at the

Taylor farmhouse was James Devant. Widow Taylor told us"—his brief pause was timed to perfection —"directly before she died."

To James, his mind muddled by pain, nausea, hunger and exhaustion, the words did not fully register.

Alma Taylor's nephew, however, Robert Hulton, reacted immediately. "Dead!"

The captain smiled. "No, not really. As far as we know, she is at this moment alive and well. It was merely a bit of intelligence we received this afternoon that the man taken at her house was you, Mr. Devant."

Terror-stricken, Robert Hulton answered, "No, I am not James Devant."

Surprise mingled with contempt in the looks and murmurs of the other prisoners. With a brief nod the captain turned over to a lesser officer the chore of returning the other prisoners to their cells. The death Robert Hulton now faced was far uglier than the one which no doubt awaited the others. The information James Devant held would be of superb value to the British—smuggling routes, names of people and ships—information Robert Hulton would be unable to give them no matter what they did to him. In the end he might even convince them they had made a mistake. How bravely James Devant would have died—suffering the tortures of the damned, yet revealing nothing.

"My name is Robert Hulton," insisted Robert Hulton, "and I am innocent of the charges against me. It was without my knowledge that smuggled firearms were hidden on my property!"

"Take him," snapped the captain.

His mind momentarily clear, James spoke loudly, "If he really is Robert Hulton, then he knows James Devant."

The group, including the captain, was abruptly silent.

It was the captain who finally addressed James. "And who are you?"

With eager, wide-eyed servility which seemed favorably to impress the captain, James answered, "Robert Smith."

Enraged—the man had made a fool of him—the captain raised his hand as though to strike him but left the action incomplete, apparently repelled by the filth which encrusted James' face. What would it take, James wondered, to communicate with poor, simple Robert Hulton? Make a deal for his own life. Identify James. James would be identified eventually. Let Robert Hulton reap the benefits. Their eyes met, a moment, a touching missed by the captain, now more concerned with Robert Hulton.

"Do you know Devant?" he demanded.

In Robert Hulton's eyes James read only fear and confusion.

The captain lowered his voice. "Mr. Hulton," he began, obviously now not sure, "your cooperation in this matter could win you a pardon. Freedom. Life."

Could. The word made the rest of the statement worthless.

Poor, stupid Robert Hulton. Tentatively, as though finally understanding and accepting James' offer, he looked directly at James. No freedom, no protection had been offered. The man was a farmer, a good farmer. Possibly he was genuinely innocent of the charges against him. Innocent and naïvc. Obviously he was unaware of the fact that among the brotherhood of prisoners, to aid their captors by identifying James Devant or anyone else in the midst of other prisoners—even men who worked for Nat Shyrie—was a sin for which, without protection, he would be torn apart. Cutting him off, addressing himself to the captain, James announced quietly, "I am James Devant."

The captain stared at him, as did two or three of the other prisoners, those still alert enough to react. In confirmation of the statement he had just made, James looked at Robert. "You are a fool, Robert Hulton," he said.

Suspiciously the captain asked him, "If you are James Devant, where is your home?"

"Near Boston."

"Married or single?"

His mind still foggy, he started to answer the truth, that he was single; however, he realized in time that he must repeat the lie by which James Devant, known throughout the Boston area as a respectable shipbuilder, avoided the attentions of overeager mothers with eligible daughters. "Married, living apart from my wife. She is in France."

The education, the selection and pronounciation of the words even more than their content set him apart from the others.

James Devant? Admitting his identity? Of course, eventually witnesses would have been brought to the fort, pressure properly applied to those who knew him. Perhaps he had realized the impossibility of indefinite concealment. Perhaps he had decided to have it over and done with.

"Bring him to the colonel's office," the captain commanded, then went on ahead, no doubt motivated by eagerness to present the news of his success.

Still wearing his chains, James stood facing Colonel John Oliver in his office. A large gilt-frame portrait of King George in military dress dominated the wall behind the colonel's desk. Two soldiers stood at attention in the doorway. A third man, in his late thirties with sensual, puttylike features, sat on a roundabout chair near the corner. His wig was heavily powdered; his clothes were not merely stylish, but high fashion. British fashion. In the relative warmth of the room which emanated from a large fireplace, James felt himself disturbingly sleepy, further tormented by lice, now warm, grown active and hungry.

The colonel, also wearing a wig, was in his late forties. He rose to his feet, then settled himself against a large, map-strewn table near the window. His voice as crisp, as arrogant as his appearance, he proceeded. "The captain informs me that you are James Devant."

James made no answer. By sheer force of will he managed to keep his eyes open and almost fully focused.

Apparently the colonel misread his silence as obstinacy. And what, James wondered without really caring, could the colonel, with his pain-free body and clean clothes, his fire, his good food and wine , possibly know of James' mind in that instant? With controlled anger the colonel continued. "We've enough against you that even an American court would probably hang you. And even if the court did not, we have heard that Nathaniel Shyrie has sworn to kill you. If you've any life ahead of you, it can only be lived in England with a full pardon and the protection of his majesty."

James had heard of a New Jersey man the British had stripped naked and chained to a rock at low tide in the dead of summer, to be baked by the sun and consumed by mosquitoes as the tide, which eventually drowned him, rolled in. To keep silent under the threat of death by drowning would be difficult for James, but no one except James knew it. Give them nothing, no words from which they might glean any information.

The colonel continued. "We are prepared to offer you such protection, Mr. Devant."

Mustering all his strength, James answered dryly, "Take your protection and go to the devil!"

The colonel drew his sword and stepped forward,

pressing the tip of the blade lightly against James' throat. "Have you ever seen a man burned to death?" he asked.

In his fogged, befuddled state, traces of a smile touched James' lips, a twisted, ironic smile. It was water James feared, not fire. He had felt water in his lungs, known the panic of a losing battle with the sea. Death by fire to James was an abstraction.

Again Colonel Oliver misread James' reaction. Quickly, adroitly, he lowered the blade of his sword to James' chest and pierced the flesh, slightly, drawing only minimal blood, a small stain on James' woolen shirt, a sting, a shock, but enough of a shock that James' body reacted, withdrew from this new source of pain. His feet still encumbered by chains, he lost his balance and fell to the floor, the pain from the cut now lost in a blur of additional pain from too many other sources. He landed with most of his weight on one thigh and his elbow, a position from which he promptly released himself by rolling onto his back.

"On your feet!" shouted the colonel.

"Go to the devil!" James shouted back. Vaguely he noticed the man in the corner chair rise and start toward him, but James' eyelids, too heavy for too long, finally closed. However, the reawakened pain in conjunction with the now even more active lice kept his nerves raw, infused his mind with a new alertness.

"We shall form our questions carefully." The colonel's voice. "He shall provide us with answers."

A second voice now. Aristocratic English, educated, arrogant. "I think not. I've seen them die in England with nothing but curses on their lips."

"He'll die with more than curses!"

Brief pause. Then the so very English voice again: "Leave me alone with him."

A faint odor of musk pervaded James' senses. English

perfume. He opened his eyes. The English dandy stood near him, holding a lace-trimmed handkerchief to his so very English nose. Poor, poor man, James thought, to have to suffer such odors. Did they stink, he wondered, when they died in England with nothing but curses on their lips? In that instant, for the first time, James Devant tasted bile born of rage. Yes, kill a redcoat. Spit on King George!

Briefly the colonel looked as though he wanted to argue. Then, with subtle nervousness, as though the other man's order might somehow have conveyed displeasure with him, Colonel John Oliver bowed slightly and answered, "Certainly, your lordship."

"No. First—" The dandy waved his handkerchief at the two guards, still posted at the door like toy tin soldiers. "First," he continued, "get him up onto a chair."

With a quick nod the colonel confirmed the order. The tin soldiers came to life, fetched a chair and forced James into it. Their hands were rough, the pain excruciating. "Bastards!" he yelled.

Settling himself into a chair opposite James, his lordship nodded toward the door. The colonel was dismissed. "Take your men with you."

Colonel John Oliver again seemed predisposed to argue. He was responsible for this English nobleman's safety. His answer, however, was merely a nervous, courteous bow.

With the door closed behind them the musk-scented dandy, still clutching his handkerchief, addressed James. "I understand you are a friend of Mr. Logan."

James remained silent.

"Damn it, man, I would like to help you."

Surprise turned quickly to suspicion. James answered, "Indeed. Why?"

As though speaking to some lower order of intelligence, the man answered, "Because I would like you to help me." Waving aside James' obvious sardonic distrust, he continued, "Allow me to introduce myself. I am Walter Williams, third earl of Ormsbee and second cousin to Lord Frederick North, who is, as I am sure you know, the prime minister of Great Britain."

Would the man next explain, James wondered, the identity of King George? For the first time, James noticed a slight physical likeness between this man and a portrait he had once seen of Lord North, the same drooping lips and heavy eyelids, the same fleshy, boneless, arrogant face.

"I am prepared," Lord Williams continued, "to grant you, in the name of his majesty, a full pardon and possibly certain monies in exchange for one small service. In a moment I shall describe that service. First, however, I must have some answers from you."

"Then take your pardon and go to the devil. I've nothing further to say."

Taken aback, angry, yet not to be deterred, Lord Williams continued. "Do you consider it a betrayal to answer one simple question? Are you a friend of Jack Logan? Of Nathaniel Shyrie?"

Vaguely, something chewed at James' brain. Yes, now he remembered. The colonel's words. *Nathaniel Shyrie has sworn to kill you.* These were test questions. Lord Whatever His Name Was already knew the answers. Something strange here—for a man of Lord Williams' stature to become this personally involved—something very strange, indeed.

Playing the game now, fighting sleep and a new surge of nausea, James answered, "I am no friend to either of them."

Lord Williams smiled. What an effort it must be, James thought, to rearrange so much flesh. "Good."

"I'll not help you find either of them," James added.

"No, no, that would not be necessary. You see? There is a service you can perform for your king which will endanger no one, betray no one."

More interested than he cared to admit, James continued to listen.

"You see, all we want"— Lord Williams paused, the tone of his voice changing, as though the subject about to be mentioned were hardly worth the effort required to speak the words—"all we want is a piece of paper. This piece of paper is, we have reason to believe, currently in the possession of a girl, a prostitute, named Isobel Browne. She is traveling in the company of Mr. Logan. The paper is a letter, a very clever forgery made by a prisoner in Newgate, a coiner long since hanged for his crimes, but we know he gave the letter to the girl before she escaped. Now unless the ship Mistress Browne and Mr. Logan boarded in London was lost at sea, and we have no evidence that it was, by now we have reason to believe the letter is still in their possession somewhere in one of his majesty's New England colonies. You see, we need someone able to move freely among the people, someone trusted and clever enough to locate Mr. Logan and obtain the letter." His voice grew hard. "Buy it from him, if you must. Should this outrageous false document be published, the scandal could prove most embarrassing, most embarrassing indeed."

"You say the letter is a forgery."

"And a most clever one, addressed to my cousin, Lord North. The forged signature is that of none other than his majesty. Even to have it read by anyone not thoroughly familiar with the true signature of his majesty—most embarrassing. The man who wrote it was hired to do so. The man who hired him has also paid for his crimes. The girl is more than a harlot; she is also a murderess and must be approached with caution."

The girl. Logan's girl. Indeed, there could not be many like her to make such a fool of Jack Logan. Still far from committed, but curious, somehow abstractedly enjoying his last laugh on Jack Logan, James asked, "Have you a likeness of her?"

Lord Williams produced a small sketch. Even in his weakened, confused state, James was impressed. "She is surprisingly beautiful for a woman of the streets."

"She was not of the streets. She was—" He broke off, then concluded lamely, "She was not of the streets."

Like a ship beginning to move with some unseen undercurrent, James' mind continued to work. Not of the streets. Of the upper class then? The aristocracy, the nobility? Were any of her clients men who might actually have had access to such a letter? Was it genuine? Although Lord Williams had not impressed James as stupid, the man's arrogance projected to James the impression that he considered James stupid, an impression James had no desire to correct. He remained silent. A faint, fair wind seemed to be blowing over the sea. Now more than an undercurrent carried his mind forward.

"There is a further possibility," Lord Williams continued. "The letter may already have changed hands. But wherever it is, I guarantee you, in the king's name, a full pardon and ample monetary rewards should you locate and present it to me. And you see? This requires you to betray no one."

Find a letter addressed to Lord North with the king's signature, perhaps genuine, perhaps forged. Probably genuine. All this effort for a forged document—no matter how clever—yet who could say for sure? Seek it out. Deliver it to Lord Williams. Why not? The only politics which really interested James were the politics of survival, although something resembling hatred for the British was beginning to take root in the back of his mind. Way in the back. "If you wish Logan to show himself," he said, "the soldiers must be withdrawn."

Lord Williams hesitated. "The soldiers also seek Mr. Logan and the whore."

Dryly James answered, "Have they found them?"

The color in his face deepening, Lord Williams answered, "One week. I shall have them withdrawn for one week. But not all. Only the additional troops sent in to seek the ship."

"Two weeks," said James. "In two weeks either you should have the letter, or what harm it might do should be done."

Lord Williams' consent betrayed his discomfort. "One other matter. Even Colonel Oliver is unaware of this false document. We wish to avoid empty gossip."

Irresistibly James asked, "How do you know I shall seek your letter? How do you know you shall ever see me again?"

Lord Williams hesitated, then answered in a voice edged with contempt, "If we never see you again, we have lost one petty smuggler."

Petty smuggler? Apparently the man had no concept of the scope of James' operation. His face, however, gave no hint of his thoughts.

"If we do see you again," Lord Williams continued, "you stand to gain much. In addition," he said quietly, "you will be watched." He rose from his chair, stepped back, then toward the door and added, "You will, of course, be given a day or so to regain your strength."

James merely looked at him. A day or so? His strength? No. His wits perhaps. But perhaps, with freedom, his wits would prove sufficient to survive.

CHAPTER ELEVEN

Without thought, Isobel took a step backward, away from Nathaniel Shyrie. "No," she said quickly, "Mr. Shyrie, please! It was you I wanted to see. Jack said you could be found through Mr. Carrington. He said to trust no one except you. I was afraid Mr. Norris was not really bringing me to you."

"How you lie!" exploded Shyrie. "Your lies don't even make sense." To Dr. Ward, he said, "I'll take her out in the woods. We'll need the body to show them she's really dead. We can deliver it to the Goddard house. They've some British officers staying there. Get all those bloody redcoats out of New England. Told Thomas she's my woman," he added contemptuously. "Never seen her before in me life."

It was because he wanted Jack Logan dead, she thought. Or maybe Nat Shyrie did make a deal with the British. Had her "lies" perhaps come far too close to the truth, a truth which might harm Mr. Shyrie in Mr. Carrington's eyes? Whoever Mr. Carrington was, he was important. Dr. Ward had told Thomas Norris that Edward Carrington, not Nathaniel Shyrie, was in charge. In charge of what?

"You cannot present her looking like that," said Dr. Ward. "The girl they seek is beautiful. She'll need a bath. Something must be done with her hair. She must have identification. Perhaps a letter addressed to her. Perhaps her name embroidered on a handkerchief."

Was he trying to help her, Isobel wondered, or did he perhaps mean only exactly what he said?

For the first time apparently enjoying himself, Shyrie announced, "I'll give her a bath. You write the letter."

"Would you kill Jack's child?" cried Isobel, her hands moving quickly to the area of her womb. "He said to trust you; he said you would care for me, see to the child's welfare!"

Initially startled, Shyrie threw his head back and laughed. "If Jack could make babies, they'd be all over the colonies. Some say was the pox done it, the fever." To Dr. Ward, he added, "And you'd take this wench to Mr. Carrington, waste Mr. Carrington's time with her fairy tales. Have your wife set up a tub in the kitchen. We'll scrub her hide off."

Whatever hope she had had that Dr. Ward might protect her vanished. Distasteful as murder might be to him, somehow she knew he had come to terms with what he now believed to be its necessity. He would not even have to see it done. Nat Shyrie would take care of it. Quickly, adroitly, her hands moved to her neck, to the gold chain attached to the leather packet which contained the letter. As Shyrie grabbed her left arm, with a toss of her head and the use of her right hand, she frantically pulled the chain over her head and thrust the packet at Dr. Ward.

"Here," she cried, "you can read. Please! Read this! This is the real reason Jack wanted me to see Mr. Carrington and trust no one else."

"More lies!" exploded Shyrie, yet he seemed uneasy. He reached for the packet, but too late. Dr. Ward held it.

Tight-lipped, Shyrie repeated, now obviously referring to the packet, "Lies!"

Dr. Ward's attitude was noncommittal, but his grip on the packet remained firm.

"Why read it?" Shyrie persisted.

"Why not?" answered Dr. Ward.

"The wench is trouble," said Shyrie. "She'd have us all at each other's throats."

"I got it from Lord North!" announced Isobel.

Incredulously Shyrie answered, "Lord North?!"

"Well, not exactly. . . ."

Apparently reassured that whatever the letter contained was probably about as accurate as Isobel's statement that she was pregnant by Jack Logan, Shyrie, although still not fully at ease, seemed willing to let the matter drop. His attention now dominated by Isobel, he shoved her ahead of him, opened the door into the main-room and continued to push her.

"Let go of me!" she cried.

He slapped her face.

"I'll kill you," she spat, tasting blood.

He laughed, seemed to be fully taking in her appearance for the first time. "No, I'll not wash you in a tub. There's no tub could hold all that dirt. There's a stream outside."

He shoved her into the kitchen. The odor of fresh-baked bread mingled with the tantalizing aroma of beef stew. Yes, the Ward family ate well. Thomas Norris, seated at a wide-plank table near the window, looked up, startled. The pewter mug and plate in front of him were empty now with the exception of a few crumbs. The Wards' housekeeper, an elderly soft-spoken woman, now as ever slightly afraid of Nathaniel Shyrie, also appeared startled. Addressing the housekeeper directly, Shyrie announced, "Fetch some soap and towels." Abruptly, irritably, as though he had just thought of it, he added, "She'll need a dress."

Norris answered, "She has one. Brought it with her from the ship."

"She look pretty in it?"

Thomas hesitated, shrugged. "Well, maybe if it had some lace." He touched his throat. "A collar."

To the housekeeper, Shyrie said, "Fetch the dress and sew a collar on it from one of Mrs. Ward's dresses."

Disconcerted, the housekeeper awkwardly placed a tin container with soap jelly on the table, then fetched two towels.

"Get the dress!" roared Shyrie.

With the housekeeper gone, Thomas rose to his feet. "What are you going to do?"

"Clean her up, kill her and give her to the British."

As quickly as Isobel grabbed Shyrie's pistol from his belt, Thomas Norris disarmed her, twisting her arm behind her back until she cried out in pain.

"Let her go," said Shyrie. Then, to Isobel: "Hear me well, girl, it's easier for me if you wash yourself, but you try anything like that again, it's your corpse I'll scrub." To Thomas, he added, "Come with us, stay with us. Watch her. Don't take your eyes off her."

Thomas Norris, Isobel realized, was embarrassed! She wanted to kill both of them! How deep was the stream? Deep enough to hide in? She could scream, once they were outside.

A scream to be cut short by a knife or pistol ball.

Numbly, carrying the soap and towels, flanked by Shyrie on one side and Norris on the other, Isobel allowed herself to be led outside, across the small cleared area into the woods to the right of the house.

The stream was small, maybe three feet wide, probably not deep at all. Pines, hemlocks and underbrush provided good cover. Abruptly the sound of a horse departing from the area of the house at a full gallop shattered the relative silence of the woods. Briefly both Norris and Shyrie froze, then apparently decided it was nothing to be concerned about.

Shyrie turned his attention back to Isobel. "Well, come on, girl. There's your soap. Be done with it."

"Don't look at me," she said.

Thomas started to turn away, a gesture cut short as Shyrie shoved him back into a proper position to watch her. "Take her clothes off, Thomas. She won't wash herself, you wash her."

The command was a reprimand, a punishment. To Thomas Norris, it seemed a punishment beyond endurance. Immobile, he merely continued to look at Nat Shyrie, Isobel still within his line of vision.

She wanted to laugh. Oh, such a *good* man! A smuggler, a killer, a grown man with a "good and godly" wife in Hartford, yet the fact that he wanted Isobel—and he *did* want her—reduced him to this, a red-faced schoolboy!

Angrily her hands moved to her boy's shirt. She pulled it over her head, then loosened and let fall her breeches. Yes, Shyrie also wanted her, would have her, she supposed. But Thomas Norris would not watch. He would turn his back. Better yet he might leave. Shyrie carried a knife. Could she get it, cut his throat with it?

No, damn him, the man was even more of a cat than Jack Logan.

Completely naked, fighting tears, now, she dipped her hand into the icy water, then quickly withdrew it. She would die of freezing!

Hands, large, strong and rough, Shyrie's hands, lifted her around her waist and half shoved, half threw her forward into the water.

She screamed. It was *painfully* cold, momentarily obliterating every other reality.

Her feet slipping and sinking into the mud below, she regained her balance and, teeth chattering, realized the water was not too deep—up to her knees, perhaps, had she been standing.

Something landed on her head. Something cold, strange. Then more of it, hitting her shoulder, this time. Still disconcerted, she looked up and saw Shyrie on the bank, thoroughly enjoying himself, holding the soap tin, throwing handfuls of jelly onto her. Without thought, trying to shield her face with her hands, she drew back.

"You've two minutes to get yourself clean," Shyrie announced. "If you're not done in two minutes, I'll come in there with you and slit your throat."

Did he mean it? Did he even know whether he meant it? The man was mad!

Unsure, frightened, she added handfuls of water to the jelly, scrubbed her scalp and hair. She stood up, soaped the rest of her body then ducked back down under the water and rinsed clean.

As one might offer a bone to a dog, Shyrie now stood on the bank and held the towel with his left hand. With his right, he motioned for her to come to it.

The early-evening air suddenly seeming even colder than the water, Isobel climbed from the stream and grabbed the towel from his hand, quickly wrapping it around her shoulders. His knife, damn him, get his knife! That fool Norris, even now, had turned his back.

The expectancy behind Shyrie's grin was unmistakable. Fighting hatred so intense it threatened to consume her, Isobel merely looked at him and waited.

The moment was shattered by the sound of approaching horses, fast, coming at a full gallop. Both Shyrie and Norris turned in the direction of the sound. Immediately

Isobel ran toward the house. A musket, a weapon. Surely Dr. Ward would have some kind of weapon about.

"Stop her!" roared Shyrie.

Had she really covered only such a short distance? This time the hands that caught her belonged to Thomas Norris. With one over her mouth, the other over the towel which covered her thighs, he pinned her to the ground. Under his hand, her mouth still moved as best it could. Sounds that caught in her throat were nonetheless audible until Shyrie arrived, drew his knife and held the blade to her neck.

Among the three of them, silence prevailed as four horses came into view. Their riders drew rein at the house.

"Stay with her," snapped Shyrie, voice low. "I'll see what they're about."

The instant he left, again Isobel started to struggle, but the pressure of his hands increased. Tears flooded her eyes. However, this time Thomas Norris was not the object of her struggles. She grabbed the edge of the towel where it covered her breasts and yanked with all her strength. Yes, it opened. Now her breasts were fully exposed to Thomas Norris' view, his hand no longer protected from her naked flesh by the towel. He drew back, released her!

She screamed repeatedly. Too late he caught her again. The screams had drawn the riders. Shyrie, trapped between Isobel's screams and the approaching riders, elected to give his attention to the riders. Feet set wide apart, pistol drawn, he held his ground.

In the lead, his face now discernible in the twilight, was Dr. Ward.

Immediately Shyrie lowered his pistol. Isobel, on her feet now, her arms pinned behind her by Thomas Norris, stared in stark horror. Somehow she had imagined the riders might be patients or anyone who, knowing nothing of the situation, might believe whatever she told them and help her. Tears of rage and frustration rose in her eyes, but her lips remained silent. Damn them, damn all of them! Even more, she was naked. Naked in Dr. Ward's presence, she felt much as she had felt in the company of "respectable" women in London—a vacillating mixture of anger and shame. How these men looked at her, all of them, some trying not to, but none succeeding. Well, let them look, and desire her, and damn all of them to hell for it! There were three of them, Dr. Ward and two others. Somehow she was sure four had arrived. Where was the fourth? And what did it matter anyway?

In a motion so smooth not even Shyrie realized what was happening until it was complete, Dr. Ward drew his pistol and aimed it at Shyrie.

"I will now thank you to drop your weapon, Mr. Shyrie," said Dr. Ward. The men accompanying him had also drawn.

Incredulously, his arm still at his side, Shyrie looked over his shoulder at Norris, whose hands were still both occupied holding Isobel.

Again as Shyrie faced Dr. Ward, his voice echoed the expression Isobel had seen on his face only seconds ago. "Have you gone mad?" he roared.

Ignoring Shyrie for the moment, Dr. Ward addressed himself to Norris. "Release the girl."

Norris complied, keeping his hands in plain sight, wide from his weapons.

"Go to the house," Dr. Ward continued, this time speaking to Isobel. "Clothe yourself," he added distastefully. "Christopher"—he indicated the young man beside him—"will take you to see Edward Carrington. You are to give Mr. Carrington the letter you gave me and tell him how you came by it. You'll not be harmed. I give you my word."

Her knees buckled. She landed on the ground, now starkly conscious of the dead grass, twigs and tiny stones against her flesh. She understood. He had read the letter, then left on the galloping horse they had heard when they first arrived at the stream. Left to secure aid to stop Nat Shyrie and Thomas Norris from killing her.

"Mr. Norris, help Mistress Browne to her feet."

Furious, Norris obeyed.

A fourth man approached from the house, carrying a pewter mug, which he offered to Shyrie.

As Shyrie stood unmoving, his pistol now on the ground beside him, his eyes asked the question.

"It will make you sleep," answered Dr. Ward. "I know you want her dead, but you'll not go after her."

Shyrie's tight lips and still-unmoving hands were his answer.

Dr. Ward cocked his pistol, raised his arm and aimed directly at Shyrie's head. "Drink it," he ordered, his aged voice unwavering, "or as you stand, I shall kill you."

Angrily, awkwardly, Nat Shyrie accepted the mug, drained its contents into his belly, then tossed the empty container onto the ground.

"And when you see Mr. Carrington," Dr. Ward went on, speaking now to Christopher, his voice no longer steady, "tell him he must find some other sanctuary for Mr. Shyrie as I refuse to have this man in or near my home any longer." The pitch of his voice rising, he continued. "Tell Mr. Carrington we are decent God-fearing people, my family and I, and in this man's presence, the very air we breathe becomes tainted by the filth of his sins. Tell him, anything else I willingly offer, even to the sacrifice of my own life, but I will not have this man—"

Noisily Shyrie collected a mouthful of saliva and spat it onto the ground by Dr. Ward's feet, then started back toward the house. He managed two steps, then fell about a yard from the spittle.

That night Isobel slept, wrapped in the smell of clean linen, her belly full of stew and apple cake eaten in awkward silence in the kitchen with Dr. Ward's housekeeper. Sleep came quickly, deep and dreamless.

The first day of the journey begun the following morning was uneventful. They traveled on horseback—Isobel, Christopher Allen, age eighteen, and John Allen, age twenty-six. Isobel wore an indigo blue wool dress, formerly the property of John's wife. It fitted well and, with the gray wool cloak, was more than sufficiently warm for what turned out to be a surprisingly mild April day. Their passes, signed by a leading member of the New London Committee of Correspondence, identified Isobel as Elizabeth Allen, John Allen's wife. With allowances for minimal rest and sleep, it was anticipated that the journey should take no more than three days. To have traveled by boat down the Sound would, of course, have been faster, but with so many redcoats concentrated in the shoreline area, a journey by land seemed safer.

Their first night was spent at a farmhouse, and it occurred to Isobel that she was learning a great deal about the organization Nathaniel Shyrie worked for in the American colonies, as she already knew a great deal about the channels through which Jack Logan had escaped from London. She knew the smugglers in the group tended to use known, well-established harbors, apparently because no one expected them to. She knew many names and even more faces, including Nathaniel Shyrie, Dr. Ward, Thomas Norris and the two Allen brothers who accompanied her. She also knew and soon would know more of the particular houses where a fugitive from British authorities could find sanctuary.

If all proceeded according to schedule, two days hence she would meet Edward Carrington, answer his questions—and then what? It had been different, before, when the letter had been in her possession. Now the older Allen brother carried it. Before, when she had had it, she had been in a position to bargain. Now, however, its deliverance to Mr. Carrington was assured, with no assurances of Isobel's subsequent treatment. Mr. Shyrie worked for Mr. Carrington. Dr. Ward said so. Was Mr. Carrington mad, like Mr. Shyrie? Or was Mr. Carrington more like Dr. Ward? And yet, before Dr. Ward read the letter, he had been willing to let Mr. Shyrie kill her, simply because he had reason to mistrust her and she knew too much. Now she knew even more.

She tried to settle herself more comfortably into the bed, but with two of their host's daughters beside her, the task was difficult at best. The smaller one, age seven or eight, snored. Would she ever fall asleep? Isobel wondered. Her thoughts raced, fought and won against the tiredness of her body. Well, at least now she could ride a horse—tensely, awkwardly, but also quickly and without the constant terror of falling which had gripped her yesterday afternoon as she rode to Dr. Ward's house with Thomas. Her wish had come true, and what an empty wish it turned out to be! Now, she was reasonably sure, she could turn her horse to the wind and lose the company of the Allen brothers, yet now even more than when she had been with Norris, where would she go? When she had been with Norris, even though it was a nebulous goal, her goal was to find and strike a bargain with Edward Carrington. But now, the letter no longer in her possession, she had nothing to bargain with.

In the early afternoon of their third day out they stopped for food in a clump of trees by the side of the road. The three of them had spoken little since the start of their journey. It was John who had set the tone—aloof, courteous. John, with his patched breeches, faded coat and callused farmer's hands. How the men she had known in London would have laughed at him! She sat on a large rock and breathed deeply of the crisp April day. Initially she had felt uncomfortable in their silent relationship, but now she was used to it. Bread, cheese, wine and cold chicken had been packed for them at the house where they had spent the previous night. What a feast! She rose to her feet and stretched. Now, her belly full, her body warmed and relatively relaxed from the wine, she began to feel the effects of too little sleep for too many nights. How nice it would be to have a blanket, to stretch out by the small stream slightly ahead and rest. The earth was alive with the promise of spring. Odd, it made no sense, but for one brief instant, bathed in the sunlight of a beautiful day, fed and for the moment intensely alive and reasonably safe, Isobel experienced something she had not felt in so long she had almost forgotten what it was like. She felt happy.

The sound of approaching horses shattered the moment. Disconcerted, both John and Christopher rose to their feet.

Instantly Isobel's mind seemed clear of the wine. Her thoughts tumbled one over the other, but somehow a pattern, a purpose began to take form. The letter. Something to do with the letter. Guided more by instinct than conscious plan, but an instinct she had long ago learned to trust, she said to John quickly, "Give me the letter."

John merely looked at her.

Impatiently she added, "If they are soldiers, if they become suspicious, they might search you. They'll not search me."

Awkwardly, yet not really suspiciously, he answered, "You're the first one they'd search."

She drew herself up to her full height and illustrated the indignant tone in which she apparently intended to answer the soldiers, if indeed the approaching riders turned out to be soldiers. "I am a respectable married woman," she said. "Your wife. If they insist I be searched, then I shall insist a woman search me. If it comes to that, before they find a woman to do it, I'll be rid of the letter."

Hesitantly at first, then quickly, as the sound of the horses grew louder, John lifted the chain over his head and handed the packet to Isobel.

She wanted to scream, to laugh, to spit on them. Quickly, quietly, her face a mask of innocent concern, she slipped the chain around her own neck, the packet beneath her dress. Untethering her horse, she continued, "I shall walk farther away from the road. Tell them your wife is with you; then call me, if necessary. I'll not be far. It's merely better, I think, if they do not see me."

John nodded, apparently respecting her good sense. Both brothers sought a better vantage point to observe the road.

Fools, thought Isobel! That she might be searched was unlikely. It was Isobel the soldiers sought. Did anyone in the colonies, other than those she had shown the letter to, even know of its existence?

With both Allen brothers now facing the road, behind their backs she grabbed some bread and cheese. All she really needed now was a place to hide the letter. Then let them find her again, let them take her to Mr. Carrington. Heart pounding, nerves tingling, she forced herself to walk, lead the horse on foot. When fully beyond their range of sight, she mounted the horse. Her timing, although unplanned, was superb. The sound of the horses on the road blended with, covered the sound of her horse as she promptly paced it from a walk to a fast trot. She continued inland, away from the road, then turned south, the direction in which she had been heading with the Allen brothers. Perhaps the real irony was, as far as she had been able to determine, the horses on the road had not even stopped. Soldiers? Probably not. Merely other travelers, as harmless to the Allen brothers as the Allen brothers were harmless to them.

An hour later much of Isobel's previous elation grew sour. She felt tense, irritable, impatient. Gradually, the enormousness of the woods, rather than its fresh, clean smell, began to dominate her thoughts. Now only vaguely aware that the road lay somewhere to her right, she realized she had lost touch with it. The occasional scurrying of animals set her nerves even further on edge.

Abruptly she drew rein. Other horses. Unable to gauge how many, she was nonetheless sure there were more than one, and they were ahead of her. Not the road. At least, not the main road. In spite of the cold, sweat broke out on her face. She must hide the letter. How alike the trees looked. No, she could not hide it in the woods—anywhere. Even should she find a place she could find again, the letter itself might well not survive the elements. She needed a house, a shop—some kind of building. A building not likely to be suspected, easy to identify when the time came to reveal it. Beginning to think as Jack Logan and Nathaniel Shyrie had taught her to think, she wondered whether perhaps the best place, the least-likely-to-be-suspected place would be the most obvious. Hide it in the home of a British official, perhaps. Or a rebel, like Dr. Ward. Or the Twin Stallion Inn.

What a dreamer she was! She must find a building, any building, quickly.

The sound of the horses grew louder, then continued away from her, and she realized they had crossed in front of her, not too far ahead. Did they follow a road? Not the main road. That, she was sure, lay to her right. Perhaps a turnoff side road. Dr. Ward's house stood at the end of a side road. Maybe the riders sought a house. Perhaps, finally, she was near a group of houses. A community? A town?

Her simple plan to hide the letter in the nearest building suddenly seemed more complicated. First, she would have to gain access to the building and then manage to be alone. Difficult, if it turned out to be a house, even more difficult if it turned out to be a shop. A barn would probably be easiest to enter and leave, but the presence of a stranger would so arouse the animals the household would soon follow. And even if she did manage to find herself safely alone, she needed a *good* hiding place, one unlikely to be stumbled upon by someone not even seeking the letter.

She wanted to cry. An hour ago, when she had broken from the Allen brothers, everything seemed so promising. Now, although she was still afraid, anger dominated her feelings. She had never really even wanted the letter. If only Lord Marlowe had chosen one of the other girls that night, Isobel might still be back home in London on her way to wealth and at least some degree of power as the mistress of some wealthy and powerful man. With luck and wit, such a relationship might even have ended in marriage, a goal attained by more than one of the other ladies Isobel had worked with. But youth and beauty were such temporary gifts. She had no time to be lost in a woods in America, virtually all her thoughts and energies concentrated on physical survival. She was almost twenty!

Slowly, on foot, she led her horse forward, toward the secondary road or whatever it was.

Yes, a road. Narrower than the main road, but obviously well traveled. On the other side she saw something which sharply caught her attention. A stream! Cool, clean water. Dip her hands in it, wash her face, drink of it. Clear her mind. Since the stream was in a relatively unwooded area, it seemed better to leave her horse on the side where she now stood. She turned back, into the cover of some trees, found a suitable low branch and tethered the animal, then stepped forward again, toward the road. Looking carefully in both directions, listening with equal care, she finally crossed the road, then ran to the stream. Swallowing countless handfuls of water, she spilled quite a bit onto her dress and did not care. Her thirst finally quenched, she started to move away, then stopped, her attention suddenly caught by her reflection in the stream. What miracle was this, her hair soft and shiny, her face beginning to glow with healthy color after only these few days of decent food and rest? A miracle indeed! But she must hurry. The stream was too visible from the road. And yet to be discovered by some casual traveler on that road might be valuable. She could tell them—what? Perhaps tell them, she was John Allen's wife and had become separated from her husband. Ask where she might find shelter and aid.

No. Better to find a house and knock on the door with the same story. A house where she might hide the letter!

With her soft striped linen petticoat, she dried her face and hands, prepared to leave.

"Hello."

A sharp cry accompanied her sudden intake of breath as she swung around. The voice belonged to a British officer, young, tall, in full-dress uniform. The thin scar over his left eye, which Sarah Carrington had found repugnant, to Isobel enhanced an already strikingly handsome face. She had heard nothing, seen nothing. It was as though by sorcery he had suddenly appeared behind her. Facing him now, she rose to her feet.

"I am sorry," he said, his tone apparently intended to comfort, although what she read in his eyes was interest in her physical form, not concern for her feelings. "I didn't mean to frighten you." When she still offered no conversation, he continued somewhat awkwardly. "About a mile down the road my horse went lame, and I've had to walk. Are you employed at the Finch house?"

Employed? Of course. With her windburned complexion, rough hands and simple country dress, she might very well have been a servant girl. In an accent suited to the role he had assigned her, she answered, "Yes, but I've the afternoon off."

"That's odd. I was sure I knew all the servants."

"It would seem, sir, then, that you were mistaken." She tried to walk past him, toward her horse tethered out of sight on the other side of the path, but the officer blocked her path.

"I can see why old Mrs. Crocker would keep you hidden from the soldiers," he continued. "A girl as young and pretty as you. Do you suppose Mrs. Crocker was ever young and pretty?"

"I don't know."

"But she is a good cook, don't you think?"

"An excellent cook," Isobel answered.

"And who," he began slowly, his voice taking on a new tone, a wariness, "is Mrs. Crocker?"

At first more confused than frightened, Isobel answered, "But you said—" She broke off. It was a trick, a trap!

"You are not employed at the Finch house," the officer announced quietly. "Who are you?"

"I—I'll not tell you!" Desperately she tried to conceal her growing panic. "Tell you, indeed," she spat, "that you might come to my home and disturb me! I'm a good girl. I've no interest in soldiers or any man other than my husband."

"Husband?" Quickly he caught her left hand. There, indeed, was the plain gold band Dr. Ward had placed on her finger when, to protect herself during the journey to the Twin Stallion Inn, she had assumed the identity of Mrs. John Allen.

Reluctantly, yet with an appropriate show of courtesy, the officer released her hand. "I am Captain George Adams," he told her, not as though he really expected her to change her attitude, but then again, one could never really be sure unless one tried. "I am a guest at the Finch house," he continued, "and shall be until tomorrow morning. Tomorrow morning I shall head south, toward Stamford. If there is any way in which I may be of assistance to you—and, of course, your husband—"

"You may be of assistance to me, sir, by allowing me to pass."

Accepting his defeat with an obvious lack of enthusiasm, but apparently no ill will, he bowed slightly and stepped aside.

She crossed the road. He was watching her. She knew it, felt it. In spite of the quantity of water she had so recently consumed, her mouth was uncomfortably dry. The Finch house. As she continued to walk, she sensed that Captain Adams had also moved, but in the proper direction, along the road. The Finch house had servants. Probably a wealthy family, a large house. She remembered Lord Marlowe's town house in London. Certainly there were a thousand places a letter could be hidden in Lord Marlowe's house.

But what about the Finch house? Carpeting, under which a letter might be slipped? No. It would make a bulge. A dresser perhaps. Pull out a drawer and hide it between the back of the drawer and the frame. Or perhaps paintings hung on the walls. Slip the letter behind a painting.

She reached her horse and untethered it. Captain Adams could get her into the Finch house.

Or could he? Surely no respectable family would permit even an honored guest simply to bring home some woman he found on the road and sleep with her.

Of course, Captain Adams had not impressed Isobel as unresourceful. Let Captain Adams supply the room, wherever it might be, where Isobel could either be alone or at least eventually awake while the captain slept.

She hesitated. In the name of heaven, the man was a British army officer. In all probability he already had a description of Isobel Browne.

She mounted her horse properly, sidesaddle, carefully adjusting her skirt. From this higher vantage point she could see him, way ahead on the road.

Who would ever think to look for Isobel Browne in the company of a British officer?

The pace of her heart quickened. Tomorrow morning he would head south, toward a town called Stamford. She had no idea where Stamford might be, but New Hereford was to the south. New Hereford. The Twin Stallion Inn.

She brought the horse, at a slow walk, to the road. Surely she had gone mad. She was bewitched! Jack Logan, from beyond the grave, reached out to muddle her thoughts, to torment and trap her.

Spit on Jack Logan! Spit into the sea and, thereby, onto his grave.

She turned her horse to the right. The previously receding red-caped figure grew larger. In response to the sound of her horse, he turned, apparently unsure of her intentions. Had she come after him, or was she merely traveling in the same direction?

She drew rein beside him. The transition in attitude from curiosity to pleasure was subtle but, to Isobel, obvious. Although his expression changed little, his stance became taller, straighter, hands on his hips. Did he even realize how he showed himself off?

"Forgive me, sir, for disturbing you," she said, her voice projecting an almost-poignant dignity. "At first I was afraid to accept your offer of help, but when you left and I found myself alone, I realized how much I do need help. I have become separated from my husband. An animal frightened his horse, and the horse ran wild. My husband is a good horseman, and I've no fear for his safety, but I've searched for an hour and cannot find him. Therefore, I hope simply to go on ahead and meet him in New Hereford, but as you can see, I am quite alone. And I don't know the way."

His disappointment showed. A virtuous colonial wife, genuinely in need of assistance. As a gentleman he had no choice. "Of course, madame, I shall do whatever I can. I am not leaving until tomorrow morning, but New Hereford is along the way, and I shall be delighted to accompany you. No doubt you may stay at the Finch house tonight."

She lowered her eyes, as befit a virtuous wife's gratitude to a male stranger. "Thank you."

"It's about another mile to the house. May I share your horse?"

"How thoughtless of me not to offer." She held out her hands that he might help her dismount.

With due propriety he lifted her down. "Don't quite know where they'll find room for you," he said, "but I'm sure you'll not mind sharing a bed in the servants' quarters."

"How nice it would be," she said sadly, but not critically, "to have my own bed. I grew up sharing a bed with three sisters and find it muchly interferes with my sleep."

Not unsympathetically, he shook his head. "I fear even the family is sharing. They are accommodating seven soldiers. Only two are officers—myself and a sergeant—but he snores, and I fear I would get no sleep. Anywhere we put him, the others would suffer the same consequences."

He made a move to mount the horse. Subtly she delayed him. Lightly, yet with a straight face, she announced, "I do not snore."

Obviously confused, he merely looked at her.

"But then, of course"— she glanced away from him and managed some semblance of a maidenly blush—"you must have your sleep."

She felt his hand on her face, gentle, yet firm in its pressure until their eyes met. With her eyes she consented to the kiss which followed, their lips barely touching. This time, her eyes brimming with laughter, he embraced her, an embrace which she returned wholeheartedly. Abruptly she shoved her hands against his chest. "Not here," she said. "What if my husband were to come along, or anyone else who knows me!"

He laughed. "The sergeant's room is across the hall from mine. If I were to stay with the sergeant, with you in my room—and then, when the sergeant is asleep—"

"No one must know," she insisted, as though suddenly frightened again.

Gently, reassuringly, Captain Adams answered, "No one will. On my honor as a British officer, I swear it."

CHAPTER TWELVE

With patronizing courtesy the Finch family seemed to accept Isobel. The captain, the sergeant and, that night, Isobel dined with the family. The five common soldiers ate with the servants, a gathering from which Captain Adams seemed to feel Isobel should be protected—not the servants, he explained to Mrs. Finch, but five soldiers warmed from the cold by wine might become indelicate in their conversation. No one seemed to doubt that Isobel was as she presented herself—a politically unsophisticated, uneducated farmer's bride from the New London area, on her way to New Hereford with her husband to collect the possessions willed to them by his recently deceased father. Yes, they did have a pass signed by a member of the New London Committee of Correspondence, but it was presently in her husband's possession. No, neither of them was really interested in politics, but provided one was neither a stranger nor known to be actively opposed to those who questioned the policies of King George toward the colonies, such passes were not difficult to come by. The committee knew of her father-in-law's death; it knew the stated purpose of the trip was genuine.

"We shall miss you, Captain Adams," said Mrs. Finch, as the serving maid cleared dishes still red from cranberry pudding. As she spoke, she conspicuously kept her eyes from her oldest daughter, Jane Finch. How attentive Captain Adams was to Jane Finch, a reasonably pretty girl of about seventeen or eighteen. Pretty and dull. Was Jane's mother seriously trying to pair off her daughter with the captain? Whenever Jane or the captain spoke throughout the meal, Isobel noticed the mother's eyes darting back and forth between the two of them, cataloguing the reactions of each to the other. Was he usually this attentive, Isobel wondered, or was he making an exceptional effort this night, to cover his true relationship with Isobel?

"We certainly shall miss you," repeated Mr. Finch, this time depersonalizing the statement by adding, "These rebel upstarts begin to worry us. I take it the girl you were seeking has been found."

"I don't really know," answered the captain, "although it would seem likely she has been. The troops brought in to search for her are being removed."

Isobel tried to hide her excitement. The soldiers were leaving, the search ended! Perhaps someone had actually convinced them the *Sally Anne* was lost at sea!

Her elation was short-lived. Certainly it was equally possible that the search had become less obvious. Perhaps a crew member with too much rum had talked about her. Or perhaps Mr. Shyrie or Dr. Ward had been captured. Both knew she had wanted to see Edward Carrington. Was Edward Carrington being watched—silently, patiently?

The rest of the conversation, to Isobel, was dull. They talked of current fashion, these silly American provincials. What did they know of fashion? And the weather. And horses.

Pleading exhaustion, Isobel retired early. The captain

and one of the maids accompanied her to his room where he appropriately removed most of his belongings to the sergeant's room across the hall while the maid spread the bed with fresh linen and started the fire.

Alone, finally, Isobel felt as though her heart would burst. The room was beautiful, predominantly blue with blue-green woodwork. The bed, against the wall in Continental fashion, was hung with pink, green and blue crewelwork in a delicate flower design on pale-blue silk. The seats of the two Queen Anne walnut chairs which flanked the small rectangular tea table in front of the fireplace repeated the bed's drapery design, as did the window draperies, each topped by a fabric-covered cornice. The room also contained a wardrobe, bureau, dressing table, desk, a third chair, a candlestand, four wall sconces and a washstand with a gold-trim flowered American-made porcelain pitcher and bowl. Although the rug differed radically in design from the bed hangings, somehow the entire room came together, harmonized.

She stood by the fire, turned and caught her breath, then realized—no, there was not someone else in the room with her; it was her own reflection. A Chinese-style Chippendale mirror was mounted on the wall beside the door, opposite the fireplace. As she turned and walked toward it, she observed her approach with pleasure. Although her appearance was still far from what it had been in England, the captain's attraction to her was understandable. The blush in her cheeks was high; her eyes were bright; her hair was shiny. In addition, the shade and fit of her dress, in which she had never before really seen herself, were most flattering. She frowned—some powder and rouge, a proper hairstyle— No, she did not look as she had looked in London.

The frame on the mirror distracted her. It was gold, an incredibly detailed tableau of scrolls, flowers and small woodland animals, somehow giving the impression of perfect symmetry, yet closer examination revealed subtle but obviously deliberate differences between the two sides. Lightly she touched her finger to a small fox on the lower left-hand side, then withdrew quickly, startled by the coldness of the metal. On the right-hand side a hunting dog stood crouched, ready to leap across the glass in pursuit of the equally exquisitely detailed fox. Oh, to own such a mirror!

Still standing in front of it, still drawn by her own reflection so magnificently framed, she reached under the bodice of her dress and removed the leather packet which contained the letter. As part of the mirror's design, a plain gold rim, perhaps an eighth of an inch thick, ran the dimensions of the frame, a subtle final touch which brought forward the glass and accented the play of light and shadow on the frame's ornamentation. With both hands, the letter packet dangling from her right arm, she lifted slightly and pulled the bottom of the mirror toward her. It was attached to the wall, she discovered, by a wire strung over a heavy metal peg.

She smiled, removed the letter from her arm and placed it behind the glass, straightening the mirror only slightly to remove any trace of its having been touched. The result was perfect.

And now she must force herself not to think of it.

Her clothing neatly laid over one of the chairs by the tea table in front of the fire, she slipped into the soft, clean linen nightgown laid out for her on the bed. The bed was at first cold, but soon warmed sufficiently by the heat of her body. She did not know what time the captain came to her, but she must have been deeply asleep, for she had no memory of his having entered the room.

His touch was gentle. "Don't be afraid, my darling," he said.

Fully awake now, in her heart she laughed at him as she was sure he laughed at her. Her deception degraded and made a fool of him, as doubtless his imagined success in conquering her faithfulness to her husband degraded and made a fool of Isobel.

"No, my dearest," she answered softly, shyly and yet caressingly, deliberately feeding his vanity with an apparent shameful passion evoked by his touch, "I am not afraid."

The following morning Isobel, accompanied by Captain Adams, the sergeant and five other soldiers set out in the direction of the Twin Stallion Inn. The morning was damp and chilly, but by nine o' clock the sun had broken through, promising to dry up the dampness and, barring the possibility of later rain clouds, to provide a reasonably pleasant day. The road was heavily traveled. At her first sight of a second group of soldiers, Isobel tensed but soon was able to relax a bit. Of course the road would be filled with soldiers. The troops were pulling out, heading for Stamford where ships would take them across the Sound to Fort Franklin. How fortunate, thought Isobel, that she had accepted Captain Adams. Without him she could not have used the road.

As she kept her horse close to his, her eyes conveyed a calculatedly shy flirtation. He had been pleased with her the previous night. She had played her part well.

An officer from another group of soldiers approached. Drawing his horse beside Isobel's, his interest in her immediately apparent, he addressed Captain Adams. "Is this the girl?"

Captain Adams responded, "What girl?"

"The one we've all been seeking. Isobel Browne?"

A spasm ran through Isobel's body. Was it visible to the two officers? Of course. It must have been.

Apparently startled and confused, Captain Adams answered, "Isobel Browne? No. Why do you ask?"

"We heard she had been captured. A rumor perhaps, but why else are we being withdrawn? This girl fits the description."

As though the thought had never occurred to him, but now seemed worth at least minimal consideration, Captain Adams took a long, careful look at Isobel Browne.

"And who, please tell me, is Isobel Browne?" asked Isobel of the second officer.

"She's wanted for the murder of a personal friend of his majesty," the man answered courteously.

"Oh," said Isobel.

"You must forgive me, please," he added. "Seeing you in the company of Captain Adams, I thought you might be his prisoner."

She could not bear it. Her mind refused to function. She must say something, but what?

Captain Adams continued to look at her as the second officer withdrew and rejoined his own men several feet behind those who followed Captain Adams.

She avoided his eyes. No good. She would have to meet his eyes. She did, in an attempt to convey innocence, an unspoken question—*why do you stare at me*? But the fear was too powerful. Instead of continuing to look at him for the extra second or so which might have been required to weaken the suspicion so obviously forming in his mind, her eyes moved forward toward the open road ahead of them. To her left and right the area was heavily wooded, but neither the road nor the woods offered any real hope of sanctuary. An attempt to outride the soldiers would be ludicrous.

Abruptly the captain pulled his horse in front of hers and drew rein. He raised his right hand, signaled for the men behind them to stop. Cut off by the captain's horse, Isobel also drew rein. The group behind them, led by the officer who had spoken to Captain Adams a few moments ago, continued to move forward.

Quietly, his tone a statement far more than a question, Captain Adams addressed her, "You are Isobel Browne, aren't you?"

She looked at him. Deny it? No good. Even if she managed to convinoe him he might be wrong, he would still be suspicious enough to keep her with him and investigate further. Eventually he would discover the truth and probably be angry at her for having made him doubt, for having made a fool of him.

With genuine tears in her eyes she answered, "I never murdered anyone. Lord Marlowe was an old man and very drunk. He fell, hit his head and died. His wife returned unexpectedly, found us together and started screaming, 'Murder.' No one listened to me. They'd have hanged me. I am innocent. Help me. Please help me!"

His voice not totally devoid of compassion—or regret—Captain Adams answered, "I cannot help you."

"Perhaps," she answered quickly, "if I help you. I escaped to these colonies with an American smuggler. I know—names. A lot of things. I—" She broke off. His eyes had narrowed as he listened. Reasons to torture her, answers to force from her. Not, she felt, that he personally intended to proceed in that direction, but the power of England was arrogant. It did not lightly strike bargains with whores.

The second officer joined them again, this time with his men at a standstill behind Captain Adams' men. "Is something wrong?" he asked Captain Adams.

"No," answered Captain Adams, "and I must thank you. This woman is indeed Isobel Browne."

Sharply, the second officer looked at her, surprise quickly changing to contempt. This time, his gaze included her body. A condemned beautiful woman. An oddly erotic object.

"I suspected it from the moment I saw her," Captain Adams continued, "but was not sure. Therefore, I kept close to her, waited for her to reveal herself. When you asked if she were my prisoner, you sped the process."

"Liar!" spat Isobel stupidly, driven by rage born of fear. "You never suspected!"

His emotional withdrawal from her was so obvious that it seemed almost as though he had put a greater physical distance between them. His stance on his horse became taller, his eyes cold. A military officer of the British Empire did not deign to argue with the likes of Isobel Browne. "You are my prisoner, Mistress Browne," he informed her with icy formality. He signaled two of his men to move forward, then told them, "This woman is Isobel Browne. You are to ride ahead, at your best speed, secure immediate passage on a boat or ship and bring the news to Fort Franklin. I shall proceed on to Stamford and hold her at Webb's Tavern until I receive further instructions."

She wanted to spit on him. She hated him. Sobs racked her body, tears which all of them could see, the ultimate infuriating, painful humiliation.

With two loyalist matrons stationed inside the room with her and four soldiers outside the door, Isobel stretched out on the mahogany Queen Anne bed and closed her eyes. Ironically, on their way to Stamford, to Webb's Tavern, they had passed, on the northern outskirts of New Hereford, the Twin Stallion Inn.

She did not know how long she slept. She had merely closed her eyes to shut out the sight of the two women, who watched her as though she might suddenly, by witchcraft, change herself to a demon and attack them. She awoke to a sense of pressure, the reality of the figure which confronted her momentarily blurring with dream images—a British soldier, towering over her, his eyes cold, lips thin, his hand on her shoulder gripping, shaking her. In the candle glow his whole face seemed to change starkly with each movement as the interplay of light and shadow accented first one, then some quite different feature.

He slapped her face.

She cried out and sat up. Like patches of fog on an otherwise clear day, the sleepiness lingered, but only briefly. The soldier, she realized, was real. At least a dozen candles were lit, six in wall sconces and at least six others in assorted holders. A second soldier stood slightly behind the first. She frowned, looked beyond both soldiers and found herself unable to move her eyes from the third man. It was he who dominated the room. In the candle glow sections of his cloak seemed to be made of solid gold, but of course, that was absurd. It was gold thread, heavily woven into the lining. Most of his other clothing also contained gold thread, woven in various quantities and patterns into beige and green silk, satin and velvet, accented at the neck and sleeves with an abundance of English lace as white as his powdered English wig. His features were fleshy, his body obviously well fed and underexercised. One might well have taken him for a lazy man but for his eyes, heavy-lidded, yet sharp, cold, arrogant, excited.

"On your feet," ordered the soldier.

Promptly, but not ungracefully, Isobel rose to her feet, her eyes never leaving the man behind the soldier. In London he might well have been a client.

"Leave us," he ordered, looking only at Isobel.

With the door closed behind the departed soldiers, alone with her now, even his breathing bespoke excitement, the excitement of a hunt rewarded, a taste, a promise of greater rewards. Oh, this fat, arrogant fool. Did he really believe she could not see his feelings? He needed the letter. She still did not fully understand its importance, but Lord Marlowe was no friend of either Lord North or King George. It was not vengeance which had brought this obviously wealthy, powerful nobleman all the way to America. It was the letter!

He snapped his fingers and held out his hand, as though attending to some minor detail. "The letter."

Stalling, she answered, "Letter?"

"The letter you took from Lord Marlowe." Ever so subtly his voice seemed to waver. Was he not absoluteiy sure she had taken it? No, that would never do. Without the letter she would be valueless to him.

"I see," she answered quietly, in her best rehearsed upper-class accent, sure her heartbeat was as fast as his. Fully awake now, she felt as though she had plunged into cold water and were now swimming. She must swim well. Her life depended on it. "I am to give you the letter," she continued. "Then you shall send me back to England to be hanged."

"As befits your crimes," he answered irritably, ungraciously accepting the humiliation of having to converse with her. "Return the letter to its proper owner, repent your sins and pray God have mercy on you."

"Better the king's mercy than God's," she answered dryly. "The king could grant me a pardon."

He stared at her as though she were mad. A *pardon*? She saw it in his eyes, read his mind. "You blaspheme the Lord!"

"No, kind sir," she answered quickly, adroitly. "As we all know, the Lord makes human beings instruments of

His justice, the king His most perfect instrument, and as God is just and my witness, I am innocent of Lord Marlowe's murder. It was in defense of my own life that I struggled with him and in further defense—that I might raise the money to escape—that I took the letter."

His voice crackled. "You sold the letter? Where? To whom?

"And who, may I ask, sir, are you?"

Obviously outraged by her continuing impudence, he drew himself up to his full, unimpressive height. "I am Walter Williams, third earl of Ormsbee, second cousin to His Lordship Frederick North."

To Isobel, his physical stature immediately seemed taller, stronger. "Is it Lord North who sent you?"

That he found her even more outrageous was written all over him. Eyes blazing, he answered, *"Yes!"*

Her voice soft, bordering on flirtation, yet subtle, the combination cushioning the directness of her words, she pressed onward. "Surely Lord North could secure a pardon for me."

The degradation was unbearable. He needed the letter. Quietly, with a bitter rein on the intensity of his anger, he answered, "Give me the name of the person to whom you sold the letter. A pardon might be considered."

"Dear, kind sir, please forgive me, for it would seem I have not found the right words to say what I desire to say." She felt light-headed, frightened, yet the words continued to flow. "As God and the king are just," she continued, "I beg your protection, for I am as you see me—wrongly accused of a most serious crime, alone and without friends in a strange land. You tell me you would consider a pardon, and I am most humbly grateful. But it is the pardon itself I must have. Otherwise, surely, I shall die."

"What you ask could take months."

He was lying. She was sure of it. Lord North wanted the letter. To send this man all the way to America without the power to pardon, the most negotiable currency among many with whom he might have to deal, was absurd. But she must not insult him. For the moment, a written promise would suffice. "I would accept your word, your lordship," she said. "A written promise in the king's name that I be pardoned of all charges against me and free to return to England. Surely his majesty would honor such a promise."

To Isobel's amazement, a touch of humor came into his eyes. "They told me you were a simple girl."

Quickly seizing on what might just be a new opportunity, she returned the look, carrying through with it in her voice. "I am simple, milord, in what I want. Life. And simple"— her tone became almost childlike— "in that I am afraid. I beg of you that I may trust you, for surely with your protection what harm could come to me?"

For a long minute he contemplated her until, with feigned shyness, she turned from his gaze. Gently, somewhat tentatively at first, he touched her shoulder, then her hair—long, lustrous, silken copper-gold hair. His voice was soft, patronizing as befitted a man of his rank, but nonetheless, it was the voice of a man making love. "It is within my power," he said, "to grant you the pardon you seek, in the king's name."

The pace of her heart quickened. Could she, dare she trust him?

"But first," he continued, "you must help me recover the letter."

But *first*, the letter. No, she decided, she could not trust him. "Oh, thank you, milord. As I trust your honor, your words give me courage."

With hands well accustomed to enjoying the charms of

whores, he now openly fondled the fullness of her breasts. The scent of musk, the feel of his clothing—she closed her eyes. His lips met hers, she might well have been back home in London. Oh, if only she could trust him. Bastard! He would see her dead and never look back, once he had the letter.

Releasing her, he asked, "Where is the letter?"

"Alas, in truth, sir, I do not know." Quickly she added, "The man I gave it to was taking me with him to the Twin Stallion Inn, where he was to collect the money to pay me, but we became separated. I pray you, sir, send me to the Twin Stallion Inn with one of your agents that I may point him out."

When he did not answer immediately, she continued. "I do not believe the name he gave me, but there are other names. Nathaniel Shyrie. James Devant." Carefully she stuck with only those names she was sure he already knew, names of people already sought or captured by the British. Chances were too great that a fresh name, at this point, might endanger her bargaining power with Mr. Carrington. "They are part of a large group which plots against the king."

"And who is at the head of this group?" he asked quietly.

Carrington, Carrington, she thought. "I do not know," she answered, "but take me to the Twin Stallion, and perhaps I can find out. They have no reason to mistrust me. They know the British believe I am responsible for Lord Marlowe's death. I beg you, sir, allow me to perform this service for my king, to prove my gratitude for his mercy. Allow me to leave—now—that I shall not miss the man who possesses the letter."

Hesitantly he answered, "The hour is late."

"The more reason to hurry, milord."

His manner now decisive, he left the room without a word.

Trembling, Isobel closed her eyes. Dare she hope? A pardon! England! As for Edward Carrington, Dr. Ward, Thomas Norris, the Allen brothers—let them die, let all of them die. After all, their behavior really was treasonous.

On the other hand, she still did not feel fully confident that she could trust Lord Williams. Better to meet Edward Carrington before making any irreversible decisions. Certainly what Mr. Carrington might have to offer, a life in France, would be better than no life at all.

The door opened, and Lord Williams, in all his golden splendor, reappeared. "It is ten thirty, Mistress Browne," he informed her. "Be ready to leave in half an hour. A suitable agent has been found to accompany you."

CHAPTER THIRTEEN

Still shivering, James Devant pulled the blanket more tightly around his shoulders and moved as close to the fire as he dared. Despite the cold, the room beneath the tower of the Twin Stallion Inn had never before seemed so comfortable, so welcome. Now, with life surging through his body, he dared think of life, of freedom, dared cherish both, and yet, cruelly, unrelentingly, his memory continued to play games with him, nip him, taunt him with what might have been. Both soldiers were dead now, the one who had accompanied James last night to the boat James was to row across the Sound and the one who had ridden so quickly to stop him with the news that Isobel Browne had been taken, that James was to be returned to the fort, to eventual death at the end of a British rope. What fools they were, those two young soldiers, to assume James Devant would peacefully accompany them back to the fort to death.

The second had been of a height and build similar to James'. After killing both, James had exchanged clothes with the second, then shot the lifeless face to obliterate any chance of recognition. He then indeed returned to the fort and boarded the ship which took Lord Williams, himself and ten British soldiers across the Sound so much more quickly, safely and inconspicuously than the rowboat could have taken James. With so many new soldiers arriving almost daily from England, the fact that none of the ten soldiers knew James presented no problem. Many of them did not even know one another. Shaved and clean, standing tall and straight in the British uniform, James had an appearance so radically different from that of the man Lord Williams had spoken to the previous evening that although once Lord Williams had briefly glanced at all eleven men in uniform, he neither recognized nor apparently even gave a second thought to James. Now not only was James free, but it was also doubtful that anyone would be searching for him. More likely it would be assumed the bodies onshore were those of James and the first soldier, the second soldier having run off, shamed by his incompetence in letting the first soldier die at the hands of an initially unarmed rebel, or having been killed, his body washed out to sea.

Two fewer British soldiers for Edward Carrington to worry about when the final confrontation took place, as James was now convinced it would. Two incompetent, arrogant, now-dead British soldiers—hardly a just price for the death of even one American-born British subject who, had his majesty not simply closed the American courts, would now be alive and free. King George was wrong. Wrong to assume that freeborn Englishmen anywhere in the world would indefinitely submit to the kind of government his majesty saw fit to impose on his American colonies. Edward Carrington was also wrong—naïve—if he really believed anything short of force could change men like Lord Williams, Lord North . . . and, of course, the king.

On the other hand, perhaps Mr. Carrington was not naïve. Perhaps he was merely willing to hope. No, not naïve. The stockpiled arms and gunpowder throughout the colonies dispelled any illusion of naïveté on the part of the Edward Carringtons of America.

Ironic. For the first time, there in the candlelit tower room of the Twin Stallion Inn, James Devant felt a genuine affinity for Edward Carrington's cause, yet he knew that if he spoke his thoughts, he would not be believed. More likely, in Edward Carrington's mind James Devant would be so completely branded a liar that the possibility of a workable relationship between them might well be shattered.

Footsteps. At least two men approached the room, their gait uneven, civilian, not military. Reluctant to part with the blanket, James rose to his feet and tossed it onto the bed. To part with it was, however, necessary. Wrapped in it, he appeared too human, weak, huddled and vulnerable to the cold. At least the clothes John McCaylan had supplied him fitted well, and his mind, refreshed by a long day filled with little more than food and sleep, was now, well into the night, clear.

Facing the door, his back to the fire, James responded as the anticipated knock materialized, "Come in."

Perhaps it was merely the unflattering angle at which the candle glow touched Edward Carrington's face, but somehow the man seemed to have aged dramatically, his features tense and drawn. Unquestionably he had lost weight, as had James in the prison at Fort Franklin. Behind Carrington stood Garth. Although neither James nor Garth spoke, James warmed to the sight of him, a reaction confirmed and returned by a subtle change in the black man's expression, in all probability picked up by no one but James. A third man, blond, of medium height, considerably younger than Carrington and well armed—a farmer, if his hands and clothing spoke truth—accompanied Carrington. It was the blond man who closed and locked the door.

"I heard you were dead," Carrington announced. "They said you were found on the shore near Fort Franklin, shot in the head."

"As you see," James answered, "they were mistaken."

"I know of no other escapes from the Fort Franklin prison," said Carrington. His tone conveyed his distrust. Was it really an "escape"? Precisely where did James stand with the British?

"At first, I was released," James answered. "They made an agreement with me. I was to help them locate the girl they've been searching for."

Visibly Carrington stiffened. He said nothing.

"Then," James continued, "word reached the fort that she had been found. I was on the shore. They tried to take me back to the prison. There were only two of them. I killed them, exchanged clothes with one of them, then went back and, in British uniform, crossed the Sound on the same ship which carried Lord Williams to Stamford."

Conceding neither belief nor disbelief in James' account, Carrington frowned. "Lord Williams? Who is Lord Williams?"

"Seems the girl has a letter—possibly a forgery, although I tend to doubt it, from the king to Lord North. It's the letter they really want. Lord Williams is a cousin to Lord North, here as Lord North's personal emissary to retrieve the letter."

"I see," said Carrington. "And where do you now stand in your agreement with the British?"

Irritably James answered, "Lord Williams promised me certain considerations in exchange for a specific service. It was not even the girl they really wanted; it was the letter—a piece of paper, a political document in which I have no interest. But when my service became unnecessary—when they found the girl—they attempted to take me back to the fort, to England, to death. It is by my own luck and wits that I stand here tonight. I have no agreements with or ties to the British."

For a long moment Edward Carrington looked at James Devant, a look which James met unflinchingly. Then, finally, the tension level throughout the room seemed to drop. "As long as they believe you're dead—"

"A few days at best," James answered. "As you receive news of them, so they receive news of you."

Carrington nodded. "The night you were taken—we had made arrangements to meet the following night."

James waited. Let Carrington take the lead. Edward Carrington needed James Devant, damn it. He needed James' ships, his organization, his experience, his contacts in Britain, France and the West Indies. He needed trained, experienced smugglers, but unlike so many of those who worked for Nat Shyrie, Carrington needed the kind of men who, on the shores of New England, worked for James—American-born, farmers and tradesmen, mainly men with roots deeply embedded in the New England area, men Edward Carrington could count on when the risks became such that profit alone was no longer sufficient motivation. At the moment, however, everyone in James' group stood guilty of bringing in, along with the goods Carrington wanted, goods Carrington had forbidden. Therefore, they feared Carrington's wrath. Without James as conduit, as negotiator, the chances of Edward Carrington's locating and establishing enough trust among them to pull the group together as a cohesive, functioning unit under his own leadership were virtually nil.

"It was you who requested the meeting," Carrington continued, not yet willing to be pushed by James' silence.

Abruptly tired of the you-speak-first game, James seated himself by the fire and answered, "You want what I have. The men, the ships, the contacts, the experience."

With a sharpness that startled James, Carrington shot back, "And I must deal with the likes of you to get them."

His voice soft, too soft, James retaliated, "Alas, Mr. Carrington, we cannot all inherit fortunes from loyalist ancestors. Some of us must make our own way."

A look of rage, reflected immediately in a visible muscular tension within both Garth and the blond man, exploded in Carrington's eyes.

Deliberately, although with obvious initial difficulty, Edward Carrington assumed a more relaxed posture. Voice low and even, he answered, "I am not in conflict with my conscience as regards the source of my income."

Matching Carrington's tone, James returned, "Neither am I. What you want of me is available to you. Shall we discuss the details?"

Although subtler now, nonetheless, Edward Carrington's anger remained in evidence—a tightness about his mouth, a noticeable edge in his voice. "Yes. Details. But not immediately. You say the British wanted you to help locate the girl—this Isobel Browne. . . ."

James nodded, irritated more with himself than with Carrington. How much wiser to have let Carrington's insult pass. Ironic! His genuine respect for the man had made James vulnerable to Carrington's opinion of him, the vulnerability provoking an emotional response where reason would have served far better the purposes of both men.

"How much do you know of her?" Carrington continued. "What did they tell you?"

"They said she was a whore, but not of the streets. And they showed me a likeness of her."

"You say she was taken prisoner."

"The soldier sent to bring me back to the fort reported this to the soldier who was with me on the shore. Also, on the ship which brought Lord Williams to Stamford, the soldiers spoke of her capture. Lord Williams was to meet her at Webb's Tavern."

Carrington frowned, turned his attention to the blond man. "Did she say anything about having been taken prisoner?"

The blond man shook his head. "Not that I know of."

Carrington also seated himself, took his time, then looked at James. "She is here at the inn. We know the letter, a letter, exists. But is it indeed a forgery? Is the girl herself no more than a British spy? Has she been one even since before she left London, collecting knowledge of our business, our ships, our people?"

James hesitated, then shook his head. "I doubt it," he answered. "Or, if she now is, I doubt that it goes back to London. No need for them to spend this kind of money to set up a spy you might believe. And the letter—forgery or genuine—might well be taken from her, published and believed. It's too dangerous."

"I would have you meet her and hear what you think of her," said Carrington. "I only just arrived and have not yet seen her. Could you recognize her from the likeness you saw?"

"Possibly. I could not really be sure, though. You suspect the girl who is here may not be Isobel Browne?"

"Isobel Browne arrived in New London four days ago. Two of our men were accompanying her to New Hereford, but they arrived with only a message that she tricked them into returning the letter to her, then ran away. They have since returned to New London."

James frowned. "Why should she run away?"

"Fear possibly."

"Fear? Of what?"

Irritably Carrington brushed the question aside. "Or possibly," he continued, "to make contact with the British in this area, to see what bargain she might strike. Seems she's a tricky wench, indeed. Quite a liar, and not stupid."

Fear. The word stuck in James' mind. Carrington's refusal to pursue the subject made sense. Isobel Browne had entered America though channels controlled by Nat Shyrie. If Nat Shyrie—James' primary competitor for Carrington's support—had frightened the girl away, doubtless Carrington was deeply disturbed by it, a bit of information Carrington, particularly at this point in their negotiations, would have preferred to keep from James. James rose to his feet. Regardless of Carrington's present relationship with Shyrie, whatever it might be, James Devant and Edward Carrington needed each other at that moment. If indeed the girl was a spy, certainly James could no more afford to have her report back to the British than could Carrington.

"You will not be able to remain here at the inn," said Carrington.

James hesitated, then decided it would be best to speak his mind now, lest Carrington later think James had not been completely honest with him. "I have decided to live in France," said James. "For a while at least."

Carrington merely looked at him.

"The operation can just as well be run from France and England," James continued, "with your organization in charge here in the colonies. You are right. I cannot remain here at the inn. Nor can I return to my home in Massachusetts."

"You could be of far more value to us here, although you could also be of value in France," said Carrington. "There are people in France whose support we seek. . . ."

"The success or failure of your operation is the success or failure of mine. I am at your service."

"When do you plan to leave?"

"Very soon after I have your assurance that no man who ever worked for me will be held responsible by you for past smuggling activities. Once I have that assurance, I can convene the men and introduce them to you."

"I see," answered Edward Carrington. Deliberately, irritably, an obvious and unconvincing debasement of James' proposal, which they both knew he had no choice but to accept, he simply rose to his feet.

For Isobel Browne, the waiting was intolerable. A while before, she heard footsteps, but they had continued past her room and up another flight of stairs. What if Edward Carrington did not respond to her message? What if he never even received it? At what point might Lord Williams' patience run out, at what point might he simply assume the letter was lost to them or move on the inn with troops to search for it? What story could she give him of information gained from Edward Carrington if she never even saw Edward Carrington? The "suitable agent" found to accompany her was actually two people—Captain Adams and another British officer, both in civilian dress, lodged two rooms down from the one occupied by Isobel. If no one visited her room, certainly both officers would know.

Seeking consolation, she reminded herself that thus far all had gone well. The officers had seen her safely into the general area of the inn, then disappeared for approximately an hour to cover any connection between their arrival and Isobel's. Thus far no words and only the most guarded looks had passed among them. Captain Adams! How she hated him, with his arrogant, sneering lips—as though he had really seduced her and thereby somehow degraded her. It was she who had used him, made a fool of him. At least now, however, he held his tongue. Lord Williams saw her as an attractive woman, an interest not unnoticed by Captain Adams. One did not trifle with even the potential property of a man as powerful as Lord Williams. Should fate be kind to her, should she actually secure a pardon and return to England as Lord Williams' mistress, then, indeed, the sneering little captain would feel her anger. Seated in front of the fire, the room dimly lit by only four candles, she threw her head back and smiled. All of them—Nathaniel Shyrie, Dr. Ward, Thomas Norris, Captain Adams—someday all of them would feel her wrath, *her* power.

A knock on the door shattered the fantasy. Startled, disoriented, she tried to collect her thoughts.

Rising to her feet, she called awkwardly, "Who is it?"

"Edward Carrington."

Heart pounding, she crossed the room, unlocked and opened the door.

The man who stood before her was not what she had expected. She knew Edward Carrington to be a man of wealth and power, yet this man's clothing, although well made, in no way reflected an aristocratic background. His body was lean; his hair and eyes were brown; his face, although not handsome, was rather pleasant in spite of its somewhat stern expression of the moment. The man who stood a step or so behind him was fine indeed to look at, starkly handsome and of a heavier, more muscular, more powerful build than Edward Carrington. His was a face and body to remember, deliberately to call to mind when the face and body of a Lord Marlowe or Lord Williams, beside her in the night, became too personal, too real. Would they kill him, she wondered, when they killed Edward Carrington? How sad. Although her eyes met his for only an instant, the instant remained distractingly vivid in her mind.

Both men entered the room, the door closed and locked behind them by the second man. Her conclusion as to which of them was Edward Carrington found confirmation as the first man spoke. "I am Edward Carrington. I understand you wish to see me."

Carefully she answered, "I had hoped you might wish to see me." With a quick glance at James she added, "May I know your name, sir?"

"Robert Smith," James answered, with no effort to make the lie convincing.

"I see you do not trust me," said Isobel, her tone sad, weary. "Nor do I blame you. But in fairness, you must understand my mistrust of you. Had it not been for the letter, Mr. Shyrie would have killed me, with Dr. Ward's consent. Certainly I ran from the Allen brothers, for once you had the letter with my explanations of how I came by it, of what value would I be to you?"

James caught a quick, uncomfortable glance from Edward Carrington. Here, indeed, was confirmation of James' earlier speculations that Nat Shyrie—the raw violence of the man—was increasingly becoming a problem to Edward Carrington.

Isobel continued, unaware of any exchange between the two men. "I tell you I have no politics. I care not who finally gains possession of the letter—you or the British. I merely wish to stay alive and free. To that end I sought you out, for Jack Logan told me that you are an honorable man." Dryly she added, "I know too many who have placed their trust in British honor and justice and been betrayed."

"Then you place no trust in it?" said James.

Meeting his gaze directly, she felt unexpected color rise to her cheeks. How pleasant it would be to have him touch her. "No, sir," she answered quietly, "I place no trust in the British."

"But, Mistress Browne, we are all British. These colonies are British," said Carrington. "Certainly our duty to our king requires that we hand you over to the first group of soldiers we can find."

"What cruel games you play with me!" she answered shrilly. "Jack Logan said the letter would be valuable to you. He said you would offer me a fair price for it."

The communication between James Devant and Edward Carrington was subtle, a glance at most. What else had Jack Logan told her? Not that any of it would be too important if she could be trusted, but could she be trusted?

Suddenly, Isobel understood. Neither of these men was really Edward Carrington. They were British agents. It was all a trap, a test set by Lord Williams to discover what she would say once she believed herself in the hands of the rebels. Now Lord Williams would know she had lied, that the rebels were not really in possession of the letter. Now he would know she could not be trusted, that she had attempted to make a fool of him, the latter, no doubt, the more dangerous offense. Oh, how cleverly these men had played their roles, how convincing their apparent caution and suspicion. So convincing that she now saw no alternative but to confront them.

"And where is the letter now?" asked Carrington.

"As well you know, that is what I am here to discover," she snapped. "Lord Williams sent you, didn't he? He sent you to spy on me, to test my loyalty to him. I suppose if I were clever, I would play your game, but he breaks my heart with his distrust. And now please go. Go and tell him I beg his forgiveness if I have in any way offended him by tricking you, but if I am ever to prove that my only desire is to serve him and my king, I must do so freely, so that he may never again in his life have reason to doubt my loyalty." Her voice softening, she added the lie, a desperate attempt to cover what she considered her initial blunder, "You see, as I told his lordship, the rebel organization is already in possession of the letter. Were you really Edward Carrington, you would at least have appeared confused when I offered to sell to you that which you already have."

Now it was Isobel who found herself confused. Both men stared at her, the handsome one better than the other at concealing whatever his reaction might be, but both were obviously startled.

Of course, they were startled. They had been sent to trick her. No doubt Lord Williams would not take kindly to their failure. Gently, but quickly, she added, "I wish you no harm, gentlemen. You played your parts well, and I shall commend you both to his lordship when next I see him." She would be a fool to antagonize them, to let them suspect their own lives might be in danger.

They continued to watch her. Neither of them moved. Then, as though suddenly exhausted, the one who had called himself Edward Carrington slumped onto a chair in front of the fire and rested his forehead against his right hand. The other man leaned against one of the bedposts, his stark blue eyes never leaving Isobel.

"But why do you—" She broke off. A new truth began

to suggest itself, like smoke or fog or the far-distant glow of a lone candle. Still, she could not be sure. *"Who are you?"* she demanded, voice trembling.

Edward Carrington stretched his legs, head back, both arms now resting on the chair arms, his hands relaxed, tired. Quietly, wearily, he answered, "I am Edward Carrington."

Without changing position, the second man said, "I am James Devant."

CHAPTER FOURTEEN

Her mouth went dry. Here was truth. The final truth. "No," she whispered. Frantically she looked at the door. She could never reach it. "*No,*" she cried. "I lied. I thought you were spies. I had to pretend I would not betray Lord Williams—" She broke off. Obviously neither of them believed her in the slightest.

Quietly James spoke to her, "You say Mr. Carrington has the letter—"

"No. He doesn't. I have it. I mean, I know where it is. I told Lord Williams the rebels had it, that it was either here at the inn or on its way and that I would try to find it. I told him this because I wanted to come here. I wanted to meet Mr. Carrington. I don't want to deal with the British. I don't trust them."

"You know where the letter is?" asked Carrington. "Then prove your good faith by telling us."

"And if I tell you? Then what?"

"What do you want?" asked James.

"France! I cannot remain in these colonies, nor can I return to England."

Carefully, James answered, "You could return to England if Lord Williams arranged a pardon for you."

She shook her head. A pretty head indeed, James had to admit.

"Lord Williams has no such power," she said.

This time James knew without question she was lying, for James had seen one of the pardons Lord Williams carried with him, signed by the king's own hand with a blank space for the name of the potential recipient. If Lord Williams had offered one to James merely to find her, surely the girl herself would have been offered one in exchange for the letter. Perhaps she had already given him the letter. Or—no. Probably not. When she believed herself in the presence of spies, the story she gave was probably the same story she had given Lord Williams. His head reeled from the confusion of her lies. Indeed, she had no politics. "Did you come here to the inn alone?" he asked.

She hesitated. "I—"

"Seems unlikely Lord Williams would permit you to travel alone," added Carrington.

Quietly she answered, "There is a British officer with me."

Yes, James thought, she would have to be killed. Quickly. To delay even a day could be dangerous. As easily as she had betrayed her officer, so also would she betray James and Edward, so also would she betray every other face and name she had known from the moment she walked out of Newgate Prison with Jack Logan. The letter was secondary. If they were unable to obtain it, the loss would be unfortunate but a misfortune Edward Carrington would have to accept. Odd. Initially James had found her attractive. Now, however, as he looked at her, a peculiar vision came into his mind: a vision of Isobel Browne decked in silk, satin, velvet and jewels, standing high on a pile of corpses, the stench of death blowing over the seas, all the way back to England. Back to the man she was reported to have murdered in England. Back to the ship on which the captain, Jack Logan and Ira all had died. Odd, how death seemed to follow her.

"And where is this officer?" asked Carrington.

How much had she already told the British? James wondered. Information the British dare not act upon as long as they believed her to be working her way into the confidence of a man like Edward Carrington, for to act would destroy that confidence. Time! A slight reprieve. Time to warn at least some of the people she had had contact with in Carrington's network.

She glanced toward the door, then aburptly shook her head. "I don't know."

"On this floor? A guest at the inn?" asked Carrington.

"No!"

"Mistress Browne, it appears that you are frightened of us," said James. "Allow me to explain. We shall kill the officer who accompanied you, and it shall be known you betrayed him."

Edward Carrington, James sensed rather than saw by any noticeable physical change, was startled, perhaps even indignant at what appeared to be James' somewhat stark usurpation of Carrington's authority, but apparently Isobel Browne was unaware of any byplay between the two men. Her eyes remained fixed on James Devant. James continued. "Once it is known you betrayed him, you cannot return to the British. You will have no choice but to work with us. But you must prove your good faith. You must give us the letter and relate to us everything you told Lord Williams of our activities."

She searched his eyes. Dare she believe him, trust him? No! If she betrayed any man as powerful as Lord Williams, where on this earth could she be safe? Surely not with these madmen. James Devant—a smuggler, a fugitive from his majesty's justice—no different, really, from Jack Logan or Nathaniel Shyrie. Merely handsomer, she concluded. As though it mattered! Handsome, intelligent, polished—as polished as a marble tombstone.

"We await your decision," announced Edward Carrington. His words supported James, told James he now understood and approved of the path James had chosen.

Calmly Isobel answered, "I must think." She seated herself by the tea table, hands folded tightly in front of her, her head lowered. No, she dare not cast her lot with these gallows-bait cutthroat outlaws. Her only real hope—no matter how slim—lay with Lord Williams, but now she must get back to him and give him the letter.

All right, give these men one of the officers. Gain their trust, at least enough to enable her to break from them and return to Lord Williams. Surely when she herself did return, Lord Williams would have no reason to believe that anything other than fate or his own incompetence had cost the officer his life. Later she would devise a story for Lord Williams to account for the letter's whereabouts in the Finch house.

But the two officers shared a room. To give one without the other would only further brand her a liar, for surely the fact that there were two would be obvious from the room—food for two, clothing for two. No, she must betray both. She must appear to be *completely* honest.

Quietly, avoiding Edward Carrington's eyes, she spoke. "There are two officers." She named and described both, concluding with: "They are lodged two rooms down the hall from this room."

Edward Carrington rose to his feet. "Kindly remain with Mistress Browne," he said to James, "while I summon someone to replace you. Then you and I shall investigate further the presence of these officers."

James nodded. The door barely closed and locked behind Edward Carrington, Isobel sprang to her feet. "Please, sir," she said, "help me. I am afraid."

"In what way might I be of assistance to you?" asked James. What foolish tricks she played. Somehow he had expected better of her.

"Even before I left England, your name became known to me. You are a smuggler, like Mr. Shyrie, like Mr. Logan. Surely if they knew Mr. Carrington was not to be trusted, you know it. I cannot believe you really trust him, work for him."

Playing the game, James answered, "Mr. Carrington is not to be trusted?"

"He wants control of your ships and men."

A logical assumption, James concluded. Indeed, she had learned much during her brief stay in the colonies.

"Once he has it," she continued, "of what further use to him are you? You are known as a man without politics. As such, as long as you live, Mr. Carrington shall know you could just as quickly turn against him should whatever currents now bring you together grow apart. I beg you, help me. Find a place where I may hide, safe from both the British and Mr. Carrington, then help me gain passage to France."

The woman was incredible. Was this how she had bewitched Jack Logan? Perhaps James had been unfair in his judgment of Logan, unfair to have laughed at him. "I see," he said, "but you neglect to tell me *why* I should do as you ask."

Lowering her head, she answered softly, "I know a man as handsome as yourself could not want for . . . the companionship of ladies, but there are others who do. Powerful men, in France. I could help you, build influence for you. Influence with men who could help you when Carrington turns on you or you are forced to turn on him." Tentatively she stepped closer to him, her lips only a whisper from his. "And I would be there anytime you might deign to honor me with your presence."

Remembering that he had entered the room unarmed, so it was not weapons she sought, he availed himself of her kiss, the pleasure of her mouth and body flooding his senses.

At last, he drew back from her. "Ah, Mistress Browne," he said, "if only time and circumstances permitted."

"But they can. Another time. Another place."

Dropping all contact with her, he stepped back, leaned against the wall and continued to look at her. "*Non,*" he said. "*Mais, dites-moi, pourquoi choisiriez-vous la France?*"

In answer to her obvious confusion, he went on. "I asked you why you chose France. For how could you truly expect to gain such influence in a country *where you neither speak nor understand the language*? No, Mistress Browne. It is not France you desire. Rather, I believe it is England, with a full pardon from Lord Williams. All you would really have of me is safe passage from this inn to a hiding place from which you could easily make your way back to the British."

"But how could I? You yourself said if I betrayed the soldiers—"

"Ah, but Mistress Browne, I did not know you then. Your 'resourcefulness' continues to amaze me." Without thought, now as he stood apart from her, he wiped his mouth with the back of his hand as though he might cleanse himself of her kiss, an act not unnoticed by Isobel. James would not kill her. That would be Carrington's job—or, rather, a job Carrington would probably assign, but with great care. No mistakes could be tolerated.

Her eyes spat fire at him. And fear. How he longed to be free of her, to forget her, to forget the touch of her lips, and somehow he knew he never would. Never before had he been party to the death of a woman or any person as defenseless as Isobel Browne. But perhaps it would not be necessary to kill her.

An idle dream. As long as Isobel Browne lived, every member of Carrington's organization she had ever seen or heard mentioned, man, woman and child, would live in mortal danger.

"I'll tell you where the letter is," she said.

Believing none of it, James answered, "Where is the letter?"

"In hell," she spat. "May God send you there soon to find it."

The door opened. Edward Carrington stood beside the young blond man who had earlier accompanied him to James' room.

Without a word to Isobel, James walked to the door and spoke softly to Carrington. "Have you not two men you could spare?"

Initially surprised, then with irritation, Carrington answered, "She is but one small woman, and unarmed."

Risking more of Carrington's displeasure, James persisted, "I tell you, her tongue is a weapon to be reckoned with. I implore you, at least allow her to be bound and gagged."

The blond man, his face disturbingly young and innocent, awaited Carrington's decision. Unlike James, this man was armed.

"Very well," snapped Carrington. To the younger man, he said, "Use your knife, and cut the sheets to meet your needs."

His hand already on his knife, he stepped into the room, closed and bolted the door behind him. If Carrington gave any of it a second thought, the thought was interrupted by footsteps. Olanthia, accompanied by Garth and two other men, one in his early twenties, the other considerably older, came into view. Addressing himself primarily to the older man, Carrington kept his voice to barely more than a whisper. "I want them disarmed and held. It might well be to our advantage to release them later. The fact that we know who they are will prove she betrayed them. Let them carry word back that she is now on our side. Then she cannot return to the British. She shall have no choice but to deal with us, give us the letter."

Yes, James concluded, Edward Carrington continued to underestimate Isobel Browne. Yet to pursue the subject and thus incur more of Carrington's anger seemed unwise. His agreement that she be bound was doubtless the best James could presently hope for. But, damn it, James' life would also be in danger should her witchcraft succeed on that boy.

Masking his concern, hoping it would prove to be ungrounded, James walked with Garth, Olanthia and the two other men Carrington had spoken to a moment ago to the room where Isobel had informed them the officers were lodged. In response to Carrington's signal, Olanthia knocked.

No answer.

Again she knocked. This time she spoke. "Gentlemen, is someone below to see you."

Inside the room the bolt slid back, and a male voice answered, "Come in."

A quick look passed between James and Edward. The occupants of the room were suspicious. Initially no one had answered, and the door remained unopen.

The entire group of men accompanying Edward Carrington stepped quickly to the side, although not completely out of view should anyone in the room look into the hallway. Each knew he would have to see into the room, quickly; that of necessity carried the danger of being seen. Those who were armed drew weapons, pistols and knives.

Olanthia opened the door. Eyes suddenly wide with terror, she screamed and threw herself against the wall, within the room, her balance gone, her knees and hands now her only support. Captain Adams faced the open door, his weight evenly balanced on each foot, a gun in each hand with a third gun in his belt. The first shot narrowly missed Edward Carrington, hitting the man behind him. The second shot went wild as both Carrington and the younger man he had brought fired almost simultaneously at Captain Adams. Spasmodically the captain's body jerked and twisted; his hands finally lodged over his heart as he fell to the floor, still writhing; a pain-racked guttural scream was cut short as the body stopped, grew still.

Stunned, the entire group merely stared at him. Had he known? James wondered. No, probably it had been a strong suspicion that Isobel had betrayed him, a suspicion formed long before Olanthia knocked on his door. James looked at Edward Carrington. The man appeared ill, his attention now fixed with an unnatural intensity on the pistol still in his hand. Apparently to kill, even when essential, was not to Edward Carrington's taste.

Garth was first to move. With one heavy protective arm he encircled Olanthia's waist, lifted her to her feet and led her from the area. Tentatively someone opened a door across the hall, while the door to the right of the room where Captain Adams lay was also opened. As though suddenly awakened from a dream, Edward Carrington spoke a few soft words to those who had appeared. The doors closed again.

Now it would become widely known, James thought. The Twin Stallion Inn, once safe for smugglers and law-abiding citizens alike, regardless of any guest's politics, was no longer a haven for anyone.

How stupidly the man had died, thought James. Had he used his wits, who could say whether or not he might eventually have been set free to return to Lord Williams? Or had he perhaps chosen to die like this, quickly, rather than face, at worst, a death selected by Edward Carrington or, at best, the rage of Lord Williams, who assuredly would hold Captain Adams, not Isobel Browne, responsible for the failure of the project. To hold Isobel responsible would be to admit she had made a fool of him. Far better, safer for his own prestige, to blame the British officer he had sent to watch her. Or perhaps the poor fool, not knowing what was on the other side of that door, had actually intended to try to shoot his way to freedom.

Carrington spoke to Olanthia, still held by Garth on the fringes of the group. Referring to the man whose shoulder had been hit by Captain Adams' first shot, he said, "See to his wounds."

James stepped into the room, checked through it quickly, then returned to Carrington's side. "The wardrobe contains two coats," he said.

The message was clear. The second officer would not have left the inn without his coat. He was probably below at this moment.

"I'd best return to my room," said James quietly. "We would have the British believe me dead. Already too many people have seen me."

Carrington nodded.

Wordlessly Garth followed James up the stairs to the tower room.

With the door closed behind them, Garth reached under his coat, produced James' pistol and presented it to him. The familiar well-worn ornamented silver handle was warm from the heat of Garth's body, sensually pleasant to the touch. James tightened his hand, checked to make sure both barrels were loaded, then tested the spring bayonet.

"Widow Taylor give it to me," said Garth. "She say you lose it the night British take you. She say you come back for it."

James smiled. Alma Taylor's faith in James' abilities to survive surpassed his own.

"Do you wish to come to France with me?" James asked Garth.

"You want me to come?"

"Might be safer for you than to stay here. Yes."

"I will come," Garth answered.

The fire had burned down to faintly glowing embers, and all five candles were low; the sixth was burned out. James placed another log in the fireplace, then seated himself on the wooden bench in front of it and hoped enough heat remained in the embers to ignite the log. A chill swept over his body, yet somehow the familiarity of the room and Garth's presence virtually eliminated the importance of any physical discomfort. The man downstairs was dead, and James was alive, miraculously alive and free. He closed his eyes as Garth joined him on the bench.

"Mrs. Carrington still want to see you," said Garth.

"Mrs. Carrington," James said out loud, his tone disclosing little emotion. *Sarah,* he thought. Why did even the sound of her name hold such power over him? Could it be because *loving friends* were so rare these days, memories—people—to be cherished so few and far between? "What does she want?"

"She wants help. Mob go all around her house last night, break windows with rocks. Set fire, little fire, not last long. Carrington think she is British spy. She want to leave New Hereford, but Carrington not let her go, not give her a pass. He think she knows too much, think husband told her much before he died. British not help her. Not trust her. Some officer claim she tell him she works for rebels. Only one servant stay. Irish girl named Mary. Mary have a brother once worked for you, get killed by British."

Stunned, James answered, "What about the child?"

"Child stay with Preacher Howgate. Safer there. Maybe."

His voice loud, James sprang to his feet. "Edward Carrington! I'll *kill* him!"

The words barely out, Garth grabbed him, one hand clamped over his mouth, the other arm confining his arms behind his back. "I think you go crazier than mob!"

Slowly James allowed his body to relax. Garth released him.

"How could the child be safer with Howgate?" James persisted. "How could Carrington leave either of them like that? The boy is his brother's child, his own flesh."

"He help now, maybe people start figure *he* work for the British. Not be able to help anyone."

"Ah, yes," James answered, more in control of himself now. There was truth in Garth's words, a truth Edward Carrington would certainly see. No wonder the man had aged so drastically. Carrington was too intelligent, too sensitive to the currents around him, saw too much of the future too clearly and was already trapped by it. If—no, *when*—war came to the American colonies, it would not be merely a war between British soldiers and American colonists, for among the colonists divided political persuasions, as in the Carrington family, would set brother against brother and father against son in a nightmare of torn loyalties and blood.

"Where does she want to go?" James asked.

"Mary say Mr. Carrington's father have friends at court. Mrs. Carrington be safe in New York with husband's father or in England."

"England," James mused. "Much safer in England."

"You help her, Carrington kill you," Garth stated flatly.

"Probably. If he finds out."

"You mean it. You go to her, you help. *Why*?"

To his own amazement James answered, "I love her. I've always loved her."

As Garth's amazement began to subside, it came dangerously close to laughter. James Devant? *Love*? Forcing a more serious mood, Garth answered, "Countryside no longer safe. A few soldiers still here, and Shyrie's men and Carrington's spies. We go together."

"Then you're a bigger fool than I am," said James, unable to express his gratitude by any more than the look accompanying the statement.

"We'll need pass from Carrington. What reason you give?"

"No reason. I shall merely tell him we need a pass."

Someone pounded on the door.

With no outward show of communication between them, both men responded to the sound, their pistols drawn and ready.

James answered, "Who's there?"

"Mr. Carrington want to see you," answered a voice immediately recognizable as Olanthia's. "Now."

Keeping well to the side, James unbolted the door and opened it. Yes, it was Olanthia, and she was alone.

"What does he want?" asked James.

"He no say. Lady you talk to earlier. Come now."

Isobel Browne, thought James. Uneasily he relaxed his weapon and, with Garth behind him, followed Olanthia down the stairs. From the hallway, outside the room where he had last seen her, he heard voices within the room. Male voices.

In response to his knock one of the voices answered, "Who is it?"

"James Devant."

A bolt slid back. The door opened. James and Garth started to enter, but both, almost simultaneously, stopped short. The window was open, the room icy cold in spite of the still-crackling fire. Stunned, James stared at the floor. The blond man Carrington had left to guard Isobel Browne lay there, his shirt drenched with the blood of numerous knife wounds, including a slit throat. The knife itself now protruded from his belly. His own knife, the one James had noticed when the man had first entered the tower room with Carrington.

James turned away, in anger as much as in repugnancy. Quietly he asked, "Where is the second officer?"

"We have him," answered Carrington. "He's unharmed. We're holding him in a room down the hall."

"And where," James continued, lips tight, "is Mistress Browne?"

Angrily, perhaps even bitterly, Edward Carrington answered, "I don't know. She's gone."

CHAPTER FIFTEEN

"Food," said Sarah, her voice firm. "Money, jewels, two blankets, a pistol and a knife. Nothing more."

Mary did not answer.

"Come back tomorrow," Sarah added awkwardly, looking about the kitchen, her face drawn and strangely hard in the dim candle glow. "Take the rest of the food for yourself."

Tears flooded Mary's eyes.

"None of that!" snapped Sarah, her voice tremulous. "I'm as frightened as you are."

"I don't trust Robert!" Mary answered. "You'll reach the coast and find there is no boat. Or worse, he'll have told others where you'll be, alone with little Charles and unprotected. They'll take everything you have, even your clothing, and leave you there to die!"

"I *have* to trust Robert," she shot back. Then, as much to convince herself as Mary, she added, "He is being well paid, but only a third in advance. He will receive the balance from the hands of my father-in-law when we reach New York. You say he desperately needs money. He'd be a fool not to take me there safely." Abruptly her tone became almost a plea for reassurance. "Mary, it was you who suggested I talk to him."

"But I told you at the time I wasn't sure he could be trusted. I know my brother trusted him. I know he needs money, and he genuinely cared for my brother—but is that enough? Is need of money and loyalty to the dead enough to make him keep his word to me? Mrs. Carrington, he believes you to be a loyalist spy."

"But you said he had no politics."

"That was before—back when they all worked for James Devant. Now it's hard to say. So many have chosen sides, because they've had to. Robert would never choose the loyalist side."

Quietly, almost wearily, yet in a voice which still seemed as though it might crack, Sarah answered, "Mary, which of us can honestly say we really know anyone anymore? I agree, I cannot argue with you. I don't know if I trust Robert, but what choice do I have? I need a boat and a man's strong arms to row that boat across the sound. I need horses on the Long Island shore to take us to the city of New York, to my father-in-law's house, to safety. I've not the strength, nor do I know the right people to manage without the help of someone like Robert. Yes, perhaps Robert will betray me. But perhaps he will not. *Perhaps he will not.* Mary, what else do I have? What other source of hope?"

Briefly, wordlessly, the two women looked at each other. It was Sarah who finally lowered her eyes. "Mary, you may leave now if you wish. I can go alone."

"To your uncle's house to pick up young Charles, then to the shore to meet Robert? Alone? At this hour? I'll not hear of it."

Quietly, fighting tears born of gratitude too deep to express, Sarah answered, "I'm not noble enough, not brave or strong enough to order you to leave me. I'm not the same person I was even six months ago. I've grown hard, Mary. And selfish."

"Selfish? To value the safety of your child?"

"It's not merely young Charles. It's myself also. To remain here, to suffer the Lord only knows what additional indignities—or worse—to what purpose? There are times when I think—" She broke off.

"What?" insisted Mary.

"I think either that I have gone mad to think such a thing or that I am right, which would mean my uncle has gone mad. I sometimes think some part of him would see young Charles and me slaughtered by drunken rebels, that we might be made martyrs. Martyrs on which a petition to the king to send additional troops into this area could be based."

"Then, indeed, it would be of value to those who defy the king to help you to safety."

"Why? Surely British troops—an army—will be sent eventually, whether or not my son and I live or die. It is only Uncle Ezra's madness that would make our deaths so important. Or have I gone mad to suspect him of such thoughts?"

Quietly Mary answered, "I don't know. I know that in some of his sermons he so attacks those who defy the king that he enrages them. Now that you speak of it—at times, one might suspect he seeks for himself the martyrdom you describe. I—I think you do well to take Charles from his household. It is not the real"—this time she slipped; in lieu of "those who defy the king," she used her own words, carelessly—"real patriots I fear. Rather, I fear those who for their own evil pleasure would harm others and now feel free to do so in the name of a cause—

any cause. At least for Robert Pollard, I can say he is not one of these."

"Robert," repeated Sarah, jolted by the mention of his name back to the immediacy of the situation. "We must go. Now."

The weight of most of her jewels sewed into her petticoats and the lining of her gray wool riding cape made both garments uncomfortable, disturbed her overall balance with each movement, tauted her already frayed nerves. First donning her gloves, she lifted the small sack containing bread, cheese and wine. Her weighted cape and colorful homespun wool dress gave no trace of her class. To the casual observer, from a distance she and Mary might well have been sisters.

A low fire still warmed the fireplace, and two candles in tin reflectors burned brightly. Although the kitchen was by no means the most familiar part of the house to Sarah, suddenly her love for the rest of the house seemed to spill into the kitchen with an intensity that frightened her. Mary lifted the blankets but made no other move as Sarah remained by the kitchen table.

"I've forgotten something," said Sarah, her voice somewhat dazed. "Something important."

Mary waited, frowned, tried to think what it might be.

It was something small, Sarah was sure. Some vitally important object small enough to hold in her hand, something she dared not leave behind. Her thoughts darted about—the buried gold, silver and glassware; the paintings carefully removed from their frames and hidden, not too well if anyone really searched for them, their frames now conspicuously empty lying about the house, not worth the energy it would have required to return them to the walls. She thought of her clothing, dresses steeped in memories of special occasions. She thought of her children, especially the one girl who had lived to the age of four, a golden-haired dream child running into the house with flowers freshly plucked from the garden. But what was the object, the one special, almost-sacred object? Could it be the christening dress worn by her first child, also a girl, dead now these many years? Or the one worn by Charles? Perhaps that was what she needed, to use for the child within her. Perhaps, with the same christening gown, this child, like Charles, would live.

Then, slowly—no, she realized, it was not any one special object. It was the house itself. Not the material building or any of its treasures, although even the architecture of the house so reflected the love and craftsmanship of its designers, that a stranger could not walk through without sensing at least a little of that love. But to Sarah, far more than the house itself, she longed for, dreaded leaving behind what the house had once represented: the eternal childhood of her marriage to Charles. Until very recently there had always been someone else to think for her, care for her, define the standards by which she was to attempt to live. First her parents, dead within months of each other, then Uncle Ezra and his wife, then Charles. Oh, not that she had never tested the reins which held her—her Whig politics in a family so strongly Tory, her meek argument with Charles as to the wisdom of returning to New Hereford in the face of Edward's warnings—but always she had given in, not through fear but, rather, through a sense of duty. Duty, as interpreted by family and, ultimately, by God, as defined and presented by Uncle Ezra.

Uncle Ezra! No. God and Uncle Ezra no longer blurred together in her mind. She did not understand God, but now, perhaps for the first time, she fully, consciously doubted whether Uncle Ezra had ever really understood God either.

A sense of duty. Duty indeed! What a coward she was.

Even now the question frightened her. Was it really duty she had surrendered to these many years, or *was* it fear? Fear of God's wrath. Now, so many years later, yet as clearly as though it were only yesterday, she remembered; tearfully she had begged Ezra to explain why God had taken all but one of her children. Her uncle had indeed explained. God took her children because she was a sinner. Yet night after sleepless night, torturously racking her brain, she had remained unable to determine what sin she might have committed of such magnitude as to warrant the unendurable agony of children who died, one after the other, until now only little Charles, frail and frightened, remained part of this world, available to hold in her arms.

But God was love. The Bible and at times even Uncle Ezra said so. Perhaps that explained it. Perhaps love had taken her children to spare them some equally unendurable agony, something perhaps even far worse than anything Sarah had ever suffered or could even imagine.

No, she did not understand God. Perhaps in many ways she still feared Him, yet whatever else He might be, God was also love.

Her voice barely audible, she whispered, "Please—guide me. Help me."

"What?" asked Mary.

Startled, Sarah answered quickly, awkwardly, "Nothing." Then, quietly, more to herself than to Mary, this time with no trace of awkwardness, she added, "There is nothing else in this house I need."

Don't look back, she thought, as they left by the servants' entrance and mounted the horses Mary had brought to the tethering rail perhaps an hour earlier.

The night air was cold, but Sarah had known worse cold. Odd, as both horses picked up speed, a sudden sense of youth and strength and health surged through her. There had been times—moments, admittedly few and far between, but nonetheless moments—when life had seemed filled with joy and love. There would be such moments again, she was sure. The child within her—how silly; she knew it was too soon for it to kick, yet somehow she was almost sure she could feel its heartbeat.

They took the shortcut, through scattered trees, then through a progressively more thickly wooded area which edged the left side of the Carrington estate. Soon they would reach the point where the shortcut met the main road, which eventually would take them to the Reverend Howgate's less impressive dwelling.

Suddenly, her heart pounding, Sarah drew rein, promptly followed by Mary. There, several feet ahead of them in a still-wooded area by a small stream several yards shy of where the main road met the shortcut, a solitary figure mounted on horseback blocked their path. It was a man, wearing a tricorn hat and heavy coat, his features made indistinguishable by shadows and distance. As Mary and Sarah waited, the rest of the woods seemed to come alive with the rustling of branches and horses' hooves. Maintaining her horse at a standstill, Sarah turned in the saddle and realized they were surrounded by six, perhaps seven men. Local residents probably. At least they were not British soldiers. Nor, at a glance, did they appear to be drunk.

In a voice which surprised her for its strength and steadiness, so foreign to the fear she felt, Sarah called, "Who are you? What do you want?" Subtly, with her left hand, she repositioned the folds of her riding cape and skirt in front of her. In her right hand, carefully concealed, she held the loaded pistol, aimed at the figure in front of her. Of course, if she used it, they would probably kill her. And yet did they intend to kill her anyway? Would the child whose christening clothes she had been so concerned about a few moments ago thus never even be born? The entire situation seemed unreal, almost absurd. The April night was too clear and crisp, the gently rippling moonlit stream too beautiful. Could she actually squeeze the trigger she held so tightly and take with her and her unborn child the life of a third human being? What perplexed her even more than the question was the fact that she had no answer. Who, indeed, could say they really knew anyone these days—even themselves?

"I am Robert Pollard," came the prompt, steady answer.

"Robert!" gasped Mary.

Addressing himself to Sarah, he continued, "We assumed you would take this route. It's faster and over less clear ground than the main road from the house. I am here to return the payment you gave me to take you to New York."

"How could you?" cried Mary, driving her horse forward. "You betrayed us! If my brother were alive, he would kill you!"

"If your brother were alive," he shot back at her, bringing his own horse closer to where Sarah remained, "he'd thank me, and well he should! More than once he begged me to care for you should he die, and I swore I would."

"I told you I'd return to Ireland as soon as Mrs. Carrington was safe in New York."

"Safe in New York!" spat Robert. "Aye! Safe in the hands of a dead man who was to pay me the balance of the agreed sum for taking her to him. Except that I'd never have arrived. It was a trap. We'd have been met by a delegation from Fort Franklin as soon as we touched land on the other side of the Sound."

Confused, Sarah asked, "Dead man?"

"Stop your games, Mrs. Carrington. I'm not the trusting child Mary is. Your father-in-law died five days ago. While you were bargaining with me, the man you said was to pay me was dead." Almost painfully he continued, addressing himself to Mary. "I wanted you to see how wrong you've been, how she's tricked you, used you. It's from you she learned my name. I work for Edward Carrington now. There's much I know and much the British would give to have me prisoner."

With eyes unable fully to assimilate the images before her, Sarah Carrington remained on her horse, as though suddenly turned to stone. Joseph Carrington dead? The words refused to come together into a coherent meaning. They became peculiar syllables, part of some odd, unknown language. If her father-in-law were dead, then, indeed she and young Charles would be anything but safe in New York. As though through a dense fog, she sensed Mary staring at her, the young girl's eyes pained, confused and questioning.

The other men who encircled them had drawn in closer, tighter.

"What did you tell her about James Devant?" Robert continued, still speaking to Mary. "Did you tell her they'd taken him prisoner? Because the British didn't know they had him, didn't know who he was. But they found out. And they killed him."

A chill ran through Sarah, icy and oddly terrifying. Her eyes stung. Some part of her soul registered the physical reaction and passed along to her mind the cold mechanical fact that her eyes stung because they were flooded with tears. James Devant was dead, definitely, without question. Was this her great sin and the ultimate punishment for it? She had loved James Devant, first tenderly, with a child's love, then, in later years, in dreams and memory, with a woman's love. She had written to him once, shortly after he left New Hereford to live in Boston—a letter she never posted for lack of courage. Rather, alone one evening in her bedroom at Uncle Ezra's house, she had thrown it into the fire, her heart pounding, hands trembling as first the edges turned brown and curled, then flame shot through the middle, momentarily illuminating the semidark room with a glow she still remembered. Yet had it really been James she loved? Or was it merely the fantasies she had woven about him in her mind? James Devant, the man, the adult—had she ever really known him? Could such things really happen—love—over time and distance and change, as surely both of them had changed. How much better had she never seen him again, never felt the quickened pace of her heart at the mere sight of him, the mere sound of his voice.

You know me, he had said to her that night at the Twin Stallion Inn. *You've always known me.*

Had she gone mad, she wondered, even to ask the question, yet the question remained, cruel and haunting—was he right? Did she know him, then, now—and forever? Know and love him, even unto, even after death.

To Mary, voice trembling, she said, "I had nothing to do with his death."

"You wanted to see him," said Mary accusingly. "You wanted him to come to you. To trap him?"

"I wanted his help," she answered shrilly. "Because I trusted him."

"And why should the likes of you trust James Devant?" demanded Robert. Without waiting for an answer, he went on, addressing himself again to Mary. "Don't you see what a fool she's made of you? If we'd known how much she was getting out of you, we'd have taken you away from her days ago, but it was only yesterday we learned he was dead. And don't fool yourself it was an easy death. The man could have had us all hanged if he'd told even half what he knew, but he didn't. We know he didn't because none of us has been arrested. He was made out of steel, that one. It was probably a blessing when they finally killed him. They took him down to the shore. Said he was trying to escape. But nobody escapes from Fort Franklin, and nobody who tries makes it as far as the shore."

Nausea rose in the pit of Sarah's belly. Why had he seemed so invulnerable to her? Made of steel. Yes. Steel could not be tortured, then slaughtered. "Mary, I swear to you—"

"No," Mary interrupted. "No, don't say it. Because I don't know what to believe. Not anymore."

His voice gentle, one of the other men in the group addressed Mary. "Is the house empty? Come, girl. We'll fetch your belongings. You can go home now. To Ireland."

Her voice tight, yet steady, Sarah addressed Robert. "And what now? On the basis of these 'facts' you present, are you to become my judge and executioner?"

"No!" cried Mary, her eyes meeting the eyes of every man in the group. Their reactions ranged from tight-lipped silence to obvious eye-averting discomfort. Addressing herself specifically to Robert, Mary said, "Give me your word she'll not be harmed."

Quietly Robert answered, "I cannot."

"Then give me your word *you'll* not harm her."

He hesitated.

"Do so, and I'll go with you." Pleading, she continued. "Do so because I ask you as I would ask my brother. My brother would not deny me."

The men exchanged glances.

"You still trust her, believe her," said Robert, only a hint of a question in his tone, his patience with her obviously growing short.

Mary shook her head. "I don't know. I'm not sure. I only know you promised to help her to safety this night."

"I promised to deliver her to a man she knew was dead!"

"I did *not* know!" cut in Sarah.

"Promise you'll not harm her this night!" insisted Mary. "All of you. Promise me."

Slowly, hesitantly, finally begrudgingly, the men nodded.

Tiredly Robert answered, "We will escort her back to her house."

To be slaughtered at daybreak, thought Sarah. "I would be with my son," she said. "He is at Mr. Howgate's house."

This time with anger, Robert answered, "Very well. I shall accompany you to Mr. Howgate's house. Mary, go with Brian."

Facing Robert, Mary answered stubbornly, "I shall ride with you. We can return for my belongings later."

"Might I impose on your kindness for one further service?" Sarah said to Robert, a discernible edge to her voice. "Would you be good enough to tell Edward Carrington I would like to see him?"

Obviously surprised, then wary, Robert asked, "To what purpose?"

A natural question, Sarah conceded. She was condemned by the forces to which Edward's life was now committed. Edward, now more than ever, would want no contact with her. Quietly she answered, "I would discuss with him the future of his nephew." Perhaps, for young Charles, at least, there was hope. Edward's wife, after numerous miscarriages, had finally died in childbirth, the child—a son—surviving her by only a few weeks. Although a distant branch of the Carrington family still lived in England, young Charles was the last of Joseph Carrington's line. Perhaps, even if Edward refused to see her, perhaps, God willing, he would at least take responsibility for the child's safety if—when—Sarah became unable to do so. As for the unborn child she carried—no, she would not tell Edward Carrington. She had not even told Mary. The child would not stop them from killing her. Knowledge that it had ever existed only to die helplessly as politics dictated the death of its mother would be an additional source of horror to Mary. To Edward—this man she had once loved as a brother—no, she would not add to his pain.

Robert's response was maddeningly noncommittal. Would he even deliver the message? She looked at Mary. Was it by chance or deliberate choice that this girl Sarah had grown to love and trust so deeply did not meet Sarah's gaze? They had succeeded in their efforts to confuse Mary, but at least they had not fully convinced her, and for that Sarah was grateful, not merely for Mary's help, but even more because of the affection and loyalty Sarah still felt toward and longed for from this very young, very decent girl, as torn and tortured by the times as Sarah.

"One further question, if I may," said Sarah, still addressing herself to Robert. "How did my father-in-law die?"

In deference to Mary, obviously believing Sarah already knew, Robert answered, "It is said his heart gave out."

Sarah nodded. Her father-in-law had been a gentle man, a good man. A quick, relatively painless death, she hoped.

Slowly at first, robbed now of her earlier sense of youth

and hope and promise, Sarah adapted the pace of her horse to Mary's and the horses of their newly acquired escorts. Unnoticed by Robert, she slipped the pistol back into the sack with the food.

With a poker, Garth rummaged through the still-hot ashes in the fireplace of Sarah Carrington's kitchen, raising an occasional spark, but primarily only ashes remained. He rose from his haunches, returned the poker to its proper place on the wide hearth, then faced James. Three candles now burned, two lit by James, the third now a tiny, flickering stub in a tin reflector left burning by whoever had occupied the kitchen prior to James' and Garth's arrival.

"Hard to know," said James, looking at the fireplace. "Might have been blazing when she left or may have been just about gone." Angrily he swung around and pounded on the table which supported two of the three candles. "She may well be dead by now. Taken by force. Who even knows which side? Could have been the British, could have been rebels."

"Carrington kill brother's wife?"

"No," James answered sharply, "but he wouldn't stop it. He couldn't. But maybe she's still here. Hiding." Loudly he called her name. "*Sarah!*"

"You already call her. Every room in house," said Garth.

"I don't *feel* she's dead," said James. "Does that make sense?"

Garth shrugged. "Man in love not want to believe his woman dead."

"Love," spat James, surprised by the sharpness of his voice. "In love with what? The memory of a child freshly arrived from England, still a child to have ever returned to New Hereford, naïve, smothered by that Tory family of hers, blindly loyal to that pompous power-mad German who sits on the throne of England and would reduce these colonies to vassalage."

"How long you look for her?"

Defeatedly, James answered, "Until I find her, or—" He left the sentence unfinished. Until he became *unable* to continue.

He started for the door, the servants' entrance.

Abruptly Garth held up his hand for silence.

James listened. Difficult to be sure. Horses? Perhaps Sarah, returning. But perhaps not.

Quickly both men left the house, mounted their horses and rode for the woods. Under cover of the trees, near the top of a slight rise in the land, they drew rein and waited, the house now far ahead of them, a mass of shadowed geometric planes in the moonlight.

The other riders arrived—perhaps a dozen. Although no words were distinguishable, the wind carried traces of voices which must have been loud. More sounds. Shattered glass? Then torches. Unmistakably torches, not candles, had been lit.

"Madmen!" spat James. "They play at terror and killing. At least, wherever she may be, she is not in that house."

"Rebels?" asked Garth.

"Could be either side. Probably drunk." Then, dryly, James added, "No longer 'rebels,' Garth. Patriots. We are patriots. Remember it."

There in the cold twisted shadows of moonlight through barren trees, Garth smiled. It was James, not Garth, who understood the white man's politics. "Patriots," echoed Garth.

"I'm going to take a chance," said James quietly. "The

way her house was left—much that was of value was gone, yet much still remained and the house itself was reasonably orderly. Not the work of looters, I think. Rather, it seems more as though her departure may have been planned. If so, I'd wager much her plans include her son. You say he is with Mr. Howgate."

"You go there, British know you are alive."

"They'll know anyway, unless Carrington's managed to stop Isobel Browne. I don't think he can. She's probably picked up help by now. All she'd need is to find one British soldier and identify herself."

"Preacher Howgate kill you."

"I'm sure he'd like to," James answered.

"And if Mrs. Carrington not there?"

"I'll speak to the child—if I can. If he's there. If not—well, the house is on the same road as the Oliver farm. As good a place as any to start the word that I am alive and we meet Thursday night at the Stanton farm."

Although he knew he must go now, still, almost compulsively, he paused for one last look at the Carrington house. A torch arced through the air and disappeared, probably into an already-broken window since no sound of shattering glass accompanied the sight. The muscles in his belly tightened. This, he knew, was only the beginning. Yes, there would be war—ugly, violent and cruel. Odd, even though James intended to be in France, he hoped Edward Carrington's side would win. With images of the Fort Franklin prison and Lord Walter Williams still disturbingly clear in his mind, he realized he cared a great deal.

Even though the wind tended to carry sound toward rather than away from them, both men slowly, as noiselessly as possible, turned their horses and started in the direction of the Reverend Howgate's house.

"The *North Star* should be in sometime soon," said James. "She carries mainly gunpowder."

"I know," Garth answered. "Only maybe one-third your men—maybe less—want unload her."

James frowned. "Why so few?"

"Some fight with each other. Some afraid. I talk to those you know longest, but nobody really able to get them to work together, lead them. Many think you dead."

Not really convinced by his own words, James answered, "Carrington can lead them."

"Carrington smart man, but not know the sea, not know the coastline, ships. Not know smuggling. Not able to smell trouble like you. Not able to decide things quick and right like you when trouble comes. Yes, Carrington can bring in new men, but without you, they get caught, killed quick."

"We have men who know the sea."

"Boss man also need talk like you, so other men listen."

"Nat Shyrie and I are not the only two men in all New England who can hold together a smuggling organization. Other groups are already in operation."

"Lot smaller. Smaller because not good like you. Many not last long."

Dryly James answered, "Then let Shyrie run it."

"Carrington don't want Shyrie. Shyrie cause trouble for Carrington."

James answered quietly, "I know." His horse closely paced with Garth's, the two men continued into the woods. Garth was wrong, had to be wrong. No man was indispensable.

He tried to picture Edward Carrington in the lead unloading a ship, hiding the contraband, and could not. The men would sense his lack of knowledge, his unsureness, and balk—possibly even run. Of course, someone else might emerge—from James' group, or Shyrie's. Jack Logan could have handled it, or possibly even one of the smaller groups could produce the necessary large-organization leader.

Yes, but when? And how many would die in the meantime, men who would not have died in the face of a correct decision—a change in where to bring the ship in, a decision to dump the cargo into the sea but into an area where later the odds would be good that it could be retrieved with minimal damage and danger—so many quick decisions, all calling for a highly sensitive mixture of instinct and experience.

No! James' only "cause" was whatever would serve the best interests of James Devant. He would go to France. Already he had an ample supply of money in French banks.

Of course, it was only a dream, but might Sarah Carrington marry him, live with him in France?

No. Not Sarah Carrington. Sarah was too English, too well bred. James, no matter how much money he might ever accumulate, was too far beneath her. In addition, should France openly support the colonies against England, ultimate war between France and England would probably result. And Sarah, so stupidly, stubbornly loyal to her king—no, Sarah would never marry James Devant.

He sped the pace of his horse. Let the sound of its hooves and the wind drown out his thoughts. He would have to be mad to remain in the colonies.

How well he knew these woods. How well he knew so much of New England. Its roads, its people, its seasons, its pulsating, living moods. Far better, certainly, than he knew either France or England. Home? Was the colony of

Massachusetts, with the small, unpretentious house he had built for himself outside Boston, really the center of the world, the point from which all time and distance were measured?

The woods behind them now, they crossed the open fields of a farm. Occasionally a dog barked, the sound soon fading into the distance. The farm had not been there when James was a child. The entire New Hereford area, like the Boston area, was growing, changing. To live abroad, even if only for a few years—would the colonies change so fast that James would no longer feel himself a part of them?

But what difference would it make? Why did it matter?

Logic gave him no answer. He only knew it did matter. If only one could free oneself from all emotion. Surprisingly, he thought of death, for what else guaranteed freedom from feeling?

CHAPTER SIXTEEN

The Reverend Howgate's house, symmetrically designed weathered clapboard, sorely in need of a thorough spring painting, appeared to Sarah dark and lifeless in the moonlight. The small barn several yards behind it, which housed a few sheep, a cow and two horses, was less distinct, more heavily shadowed by neighboring trees and overgrown winter-barren bushes. Had the house ever seemed warm and welcoming? Sarah wondered, surprised by the thought. Yes, she decided. Briefly, when she had first arrived from England.

Odd, the treasures she and Mary had so painstakingly buried meant nothing to her now. All that really mattered was her son. Within moments she would hold him in her arms. The thought warmed her, flooded her whole existence. The men who rode with her in tight-lipped silence and Mary, so confused, yet unwilling to relinquish all loyalty—these were dream figures, part of some other world, a world from which the wind would soon carry her soul, free and forever entwined with the souls of her parents and children. Nothing could hurt or frighten her, not now.

Abruptly she wondered, had she gone mad? As mad as her uncle perhaps. Did she, like him, seek death?

No, she thought, suddenly angry. Perhaps the obedient, dutiful child, still so much a part of her, had started to prepare for the martyr's death Uncle Ezra seemed to have chosen for her, but now the woman Sarah had become recognized that child and, with compassion, refused the child's frightened plea, denied the child's will to please Uncle Ezra, to win and hold his love at any price. It was life Sarah wanted. Life and freedom!

The sound of Ezra Howgate's dog barking became distinguishable above the sound of the horses. By the time the group reached the house a dim light could be seen in the right upstairs front bedroom window. Uncle Ezra's room.

In front of the house Sarah drew rein and faced Robert Pollard. "My uncle is an old man," she announced, her voice strong and clear. "So many of you, at this hour—you'll frighten him. May I ask you to leave, please? Now."

After only a split second's hesitation, Robert Pollard nodded, an incongruously courteous gesture. He raised his hand in signal to the rest of the group. As they responded, turned and rode away from her, she dismounted, then hitched her horse to the hitching rail. Later she would take it to the barn, but now she must reassure the household. The light from the upstairs bedroom window was gone. Doubtless, her uncle had left the room, carrying the light with him. By now, from some other window, he had probably seen the others depart. She lifted and let fall the tarnished brass door knocker. "It's Sarah," she called over the last reverberation of metal against metal in the now oddly ominous silence of the night. "I am alone."

The door opened. Only one candle lighted the entranceway. It was held unsteadily by Ezra Howgate, a gaunt, poignant, yet strangely frightening ghostlike figure in his nightcap and tattered woolen robe. Fully awake now, his eyes seemed to glow with some inner fire far brighter than any candle flame.

The door closed, as though of its own accord. Startled, Sarah swung to her right and saw, for the first time, John—the boy of fourteen or fifteen who had been at the church the day she learned of her husband's death. In his hand he held, now loosely, a steel military flintlock pistol, its barrel about thirteen inches long. In the upstairs hallway a door opened; another figure appeared. In the light of the candle he carried, Sarah vaguely recognized him as William Dorman, a man in his mid-forties whom Sarah had known for many years. In his right hand he held a musket. William Dorman, confirmed loyalist, staunch church supporter.

Quickly Sarah faced her uncle. "What's wrong?" she asked. "Where's Charles?"

"The boy is asleep," Ezra answered. "Why do you come here at this hour? Who accompanied you?"

Without answering, she started up the stairs carefully, her riding cape with the jewels sewn into the lining uncomfortably heavy, as were her petticoats, her path poorly lit by only the two candles, the one held by Ezra, still in the entranceway, the other held by William Dorman at the top of the stairs.

"Stop!" Ezra ordered. "I'll have an answer and proper respect from you, if it need be beaten from you!"

Preoccupation, the desire to be with her son, not disrespect, had prompted her silence. Now, however, her nerves too frayed to be dominated by rational judgment, she was angry. She paused only briefly, then continued up the stairs, still silent but now motivated by fear that the words which filled her mind, once spoken, might never be forgotten or forgiven. Beat her indeed! As though she were still a child. How dare he!

Ezra Howgate's voice resounded throughout the hallway. "John, stop her!"

Slowly, midway up the staircase, she turned and faced John, still in the foyer below. Apparently at a loss as to precisely what was expected of him, awkwardly he raised the gun. "Mrs. Carrington—"

What a picture he made, so young, confused and intimidated by Ezra. Compassion mingled with bitter amusement. "Would you shoot me, John?" she asked quietly. Without waiting for an answer, she turned again and gave her attention to the stairs.

As she reached the top, the light below grew starkly brighter, bright enough to draw her attention. The housekeeper, old Mrs. Griffin, had arrived, apparently from the servants' sleeping quarters behind the kitchen. She carried a kerosene lamp.

"Why, Mrs. Carrington!" exclaimed Mrs. Griffin.

Warmed by a sudden welcome flood of memories, Sarah started to respond but was interrupted.

"Mama!"

She swung around. Tears filled her eyes. Robeless, barefooted and sleepy-eyed, but smiling, young Charles ran to his mother's outstretched arms. Down on her knees now, she held him, ran her hands through his hair and over his small back and shoulders. Deliberately she loosened her grip in fear that the strength of her embrace might hurt him.

"Does this mean we can go home now, Mama?"

She drew back slightly and looked at him. Was it merely the candle glow, or had he actually grown paler, thinner in the week or so since she had last seen him? As their eyes met, his grew wide and worried. "Why are you crying, Mama?"

"Because I'm so glad to see you."

"Will we stay together now?"

The question caught her off guard. How could she tell him? For some reason she did not understand, the extra troops that had so recently been brought into the area were now being withdrawn, leaving the rebels the real power in New Hereford. For the moment at least, Charles would be far safer with his Uncle Edward.

"I . . . don't know," she lied. A lie. Another sin. Why was she always so conscious of her sins in Ezra's presence, even during moments when he did not speak of them? She drew Charles into her arms again and rose to her feet. Ezra, every step showing his age, started up the stairway.

"I came to see my son," she said. "The men who accompanied me work for Edward Carrington."

Ezra Howgate stopped, gave his full attention to Sarah. "Then it's true. You have turned away from your king. Away from everything your brave and loyal husband died for."

The sudden tension around her was so strong it was almost visible, bright and burning, like raging flame. John, William Dorman, Mrs. Griffin—but why should they support Sarah, believe Sarah, when Ezra Howgate did not?

Quietly she answered, "My husband lived and died in accord with what he believed to be right. I pray God may grant me the guidance to know what is right for me and the courage to live and, if necessary, dic accordingly."

"And so you ride with rebels to this house!" cried Ezra. "An odd hour, indeed, for you to drop by to see young Charles."

"Rebels who might well have killed me, had it not been for Mary!" she shot back. "I am no rebel!" Voice trembling, she added, "Do you really believe I would betray you, ever willingly harm you?" Quickly she glanced about at the others. "Ever willingly harm any of you?" she added awkwardly.

Some of the tension seemed to subside. This time Ezra answered quietly, "You have become a willful, headstrong and vain woman, Sarah. Vain to believe the Lord would make known to you His will so easily. Pray not for guidance, my child, for you are too young to sort the wily answers of the devil from the truth of the Lord. Pray rather for grace, humility and forgiveness. Your path, your duty in the sight of the Lord, is clear. If we, who support his majesty, run at the first test of that support—" He left the sentence unfinished, his eyes never leaving hers. Had he, she wondered, heard of her desperate efforts to escape from New Hereford, in direct opposition to his will? Probably.

We who support his majesty, she thought bitterly. And where was his majesty's support, his protection for them?

"As you see, Uncle," she answered quietly, carefully, "I am here." Her arms began to ache with the weight of her son, yet to put him down, to lose even a moment of his physical closeness, was unthinkable.

Ezra's anger toward her seemed to soften. Not that he believed she was truly repentant, she was sure, but nonetheless, she was still the only surviving child of his brother's son, young Charles the last of the Howgate line. Gently, tiredly, he spoke to her. "Go to sleep, my child. Take the room with young Charles. In the morning we shall talk."

And once again, she thought, *I shall fall under your spell. No! For you are mad. You are death.* A sudden chill swept over her, a coldness of the soul, unconnected with the drafty house. "May I have something hot to drink?" she asked.

"Of course," answered Ezra. He waved his hand at Mrs. Griffin, an instruction that she was to prepare something. He continued up the stairs.

"And I must put my horse in the barn," Sarah added, reluctantly returning Charles to his feet.

"John can tend to it. It's best you not go out alone."

"The night is cold, and John is not dressed," she answered, immediately regretting her words. Ezra, of course, would see it as argumentative, another show of willful disobedience.

She had misjudged her uncle. Or perhaps he was merely too tired to pursue the subject of her deteriorating character any further that night. "Then so be it," he answered with only minor irritation. "May the Lord go with you." At the top of the stairs now, he gently disengaged young Charles from his mother's skirts and steered the child toward the room Sarah would soon share. The gentleness of his touch brought unwanted tears to Sarah's eyes. In his way, she supposed, even through his madness, Ezra loved the boy, as, she supposed, he also at least believed he loved Sarah.

"Thank you," she said, her voice brimming with emotion. *Thank you,* she thought, *for loving my son and for trying to love me.* Impulsively she kissed her uncle's cheek, her hand resting on his back in what was almost an embrace. Startled and disoriented by such an overt display of unquestionably genuine affection, Ezra Howgate stared at her, as did the rest of the household. For perhaps a second or two the instant hung suspended. Then, as though orchestrated by some unseen conductor, Mrs. Griffin started back toward the kitchen, John lit two candles in a wall sconce near the door, and William Dorman returned to his room. Movement, the business of a household preparing to retire, was restored.

By the time Sarah reached the bottom of the stairs no one else was in sight.

As she closed the door behind her, she allowed a few seconds for her vision to adjust to the moonlight. The chill which had begun in the house was worse, now intensified by the wind. Her back and shoulders ached with it, in spite of her woolen riding cape and the fact that she had managed to survive far colder nights in the past. After untethering her horse, she took two steps, then stopped. Had she really heard something out of the ordinary coming from the direction of the heavily shadowed barn? Out of the ordinary? What did that mean? Some small woodland animal scampering across dried brush was hardly unusual.

Or had she misjudged the source? Probably. Most likely the source was no more than the pounding of her own frightened heart. Yet, still, she sensed she was not alone. Tears flooded her eyes, stinging, burning in the wind. Of course, she was alone. Alone with her own exaggerated fear. Fear of the dark.

"The Lord is my shepherd," she whispered. As a child, alone and afraid in the dark, the psalm had comforted her. Now, however, the words seemed empty.

Her uncle had called her vain. Obviously he was right, for pride alone prevented her from returning to the house, admitting her fear and asking John to put the horse in the barn, as Ezra had initially directed.

Back straight, head high, yet with hands that trembled, she led the animal toward the barn, grateful for the sound of her own footsteps which mingled with the horse's hooves. Other sounds were drowned out, no longer able to tease and torment her. It was only a few yards. A walk of about two minutes.

She stepped into a heavily shadowed section, only about an arm's length from the barn door.

Suddenly she wanted to scream, but both voice and breath were momentarily smothered by the hand which covered the lower part of her face, including her mouth and, briefly, her nose. Then, although her mouth remained covered, at least she was permitted to breathe. A second hand, an arm like steel, pinned her arms to her sides. The man who held her had a companion. The companion, a tall, well-built man in a tricorn hat and heavy clothing, grabbed the reins of her horse as she dropped them. Quietly he steadied the startled animal, his face still indefinable in the darkness.

She ceased to struggle. Was it to be now? A knife probably. A knife would be slilent.

A voice, male, barely more than a whisper. Not the man who held her—it was the other who spoke. "Sarah. Don't be afraid. Don't scream. Do nothing to arouse the household."

She could see his face now, very close to hers. The face of a dead man. James Devant. But was he real, she wondered, or had she indeed gone mad?

The second man released her. A black man, she now saw. It was the man who had been with James that night at the inn.

Numbly she stared at James, afraid her knees would no longer support the weight of her body. Yes, he was real. Alive! "They told me you were dead."

"It was intended that many should believe it," he answered, grateful for the deceptive steadiness of his voice. He could see she had been crying, feel her fear. How wrong that Sarah should ever be afraid, that anything should ever hurt her.

Turning the care of her horse over to Garth, who proceeded to open the barn door, James took her arm, delighting in, yet at the same time shamed by the pleasure even such minimal physical contact with her evoked in him. Keeping well within the shadows, he led her around to the side of the building, a section not visible from the house. Respectfully he released her arm.

"No," she said, facing him. Quickly she raised her hands to his chest, his shoulders. "Allow me to touch you," she continued, "please!" Her voice cracked, a new wellspring of tears in her eyes. "They said you were dead. Dead! I believed them." Awkwardly, withdrawing her hands as quickly as she had raised them, she added, "Forgive me. Sometimes I think I've gone mad."

"You cry to find I am alive?" he asked gently, teasingly, his heart pounding, his arms remaining at his sides only by the most rigid exercise of will.

A light touch came into her still-unsteady voice. "God is good," she said. "I shall survive your teasing. Once you teased me with a spider."

He raised his gloved hand, a fist, then opened it, palm upward. "I had no spider."

"What?"

"My hand was empty."

She laughed, the sound of it uncanny to her own ears. How long since she had experienced real laughter, with joy and warmth?

It was James who broke the mood. "Time is short," he said. "I understand you wish to leave New Hereford."

Dare she hope? "Yes!"

"England?"

"I've no choice now. Only tonight I learned Joseph Carrington is dead."

Some distant corner of James' mind catalogued the fact. Edward Carrington's father was dead—doubtless a further explanation of the accelerated aging process so starkly apparent in Edward.

"I—I have some money in England," Sarah continued awkwardly. "It was left to me by my parents. And some Carrington money which will go to Charles when he's of age. I'm not sure how much. It could be sizable. And I've a small house by the sea which Charles and I bought the first year we were married."

Barely perceptibly James' lips tightened. A small house by the sea. Young, beautiful Sarah Howgate Carrington, the dutiful recipient of her husband's passion. Or had she enjoyed it when Charles made love to her? James' thoughts shamed him. Sarah Carrington was no seaport whore, no Isobel Browne, no bored titled English or French wife cuckolding her husband in the bed of a tall, dark-haired American shipbuilder.

Unaware that James had reacted at all, Sarah continued, "Young Charles and I could live in that house. We could be safe, there. I'll pay you, of course. I've not much money here, but—"

"Oh, yes," he answered, again teasing her, "you must pay me well." Seriously he continued. "But I must warn you. My own position is . . . unsafe. The British would have my life, and Edward Carrington does not fully trust me. Tell no one of this meeting."

"Edward will never let me leave."

"Edward Carrington does not yet control my ships," James answered, deliberately misleading her. It would be safer, far safer than a smuggling ship, he had already decided, to change her appearance and his, to travel on a legitimate vessel, with the child, as a family under some other name. He could take her with him to France. From France, he could send her with reasonable safety to England. "Can you be prepared to leave within a week's time?"

Tearfully she answered, "I was prepared to leave tonight."

He smiled. "We speak now of England, not New York."

She returned the smile. How different his face looked. Softer, younger, incredibly handsome. She felt briefly as though the years had fallen away. They were children again, yet—no, not children. She was a woman now, with a woman's desire for this man, a desire she had never felt for Charles. The realization shocked her. Could a decent woman really feel such things? On impulse, she said, "I wrote to you. A month or so after you first left New Hereford."

Surprised, he answered, "I received no such letter."

Embarrassed, she turned away. "I never sent it. It doesn't matter. So long ago."

His hands braced her shoulders, gently turned her face toward his. "It matters. Why did you not send it?"

"We were children. I—it seemed somehow improper, when you had not asked me to write, nor had you written to me. It was nothing, really. Some local news. And I said I missed you."

Afraid of the intensity with which he longed to take her into his arms, he released her. "I wrote to you," he said. "One letter. Much the same as what you say you wrote to me. What I wrote, however," he added, "I posted."

Her eyes and open mouth eliminated any need for words. No doubt, James thought, Ezra Howgate had received and read it.

Again Sarah laughed. "Uncle Ezra was never overly fond of you." James, however, did not laugh. How seriously he watched her. Why? The question was a farce, the answer so obvious. He cared for her, desired her—as she desired him!

Grateful for the shadows which hid the sudden flush of color in her cheeks, she again turned from him.

"No," he answered. Gently, with his hand, he brought

her face back into close alignment with his. He had removed his glove.

How sweet, how warm the touch of that hand. How she longed to return the contact, how easy it would be to press her lips against his fingers.

"Not again," he continued. "Do not turn away from me. Not now."

Her eyes met his, and in hers he found the truth he sought. She wanted his kiss, his embrace. His love? Yet something was wrong. What? Fear? Yes. But why? "You are afraid of me," he said. "Why?"

"No," she answered quickly, too quickly. "I am not afraid of you. I—" Overpowered by a surge of emotion she had never before even dreamed herself capable of feeling, she threw her arms around him, clung to him, shamelessly accepted his lips against hers, his mouth, the tightly controlled passion of his hand beneath her riding cape. "No," she begged, not meaning it. "Stop," she cried, fearing she would die if he released her, *ever* released her.

"Then let me hold you," he answered. "Nothing more."

She clung to him. "You shame me," she said. "I behave like a whore."

His laugh was gentle, almost patronizing. "And what do you know of whores, Sarah Howgate?"

"Less than you, I'm sure," she answered, regaining some semblance of control.

Her words surprised him. Here were a quickness, a wit, a new dimension which in no way displeased him. Nor did her response to his body displease him. Again, as though she had read his thoughts, she seemed unable to look at him.

"I say things to you," she whispered, "things I should not say. I think about you. Thoughts I should not have.

When they told me you were dead, I felt—I felt somehow as though I also had died."

His heart pounding, James answered, "Sarah—"

The moment was shattered by sharp, swift footsteps, a voice, low and urgent. The black man. "Someone come from house," he said. "Big man. Carry pistol."

James' disorientation lasted only an instant. From his ungloved hand, he withdrew the only piece of jewelry he wore—a gold signet ring, once the property of his father, returned to his English mother by a French officer, following his father's death. Thrusting it into Sarah's hand, he said, "If you need me, send your message with this ring to John McCaylan at the Twin Stallion Inn. Do not use your name."

"No time," cut in Garth.

His instincts in full charge now, James shoved her, not gently, toward the front of the barn. His roughness seemed to help. The momentum, the alertness she needed came to her. By the front of the barn she stopped, remained in the shadows. The man was now only a few feet from her.

"Mr. Dorman," she said quietly, still warmed and shamed and elated by the memory of James' arms, his lips, his voice.

Initially William Dorman's body stiffened, then seemed to relax, but only slightly. "Are you all right?" he asked.

"Yes."

"We began to worry." Carefully, yet firmly, he continued. "May I ask, what were you doing here for so long?"

She stepped from the shadows and met his eyes. Head high, she answered, not untruthfully, "I was crying." More softly, her voice edged in bitterness, she added, "I would not have my son and uncle see me in tears. Please forgive me for whatever inconvenience I may have caused the household."

His eyes left hers and glanced behind her, toward the side of the barn. Then, apparently satisfied, he lowered his pistol.

"May I have your arm please?" she asked.

Gently, sympathetically he answered, "Of course."

His kindness touched her, his arm steadied her.

That night, her son in bed beside her, sleep came slowly to Sarah Carrington. Her courage—or shamelessness—continued to amaze her. Dare she pray—had she the right to pray for the safety of James Devant? James Devant, smuggler, rebel. James Devant, who, if he could, would see her safely to England while he remained in the colonies, committed to Edward Carrington, ready to kill—if his own survival depended on it—good, decent men like William Dorman, who, just as quickly, would kill James Devant. Perhaps it was not merely her uncle; perhaps the whole world had gone mad. James Devant, James Devant. How painful the realization that she would probably never see him again once she reached England. Should he even try and Edward learn of it, doubtless Edward would kill him, not merely because he thought him a spy, but because whatever tattered family honor might still exist toward his brother's widow would require it of him.

Tears filled her eyes, spilled onto the pillow, more and more tears. Tears born of what? Fear? Guilt? She did not know, yet the tears continued. Vaguely, some distant distorted memory of an Irish Catholic childhood acquaintance at prayer came into her mind and refused to leave. *Mary, Mother of God,* she thought, *cry for us all.*

CHAPTER SEVENTEEN

"With these hands, I could kill her," spat Edward Carrington.

Silently James watched him. The two men were seated on rough-hewn stools by what remained of the fire in the kitchen of the Miller family's small farmhouse approximately half an hour's ride from the far larger Stanton farm near Norwalk, where James' grcup was already beginning to assemble in the underground room designed by Thomas Kyle so long ago when smuggling of any kind was considerably less respectable. It was Friday, April 14, 1775, a little after 8 P.M. Knowing only that for an hour or so the house was to be used by some important personages, the Miller family had discreetly left earlier that night. Of the Miller family, James knew only that it was part of Edward Carrington's network. Two other members of that network were due to join James and Edward at the house soon, the entire group then to continue its journey to the Stanton farm. Although the British, as far as both James and Edward knew, had no reason to be suspicious of the Miller house, still, Garth and the young man who had accompanied Edward Carrington from New Hereford both stood watch, Garth by the front window and the young man from an upper back bedroom window.

Edward Carrington stared quietly into the fire, clenching and unclenching his hands. Was he even conscious of the movement? James wondered. Such an open show of emotion was uncharacteristic of Edward Carrington. Unlike men such as Samuel Adams, Patrick Henry and Thomas Paine, Edward Carrington, James suspected, derived little, if any, personal satisfaction from the position of power and leadership in which he found himself. Yet even as far back as 1768, seven years ago, when Thomas Hutchinson willingly abdicated the governorship of Massachusetts to General Gage and his despised British troops, the signs of where Edward Carrington's leadership must one day take him had been present. Had the man really hoped the tide might turn? James wondered. Had Edward Carrington really hoped that Lord North might fall from favor, that King George might one day attain the political sophistication to realize that his American colonies would not indefinitely submit to so many injustices?

"Are you absolutely certain your information is correct?" asked James.

"Absolutely certain," Carrington replied. Then, softly, but with no slackened intensity, he added, "And yet perhaps after all, God is merciful. His heart simply stopped. He never even saw the fort, only the ship that was to take him there. The body was returned. He'll have a decent burial."

James had never met Dr. Ward, but the name was not unfamiliar. A loyalist in his political inclinations, James had always assumed, as had many others, an opinion carefully nurtured, no doubt to enhance his value to Carrington's organization. A good man, well loved. Dead now. Dead at the hands of Isobel Browne, as surely as though she herself had placed the chains on his wrists, then taken him to the ship.

"They say Mistress Browne is well cared for these days," offered James dryly.

Matching James' tone, Carrington answered, "She remains at Webb's Tavern, in Stamford. The tavern is become a fortress. I have heard on good authority that Lord Williams plans to return to England soon and take her with him. In the meantime, she is visited by hairdressers, jewelers and dressmakers. And Lord Williams—frequently."

"How much harm has she done?" James asked.

"The same night she escaped from the Twin Stallion, we sent a messenger, bound for England, to warn all who had helped her escape from Newgate with Jack Logan. But the ship he was to take—something went wrong. I would now say it is unlikely our warning arrived in time to make any difference, if ever it did arrive. As for the ship which brought her into the harbor at New London, it's sailed under many names. That day it was the *Wayfarer.* Most of its crew have either been taken or are being hunted. Those who've been taken will all be hanged, of course. From the harbor she went to Dr. Ward's house." With no further amplification on that point necessary, Carrington concluded, as though the entire subject were too disturbing to pursue further, "It would seem, everything she could tell his lordship she told."

"Is John McCaylan safe?" James asked. "Are you?"

"It would seem so—for the moment. The soldiers who accompanied her to the inn are both dead—and buried. They've no real proof against John or me. Only her word."

"What proof had they against the others, except her word?"

Dryly, with a political sophistication James had to admit was superior to his own, Edward answered, "None of the others were named Carrington, a name not unknown at court. My late father's name and my dedicatedly loyalist brother's name. Connecticut has its own charter. The Committee of Correspondence of which I am chairman in New Hereford is perfectly legal. Granted, I could be taken and sent to England, but the mock trials by which those poor farmers and sailors rotting in the prison at Fort Franklin will eventually be hanged—more than that would be required to hang me. Considerably more."

"And John McCaylan?"

"John McCaylan, through his family—his brothers and sisters, his children, his nieces and nephews and all their ties by marriage—John McCaylan is one of the most powerful men in Connecticut. In England, granted, that power would be worth little, but John McCaylan is not in England. Personally I should dislike to be part of any group of British soldiers sent to arrest John McCaylan on Connecticut soil, even with *very* tangible proof of his guilt, which they do not have."

"Yet they took Dr. Ward."

"They took Dr. Ward," Carrington answered, his voice sharp, "because we have no army to stand up to them and tell them, this man is an American. He will not be charged or tried except by other Americans."

Again the flash of emotion, the fire. Uncharacteristic? Certainly no patriot-dominated court would ever have convicted Dr. Ward of treason. Treason against whom? England, perhaps, but not America. Odd, to think of America as separate from England. A separate country, with the right to bear arms in defense of itself, even against England.

Edward Carrington rose to his feet, warmed his back at the fire and took a hard look at James. "You seem deep in your own thoughts," he said.

Quietly, meeting Carrington's gaze directly, James answered, "'They tell us . . . that we are weak; unable to cope with so formidable an adversary. But when shall we be stronger? Will it be next week or the next year? Will it be when we are totally disarmed, and when a British guard shall be stationed in every house?'"

Edward was obviously startled, but his response was immediate. "I had no idea the proceedings of the Richmond convention were of such interest to you."

"Mr. Patrick Henry interests me," James answered. "Indeed, in the face of a military force such as the British Empire could raise against us, we *are* weak. But I find I must agree with Mr. Henry. When shall we be stronger? The troops so recently withdrawn from this area and returned to Fort Franklin are not returning to England. Rather, more troops, more ships arrive almost daily. 'Has Great Britain any enemy, in this quarter of the world, to call for this accumulation of navies and armies? No, sir, she has none. They are meant for us; they can be meant for no other.'"

"It would seem you know the speech as well as Mr. Henry."

"I read it many times," James answered pensively. "I remember Boston when it was occupied by General Gage's troops."

With no effort to hide his continuing surprise, Carrington asked, "Then you agree with Mr. Henry?"

"Not completely." James rose to his feet, impatient for the arrival of the men they awaited. "If the only choice were really liberty or death," he continued, "I must admit, I would choose liberty in France over death in America."

"Are you truly convinced that to remain in America would mean your death?"

Taking his time, James answered, "My name is not

Carrington. Nor have I a family to compete with John McCaylan's. I have no family."

"Except for your wife. I understand she already lives in France."

James hesitated, then decided it would make no difference to Edward Carrington. He smiled. "She now lives in America and refuses to come with me to France." In response to Edward's look of obvious confusion, James laughed. "I have no wife," he said, "nor would I be driven into marriage by the social pressures of whatever community I live in."

Edward Carrington also smiled. His face seemed softer, less haggard, yet the accelerated aging process was still evident. At their first meeting—was it really less than three months ago?—James would have taken the difference in years between them to be slight—perhaps only three or four. Now, however, Edward Carrington might well have been ten years James' senior.

Odd, for the first time, James looked at Edward Carrington with mixed feelings. Quietly he said, "I wish you well."

His eyes suddenly guarded, Carrington asked, "In what respect?"

This was the "other" Edward Carrington, James quickly realized. The man who once so easily, that night of their first meeting, condemned James to death. The man who even now kept his own sister-in-law a virtual prisoner in New Hereford, where well he knew she could not survive indefinitely. This was a man who put country above all else. Yet only three months ago Edward Carrington had been human enough to jeopardize his own position within his organization by bringing his brother, sister-in-law and nephew, at his brother's insistence, into New Hereford.

Three months. Time enough for a man to go mad? Perhaps, if in some way he blamed himself for his brother's death and his father's death. Was it true, James wondered, that Joseph Carrington had died denouncing and disowning Edward, as James had heard after checking into it on Sarah's behalf?

And yet—mad?

No, James decided. Edward Carrington was sane. Merely callous. As callous as the times, and his country, required. As callous as James when James' own survival and now the survival of Sarah Carrington and her son might require him to be. Perhaps Edward Carrington and James Devant were not really as different from each another as James had once imagined.

"I wish you well," James repeated, "in your endeavors to enlist the support of everyone at the meeting tonight. It's more than an efficient smuggling operation you want. It's an army and navy. Men who know how to fight and can train others."

"Men like you," Carrington snapped. "You call yourself French, yet your mother was born in England. Yes, your father was French, but he left your mother before you were old enough even to remember what he looked like. And you, of course, were born and have spent most of your life in America."

"All right," James conceded, impressed that Edward had bothered to check so carefully into his background. "Perhaps you are right. Perhaps I am more American than French."

"And if America falls under complete British domination—'with a British guard stationed in every house'—what are you then, Mr. Devant? American, British or French?"

"French, I suppose," James answered irritably. The conversation was beginning to bore him, or so he told himself.

"And should another war break out between France and England," Carrington persisted, apparently unperturbed by James' obvious distaste for the entire subject, "on which side do you think a defeated, British-dominated America would fight? On the side of the English, sir, for it would have no choice. Oh, I'm sure the French would accept your help," he went on, "but would they accept *you?* Or would they see you as a British-American traitor? And what if France should fall to England? What are you then? English? But would they have you? What *is* your country, Mr. Devant? Where do you draw the line? At what point do you say, this piece of earth is mine, I belong to it and it to me, live or die on it, I shall not be moved?"

"I find your conversation exceedingly dull," snapped James, startled by the stupidity of his own emotionalism.

Edward Carrington smiled. "Do you indeed?" he asked pleasantly. And why should he not smile? James realized. Edward Carrington had just won a victory over James Devant, a clear-cut, uncompromising victory—his first.

It was James who finally broke the ensuing silence. Quietly he asked, "And this is why you remain and fight?"

"Not completely. I would have more, much more. Not only would I have that piece of earth which is mine, a part of my country, but I would live in my country with dignity and freedom."

"Liberty or death?" mused James, more a statement than a question. "You've changed, Mr. Carrington. The night I met you, you spoke of boycotting English goods. Your approach in all areas was known to be . . . more conservative."

"Yes," Edward Carrington answered in much the same tone, yet an icy, bitter edge was clearly discernible in his voice, "I have changed."

Garth's sudden presence in the doorway startled both James and Edward. "Two men come," he said. "Slow. On horseback."

Without a word Edward Carrington extinguished the candles and drew his pistol, his tall, slightly stooped figure a silhouette now in the dim glow from the fireplace. As quietly as he had arrived, Garth left to join the young man who had accompanied Carrington and was now in position at the front door. James, his own pistol drawn and ready, stood by Edward's side.

As the two riders drew nearer, Edward Carrington visibly relaxed. "Looks all right," he said.

The men they had been waiting for, thought James. Edward Carrington's men. Yet somehow the riders continued to receive little of James' attention. Rather, he found himself looking around and beyond them, at the moonlit land, the winter-barren fields and leafless trees, the land, this small stretch of earth, this single farm in the colony of Connecticut. This colony. This country? James' country. The thought disturbed him deeply.

Sarah Howgate Carrington stared at her uncle in open amazement. "Surely you can't be serious," she protested.

It was Friday evening, April 21, 1775. The male armed church member spending his nights in the Howgate household this week was Raymond Brooke, MD, a man nearing fifty, born in America, but educated in England. He also looked uneasily at Ezra Howgate. John, confused by his personal agreement with the sermon Ezra had just read to the three of them and the obvious disfavor with which both Mrs. Carrington and Dr. Brooke seemed to view the old man's intention to deliver it in church this coming Sunday, remained silent.

His features stark, hawklike and oddly waxen in the glow of the whale oil lamp on his desk, Ezra Howgate lowered the pages in his hand and faced his niece. "And what would you have me say?" he demanded. Without waiting, he continued. "We are at war! When a governor, a military commander lawfully appointed by the king of England sends troops to confiscate arms and gunpowder blatantly stored by an entire town and the populace of that town, yea, if the entire colony of Massachusetts rises to defend their unlawful arms and fires on—murders—British troops, what would you have me say? Would you have me ask God to forgive their sins? No!" Voice rising, he went on. "I speak as the Lord directs. It is said that even men from Connecticut joined their ranks. It is further reported that throughout these colonies there are others, equally mad, equally determined to murder British soldiers. Patriots, they call themselves. Patriots indeed! Traitors! Their acts be *treason!*" With obviously forced control, he continued. "In the pages of history, few deeds will leave a stain to compare with the infamy of those who took arms against their ordained ruler at Concord and Lexington last Wednesday. *Now* is the time for every decent God-fearing loyal subject of his majesty to speak out, to offer full support even to the laying down of his life in the cause of honor, order and justice. As a minister of the Lord I've no choice but to say so!"

Sarah closed her eyes. Knowing her words would fall on deaf ears, she nonetheless felt the words must be said. "Dear Uncle," she began quietly, "I love you and would not have you doubt it, not ever, yet I must tell you, you frighten me. The times are explosive, tempers are sharp—perhaps now more than ever before in the history of these colonies. You know there are those who attend our church merely to report to others what is said there. The sermon you propose could inflame them. I would fear not only for your personal safety, but for the safety of every member of the congregation."

"Perhaps," Dr. Brooke added awkwardly, "later. When troops are stationed in this area. As for now, however, I can only suggest, of course, but I suggest and hope you might reconsider. To lay down one's life in support of the king—if this eventually becomes necessary, then, yes, both of us know many willing to make such a commitment, including ourselves. But to speak the commitment now, here, in New Hereford, where we are so sorely outnumbered—Ezra, if we are openly to join the fight, let it be when we have at least a chance to win. If we who support the king are to die at the hands of these mad rebels, at least let it be at a time and in a way that our deaths might have meaning. Right now—" He held out his hands, let the sentence hang. What more could be added?

Surprised, angered and humiliated by their reactions, Ezra fixed his gaze on Sarah, the primary and most cutting source of his humiliation, his own niece and a woman. "And you," he demanded quietly, his tone accusing her well in advance of any answer she might give, "you, who love me so dearly you would never have me doubt it, are you prepared to lay down your life in support of your king?"

Again she closed her eyes, this time in weariness. At that moment the king somehow seemed so far away. Were the requests the colonists had made of him really so unreasonable? Such a short while ago, less than a year, during her last visit to England with her husband, even in England, she had met many who sympathized with the colonists. Did it really have to come to this? War! For what else could anyone call it? A war between England and its American colonies! Yet, even more horrifying, it was also a war between Americans, with neighbor against neighbor—even brother against brother, father against son. "I am tired and confused," she answered finally, quietly. "There is too much I do not understand."

"Of course," offered Dr. Brooke quickly. It was not the first time he had come to her defense. After all, his protectiveness seemed to say to both Sarah and Ezra, Sarah is only a woman, and women were never meant to concern themselves with politics.

In hopes that she might avoid any further arguments with her uncle, at least for this night, Sarah rose to her feet. "Forgive me, please, if I retire now. I really am quite tired."

"And it is not even yet nine o'clock," snapped Ezra.

"Yes, but I—" She broke off, her body suddenly tense, fully awake. Immediately John jumped to his feet and drew his pistol. In the same instant both Ezra and Dr. Brooke seemed to realize they had not brought weapons with them into the old man's study. The sound of horses' hooves stopped, directly outside the house. But perhaps it was only one rider—two, at most. Certainly not a mob.

Be still, my heart, thought Sarah. A week, James had told her. Be prepared to leave in a week's time. Yet the week was more than past. Of course, she understood he was waiting for a ship, and the arrival of a ship was rarely predictable. James! Even to think of him made life a miracle rather than a burden to be endured.

Odd, that night when she last saw him—to go to England had been so important to her. But now, with the shooting actually begun, everything seemed different, painfully confusing. To live permanently in England now would be to disown America. America. Her home. James' home. Of course, perhaps someday she could return, accompanied by her two strong, healthy children. Yet, if America lost, could it ever again be a place in which she might wish to live?

With all three men gone now and the lamp extinguished, she remained in the darkened study and listened as Ezra responded to the knock at the door.

A voice, very young, frightened, answered Ezra's greeting with, "May I see my father, sir?"

She stepped from the study as Dr. Brooke came quickly down the stairs. "Thomas! What is it, son?"

Now she saw him, a small boy, cold and frail—no more than ten or eleven, at most.

"Some men came to the house," he said breathlessly. "They broke some windows and tried to set a fire; then they left, but Elizabeth was badly cut, and Mother's afraid they'll come back. She sent me to fetch you."

"Of course," answered Dr. Brooke. With a quick glance at Ezra, he added, "I must leave. Perhaps it would be best if you and your family also left, sought sanctuary elsewhere, at least until morning. Sometime tomorrow we can meet at the church and decide what to do. Certainly we can send a request for protection to Fort Franklin. And perhaps it would be wise to select one house which would be defendable, where all of us might stay together. Or several houses. I—" Whatever additional thoughts he may have had on the subject, he left unspoken, the urgency of his own personal situation too vividly before him in his son's frightened eyes. "Tomorrow," he concluded. "One P.M., in the church."

As though still not fully adjusted to the reality of the moment, Ezra nodded.

As father and son rode off, Ezra stood with his back against the door, facing Sarah and John. "Come," he said, his voice somehow too calm. "We'll go to the church. Fetch some extra blankets."

"What about Mrs. Griffin?" asked John.

"Yes," Ezra answered. "Best if we clear the house. Her son and his family live nearby. She'll probably be safest with them. It's us they'd be after, not her. Sarah, go fetch her."

With Mrs. Griffin safely lodged at her son's house,

Ezra, John, Sarah and Charles, the boy still sleepy in his mother's arms, resumed their journey to the church. Although the roads supported a surprisingly large number of travelers for an April night at this hour, most seemed intent on their own business, none eager to confront anyone they did not recognize. Sarah, she soon discovered, was not the only woman with a child in her arms. Rebels or loyalists, she wondered abstractedly, as one particular group—apparently a family consisting of father, mother and four children—passed them. Certainly rebels, loyalists and, perhaps particularly, those who had attempted in the past to remain politically neutral had reason to be frightened. Houses where lights could usually be seen at this hour seemed ominously dark, their doors double-bolted. Doubtless, inside, occupants were still awake with muskets and pistols ready for use.

As Sarah's group approached the rocky slope which led to the church, the surrounding land barren except for the most determined trees and shrubs, Sarah felt the beat of her heat quicken. Had she imagined it, she wondered, or had a man actually ducked quickly into the building? But the church was locked. Ezra had the key.

Apparently John had also seen it, a brief, but clear, silhouette in the moonlight. Slowing the pace of his horse, he called quickly, yet softly, cautiously, "Mr. Howgate . . . Mrs. Carrington. . . ."

Sarah also slowed her horse, gave her full attention now to John. How young he was, she thought, somehow surprised by her sudden awareness of it, yet there in the moonlight, his teenage face seemed considerably older, stronger. The face of a man. Doubtless he would soon join the British army. *God, keep him safe,* she prayed.

The sheltering shadows of the trees several yards behind them, the church perhaps half a minute's ride ahead of them, the entire group came to a complete halt.

"I think—" John whispered to Ezra, his voice barely audible to Sarah.

Abruptly, John's sentence unfinished, the relative silence of the night was shattered as a voice cried out from behind them, "Be still, or we'll kill you all as you sit."

Startled by the sound, John's horse suddenly reared and turned as John, also startled, yanked awkwardly on the reins, the movement of both horse and rider immediately followed by the crack of exploding gunpowder. Beyond control now, Sarah and Ezra also turned, barely in time to see John fall, screaming in pain, his hand clutching his chest. As the horse ran off into the night, the screaming continued, the boy's body now no more than a shadowy, tormented form writhing on the ground. A second shot rang out. The screams ceased, and save for one final spasmodic convulsion, what remained of John Harris lay still and silent on the rocky slope.

Incredulously Sarah looked from John's corpse to the two men in front of her. All of it, of course, was a dream. It had to be. John Harris could not possibly be dead. She had known him too many years. Only a moment ago he had spoken to her.

Young Charles started to cry.

In a movement so quick Sarah barely had time to realize what had happened, the second man raised his pistol.

"No!" she screamed, finding her voice at last, her arms so tightly around her son she might well have harmed him. "Please," she went on, "I beg you. I'll do anything you ask." More quietly, but with a hand that trembled, she covered Charles' mouth and continued. "Be quiet, darling. At once!"

The man hesitated, then lowered his pistol, as Charles' cries turned to a mere whimper, muffled still by Sarah's hand.

The two men strongly resembled each other. Both were

unshaved; both wore sailor's jackets and heavy boots. The one on the right, however, was older, taller and leaner, his mouth and eyes more obviously cruel.

"Dismount," ordered the taller one.

"Yes," said Sarah quickly. With Charles to manage, the job was difficult, awkward. They gave her no help, and she was grateful.

"Dismount," echoed the second one. She saw his command was directed at Ezra, still on his horse, his eyes glazed.

Leaving Charles only for an instant, quickly she took Ezra's hand "He . . . can't hear well," she told them. "He'll do as you say. Exactly as you say. He's an old man." Her voice shrill, she yanked at her uncle's hand. "Come down, Uncle Ezra."

Almost as meekly as Charles, Ezra permitted himself to be drawn from his horse. *He will be all right,* Sarah told herself. *In a moment. They will not kill him. He will do as they say.*

His words accompanied by a nod of his head, the taller one ordered, "Into the meetinghouse."

Meetinghouse? At first the words did not register. Then she realized he meant the church. But no one in New England could make such a mistake. The Congregationalists had a meetinghouse; the Anglicans had a church. The architecture of the two was radically different. Meetinghouses did not have spires.

"Yes," she said quickly, the instant she realized he meant the church. With one of her hands holding Ezra's and the other intertwined with her son's small fingers, she started up the slope. Several feet short of the main entrance, however, now quite clearly visible in the moonlight, she stopped briefly, promptly prodded forward again by the two men behind her. Yet it was the sight ahead of her which had caused her nearly to lose her balance. At least three men, possibly more, flanked the open doors, all with weapons aimed in her direction. But how absurd, she thought. She wanted to laugh, to scream at them, to cry. So many men, so many weapons, all trained on a seventy-two-year-old man, a perfectly defenseless woman and a five-year-old child.

But who were they? she wondered, her feet somehow miraculously continuing to carry her even closer to them, these unshaved men in sailor's jackets who did not even know the difference between a meetinghouse and a church.

The answer came to her so quickly that she felt like a fool for not having seen it immediately. They were smugglers! A smuggling ship had come in earlier that night. The two men still behind her who had killed John Harris were part of the crew. They were English, cockney English, not American. The cargo had been unloaded and was being taken to—or from—the church.

A smuggling ship. James' ship? The one he had been awaiting? Might James actually be in the church?

Her instant of hope and joy was shattered by a fear that she might vomit. God in heaven, was this how the man she loved served Edward Carrington?

No! She must not judge him. There was too much she did not understand. John Harris might well have drawn his pistol before his horse reared and turned. The men who killed him could not have known, could not have been sure. They took no chances. Cold, brutal and quick to kill, they themselves survived and would continue to survive, to smuggle into America the supplies which, in the eyes of James Devant and Edward Carrington, America desperately needed.

Numbly, with a still-sinking feeling in the pit of her belly, Sarah concluded her brief walk to the church entranceway. Now she saw the wagon by the front door, well placed in the shadow of one of the few trees which somehow continued to survive in the eternally inhospitable soil. The wagon was loaded with barrels. She had seen such barrels before. Gunpowder?

A voice from within the darkened church called, "That's the last of it."

A man with a tricorn hat walked out of the church. As though distracted from some other line of thought, he stopped directly in front of Ezra, Sarah and Charles. His clothes and voice were American; his face was hard but not really cruel. Or was it merely her interpretation? Sarah wondered. A wish, a hope. "And what are we to do with you?" he asked.

"Rebels, aren't you?" spat Ezra.

Desperately Sarah glanced at her uncle. He must be silent, he must not anger them, yet she knew there was no way she could stop him. Quickly, fighting hysteria, she addressed herself to the American. "May I see Mr. Devant, please? Is he here?"

The man looked startled. Carefully he answered, "You seek James Devant?"

Barely able to think, she reached into the bodice of her dress and withdrew James' ring. "Please," she said, "give this to him. It's his. He gave it to me. He said, if ever I needed his help, to send it to him. Is he here?"

Ezra's astonishment turned quickly to rage. "Traitor!" he screamed. "How long and how well do you know that whelp, that swine?"

Her own voice matching his in pitch and intensity, she cried back at him, "Uncle, do be silent, I beg of you!"

Obviously irritated by the outburst, but not really distracted by it, the man accepted and carefully examined the ring. Then, finally, still holding it, he answered Sarah. "No, Mr. Devant is not with us tonight. Where did he tell you to send the ring?"

"To John McCaylan, at the Twin Stallion Inn," she answered quickly, to prove, she hoped, that it really was James' ring. "He said to send it with an unsigned message—that if the message came with the ring, he would know who it was from and he would come to me."

"Where?"

Something was wrong. She felt it. "Wherever . . . the message said to meet him," she answered awkwardly. Something was very wrong. "Will you—" The words "take it to him?" died on her lips.

The man's fingers closed over the ring. "Come with me," he said to Sarah as he led the way back into the church.

With startling force Ezra caught her arm, swung her around to face him. Eyes blazing, he cried, "You are damned, Sarah Howgate Carrington, your soul is damned for all eternity. Oh, God, what agony the Lord hath bestowed upon me that ever I was bewitched into loving you!"

Clutching her son's hand so tightly now that he tried to draw free of her, Sarah answered in a voice choked with tears, "As God is my witness, I never betrayed you!"

"You are damned," he repeated in a voice which now, amazingly, carried the thunder of much younger days. He swung around, faced those who now watched him, almost hypnotically, from the bottom of the church steps. "All of you are damned," he cried even louder, "all of you who betray your king, who murder his loyal servants, who defile the house of the Lord with your filth—"

The explosion of a pistol shot ended his statement. He jerked backward, then fell forward, his face gone, completely gone. Sarah dropped to her knees. Gagging, retching, she clung to the open door as the contents of her belly spewed from her lips onto the same steps where Ezra now lay. An arm lifted her, a sailor's jacket, cold and rough against her face.

"Mama, Mama—" The voice was frantic. Charles followed them all into the church—the first of the two sailors who had initially told them to dismount, the American in the tricorn hat and Sarah. No, she thought, as the sailor dragged more than carried her toward her uncle's office. Charles must not follow. Let him run elsewhere, hide somewhere within the church. God willing, the men would forget he had even been with her. He could remain safe, alive!

The door to her uncle's office was open, the room lit by two candles, one on the tea table and one on the desk. A heavyset unshaved gray-haired man, well into his fifties, stood in front of the desk. The drawers were pulled out, except for one which he had just succeeded in prying open as the sailor, the American, Sarah and Charles entered the room. His attention distracted from the drawer, he looked up at them. Piled on top of the desk near the candle—a small pile indeed—was everything of value he had taken from the desk: a few coins, a gold cross on a chain, even the sweets Ezra had dipped into often to provide a treat for young Charles.

Still sick, dizzy, desperately trying to coordinate her thoughts, Sarah looked at him. The man in the sailor's jacket half shoved, half dropped her into the desk chair. Young Charles ran to her, no longer crying, merely clutching her, his face hidden within the folds of her riding cape, his hands frail and birdlike.

"What's this?" demanded the man by the desk. By his voice and dress, he also appeared to be American.

Closing the door before he spoke, the younger American answered, "She's got a ring Devant give her. She's to send it to John McCaylan with a message if she wants Devant to meet her someplace." He held out the ring.

The man at the desk suddenly took on a catlike quality, in spite of his bulk. A cat ready to spring. "Where's the meeting place?"

Sarah did not answer.

The man's hand smashed across her face. The force of the blow seemed incredible. She cried out, tasting blood, yet like her own voice when she had screamed, even the pain seemed distant. Someone else sat in that chair, not Sarah. Sarah merely watched.

"I said, where's the meeting place?" he repeated.

The second American answered, "She's to name it. In a note to be sent with the ring."

The older man nodded. "Then we'll name it. Someplace he can get to tonight. That means near the Twin Stallion, but not too near. He's too many friends there, now. Damned half-breed bastard. Thinks he's all set with Edward Carrington, thinks I'm over and done with. Near the Twin Stallion. Where?"

Edward Carrington? For the first time it occurred to Sarah, not one of them had asked her name, nor, she imagined, would it make any difference if they knew it.

Silence hung heavily in the room. Then, abruptly, the man who had asked the question answered it. "Cotter's Hill! By the six pine trees. Aye, and close enough to the shore; we'll take his body and dump it into the sea." He cleared the desk by emptying into his pockets the objects he had withdrawn from the drawers, then shoving what remained that blocked the writing surface onto the floor. Laying out paper and pen, he nodded toward the desk. "Write the note," he ordered. "Tell him to meet you on Cotter's Hill by the six pine trees at midnight tonight. Tell him if he can't come tonight, come tomorrow, same time."

Incredulously Sarah stared at him. *Dump his body into the sea.* She dared not speak.

Following a nod from the man who seemed to be giving the orders, the sailor, stumbling over Charles, lifted Sarah with one arm around her waist. With his other hand he moved the chair into proper position in front of the desk, then shoved her back into it.

Another slap across her face by the older man followed. This time, quietly, she answered, "Do as you will with me. I shall write no such note."

Irritably, impatiently, he looked about the room, then suddenly focused on young Charles. To the sailor, he said, "Cut the boy's throat. An inch at a time."

Before Sarah could move or even speak, the sailor gripped her son by his hair, braced one knee against the boy's spine and forced the child's head back. With his other hand he drew a knife that was long and looked very sharp. Her instincts told her what her mind still somehow refused to accept. He would actually do it.

Almost immediately the knife drew blood, but from Charles' hand with which he had sought to defend his throat.

"No!" screamed Sarah. She tried to rise from the chair, but the younger American held her. "Then you'll write the note?" demanded the older man, obviously long ago out of patience with her.

With hypnotic efficiency, even as Sarah and the gray-haired man spoke, the sailor simply pushed young Charles' hand away and found a new hold which precluded further interference. Again he raised the knife.

"Yes, yes! I'll write it! I'll write whatever you say! Only release him!"

The knife stopped, poised at the boy's throat. The man still held him.

With a strength that amazed her, Sarah rose to her feet and faced the man who gave the orders. *"Release him!"* she demanded.

He hesitated, then nodded to the sailor. Charles ran to his mother, sank onto the floor beside her and tried to stem the bleeding of his cut hand with his other hand. His tears were back now, low, racking sobs.

Numbly, her whole sense of time and place dreamlike, Sarah wrote as the younger American dictated. When she was finished, he read it.

I am damned, she thought. *My soul is damned for all eternity.* Tears fell from her eyes. Silent tears, born finally of rage as she glimpsed the sailor's face. To the gray-haired unshaved man, the letter was business. To the second American, the entire business seemed distasteful. But the sailor was enjoying it.

The gray-haired man grabbed an envelope and shoved it in front of her. "Write 'James Devant,'" he ordered.

She complied.

With both the ring and letter packed into the envelope, he handed the envelope to the second American. "Get the young Stephens boy to deliver it," he said. "McCaylan don't know him. Don't know he works for me."

As the younger man started to leave, the older one called after him, "You're a valuable man, Thomas Norris. You know how to read." His tone was contemptuous. Obviously the older man could neither read nor write; therefore, any man who could was to be looked down upon.

Now only Sarah, Charles, the older American and the sailor remained. The older American looked at Sarah, then beyond, at the sailor. Something passed between them, a look which communicated all, without words. It was the gray-haired man who finally spoke. "All right. When you're finished, go back to the ship." With a sidewise glance at young Charles, he added, "Both of them."

On his way out he closed the door behind him.

The sailor smiled openly. "Pretty wench like you. All

them bruises on your face. Mr. Shyrie, he don't like it when people don't do like he says."

As he removed his jacket, Sarah heard the wagon and numerous horses begin to leave the church area.

"You stink," she said, amazed that the words had actually taken form, been spoken. "From here I can smell you."

With his cut hand Charles reached for the handle on the door. So quickly that none of his exact movements were really discernible to Sarah, the sailor reached the door, grabbed Charles and threw him across the room. The child hit the wall, cried out, then landed on the floor, his voice abruptly silent, his body motionless.

Rage predominated over love. Her face so contorted that probably no one who knew Sarah Carrington would recognize her, she leaped from the chair and threw herself onto the sailor, her fingernails raking deep into his flesh. He hit her, knocked her off-balance, then drew his knife. Bracing herself against the wing chair in the corner, she watched him, seared him with her eyes.

"Inch by inch," he said with a grin. "That's how I'll cut your boy's throat. And then yours. Unless—" He opened his belt and crooked a finger at her.

"Then cut his throat," she answered quietly. "And mine. And be damned with you."

His grin turned to straight, tight lips. He lay the knife on his jacket with himself between Sarah and the jacket. "I'll have you first," he said.

"I'll see you in hell," she answered. "For I, too, am damned. James Devant trusted me, and I betrayed him—and for what? A few more moments of life for myself and my son. But I swear to you, I shall wait for you in hell. And whatever the torments may be, to know you also shall someday suffer them will make them easier for me."

His face paled. He was a sailor. Most men who lived with the sea, Sarah knew, believed in some kind of God, heaven and hell.

Now it was Sarah who smiled. "To violate and murder a defenseless woman and child in the house of the Lord," she went on quietly. "Do you really believe God could ever forgive you? Through all eternity, you shall suffer. Guard you life well, for when it ends—"

"I'll hear no more!" His voice was like thunder, his strength beyond anything she had ever imagined, as he grabbed her, flung her to the floor.

In rage and helplessness, she screamed, fought with him as he tore at her clothing, felt his flesh clog under her fingernails as she raked his face. He struck her a blow so hard it stunned her. Tasting blood, her mind reeling, she wondered, why did she fight him? Let it be done with. Had God in his infinite mercy already taken young Charles?

As she ceased to struggle, he responded, breathless and sweating, "Aye, that's better." He grabbed at her skirt and petticoats, then, suddenly, unexplainably, stopped, his eyes wide and startled. He simply removed his hands from her, rose to his knees and turned.

It was then that Sarah saw the knife in his back. It was not deeply embedded, but considering that only the strength of a five-year-old boy had been behind the thrust, neither was its penetration shallow.

Weak, dizzy, bleeding from her nose and mouth, Sarah tried to pull herself to her feet and found she could barely move. Her head was like stone, her neck and shoulder muscles somehow too weak to support it. But the sailor was on his feet, facing Charles. As wide-eyed as the sailor had looked when the knife first struck him, Charles' eyes were now wide as he backed away toward the desk.

Sarah, by some miracle of will, of strength beyond her

own, reached her knees. Frantically she sought anything nearby with which she might find the necessary support to rise to her feet. She needed a weapon. Anything!

A sound, quick scrambling—then an explosion. The explosion of a pistol shot.

Charles' aim had been poor. The pistol ball hit the left side of the sailor's head. Still alive, but badly stunned and bleeding, the man fell directly backward, only to meet some far greater pain, greater shock. It was there in his eyes—pain, shock, then nothing. Nothing, as his arms and legs abruptly ceased to move, all sound gone from his body. One final movement, but not the movement of a living body. Rather, it was an act of gravity. The force of the fall had driven the knife all the way into his back, except for the handle, now visible as the body slumped to accommodate the laws of balance, which did not allow a man of his size to rest indefinitely on a five-inch knife handle.

Obediently, almost apologetically, Charles returned the pistol to the desk drawer. It was the drawer Shyrie had just succeeded in prying open as Sarah entered the room—the one drawer he seemed to have forgotten to empty, in his haste to find and kill James Devant. Once before, Charles had held that pistol in his hands. Uncle Ezra, Sarah remembered with an ironic clarity that startled her, had been angry at him for touching it.

"Charles . . ." she whispered. Suddenly, hysterically, helplessly, she started to cry.

He ran to her, his gait unsteady. "Shall I get Dr. Brooke, Mama? I can ride by myself."

Still unable to speak, she shook her head.

"They're all dead, aren't they?" he asked quietly. "John Harris. Uncle Ezra."

James Devant, she thought. Finally able to voice the

words in her mind, she answered, "Yes, darling. We must go somewhere."

"Where?"

"It's an inn. We must hurry. Let me see your hand."

He held it out. She winced. With her teeth and a strength in her fingers which surprised her, she tore a section from one of her petticoats and made a bandage. At least the bleeding had stopped.

Again, she tried to rise to her feet and found she could not. Panic swept over her, then, abruptly, deliberately, she took control of her thoughts. "The Lord is my strength," she whispered. Yes. The words helped.

Pain-racked, weary and dizzy, she rose to her feet.

"Lean on me, Mama," said Charles.

Again tears flooded her eyes. Tenderly she touched his head, then quickly withdrew her hand only to return it again for closer investigation. The boy winced. She could feel the swelling. The stickiness matted into his hair, she knew even in the dim candle glow, was blood. Rage boiled inside her as she remembered the now-dead cockney sailor throwing her son across the room. She looked at his corpse, felt somehow oddly detached from it. Words came into her mind, as though from somewhere beyond her, yet she recognized them, welcomed them . . . *a time to every purpose under heaven . . . a time to kill . . . a time to love.* She looked at her son.

"Say it with me, darling," she said as they started from the room. Very quietly she began, "'Yea, though I walk through the valley of the shadow of death. . . .'"

His small voice joined hers. "' . . . I will fear no evil: for thou art with me; thy rod and thy staff. . . .'"

"' . . . they comfort me.'"

Together, they walked out of the church.

CHAPTER EIGHTEEN

"My dear, words to describe your loveliness fail me."

Isobel Browne smiled and bowed, a mock bow intended primarily to give Lord Williams a titillating view of her bosom, now white and soft, lotioned and powdered, under her low-cut silk brocade gown threaded with gold and trimmed in jewels, aflame with its own special glow in the candlelight.

"Is it time to leave?" she asked.

"In a moment."

"But the ship has arrived?" He nodded. She smiled. The schooner which would take them from Stamford to Fort Franklin. Soon she would be free of this room at Webb's Tavern, which, in spite of all the luxuries his lordship provided, had still begun to feel like a prison. From Fort Franklin, they would leave for England in the morning. England! Not only England, but as Lord Williams' mistress she would actually attend court functions. *She,* Isobel Browne! The nightmares would disappear. The day would come when she would be able to smell the sea without wanting to run from it in eerie, sickening fear. Perhaps it was just as well that those stupid colonials had dared fire on his majesty's troops at Concord and Lexington. Their actions and the subsequent disquiet, apparently throughout the entire thirteen colonies, seemed to have sped Lord Williams' decision to leave. It was Friday, April 21, 1775. With luck, their ship would reach England by late May. Spring in London. Home!

Lord Williams handed her a mirror. It was hers, a hand mirror trimmed and backed with intricately patterned gold and jewels, an earlier gift from him. "Now look at yourself," he said.

She looked into the mirror, but her eyes focused flirtatiously on the reflection of his eyes.

"No," he said, returning the flirtation. "Yourself."

Her own reflection, there in the candle glow, was indeed pleasant, her copper-gold hair styled high upon her head, except for the few perfectly formed curls which touched her shoulders. Her complexion was clear and smooth now, softly powdered, her cheeks appropriately rouged. How young she looked. And she was young, she felt young. Barely twenty. How old twenty had seemed, even a few weeks ago. The reflection of Lord Williams' hands distracted her from her own image. Her eyes widened; a cry of pleasure escaped her lips. The necklace he had fastened about her throat was exquisite.

"Emeralds," he whispered, apparently delighted by her joy. "To match your eyes," he added.

She tossed the mirror onto the bed and threw her arms around him. "I love you, I love you!" she cried. "How you spoil me!" His lips, wet and sensual, met hers. His touch, although not pleasant, at least no longer repelled her.

"I would see you happy, Isobel," he whispered, still holding her close to him.

"I am happy," she answered quickly. "I have never been so happy."

Gently he disengaged himself, then stood away from her and looked at her. Odd, something about the way he looked at her, as though he were embedding in his mind a picture to remember.

No, it was not at all odd. She *was* a picture, gowned and jeweled in the candle glow. She smiled.

A knock sounded on the door, followed by a man's voice, "All is ready, your lordship."

Lord Williams started toward the door.

"I'll get my cloak," said Isobel.

"No, not just yet," answered Lord Williams. "I've one or two other matters to attend to."

Odd, he seemed to avoid her eyes as he spoke. Oh, in the name of heaven, she must control her silly fears. Women like Isobel to Lord Williams were merely a source of pleasure, like fine wine or good food. Of course, the man would not always meet her eyes when he spoke. It had happened before, would doubtless happen again. His mind had merely shifted to other concerns, to him far more important than any woman. She must grow accustomed to it.

The door opened. But as Lord Williams walked out, two other men walked in. Incredulously Isobel stared at them. They were ruffians. She had known such men in the streets of London.

Drawing back, swept by a wave of icy terror, she asked, "What do you want?"

Addressing himself to his companion, the taller of the two said, "Move! His lordship said make it quick."

The man who had not spoken drew a knife.

She screamed. Before either had time to react, she shoved a heavy chair against one and struck the other such a blow with a silver candleholder that he dropped the knife and staggered backward. Blind with rage and fear, she sought the door, found it, swung it open.

Directly in front of her stood Lord Williams, his face a mask of rage equal to hers. To the men in the room, he cried, his voice shrill, "I told you, quickly, with as little pain and fear as possible!"

Stunned, bewildered, Isobel staggered backward, her eyes wide with terror, *"Why?"*

Initially she thought he was not going to answer. Then, "My dear," he said, gently, almost painfully, "at the moment, there are rumors. Rumors of a particular document"—he touched his chest where now, in the same pouch once carried by Lord Marlowe, a corner scrap of the letter, the corner which contained the king's signature, rested, merely a scrap—of danger to no one should it be taken from him, yet tangible proof to Lord North, once Lord Williams reached England, that the letter had actually been recovered and destroyed—and a girl named Isobel Browne. At this moment, merely rumors, and as such they shall soon die. But should the girl—Isobel Browne—return to England, especially if she were to return and mingle with London society—"

Her eyes suddenly flooded with tears, she whispered, "No!" Backing away from him, she cried out, *"No!* You fat, stupid swine! How my flesh crawled every time you touched me, how I longed to—"

A hand grabbed her hair, pulled her back into the room.

"Be thorough, be sure," barked Lord Williams, slamming the door in her face.

"No!" The pain, the sting, like fire, such pain, incredible pain, her throat, first, then other parts of her body, the knife long, sharp, and swift in the hands of the bearded one while the other held her.

Lord Williams' words, echoing, echoing through her tortured still-living brain: *Be thorough, be sure.*

Thorough.

Sure.

Then . . . nothing.

When Sarah Carrington entered the taproom of the Twin Stallion Inn that night, Friday, April 21, 1775, all conversation ceased. Aside from the bruised and bloodied appearance of both mother and child, ladies did not enter taprooms.

"John McCaylan," she said, addressing herself to no one and everyone. "Please. I must find John McCaylan."

The man who finally responded seemed featureless to Sarah. She remembered only that he was wearing a large white apron. "Please," she begged. "Is James Devant here? Or my brother-in-law?"

His voice, also, seemed nondescript, although much later, she did remember a faint Scottish brogue. "And who might your brother-in-law be?"

"Edward Carrington."

If possible, the room grew even more quiet.

It was McCaylan who finally broke the silence, but it was not Sarah to whom he addressed himself. "Olanthia," he said, "show Mrs. Carrington and her son to a room. There's still one empty on the second floor." Awkwardly he added, "And bring a basin. Warm water. Towels."

"*No,*" she insisted. "I must talk with you. James Devant—"

"You'll not talk with me now," he answered brusquely, almost harshly. "I've other business to attend to."

"Oh, please," she said, "*please!* There's no time!"

But the man was already gone. She tried to go after him but felt an arm around her, the black woman's arm, leading, steering her away from the taproom, into the hall, toward the stairs.

"Charles?" she called.

"Boy right here," said Olanthia.

Sarah reached out her hand and caught his. For a moment there she had lost it. James. Edward. Her thoughts spun, wearily, senselessly. Would no one listen?

The room to which the black woman took her had already been prepared. The inn was crowded that night, from the fireroom to the taproom. Like the roads. So many travelers. She sank onto a roundabout chair in front of the fireplace, afraid that if she lay on the bed, she would fall asleep. Here, in the warmth of the fire, she began to recognize and miss the advantages of the cold outside. The cold had been kind, numbed her aching body, cleared her head. Young Charles now also seemed to feel the fatigue. Did he also feel the throbbing, she wondered, the renewed awareness of pain with each heartbeat?

"Come, dear," she said, grateful for the warm water and towels Mr. McCaylan had thought to provide. She tended first to Charles, then to herself, removing at least most of the now-caked blood from her face. The job complete, she started to tremble uncontrollably. Tears flooded her eyes. But what new madness was this? she wondered, desiring neither to tremble nor to cry, yet now even her thoughts seemed barely her own.

Frightened, Charles asked quickly, "Mama, why are you crying?"

"I love him," she answered.

"Who?"

"The man they're going to kill because no one will listen to me. It's after midnight."

A knock sounded at the door.

Demons clouded her mind. Surely behind that door stood Uncle Ezra, dead, looking as she had last seen him on the church steps. Uncle Ezra had come to take her, come with her husband and John and all the others. Using the chair for support, she forced herself onto her feet. She must not greet him so meekly, must not let him see so easily that the torments of hell he had promised her were already begun. Yes, she was sinful. In that instant, above all else, her sin was pride.

"Come in," she said.

The door opened. Edward Carrington stood in the hallway, and yet—Edward? How much older he seemed. He also stared. It was then that jolted back by the sight of him into full contact with the immediacy of her own situation, Sarah realized how she must look to him, her face bruised, cut and swollen, her clothing still stained with blood.

Charles' reaction was immediate. "Uncle Edward!" he cried joyfully. Every step reflecting pain, he nonetheless ran the length of the room. With his hands, the cut one now bleeding again, he reached up to be embraced, an embrace which his uncle refused.

Closing the door behind him, Edward addressed Sarah. "John McCaylan said you wished to see me."

Ah, so this was how it was to be. Odd, she felt no anger at his coldness. Merely the numbing realization that Edward Carrington, a man she had once dearly loved as a brother, was now as dead as her husband. With a calmness that amazed her, she answered the stranger in front of her. "I understand James Devant is of value to you. Tonight Uncle Ezra and I went to the church for sanctuary. When we got there . . . a group of smugglers . . . we hid, and heard them talking. They plot to kill Mr. Devant. Tonight."

Unimpressed, Edward responded, "Plots to kill James Devant are not uncommon. Thus far none have succeeded."

"You don't understand," she cried, the controls suddenly weakening, some shattering. "They plan to get him alone—some hill, somewhere near here. Tonight! At midnight!"

"I see. What hill?"

"I don't know, I can't remember." She sank back down onto the chair. "Carlton? Cotton? Pine trees. Six pine trees."

"Tell me, why do you concern yourself with James Devant?"

"Does it matter?" Her voice was high, almost shrill. "Is he not important to you? Do you not want him alive?"

"Ah, *now* I see." Open anger replaced his previous wariness. "You would connect me with James Devant, a wanted smuggler, a fugitive, for your loyalist friends. And what would you say were I to tell you I have never met the man?"

"I would say you lie!" she spat. "And I tell you again, if he goes there alone tonight, they will kill him."

Obviously preparing to conclude their meeting, Edward replied, "The hill you speak of is called Cotter's Hill. And rest assured, my dear sister-in-law, there is no way anyone could get James Devant alone on Cotter's Hill at midnight. At least," he added, "this is what I believe from what I have heard of the man."

Tears filled her eyes. "Dear God," she whispered, "give me the words, show me the way."

The brief ensuing silence was broken by Charles' voice. "Mama, is this the man you said you love?"

With a look bordering on astonishment, Edward turned his attention to the child.

"Be silent!" Sarah ordered her son with a shrillness far beyond anything she had intended.

On his knees now, in front of the boy, Edward Carrington laid both hands gently on his nephew's shoulders. "And what do you know of all this?" he asked.

"No!" said Sarah, again rising to her feet, stumbling toward her son.

"But, Mama, tell him about the letter they made you write."

Quickly Edward Carrington stood, caught her arm and swung her around roughly. "I repeat," he began, his voice ominously low-pitched, "what have you to do with James Devant?"

With a fire in her eyes that seemed to amaze, perhaps even at least partially to disarm him, she answered, "Go ahead. There is nothing you can do to me this night which has not already been done, save violate and kill me, and both of those have been tried."

The pressure of his hand on her arm lessened.

"But tell me," she went on, "why do you question me? You, who already know everything. Oh, how thoroughly you see into the human soul, so much more thoroughly I'm sure than God ever could. Tell me, what do you find of good and evil? Tell me, please, for I have not your gift to judge a man's character by his politics. *I* am confused. Love confuses me. I loved your father and your brother, my son is your nephew, and as God is my witness, until this moment, I loved you."

He released her. "Sarah, forgive me."

Tears flooded her eyes. "*Help* me."

"I—" Floundering, he broke off, then continued. "You must be truthful with me. What letter? What is the boy talking about?"

"How can I tell you," she exploded, "when you have gone so mad you will kill him? I am no British spy, not now, nor have I ever been. But if you would kill James, then you must also kill Robert Pollard, for Robert Pollard also agreed to help me leave New Hereford. For a price, Mr. Pollard was to take young Charles and me to your father. I did not know your father was dead."

"I am aware of the incident with Robert Pollard," Edward answered, offering no further explanation. "And where did James say he would take you?"

Her mind reeling, she answered, "England. But he said to tell no one we'd even met. He said you did not fully trust him. We both knew you believed I was a spy. We saw each other only briefly. He gave me his ring and told me if I needed help to send it with an unsigned note to him through John McCaylan. I lied about the church. We didn't hide. They found us right away. They killed Uncle Ezra and John Harris. I thought they were James' men, and gave them the ring, told them what it was for." Her voice, cracked. "I cannot say they made me write it. I could have refused, but they cut Charles' hand, tried to cut his throat, they beat me, then left someone behind to kill us, only—"

His face gone pale, Edward answered, "Can you recall a name? Any name any of them may have used to another?"

She hesitated. "Yes! That's it! 'Mr. Shyrie, he don't like it when people don't do like he wants.' That's what the sailor they left behind to kill us said."

"I killed him," said Charles, with neither pride nor shame. It was merely a statement of fact. "With a knife, then a gun Uncle Ezra kept in his desk."

Without a word Edward started toward the door.

"No!" cried Sarah, grabbing his arm. "Don't hurt him. He is loyal to you!"

Briefly Edward Carrington stopped. "You say you love him. Tell me," he continued, "how do a devoted loyalist and an active patriot reconcile such differences?"

"I think you have me confused with your late brother," she answered. "No responsible king could let happen what has happened in these colonies."

For a long moment he looked at her. "But you choose to live in England," he said finally.

She shook her head. "Not King George's England, not now. But if I have to, then, yes, I'll live there. I've young Charles to care for, and"— gently, she touched her belly—"and a second child, still within me. Charles' child." Again choked by tears, she cried out, "It is after midnight. Well after midnight!"

Without another word, quickly, Edward left the room.

A cloud bank drifted over the moon. James Devant used the momentarily intensified darkness to rise from his belly to his elbows, listening as much with instinct as physical senses for any sound from the top of the hill.

Nothing.

He sank back down to his former position, Garth beside him. Although this particular section, maybe twenty feet from the base of Cotter's Hill, was well shadowed by underbrush, it remained an unlikely hiding place because the trees were few and scattered. James' horse, tethered beside Garth's fifty feet behind them where trees grew more thickly, was close enough to the path for any sound the animals might make to blend with the sounds of other horses. It was Saturday morning, well after midnight, April 22, 1775, the roads still unusually heavy with travelers, most of them peaceful, but cautious and armed. The eight men who had accompanied James and Garth also lay in the surrounding area in groups of two, forming a complete circle around the base of the hill, their horses, like James' and Garth's, also tethered at a distance.

"Maybe he already there," whispered Garth, indicating

the top of the hill, particularly the dark area of the six pine trees.

"Good chance of it," James answered, his eyes blazing. "How long have we been here? Must be well after midnight now. Maybe he got here early. Maybe even before the letter was delivered."

"You *sure* Shyrie send that letter?"

"I can think of no one else." Clenching his left hand, he ran his thumb over the ring now back on his finger. Initially after reading the letter, he prepared to leave. Within minutes, however, he realized something was wrong. Cotter's Hill was wrong. Used for many years as a signal base for smugglers, long before the Twin Stallion had been built, Cotter's Hill was well known among smugglers. But Sarah Carrington was not a smuggler. Even if one operated on the unlikely assumption that she might ever have heard the name, it was still not an area with which she would be familiar, and to chose a meeting place so unfamiliar and so far from New Hereford, in times as dangerous as these, made no sense unless she planned to come from and return to somewhere else in the same area—but where? Except for the inn, a mile or so to the south, where Sarah Carrington would be anything but safe, and one patriot stronghold farmhouse about two miles inland, Cotter's Hill was exceedingly isolated.

No, Cotter's Hill had not been chosen by Sarah Carrington. Of course, some military or loyalist group might choose it, but why? Why not, rather, a place where reinforcements or medical aid could be readily summoned, should either become necessary?

"Perhaps he wait on road between the hill and the inn," Garth suggested.

"I doubt it," James answered. "Odds are too good he

might run into some of Carrington's men. Carrington finds out Shyrie tried to kill me, he'll have to kill Shyrie."

Again confused by the white man's politics, Garth asked, "Why?"

"Because he's already told Shyrie *not* to kill me. If Shyrie disobeys him and Carrington doesn't kill him, Carrington's authority, his honor, his protection—all become as nothing in the eyes of too many people who must follow him, respect him, even fear him, if he is to maintain an effective organization."

The strain of waiting beginning to take its toll, James rolled onto his back and looked up at the stars. The earth against his body felt good. Soon it would be warm with spring, then summer sunlight. Warm and green. God in heaven, if there was a God, why bring him so close to Sarah, after all these years, only to take her away again—forever? He knew she was dead. Shyrie had obtained from her the ring and the information on how to use it. Nat Shyrie was a butcher. This torturous, nagging, otherworldly sense that she was *not* dead was, he knew, no more than what Garth had told him when together they found her house empty those few weeks ago. Because James loved her, he did not want to believe the truth.

He knew he had come here this night to kill Nathaniel Shyrie. It would save Carrington the trouble of seeing to it himself and would protect James from Carrington's ever learning of James' association with Sarah. If Shyrie did come, James knew he would bring only a few men with him. Only men he could fully trust. Or perhaps only one man. One man Nathaniel Shyrie could kill after the two of them had finished with James Devant. Yes, that seemed most likely. No witnesses, no proof. The irony of it! The trap Shyrie had set, at the price of Sarah Carrington's life, to surprise, outnumber and kill James had reversed itself. It was Shyrie who would now be outnumbered and dead before the sun rose. Or dying. It must be slow, James decided, with a vindictiveness which amazed him. As slow and painful as whatever the man had done to Sarah. *More* painful.

"Whoever he may have with him," James whispered to Garth, "it's Shyrie I want. *I* want him."

Silently Garth nodded.

Distant, at first—was it instinct or actual sound? Yes, sound! The night was shattered by sound, horses, at least a dozen, possibly more. They came at top speed from the south, the direction of the inn. Lips tight, James flattened himself against the ground. Had Nat Shyrie outmaneuvered him after all? Rage choked him. With luck, he and his men could make it back to their horses and escape with their lives, but Shyrie also would escape death this night.

As the horses galloped nearer, voices cried out. Well positioned to rise and break into a run, he waited. But what was this? Two men, recognizable as part of the group which had accompanied James because they had no horses with them, were on their feet speaking with three men on horseback who had drawn rein as the rest of the newly arrived group continued up the hill.

One of the riders who had been speaking approached the general area where James and Garth remained concealed, the man's voice sounding through the night air. "Mr. Devant—"

Garth backed off, loosed his machete into his hand and waited.

Within seconds James signaled him to relax his weapon. The man who approached was known to James. Robert Pollard.

"Mr. Devant," said Robert, "is Mr. Shyrie on the hill?"

Startled, James covered the reaction well. "I strongly

feel he may be," he answered calmly, carefully. "I am not sure."

"Mr. Carrington went to find out."

"Mr. Pollard," said James quickly, "might I trouble you for the loan of your horse? My own is tethered by the path. Garth will show you the way."

Surprised, Robert Pollard nodded and dismounted.

At the top of Cotter's Hill, Nathaniel Shyrie, accompanied only by Thomas Norris, was in the midst of a sentence directed to Edward Carrington. " . . . on me way to the inn to find you, to tell you I've a good cargo, safely landed this night."

Gently, slowly, James guided his horse through the assembled group until both Nat Shyrie and Edward Carrington saw him. Drawing even closer, close enough to touch both of them, in a voice edged in steel, James addressed Nat. "Good evening, Mr. Shyrie."

Eyes narrow and catlike, glistening with hatred, Nathaniel Shyrie answered, "I'd like to kill you, lad, but Mr. Carrington here says it's not allowed."

"How good it is to know we now work for the same man," said James, intensely aware of Edward Carrington's unwavering attention. "Good to see you know how to take orders," James continued, still unaware of why Edward Carrington had come. Somehow, he must have known, but how much did he know—and from whom? If Carrington knew there was a woman involved, could James deny that the woman had been Sarah? Maybe. "Good to see you know your proper place," James went on, deliberately goading, prodding the older man. "Why, I can remember when you thought you owned the entire New England coastline. But now, of course, we'll work together."

"I'll see you in hell first!" spat Shyrie.

Another moment, another few sentences should do it.

Shyrie would go for his pistol, and so would James. Let God, if there was a God, decide the outcome.

"That's enough," said Edward Carrington quietly.

Briefly James closed his eyes, barely breathing. Damn him! Damn Edward Carrington!

"I am in need of some explanations," Carrington continued, addressing Shyrie. "You say you were on your way to the inn to see me, yet you came from New Hereford. Why are you a mile and a half *above* the inn?"

Slowly, his teeth suddenly bared, Shyrie answered, "It would seem you already have your explanations since it weren't I told you the ship come in at New Hereford."

"Then you confess that in direct opposition to my orders you and Thomas Norris came here to kill James Devant?"

"And kill him I will!" exploded Shyrie. He reached for his pistol, but it was not James' shot that killed him. So many shots, so many pistols, one of them Edward Carrington's. James had not even had a chance to draw. Thomas Norris and Nat Shyrie, both dead.

Eyes blazing, James Devant faced Edward Carrington. "He was mine to kill," said James. "*Mine!*" Enraged beyond control, he turned his horse and galloped down the hill, neither knowing nor caring what direction he might take. A full minute later he realized someone else was behind him, one lone rider rapidly closing the distance between them.

His feelings more in hand now, he drew rein, waited as Edward Carrington joined him.

"The inn is to the south," said Edward. "You ride north."

"Then indeed I have made an error and will ride south," James answered.

"And why, may I ask, was it so important to you to kill Mr. Shyrie?"

"Indeed you may ask, but I shall not answer."

"And if I order you to answer?"

"Then I order you to go to hell."

Startled, but covering it fairly well, Carrington continued. "How did you know it was a trap?"

"I knew."

"I find you difficult to talk with, Mr. Devant."

"Perhaps because I find your conversation exceedingly dull, Mr. Carrington."

"Sarah and the boy are alive. Both were beaten, but doubtless shall soon be well."

Taken aback, James stared at him.

"Does my conversation become less dull, Mr. Devant?"

A new kind of tension, a wariness replaced James' previous anger.

"You bring to mind a snake, ready to spring," said Edward Carrington. "How well I grow to know you. Right now, if you felt it necessary, you would draw on me, kill me, would you not?"

Carefully James answered, "If I felt it necessary, you know I would."

"But Sarah would be so disappointed. For then surely others would kill you." He laughed. "To think of you, in my family, stepfather to my brother's children. She carries one inside her, yet unborn, your know. Or did you not know? Or does it not matter to you? For if your intentions toward her are less than honorable, then you'll stay away from her, or by God, I shall give you cause to draw on me."

Bewildered, again James merely stared at Edward Carrington. Then, finally, he answered, "Sarah wishes to live in England."

"Sarah wishes to live with you. She is much changed,

in mind and politics. She would prefer to remain in America but doubtless would go to France with you, if you insisted. She would be lonely, there, however. She does not know the country, does not speak the language."

"You assume she would marry me. I've no name, no family—"

"You balk at marriage."

"To Sarah? Never. From the time she and I were but children, I—" He broke off, oddly embarrassed. Never had he intended to reveal so much of himself to anyone, least of all Edward Carrington.

"Then go to her. Tell her."

"You . . . accept this?"

"Alas, although her politics are much improved, a most stubborn will shows itself. She believes herself in love with you and will have no other. No, I'll not stand in her way."

His head light, heart pounding, James asked, "Where is she?"

"At the inn."

Confused, the words not fully registering, James repeated, "The inn?"

"Bruised and bleeding, she rode all the way from New Hereford with the child to seek help for you, to warn you that the letter was a trap. She is now lodged in a room on the second floor, awaiting news of you."

Slowly, numbly, James turned his horse south. Sarah? Alive? Sarah Carrington. Sarah Devant? His thoughts overwhelmed him, too many thoughts, too much to absorb and sort out.

Quickening the pace of his horse, Edward Carrington soon far behind him, the night air poured into his body like fine wine. The entire countryside had never before seemed so beautiful, not by sun or starlight in any season. Now it was clear to him. All of it. His countryside. His country. Yes, he would stay in it, fight for it, die for it, if need be.

Indeed, the morning was heavy, yet heady with commitments.

His country.

His wife.